HE IMMOR   d
gain, the two   y
his time thing   y
o overcome t   -
essly by while comrade after comrade faced the deadly chal-
enge alone. . . .

HE STAINLESS-STEEL KNIGHT by John T. Phillifent—A
ance was the perfect weapon for jousting with the local
nights, but when it came to taking on "dragons," a little
echnological wizardy went a long, long way. . . .

DIPLOMAT-AT-ARMS by Keith Laumer—The Empire would
oon rise again, spreading rebellion to the stars unless Jame
Retief could best the Crown's new champion and win the
iggest gamble of his long career. . . .

DIVIDE AND RULE by L. Sprague de Camp—The hoppers
ad turned America into a place of petty lords and feuding
tates. Yet all mankind needed to overthrow these masters
vas a little luck and a very special ally. . . .

eluctant dragons, brave warriors, beautiful damsels in distress,
reacherous wizards, all these and more you will meet in—

COSMIC KNIGHTS

Isaac Asimov's
Magical Worlds of Fantasy #3

Great Science Fiction from SIGNET

(045)

☐ **INTERGALACTIC EMPIRES: Isaac Asimov's Wonderful Worlds of Science Fiction #1** edited by Isaac Asimov, Martin H. Greenberg and Charles G. Waugh. (126246—$2.95)

☐ **THE SCIENCE FICTIONAL OLYMPICS: Isaac Asimov's Wonderful World of Science Fiction #2** edited by Isaac Asimov, Martin H. Greenberg and Charles G. Waugh. (129768—$3.50)

☐ **SUPERMEN: Isaac Asimov's Wonderful World of Science Fiction #** edited by Isaac Asimov, Martin H. Greenberg and Charles G. Waugh. (132017—$3.50)

☐ **WIZARDS: Isaac Asimov's Magical Worlds of Fantasy #1** edited by Isaac Asimov, Martin H. Greenberg and Charles G. Waugh. (125428—$3.50)

☐ **WITCHES: Isaac Asimov's Magical Worlds of Fantasy #2** edited by Isaac Asimov, Martin H. Greenberg and Charles G. Waugh. (128826—$3.50)

☐ **COSMIC KNIGHTS: Isaac Asimov's Magical Worlds of Fantasy #** edited by Isaac Asimov, Martin H. Greenberg and Charles G. Waugh. (133420—$3.95)

☐ **THE SLEEPING DRAGON: Guardians of the Flame #1** by Joel Rosenberg. (125746—$2.95)

☐ **THE SWORD AND THE CHAIN: Guardians of the Flame #2** by Joel Rosenberg. (128834—$2.95)

☐ **TIES OF BLOOD AND SILVER** by Joel Rosenberg. (131673—$2.75)

*Prices slightly higher in Canada.

COSMIC KNIGHTS

Isaac Asimov's
Magical Worlds
of Fantasy #3

EDITED BY
Isaac Asimov,
Martin H. Greenberg
and Charles G. Waugh

A SIGNET BOOK

NEW AMERICAN LIBRARY

Acknowledgments

"Crusader Damosel," by Vera Chapman. Copyright © 1978 by Vera Chapman. Reprinted by permission of the author and her agent, Carnell Literary Agency.

"Divers Hand," by Darrell Schweitzer. Copyright © 1979 by Gerald W. Page. From THE YEAR'S BEST HORROR STORIES SERIES VII. Reprinted by permission of the author.

"The Immortal Game," by Poul Anderson. Copyright © 1954 by Fantasy House, Inc., renewed © 1982 by Poul Anderson. From THE MAGAZINE OF FANTASY AND SCIENCE FICTION. Reprinted by permission of the author and his agents, the Scott Meredith Literary Agency, Inc., 845 Third Avenue, New York, NY 10022.

"The Stainless-Steel Knight," by John T. Phillifent. Copyright © 1961 by UPD Corporation. Reprinted by permission of James Allen, Literary Agent for the Estate of John T. Phillifent.

"Diplomat-at-Arms," by Keith Laumer. Copyright © 1982 by Keith Laumer. Reprinted by permission of the author and the author's agents, Richard Curtis Associates.

"Dream Damsel," by Evan Hunter. Copyright © 1954, renewed © 1982 by Evan Hunter. Reprinted by permission of the author and his agent, Jane Gelfman.

"The Last Defender of Camelot," by Roger Zelazny. Copyright © 1979 by Davis Publications, Inc. Reprinted by permission of the author.

"A Knyght There Was," by Robert F. Young. Copyright © 1963 by Conde Nast Publications. From ANALOG SCIENCE FICTION. Reprinted by permission of the author and his agents, the Scott Meredith Literary Agency Inc., 845 Third Avenue, New York, NY 10022.

"Divide and Rule," by L. Sprague de Camp. Copyright © 1939 by Street & Smith Publications, Inc., renewed © 1966 by L. Sprague de Camp. Reprinted by permission of the author.

CONTENTS

INTRODUCTION
IN DAYS OF OLD

by Issac Asimov

There are some words that reek of romanticism, and "knight" is one of them. Yet its lineage is rather low. It is from the Anglo-Saxon *cniht*, which meant "boy" or "attendant." He was someone who attended his master and waited upon his needs. The German homologue, *Knecht*, still means "servant" today.

Of course, if it is the king we are talking about, his attendants were often fighting men, and in medieval times, that meant someone who could afford a horse and armor, and that, in turn, meant an aristocrat.

In other languages, it is the horse that was stressed rather than the service. In ancient times, to ride a horse was the surest sign of aristocracy (a war-horse, of course, and not a plow horse), just as driving a Cadillac or Mercedes (not a Chevrolet or Volkswagen) does the trick today.

In literary Latin, the word for "horse" is *equus*, but in soldier lingo, a horse was *caballus* (equivalent in English to "nag" or "hack"). It was the latter that came to be used for "war-horse." In Spanish, *caballus* became *caballo*, in Italian it became *cavallo*, and in French it became *cheval*.

Consequently, a horseman was *caballarius* in Latin, *caballero* in Spanish, *cavaliere* in Italian, and *chevalier* in French. All were equivalent to the English "knight." If we want to speak of

1

the whole body of knights, you might talk of the "knighthood" of England, but it is more common to turn to French (for Norman-French, at least, was the language of the English aristocracy from the twelfth to the fifteenth century) and speak of "chivalry." To behave like a knight—that is, with courtly manners, instead of with the boorish behavior of malapert peasant knaves and varlets—is to be "chivalrous."

Actually, however, the romantic glow that makes knights seem so wonderful is totally a matter of fiction. In actual fact, knights, presuming on their horses and armor, were arrogant and insufferable in their behavior, especially to people unarmed and on foot. In English, we have another word for "knight"—"cavalier" (usually used for the arrogant fools who fought for King Charles I)—and we all know what "cavalier treatment" means.

Incidentally, I made use of the word "knave" a few lines back. This means "boy" or "attendant", and the German homologue, *Knabe*, means "boy" even today. As you see, "knave" and "knight," which are now treated as opposites, meant precisely the same to begin with. (The German word for "knight," by the way, is *Ritter*, meaning "rider.")

Ever since 2000 B.C., aristocrats did not fight on foot in the way the peasant-scum were forced to. The Homeric heroes fought in chariots whenever they could, and the Greek and Roman aristocrats were in the "cavalry" (the Latin equivalent of the French/English "chivalry").

Nevertheless, until the end of ancient times, the cavalry never served anything but a supporting role. They were mainly important because of their speed of progress. They could spy out the enemy, and they could pursue an already broken and fleeing foe. The actual fighting, however, was done by the steady and disciplined "infantry," the Greek line of hoplites, the Macedonian phalanx, the Roman legion. (The very word "infantry" is akin to "infant" and is another word meaning "boy." The term is a measure of the contempt held for the foot soldier by the aristocrats.)

The role of the cavalry changed with the invention of the metal stirrup by the nomads of central Asia some time in the early centuries of the Christian era. What a difference it made. Without a proper stirrup, the cavalryman was insecurely balanced on his horse, and if he used a spear too incautiously he ould be easily pulled or pushed off his mount. Under those onditions, horsemen were better off using arrows, as the Parthian avalry did. With a good stirrup, on the other hand, the avalaryman could wedge his feet securely and place the full weight of himself and his horse behind the spear. No footman of he period could stand against that.

When the Goths were fleeing from the Huns in the fourth entury, they did manage to borrow the Hunnish stirrup, and in '78, the Gothic horsemen demolished the Roman legions at the Battle of Adrianople. The cavalry was then supreme for a thou- and years, and the era of knighthood began.

Still, however much knights were idealized and heroicized in iction, in actual life they were cruel, despotic, and ferocious in heir treatment of the lower classes, and when they were finally nd disgracefully defeated, we all cheered.

The time came when the lower classes learned to fight the orsemen by keeping them at a distance and skewering them. In his the lower classes were greatly aided by that inevitable ccompaniment of arrogant aristocracy—invincible stupidity. The 'lemish burghers learned how to use the long pike in a steady ine (the rebirth of the Macedonian phalanx) and slaughtered the 'rench horsemen at the Battle of Courtrai in 1302. The English ongbowmen massacred French horsemen from a distance at the Battles of Crécy (1346), Poitiers (1356), Agincourt (1415), and Villeneuve (1420). The Swiss pikemen demolished the Burgundian orsemen in 1477, and by then gunpowder had established itself nd knighthood was all over.

But we still remember it in a golden glow of romance and, most of all, in the Arthurian legend—the tales of King Arthur of Britain and his Knights of the Round Table. In fact, anytime we peak of "knights" we think of those tales and, most of all, of ir Lancelot.

The Arthurian legend began with Geoffrey of Monmouth, vho, in about 1136, wrote his *History of British Kings*, and in ne process talked of Uther Pendragon, his son Arthur, and their elpful wizard, Merlin. It is not history, but myth and legend, et it fascinated its readers, who then, as today, would rather ave history appeal to their superstitions and patriotism than to ny abstract and bloodless passion for truth. If you want an excellent modern retelling of Geoffrey's tales, read *The High Kings* by Joy Chant (1983).

About 1170, a French poet, Chrétien de Troyes, took up the tale and added straightforward romance. It was he who first invented the adulterous passion of Lancelot and Guinevere, and the mystical tale of the search for the Holy Grail. Since Chrétien made no pretense to even the shadow of historical truth, his tales were even more popular than Geoffrey's.

Sir Thomas Malory put together the scattered fragments of the Arthurian legend into *Morte d'Arthur* ("The Death of Arthur") and it is his version, published in 1485, that we know best today

The legend has never died, and in each century it has been retold. In modern times there are Alfred, Lord Tennyson's *Idyll of the King* (1859), Mark Twain's *A Connecticut Yankee at King Arthur's Court* (1889), and T. H. White's *Once and Future King* (1958). From the last of these, the musical *Camelot* was taken Most recently, there is Marion Zimmer Bradley's *The Mists of Avalon* (1982).

The Arthurian legend is strictly fantasy. It is loaded with wizards, enchantresses, spells, and magicking. Those who at tempted to remove the fantasy and present the legend in a realistic manner were least successful. I found Tennyson to be dishwaterishly dull, for instance. Twain introduces the time travel motif, which makes for anachronistic amusement, but by turning Merlin into a flim-flam faker, he greatly detracts from the interest of the tale.

White, on the other hand, especially in *The Sword in the Stone* (1939), which is the first volume of his tetralogy, even adds to the fantasy, and his version rises superior to Malory for that reason (in my opinion). The same can be said of Bradley' painstaking *tour de force*.

It is not surprising, then, that modern fantasy writers turn every now and then to knightly romanticism and, in particular, to aspects of the Arthurian legend and try their teeth on it. Here in this anthology, for instance, we have ten stories of different types, all united by their possession of knightly heroes.

Zelazny, for instance, adds a moving epilogue to the Arthurian legend. Young, on the other hand, repeats Twain's attempt to deal with it anachronistically and humorously, but does so more successfully, I think. There are satires on the whole notion of knightliness from the careful self-consistency of de Camp to the rollicking implausibility of Hunter and the delightful ingenuousness of Grahame. There is even the straight science fiction (however fanciful it may seem at first blush) of Anderson and the horror tale of Schweitzer.

I am quite certain you will enjoy this collection even though you may not ever again be able to think of knights in quite the fashion you used to.

CRUSADER DAMOSEL

by Vera Chapman

Now retired, Vera Chapman (1898–) is an Oxford graduate and former missionary wife and welfare officer. She turned to writing late in life, probably as a result of activities in the Tolkien Society, which she founded in 1969. Her major work is the Three Damosels Trilogy (The King's Damosel, 1976, The Green Knight, 1978, and King Arthur's Daughter, 1978). It retells Arthurian legend from the viewpoints of three young women of the court.

The following historical fantasy presents a love story against the factual backdrop of the battle of the Horns of Hattin (1187).

When Adela learnt that her father was to go to the Holy Land, taking her and her mother with him, she was delighted. Her mother, Dame Blanche, was less delighted, but there was not much choice in the matter. Sir Brian de Bassecourt, of Stoke Bassecourt in the county of Kent, had been ordered by the Abbott to go on the Crusade, or else build an expensive chantry for the abbey—for Sir Brian had killed a monk. He hadn't really meant to kill the monk, he said, but when he found him halfway up the stairs to Dame Blanche's bower, he had given him a little push down, and—the man had broken his neck. The Abbot acquitted him of willful murder, but ordered that he should either build a chantry or go on the Crusade. Sir Brian wasn't a rich man, so although the Crusade might cost a good deal of money, the chantry would cost far more. Besides, there were advantages, as he pointed out to Dame Blanche.

"Just think—we get all our sins forgiven, all of them—yours too, and Adela's. And if we should die on the journey—"

Dame Blanche gave a shriek.

"*If* we should, we'd all go to heaven at once—no Purgatory at all. Think of that!"

"I'd rather not think of that," said Dame Blanche.

"Don't, then, my dear—never mind. There's other things. Almost everyone that goes out to Outremer comes back with a fortune. There's plunder, and ransoms—there's even lands and castles for the picking up. *And* we'd be sure to find a husband for Adela, which is more than we'll do here."

So Dame Blanche went about her preparations, tearfully at first, and later with zeal and fervour—and Adela watched the preparations with mounting excitement.

Adela was fifteen, and had never been outside Stoke Bassecourt, where they lived in a humdrum little farmhouse dignified by the name of Manor, which Duke William had bestowed on Sir Brian's great-grandfather. Adela had a fine Norman profile, jet-black hair, and blue eyes inherited from a Saxon grandmother. She was a bold girl, something of a tomboy, a good rider, and afraid of nothing she had met so far. But attractive as she was, she might as well go into a convent and be done with it, in that dull little corner. She'd never find a husband there.

So, after an overwhelming fuss and bother of preparation, they set out—Sir Brian in armour on his big charger, Dame Blanche in a mule litter, Adela on a palfrey. She had devised herself a dress like that invented by Queen Eleanor some seventy years before, when she and all her ladies went on the First Crusade with King Louis, before she became Queen of England. Well-cut leather breeches, discreetly covered by a long, voluminous divided skirt, so full and flowing that no one could see that the wearer sat easily astride on a man's saddle underneath all that brocade. There was also a light corselet of soft leather, shaped so as to enhance the figure very discreetly, and covered with a silken surcoat. In that outfit, with a hooded cape for the rain, Adela sat proudly and confidently on her pretty black mare.

The first rallying point was at Wrotham, for the Kentish levies. Here the Crusaders made their vows and "took the Cross—." Sir Brian had a bold red cross, made of two strips of red cloth, stitched to his mantle, while he took the Crusader's Oath in the church.

Adela wanted to be enrolled as a Crusader too. She saw at least two imposing ladies going up and receiving the Cross. "Why can't I?" she asked Sir Brian. "*They* can."

"Oh, yes, my dear, they do let ladies take the Cross, but only if they bring their own retinue of fighting men, as those two ladies are doing. I'm afraid my small following is barely a quota for one—besides that, you are under age."

But the noble words of the Crusader's Oath stayed in Adela's mind and haunted her. She wove daydreams about riding out to help King Guy to defend Jerusalem, with a long sword at her side, fighting to keep the heathen from regaining the Holy Sepulchre, the holiest spot on earth.

Somehow the milling crowd got across the Channel, and in the fields of France a long caravan formed, and slowly made its straggling way across Europe. It was an astonishing assembly—knights and noblemen with their soldiers, bands of volunteers from the country trudging with their bows, monks and clerics of every order, pilgrims, peddlers, hucksters and sutlers, wives and families of fighting men—and, of course, a number of dubious ladies who travelled with the wagons and were discreetly known as "baggage." Then there were smiths and cooks, with their furnaces and cauldrons, and flocks of sheep and herds of cattle to provide meat on the hoof—and Lord-knows-what besides. It was like a slowly moving town. Every day saw them strung out along the road, all in their accustomed order, with marshals riding up and down the line to keep them together. At night there could be the most astonishing variety of resting places. Sometimes they would reach a town or a castle, and then some of them at least (particularly the ladies, such as Adela and her mother) would be guests in comfort—or in more or less discomfort, as the luck was. Sometimes the company would halt in the open country, and make camp—everybody would pitch their tents, and once you got used to this and got organized, it wasn't bad at all. When a camp was made, it was a good opportunity to go up and down the lines and call on one's friends. Blanche did a good deal of visiting, with Adela beside her, rather overwhelmed with the newness of it all, and for the time being, diffident and a little withdrawn. Sir Brian brought young knights to their tent and presented them, ceremoniously, to Blanche and Adela. They were fine to look at, but Adela could find nothing to say to them.

Every morning began solemnly with Mass, either in the church of the town where they happened to be, or in a great pavilion set up with an altar and all the holy adornments—the knights and ladies devoutly kneeling on the grass outside. (But Dame Blanche took care to have a cushion.) It was one morning halfway through France, when Mass was being celebrated in the pavilion, and all the company was ranged in order outside, that Adela looked over her right shoulder, and saw a phalanx of men, standing foursquare together, in straight rows. All were in armour, and over the armour a white tunic and a long white mantle, emblazoned with the red cross. Their helmets were round, and cut straight across the top, like round towers. Something grim and resolute marked these men out from the rest. Adela ran her eyes along their faces, such of them as she could see. Mostly bearded, greyish, lined, some of them scarred. But one—he was young, bright-eyed. Something about him said to Adela: "This is the one."

She had turned half round—very naughtily—and for the life of her she could not keep herself from fixing her eyes on his face. And he looked at her for one moment—dark brown his eyes were—and a flash of understanding passed between them. Then Dame Blanche was pinching Adela's arm quite painfully, and jerking her round. Adela returned to her devotions—but she hardly knew what she was doing.

At the end of Mass, Adela stole a discreet glimpse over her shoulder—but now the crowd in general turned to see the men in white mantles, frowning and aloof, marching away in disciplined ranks. She tried in vain to see the face she had noticed.

"Adela," her mother said, "you mustn't look at those men. Don't you know what they are? Those are the Knights Templars."

"Are they? Well, what's wrong with them?"

"Nothing *wrong* with them—but don't you understand, they mustn't look at women, or even let women look at them. They are under a vow of poverty, obedience, and—chastity. You keep your eyes away from them, my dear."

But Adela had looked once too often already.

The Templars, part of whose duty it was to protect pilgrims, and the relatives and dependents of Crusaders, on their way to the Holy Land, now constituted themselves a guard to the company. Strung out at intervals, they patrolled the borders of the road, as well as going ahead and also covering the rear. They changed their positions often—and so one day Adela saw that face again, and then again, and found out from some of the servants that his name was Hugo Des Moulins, and that in spite of his French name, he was an English knight from Sussex. She looked him in the face, but the first time he answered her look with a kind of breathlessness, and the second time with a frown of anxiety, almost of pain. She knew she ought not to let her mind dwell on him, but how could she help it? And as they continued on their way, and reached Venice, and took ship (a dreadful passage it was) to Acre, her case grew more and more desperate. Until at last, at Acre, as soon as they were settled into their humble quarters in the great stony fortress, she felt she must take action. So, as soon as she knew where that lady would be quartered, she sought out the Abbess of Shaston.

The Abbess of Shaston was a remarkable woman. She knew a wonderful great deal about a great many things—people came to her to be cured of illnesses, and of heartaches—to resolve doubts, and points of law, and settle quarrels; to seek love, or to be delivered from love; she was sought by women who wished to have babies, and, it was whispered, by those who did not. She could not be called a midwife nor a leech, for such occupations would be beneath the dignity of an Abbess; but it was thought that she knew more than all the wise-women and all the doctors together. She went back and forward to the Holy Land as it pleased her, and it was said that she knew the secrets of the Saracens as well as of the Christians. She was certainly not a witch—nobody dared say such a thing, for she had high connections. She obeyed no authority lower than the Pope's—if his, seeing that she was perhaps his cousin. She was strangely beautiful and very stately. Adela sought her out, taking with her the little jewel-box she always carried with her, containing such modest jewelry as she possessed. She opened this, and left it lying open before the Abbess.

"Put those things away, child," said the Abbess. "Now tell me. You're in love, of course?"

So Adela told her.

"A Templar? That's difficult. Why did it have to be a Templar, you silly girl? You know he can't marry you. Do you want to be his paramour?"

Adela blushed. "Oh, but Templars don't have paramours."

"Don't they, then?—There's a lot you don't know about Templars.—But that wouldn't do for you, nor for him, I think. What do you want, then?"

"Can't a Templar ever be absolved from his vows?"

"Oh, yes, he can. The Pope can dispense his vow. I'd see it done myself—the Pope would do it for me." She spoke with airy assurance. "Only—the petition must come from him, not from anyone else. He himself must ask for it. Would he do that—for you?"

"He doesn't know me," said Adela with her eyes downcast.

"No.—Oh, but he does, though. He dreams of you."

"How—how on earth do you know?"

"Never mind how—but I know. You and he know each other quite well, on the Other Side of the Curtain. But that's no good for earthly matters."

"What do you mean—the Other Side of the Curtain?"

"The other side of life and being. Even beyond dreams. Out of the body. You and he meet together, night after night, while your dreams hang a misleading curtain before your mortal minds."

Adela felt as if a great window was opened before her, full of beauty and wonder.

"Oh, if only I could know—if only I could remember! Could you not send me through the Curtain in my waking mind, or make it so that I remembered?"

"My child, I believe I could. But you must attend and do exactly as I say."

So then she gave Adela certain instructions, and taught her certain words and certain signs. And once again she waved aside Adela's jewel-box.

So that night, Adela, lying on her bed wide awake, and having done all that the Abbess told her, felt herself rise out of her body, like slipping a hand out of a glove. She looked down at herself lying peacefully asleep on the bed, and then she stepped over herself, and was lightly out of doors and across the night and into a moonlit orchard, where Hugo was waiting for her.

"Welcome, my dear companion," he said, and clasped both her hands, but did not kiss her. It was enough for her, so far—just to feel his happy fellowship.

"I knew you would come," he said. "You always do."

"Yes," she answered, feeling quite sure that they had known each other quite well for a long time. "But this time I shall know what I am doing, and remember it afterwards."

"I wish I did," he said. "I never remember anything when I am awake. I don't know even that I know you."

"What do you call me—here?" she asked.

"Why—Adal, I think," he answered.

"And am I a boy or a girl?"

"A boy, of course—no, a girl—oh, to be sure, I don't know," and he laughed in confusion. "But come on—the trumpets are sounding—we must ride against the infidel."

By his side was a horse, saddled and ready, and she got up behind him. It seemed that they were both armoured and accoutered in the Templars' armour, and she had a long sword by her side. She remembered the device on the Templars' seal—two knights riding on one horse.

They galloped out of the orchard, and it was daylight. Before them lay a wide plain, and far off a little compact city on a hill, which she knew must be Jerusalem. Behind them rode the squadron of the Templars, but she could not see them clearly because they were behind her. Suddenly, as they rode toward the City, there rose up before them a host of ugly little black men. They were apelike and dusty-looking, their clothes black as well as their faces, and on their heads were small red turbans with golden crescents. They all looked alike, and all had horrible grinning faces, and sharp crooked swords.

"Oh, what are these?" exclaimed Adela.

"Paynims, Saracens—have no fear of them—charge for the Cross!" And he drew his sword and galloped into the thick of them. She drew her sword too, but passed it into her left hand so that as he slashed on the right she could slash on the left. In the body which she now seemed to have, her left arm was as good as her right.

They hewed at the little black men, who fought fiercely and shouted, but fell as they slashed them, without any blood—they seemed to be made of something like soft wood, or wax, and never bled, nor did their expressionless faces show any pain. More and more came up on them, but they hewed them all down, and rushed on through them with a fierce delight. Behind them came the other Crusaders but never overtook them. At one moment Hugo drew rein, and Adela was able to look behind them—there were a few of the Crusaders fallen, but over each one hovered a fine white-winged angel, just like those in the church paintings at home—gently drawing the man's soul out of his body, and carrying it upward.

The Holy City was nearer now, and shone with gold; on a pinnacle in the midst Our Lady stood, in a robe of blue, with the Holy Child in her arms. As the Crusaders fought their way towards the City through the tumbling black men, Our Lady smiled at Hugo and Adela and flung a handful of rose petals.

And then Adela was suddenly awake, and it was all a dream—or was it? The tips of her fingers smelt of roses.

There were galleries all round the great courtyard, and there Adela, her mother, and all the ladies of the company, were seated on the chairs to watch a spectacle. Down below, the courtyard was thronged with armed men. With pomp and pageantry, a procession entered below. Count Raymond himself, with all his peers, glittering with metal and coloured silks, and a tall swordsman by his side, and men with a brazier. Adela supposed the brazier was to keep Count Raymond warm out there.

Then were led in a long line of tall, dignified men, in long white robes and turbans. Their arms were tied, and the foot soldiers led them along. Their faces were sallow but pale, and their eyes dark, and all had beards, some black, some grey. They

held themselves with sorrowful composure, and reminded Adela
of pictures she had seen of Christian martyrs.

"Oh, who are these?" she asked.

"Paynims, child—Saracens, Mussulmans and heathens. These
are the enemy."

"Oh—" But these were not in the least like the little black
men in the dream.

The first was led before Court Raymond in his chair. Now,
Adela thought, he will loose his bonds and set him free. The
paynim man made a low obeisance—Count Raymond gave a
sign to the man with the sword—the sword fell, and the paynim's
head toppled horribly to the ground. Indeed these were not like
the little men who did not bleed. . . .

Another and another. . . . There were some whose hands were
chopped off. . . .

"They don't feel anything, those paynims," said Dame Blanche.
'They'd serve our own men the same if they caught them.
Anyway they've refused baptism. Now this one will be a differ-
ent punishment, look—"

"Let me go—I don't feel well," Adela said, shuddering, and
escaped to her room, where she cried for hours.

It was some nights before she could get "through the Curtain"
to Hugo again, but when she did, she told him about it, and all
her horror and revulsion. And he looked serious and worried,
and said, "How can we understand? All we know, when we are
awake, is that we must obey and fight. But I know—I have felt it
too."

But then the little black men crept up on them, and once again
they had to fight their way through them. And this time they
broke right through the Saracen army, and came to the golden
walls of the Holy City—and the gates stood open, and they went
in. There was nobody to be seen there—all stood deserted, all
the houses of gold, with their windows of jewels—but from
somewhere, high up, a sound of heavenly music and joyful
singing filled the air. From every part of the city could be seen
the pinnacle where Our Lady stood.

"Come," said Hugo, "we must seek the Sepulchre of the
Lord," and they went on through the golden streets, but some-

where the ways diverged, and Adela looked round for Hugo and
he was not there. She went on, calling for him, and found herself
outside the City on the other side, looking back at the walls.

And there before her, but facing the City, was the host of the
Saracens—those same tall, turbaned, white-robed men, with pale
faces and dark beards. They were armed and on horses, and
galloping, galloping towards the City. Out against them came a
horde of little black men, just like those she had fought against
with Hugo, just as ugly and just as wooden, but these had round
red caps on their heads with silver crosses on them. And the
Saracens charged into them, hewing and slicing off heads, arms
and legs as before; and as before, the little black men fell
without bleeding and with no sign of pain. Before the Saracens,
as they fought, stood the Holy City, but on the pinnacle where
Adela had seen Our Lady was a tall tree full of flowers. Some of
the Saracens fell, and over each one hovered a beautiful girl,
with butterfly wings and clothed in rainbow silks, who drew out
his soul and carried it aloft.

Two Saracens closed up beside her.

"Come, lady," they said, "we welcome you with all honour."
They led her away from the battle, to a richly decorated tent
where sat Saladin himself on silken cushions. He smiled and
bade her welcome, and as she thought of the tall men slaughtered
in the castle yard, her eyes filled with tears.

"Lady of the Giaours," he said, "if we all pitied our enemies,
there would be no wars."

"And would not that be a good thing?" she said with the
boldness of a dream.

"Ah, who knows? But we know that Allah made soldiers to
fight. What else would they do?"

He made her sit on cushions by his side, and sip a strange
sweet drink, and he told her a password which she was to
remember. Over and over he said it—and she woke up saying it.
In the moment of waking she wrote it down, in a sort of fashion,
in such letters as she knew, just so that she should not forget it.

Everything was astir in the castle and town of Acre. "We
shall have to move as soon as we can," said Sir Brian. "Get
boats and be off to-morrow early. It isn't safe here. Saladin's

forces are between us and Tiberias. We're cut off. Tiberias is besieged, with Count Raymond's wife and family in it. Some say the army is to march on Tiberias—some say not. I know what *we'll* do. Get packed.''

So the rest of the day was full of bustle. But Adela, whose heart was heavy with foreboding, went to sleep early.

When she slipped out of her body, and went in search of Hugo, she knew there was a difference. She did not find herself in the moonlit orchard—she was not in the magical world of visions, but hovering over and wandering through the real world, like a ghost, unseen. She was watching the army of the Crusaders on the march, through the night, the Templars leading. Hugo was there, on his horse, but not riding gallantly. They were none of them riding gallantly. They laboured through the night on tired horses, and drooped in their saddles. She heard them talking.

"Why on earth did we have to leave Sephoria? Plenty of water in Sephoria, and a good defensive position. But no—before we'd time even to water the horses—"

"And after marching all day—hardly time for a mouthful to drink, and God! I'm thirsty . . ."

"They say the Commanders quarrelled. Count Raymond, like a sensible man, said stay in Sephoria, with the water, and wait a bit—though, mind you, it's *his* wife and children who are in Tiberias. He said it was a trap to get us to move out. And King Godfrey listened to him, didn't he?"

"Yes, but then Count Gerard came in, and said Raymond was a traitor and had sold out to the Saracens. So King Guy got in a panic and ordered us to march on Tiberias at once, before we'd had any rest."

"What can you do, when your Commanders disagree?—Oh, what would I give for a drink. Never mind ale or wine—just water."

"If we can get through to Galilee, there's plenty of water."

"And all the Saracens between us and Galilee. The horses will founder first."

"What's this place we're making for—the top of that hill?"

"They call it Hattin—the Horns of Hattin—the Horns of Hattin—"

She moved through the ranks and hoverd over Hugo, trying to enter his mind. But all that came across to her was thirst, thirst, thirst—and the oppressive weight of his armour, the heat inside it, the weakness of the body that had sweated all day and was now drained dry. The grey-faced old Templars rode beside him, bidding him cheer up, for the more the suffering the greater the glory. He listened dull-eyed.

She woke, dry-throated, crying out, "Water, water—the Horns of Hattin, the Horns of Hattin . . ."

She knew what she had to do. Quietly she slipped out of bed and dressed in her riding breeches and corselet, but without the skirt, and threw a hooded mantle over her. Stealthily she slipped out to the horse-lines, found her own black mare, saddled her, and before she mounted, slung on her saddle two small casks full of water. It was as much as she could require the mare to carry.

The sentry at the door barred her way.

"Oh, please—" she said.

"Oh, a lady. By heaven, the Lady Adela—"

"Soldier," she said, "you know why people sometimes have reasons to slip out alone—"

Certainly he did—with half the Castle engaged in love affairs. "Surely—but *you*, Lady Adela—I'd never have thought *you*—" In the dark he could not see her blush.

"All right, my lady—not a word from me. But take care of yourself, won't you?" He let her past.

Then she rode like the wind towards Tiberias.

From daybreak to noon she rode, and that noon was fiercely hot. It was July, and the grass was dry and the earth was splitting. Once in sheer exhaustion she dismounted, drank from a wayside spring and let the mare drink, and rested a short time. She could not have eaten if she had had food with her. Then she went on eastwards, and as she went she could smell burning grass. Nothing unusual in that—the grass caught fire very easily at that season. But now the smoke was denser—soon it was a choking smother. As she came up a hill, and saw Galilee below her, she also saw the battle. It raged fiercely over the plateau— the Horns of Hattin! The army of the Cross, fighting fiercely, fighting desperately against the vast, overwhelming army of the

Saracens. As they fought, the smoke from the grass-fire, blowing away from the Saracens, covered the Crusaders in its stifling, throat-drying fog.

The foot soldiers had broken and fled. Most of the horses lay exhausted on the ground, and the knights were falling one by one, or lying, helpless heaps of clashing metal, at their enemies' feet. This was no battle of little black bloodless men—far from it. Adela was spared nothing of the blood and horror.

Alone among the rest stood the Templars and the Hospitallers, grouped around the black-and-white banner, isolated in the field like the last sheaf to be reaped. They were laying about them fiercely, and Hugo was amongst them—but they were failing. As she watched she saw him fall.

Without a moment's hesitation she spurred forward, forcing the unwilling mare to face the smoke. But there was rough cliff in front of her, and a drop—no way down. She had to go round, and the only way she could go led her in a curve to the opposite side of the battlefield. She found herself dashing into the lines of the Saracens. Hands reached up to catch her bridle-reins.

"Oh, let me go!" she exclaimed, not at all sure if they understood her language. "I must get to him. I must save life—save life, do you understand?" The dark faces grinned, not comprehending. It seemed the battle was over—the Saracens were coming back from the field, leading prisoners.

Then Adela remembered the password she had learnt from Saladin in her dream, and spoke it.

The men fell back in astonishment, and let her through.

Down that grim hillside she went, the smoke still all about her. She tried to remember the place where she had seen Hugo all by the black-and-white standard. The worst was having to pass the other men, wounded, dying, ghastly, who cried to her from the ground for water. Some of them were too parched to cry out. Some seemed to be unwounded—it was only the heat and the smoke and the drought that had killed them. But she could not spare any water at all. There were one or two with still enough strength to scramble to their feet and try to snatch the water-barrels. But she beat them off with her riding-whip—they had not much strength after all and could not run after her.

And at last she found him.

He lay on a horrible heap of dead men, and he did not move.
She dismounted, and dragged him aside to a clean patch of
ground, and bathed his face, and trickled water into his mouth,
and freed him from his armour—she had to take his dagger to cut
its lacings, and even when she had unfastened it, the metal was
still hot to the touch. She flung each piece away from him. He
began to stir, opened his eyes, and then was able to swallow the
water she held to his lips. She laid a wet kerchief over his
nostrils against the smoke. And when at last he showed enough
signs of life, she helped him on to her mare, and mounted behind
him, holding him, and so rode slowly and carefully away from
that dreadful place, once again like two Templars on one horse.
She went boldly through the camp of the Saracens, and spoke
that password. The Saracens buzzed and chattered in amazement,
and some of them sent messengers to tell Saladin, but they let
them through.

And after a long time they halted by the sweet shores of
Galilee, and she laid him with his back propped against a
sycamore tree, and let him drink again. And then he took notice
of her at last.

"Adal," he said. "My good comrade. But I thought truly that
we had been through Purgatory together, and were entering
Paradise. But now I know that you are a woman."

"Are you glad or sorry?" she said.

"Oh, I'm glad, I'm glad!" he cried. "And yet—what am I
saying? My vow—the Templars—"

Very gently she told him how the Templars and the Hospitallers lay on the battlefield. He crossed himself, and wept. Then
he held out his arms to her as if she had been his mother.

"And now—but what shall we do, my love, what shall we
do?"

"I know what we must do," she said. "We'll go to the
Abbess of Shaston. She'll make everything right for us."

DIVERS HANDS

by Darrell Schweitzer

With the lean and hungry look of Cassius, Darrell Schweitzer (1952–) provides a good example of the drive necessary to succeed as a freelance writer. Immerse yourself in the field: write stories for small magazines (such as Whispers*), write nonfiction about the field (such as* Conan's World *and* Robert E. Howard*), conduct author interviews for larger magazines (such as* Amazing*), and support yourself by assisting in the editing of SF magazines (such as* Isaac Asimov's Science Fiction Magazine *and* Amazing*) while you try to write some more.*

No wonder Sir Julian (the protagonist of We Are All Legends*, 1981) is seized with the compulsion to strangle people in the following story.*

"In what battle was it, Sir Knight, and to what foe did you lose your hand? Did you slay him who maimed you thus?"

The speaker was seated before me, a short, hooded man with a copious gray beard. I could not see his face in the fading twilight. He was the last one to come that day into my tent, at the crossroads fair in the mountain country beyond the empire of the Greeks, which is called Byzantium. The circumstance was

21

a strange one: I, Julian, of various names and titles, long since lost to chivalry and my God, was reduced to beggary, shunned by the folk of every land. Who would trust this grim, hook-handed knight in tarnished mail, whose shield and surcoat bore not the emblem of the cross? What is he doing here? Is he really a man, they would ask, or some creature out of the darkness? Why goes he not with his comrades, to the east to fight the pagans? At the fairground, in that tent in a strange land near a strange city, and speaking a tongue I knew but rudely, I seemed to fit in, at least for the moment. I could not admit to myself that mere existence had become an end in itself, and each hour of peace a worthy goal for a long quest.

To make a living I told tales of my travels and of the adventures of others, and sometimes when these failed I invented, but no one could tell when I lied and when I didn't. Ever popular was my sojourn in the land of darkness, where dwell folk marvelously transfigured, so that their heads grow beneath their shoulders, and their ears, appended to their arms, stretch wide like the wings of bats, enabling them to fly. Also there were the salt maidens of Antioch, whose tears filled up their entire forms, so that they were left pillars of salt, like Lot's wife, when they mourned a blasphemer struck dead by the Apostle Peter. As each tale concluded, the listener would drop a coin in the bowl I had set out—and the telling was rewarding in another way too.

Being a storyteller is like confessing to a priest—nay—more like the fool in the fable who buried his head among the reeds and whispered *King Midas has asses' ears*. Everyone knows, but it is a fanciful thing. Who believes what is said by the wind in the reeds? Thus one can be unburdened of truth. So I told the questioner the true answer:

"Long and long ago it seems, but not very long ago in fact, there was a knight who met the Devil face to face in a ruined hall deep in the forest, and there he gave himself to him, to ransom a maiden who had been wronged. This was, by his faith, and his faith was a terror to him thereafter, the only chivalrous thing he had done in his entire life, for all his ideals, all his training, all his deeds. And for this he was damned, so that the Devil did not take his soul just then, so sure a thing it was, but instead commanded him, '*Go wander the world which shall this day be made anew, and forever be a stranger, until at last you come to me.'* And in his travels he met an evil thing, which in the guise of a lady comforted him, but in truth drank away his blood and his years. When the thing was slain, as needs it must be, the knight woke from a blissful dream in those false arms, and was confused, and in misguided wrath killed his deliverer, and for this was again damned. Then, on one of the occasions when he wished his life would end, but knew it could not, lest the Devil have him at once, he sought the Vale of Mistorak in the farthest East, and there conversed with a spirit, but bought those words with his own flesh, and that is how he lost his hand.''

"And was the bargain well made?" asked the listener. "Was the answer satisfactory?"

"If it were, would I be here in the tent telling such wild tales?"

The hooded one wheezed what was supposed to be a laugh.

"I have no coin for you," he said, "but in exchange, a tale of my own. There was a king, whose name was Tikos, who ruled over a very ancient land. To the castle of his fathers came all the great lords of the world at one time or other. Alexander came there as a boy, and saw the wonder of it, and when he grew older turned his armies away from it, toward the east. But at long last, through treachery wrought by the priests of a new god, against whom the old gods were powerless, the people seized the king and mutilated him according to their custom, cutting off his right hand so that he might never again raise a sword, cutting off his left so he could hold no scepter. Thus was the king reduced to misery and scorn, until he found a way to gain his revenge. He swore himself to a new master. He became *Nekatu*."

"Nekatu?"

"As such he had vast powers, including prophecy. It has been prophesied that the knight of your story will come to the castle of the king of mine, and learn what that word means."

With that, he rose and left the tent. The flap waved like a flag with his passing.

"Wait!" I sprang up and went after him, bursting out into the evening air. It was intensely cold already, as it gets so quickly in the mountains. Beyond the peaks, the sun had set in a splash of gold. Overhead, the stars were already out, and I was sure the chill wind I felt came from between them, from beyond the mortal earth, where winged demons freely traffic. Such a demon my listener must have been to get away so fast. There was no sign of him anywhere.

Nekatu, he had said. That was the first time I ever heard the term.

That night as I slept I was haunted by evil dreams, at first, a recurring vision of a meadow strewn with the newly slain, all of them rising up as I approached, their wounds unhealed, to fight again in hopeless misery. Their cries at last drove me from the dream, and I awoke, bewildered for an instant, finding my tent an unfamiliar place. Then I listened to the night noises, tethered horses stamping in the cold, the crackle of campfires, a dog barking, someone singing. Beyond all that, an owl hooted.

I slept again, and this time I was riding through a dark wood, where every tree seemed to lean low with the weight of monstrous menace crouched in the branches, and inhuman faces peered fleetingly between the trunks. I had seldom known such terror in the waking world. My horse wanted to rear up and bolt, and only with utmost effort could I retain control. I gave in to the animal's instincts some, letting it speed up to a trot, then a canter, and finally a full gallop, as its panic and mine were one, and we thundered through the forest in a rain of great clods of mud thrown up by the hooves, and still there were the feeling of suffocating dread, and the half-glimpsed forms between the trees. Then I turned around in the saddle and looked behind me, and saw that I was indeed pursued, by another knight clad all in black mail and a black surcoat, mounted on a black steed, with his visor raised and a bare skull for a face. Then I screamed, and awoke again into the tent, and there was absolute silence in the camp, with every ear turned my way. Was the strange knight wrestling with a demon in his bed? I knew I would have to leave in the morning, before the tale grew in the retelling and reached the ears of a priest, and too many questions were asked.

Just before dawn I dozed off again. I was still riding through the forest, the apparition just behind me, and I was exhausted, as if my dream self had been fleeing on the foam-flecked dream horse all the while I had been awake. The terror was still there, and every instant seemed my last, until finally the forest broke

into an open plain where two rivers joined. Where they joined
stood a walled town, and beyond it, with a river girding it on
either side, was a lone mountain. Three of its sides were sheer
cliffs, but on a fourth a road wound down, crossed a bridge, and
entered the far side of the town. Atop the mountain perched a
castle of black stone. As soon as I spied this place it seemed a
great weight was lifted from me, and another glance over my
shoulder revealed that my nemesis had vanished. I let my horse
slow to a walk, and as I approached the town and castle, the sun
rose behind me, out of the forest, banishing all evil.

The last thing I saw—and I don't know if I imagined or truly
dreamed it—was the hooded stranger rising from where he sat
over a steaming caldron, stretching his cramped legs, while
within all the things in my dreams, the knight, the horse, the
forest, the castle, and even myself, sank slowly through the
broth to the bottom and there dissolved away.

I had no more visions that night.

There were people milling about when I awoke the third time.
When I emerged from my tent they steadfastly refused to look
directly at me or speak a word, even if questioned. And I knew
not to persist in questioning. Some were breaking camp, piling
unsold goods into carts, making ready to go even before the fair
was over. I didn't have to ask the reason. An ill omen. There
would be no luck in this place, and perhaps a curse for those
who lingered. Next year the fair would doubtless be held somewhere else.

I didn't linger either, but instead packed what supplies and
money I had into saddle pouches and rode away, leaving my tent
where it stood. I couldn't take it with me in any case. For all I
cared, the old bread-seller from whom I'd bought it could have it
back. He might want to wrestle a devil in there sometime.

I knew that in such dreams, from wherever sent, something of
import had been revealed, if a little vaguely, as is the manner of
dreams. But such things cannot be without meaning. Indeed, as
had been prophesied, I rode west, and that very afternoon came
to the forest I had seen. It was not as sinister as its dream self,
but always in the periphery of my sight there was a suggestion of
a shape that set me ill at ease. I glanced back now and again to

see if I was followed. I was alone, but my steed was as nervous as I, and difficult to control.

Beyond the wood was a plain, as I had foreseen, and two rivers met, and a mountain reared above all. One could only reach the castle atop it by passing through the town, as if the castle were the innermost keep of a larger fortress surrounding it.

Soon I came upon peasants bringing their crops to market. The folk on this side of the forest seldom dared venture to the other, so they were not the same who had been at the fair, or so I hoped. There were all sorts going the same way: two priests—and I recoiled unconsciously at the sight of them—a boy with a mandolin slung over his shoulder, obviously a minstrel, and every variety of low-born person, afoot, astride mules and plow horses, or in carts.

As the traffic increased there were even a few of the wealthy in their ponderous, solid-wheeled carriages, surrounded by troops of men at arms. It occurred to me to seek employment as one such, but first I knew I must discharge whatever supernatural obligation had been laid on me, the dreams would continue, the skeletal rider overtake me as I slept, and at the very least I would awaken mad.

There was a soldier at the town's gate leaning lazily on a pike, asking each man what his business was. A farmer would drive up with a load of cabbages, announce that he'd come to sell cabbages, and be passed through with a bored wave. The nobles in their carriages would be known by the signs of their houses, inevitably on a banner carried by one of their horsemen, and not challenged at all.

In my case, it was not that simple.

"What do you want here?" Seeing that I wore a mail coat under my cloak and a steel cap on my head, and carried a sword, and eying the plain black shield that hung by my saddle, and all the while knowing by the most cursory glance that I was a foreigner, the guard stood up attentively, and raised his pike to block my way.

An equally cursory glance on my part revealed no other guards nearby, and none of the men at arms attending the carriages were close enough to come immediately to his assistance, or even ascertain at once what was going on.

So I reached up with my right hand—my only hand, the hook being hidden beneath the cloak—and pushed the pike away. At the same time I feigned a rage and glared at him.

"You filthy churl! How dare you question your betters?" My Greek was rough, but I was understood. The pike dropped limply away, and the fellow's mouth hung agape. He didn't know what to do, and alone he dared do nothing. So I took reign again in hand and spurred my horse quickly into the city before he could recover his wits. Almost as quickly I wondered if I had done the right thing. Would the guard brave his master's wrath and report his incompetence? Well, the die was cast, as Caesar had once remarked, and I had done what I had done. If my strange saga were known, I surely would not be welcomed here, but first I wanted to know what sort of place this was before seeking out its lord and making my way to the castle.

In the main square something was going on which wasn't standard trading or entertainment.

A large crowd had gathered and there was much excitement. I stood up in my stirrups to see more clearly. It was an execution. A man was being drawn and quartered between four separately harnessed oxen. Even over the yells of the mob I could hear his shrieks. As he hung there above the ground, and hooded executioners stood by with switches ready to prod the animals on, another, presumably the Master Executioner, had slit his belly open, yanked out an end of intestine, and begun coiling it around a stick. With every firm, jerking turn came another scream. Then one of the prisoner's arms slipped from the ropes, and I saw why—he had no hand, so the wrist slid right out of the knot. Gesticulating furiously, the master rose from the disemboweling, kicked one of his assistants aside, and retied the rope, below the elbow this time.

As if this sight reminded them of something, the crowd began to shout with one voice a single word: *"Nekatu! Nekatu!"*

I sat down, startled. That was the second time I had heard the name, or term, or whatever it was, and I liked the circumstance even less well than I had the first. I took care that my own lack of a hand was concealed. I doubted this was the criminal's offense, but instinct counseled caution.

Disgusted, I rode around the edge of the square and along a

narrow street filled with booths. Behind me the shouts of the crowd came to a crescendo, then stopped.

Now, most cities I have seen are vast caverns of wood and stone, and this one was no exception. Night begins early in a city. Even the great capital of Constantinople is lighted only around the palace and guard houses, and in a few principal squares. The common people grope like the blind through muddy, treacherous streets. In this place the upper stories of the houses leaned over the back street, the all but touching roofs shutting out all but the light of noontide. As I rode it was well into the evening, the fading sunset reflected only from those high gables and rooftops which caught the glow.

I came to a gap in the buildings, where I could get a full view of the castle on the hill beyond the town. Now it was silhouetted starkly against the western sky. Even as time passed, and the light faded even more, the place remained dark. Not a torch was lit in a tower; not a lantern glowed from any window. It seemed simply impossible that it could be deserted with a thriving town at its feet.

"Hist!" someone whispered. "Don't be staring at that! Ye'll bring a curse down on yer head."

I looked down, astonished that anyone would speak to me in such a manner. It was an old woman, her hair a tangled white explosion, with a bundle of sticks on her shoulder.

"And what ill can come from looking at the house of your lord? Woman, do you speak treason against him?"

Her face all but split apart with an irregularly toothed grin.

"Our *lord*? Ha! Our mortal lord lives here in the town. Only the wicked call *him* lord!" To make herself more clear, she pointed at the castle with her free hand.

"Does Satan himself roost up there then?" I laughed back at her.

" 'Tis no subject for a jest, good sir. That one they quartered today—that's what happens to people who take too much interest in evil places." She crossed herself hastily.

"For merely looking at it?"

She grinned again. Now I was sure she took me for a fool, for all my higher birth.

"He *went* there. He was *Nekatu!*"

As soon as she uttered that word, the exchange was no longer a joke. I leaned over in the saddle and faced her intently. Despite the gloom I could see her eyes well enough to tell she was suddenly frightened of me.

"I have heard of this *Nekatu* many times. Twice since I came here. Old woman, there is gold in this for you if you will kindly tell me what—may the saints perserve us—everyone is talking about. What is *Nekatu?*"

She put her hand to her mouth and said nothing. Ah, I thought. Her tongue is suddenly tied in knots. Thinking to loosen it, I reached into my purse for one of my few coins. But the leather thong was too tightly drawn. I couldn't get it open with one hand. So without giving it any thought, I slipped the tip of my hook between the thong and the bag to work it loose.

And the woman screamed. At the sight of the hook she dropped her bundle and ran down the street shrieking "Nekatu! Help! Help! Another one! Nekatu!"

Instantly what seemed an empty alley filled with people. Some grabbed at my horse's reins. I drew my sword and slashed, and there was a howl of pain, but by then dozens of others had swarmed all around. Hands were pulling me from the saddle. My horse reared up in terror, which only helped them, even if a few skulls were split beneath the hooves. I tumbled over backwards out of the saddle and into the muddy street, striking furiously with sword and hook.

This had a temporary effect. No one was holding me when I hit the ground. I struggled to my feet. Whirling steel kept my foes temporarily at bay. None of them were armed with anything more fearsome than some of the old woman's firewood.

This changed almost at once. Nearby mail clinked, and I glanced quickly in the direction the crone had run. The pikes and steel helmets of the city guard were working their way through the jostling crowd.

With renewed fury I cut my way through the wall of my assailants. My horse had run off. I would have to escape on foot. An iron shoe in the groin, a chop at an upraised arm, a raking slash across the face with my metal hook, and I was no longer surrounded. A shout went up from the guards, and all the people regained their courage and surged after me. The chase went along that street into a narrower one, splashing through the mud, pushing passersby roughly aside until they understood what was happening, and joined in. The cry of *"Nekatu!"* seemed to be a kind of universal alarm, and every citizen stopped what he or she was doing and united against the common enemy.

My mail and my iron-covered shoes weighed me down, and I surely would have been overtaken before long had the chaotic fray not spilled into a lane so narrow that there was barely enough room to squeeze a cart along it—and there was a cart heading straight toward us.

Some of my pursuers hesitated, but I lunged forward with desperate speed. The cart driver drew reins, unsure of what was going on. Before he knew it I was alongside him. I flattened myself against a wall, then gave his horse a long, shallow swipe on the rump with my sword. Of course the enraged animal charged forward, completely out of control, right into the mass of my foes. As it clattered past, the protruding axles of the cart missed me by scarcely a span.

Breathing heavily, but still maintaining the strength which had brought me through countless battles, I came at last to the far end of the town, where a gate led to the bridge over the river, then to the winding road up the one less than utterly sheer side of the mountain. This gate was barred from the inside. Now the bridge itself was fortified, and a small number of soldiers thereon could surely prevent an enemy from climbing up onto it from barges. This side was otherwise completely inaccessible. The thick, slippery wall of the town dropped straight to the water's edge, leaving no more than a foot or two of muddy bank. In any case, I'd seen no indication that this was a time of war.

Not hesitating to ponder this idiocy of siege design in a town that seemed completely crazy anyway, I placed both shoulders beneath the massive wooden bar, and with all my strength forced it up until it rose free of its supports and fell to the ground with a thud. The gate swung outward and I staggered backwards through it, onto the bridge.

By now those who hadn't been trampled by the runaway cart had found me again. With long strides I ran across the bridge and partway up the mountain. Then I turned to look. They

'eren't following. The crowd now filled the gateway, but none
'ould venture forth. A tangle of faces stared up at me, sullen
ıd quiet. It only seemed fitting that people who so irrationally
:ared men who were missing hands, and who so shunned the
ıstle around which their town was built that they condemned to
:ath anyone who went there, should behave in so ridiculous a
'ay. I was sure they were all lunatics. With a contemptuous
ıort, I turned and made my way up the mountain at a leisurely
ıce.

It was only after I had gone a ways and the castle loomed huge
ıove me, blotting out the stars, that it occurred to me that the
:ople might have been sensible after all. Could there be some
ınger lurking among those towers such that one going the way I
'as would be ensured a more frightful doom than anything the
xecutioner could contrive?

If so, I was in a terrible situation, like a man who cannot swim
apped on a burning ship. I could not return to the town. There
'as no way to go but up, into the castle I had first glimpsed in a
ream. In that dream it had been a place of relief and refuge, but
ow I was not so sure.

There was a little door beside the main gate of the castle, with
 heavy metal iron for a knocker. I clanged the thing until the
ıund must surely have echoed throughout the whole land.

There was a stirring within.

"Nekatu," I said.

A bolt slid aside and the door opened.

This is how I found refuge among the *Nekatu.*

II

"The phrase *'nekatu'* literally means 'messenger,' not in Greek,
ıt in the older language of these people. As you see, I have
ıade good my promise. As soon as you arrived here, you
arned the definition."

The same hooded stranger who had come to my tent the night
:fore now led me up a winding flight of stairs, and into a large
»om. I couldn't tell how large. He carried only a small oil lamp,
ıd nothing was lighted. The castle was clearly in a state of

considerable disrepair. I could dimly make out fallen beams
stones, and tattered draperies scattered about.

He put the lamp down on a bare wooden table, pulled out
high-backed chair, and indicated that I should sit. The onl
sounds were the scraping of the chair, the clank of my shoe:
and the soft pad of his slippers. He stood and I sat absolutely sti
for a moment, and the only sound was a slight fizzling from th
lamp. Then there was something else: a faint pattering, like th
scurrying of rats. At first I thought it to be that, but there wasn
enough scratching. Too soft, without claws. More like mar
people drumming their fingers nervously on wood.

I watched my host's every move with utmost suspicion. A
this had been his contrivance. He wanted something. I was beir
brought here as surely as a fish on a hook. To make the poi
that I was not utterly helpless, I did not sheathe my swor
which I had carried in hand all the way up the mountain, b
placed it in clear view in front of me. It clattered, and for ¿
instant the tapping sound in the background stopped. Then
resumed, somewhat closer.

The hood fell back, and a thin, bearded, ageless face wa
revealed. Atop silvery hair rested the thin band of a golde
crown.

"King Tikos, I presume."

"The unhappy knight of the tale, I presume." Another cha
was dragged, and he sat down across from me. "But let us s
aside all pretense. Look at this."

He leaned forward into the light, pushed up both sleeves, ar
held his wrists up to the lamp, so I could plainly see.

"Look very closely," he said.

I let out an inadvertent grunt of astonishment. There was
thin line across both wrists, and he turned both hands over
show that these lines went all the way around. No one cou
have scars like that. They were *seams*.

"Sorcery! Not even the greatest doctors of physic . . ."

"Most not-so-noble knight, if your tale is as true as I think
is, you are not wholly godly yourself."

"That is . . . true. But how?"

"This is one of the many powers of the *Nekatu*."

"Messengers?"

"A kind of brotherhood, set apart from the rest of mankind. This is why I have brought you here, why I sought you out when saw you in the fair and noticed that your left hand was missing."

"Are you some kind of ghoul that you are fascinated by mutilation? Go to the wars in the east, and you'll get your fill."

"No! No! You fail to understand! I offer you a great gift. Look again!"

He reached under the table and drew from someplace a wooden box. The hinged lid came open. Inside there was a left hand carven out of a single piece of crystal, glittering with a thousand facets. It was a stunning piece of work, something with which to ransom empires.

I was not at all sure that it was a trick of the poor lighting that the thing seemed to move. Had the fingers been entirely outstretched? Now they seemed somewhat curled.

"By a most secret art," he said, "I have learned to make these. Contrary to what the philosophers will tell you, that which glitters has substance. Each ray of light captured within the crystal is a living thing, giving the hand itself life. This hand I have exposed to the stars for a hundred nights, giving it the life of the *Nekatu*. When joined to a wrist it becomes as living flesh in all ways."

"Joined? How so?"

"It naturally adheres, as you shall see. Take off that hook and bronze cap, and be healed and whole again."

The intensity of his gaze, my exhaustion, and the perils I had passed through must have bewitched me, for I thought of little else but having a living hand again, even if there would be a seam around it. I forgot the treacherous, extreme outrageousness of my situation, the childishly obvious fact that the king was not doing this out of charitable commiseration over my wound.

Hardly realizing what I was doing, I pulled the hook and cap off my left wrist, exposing the healed stump. Tikos took the arm in his hand—I did not resist—and joined it to the crystal hand over the flame of the lamp.

I felt no pain. First there was a numbness, then a tingling, a sort of melting, as the flame licked over the wrist and hand, and the substance flowed like hot wax. Even as I watched the crystal lost its luster, the facets smoothing over, the color fading. It was turning into flesh. I seemed far away from everything, drifting in abstraction. I wondered in bemusement if this were tried on a Negro, would the hue be right?

When the King let go, the hand seemed as if it had grown there. Thrilling at the situation, I flexed the fingers, then made a fist and banged with all my might on the table. The sword and the lamp bounced.

"A miracle! I am restored!"

"Yes, miraculous. By the way, are you hungry? I doubt you've eaten."

I made no answer. It seemed such a silly question, like the hues of Negroes. Who could care about food now?

King Tikos snapped his fingers and a tray was set before me. My heart skipped a beat when I saw that it was placed there by *hands*, but nothing more. They floated in the air as if creatures were reaching through from some invisible world into our own.

"Christ and Satan!"

"Swear by whomever you like," laughed the King. "Why not Jupiter, Thor, Mithra, and Ahura-Mazda also? It'll do you as much good. Those hands, I can safely tell you now, are simply *Nekatu*, like yourself, only in a far more advanced stage of development. The body withers away—it is unimportant—and is absorbed entirely into the hand. Why has this not happened to me? I remain whole because the Master, whom we all serve—yes, even you now—wills it. I recruit new slaves for him, even if sometimes, like that fool in the town today, a few are lost. He tried to run away."

With a howl of rage and despair, and every curse I could think of garbled together, I grabbed my sword and lunged across the table at the laughing monster, bent on total dismemberment. But before I could even get to my feet a frigid shock ran up my left arm and through my body. I staggered numbly for a second, the sword dropping from senseless fingers, then collapsed forward onto the table, smothering the lamp. That was the last thing remembered.

For a second night then I was tossed like a cork on a sea of nightmares. At first there was complete darkness, and a feeling of being long dead and very *soft*, trapped far underground, and clawing my way to the surface, until all the putrid flesh of my body had been sloughed off, and only my diamond-hard *hands* emerged from the earth. Then the scene changed and I saw myself lying where I had fallen on the table, my left arm, with that accursed hand, dangling over the edge. Again came a numbness at the wrist, and a sensation of melting.

The thing dropped off, landing on the floor upright on its fingers, like a cat dropped from a rooftop. It stood there like a living thing—which indeed it was—and there was an instant of confusion and disorientation: I was wrenched from where I lay, drifting, falling, floating upward into warmth; and then I was looking up into the gloom at an enormous table with an unconscious giant sprawled over it, and the stump of a left wrist hanging over me.

My soul, my self, was now a prisoner in the hand. I was not in control. Another mind was at work. Following a way the fingers knew, I was carried away from the table and my body, into utter blackness as the hand passed through a tiny crevice in the wall. I could ''see'' nothing else until I/we/it emerged on the outside of the castle. All the while the sensations of fingertips on damp stone were intense, very real. Then there was the vast panorama of the town and surrounding countryside viewed from a height, and a brilliant full moon in the sky.

The hand wanted to avoid the light. It stayed in the shadows as much as possible as it climbed down the outside of the castle wall, each finger seeking and finding holds sufficient to sustain the weight of the thing. Like a monstrous spider it crept over the stone until it was just above the door through which I had first entered the castle. There followed a sickening, terrifying drop through space as the grip was released, then a jolt as the hand landed upright, as it had done beneath the table.

It crawled down that road up which I had come, scurrying as fast as a rat. For all the distance and its small size, it was at the barred gate of the town very quickly. The closed gate posed no obstacle. The rough outcroppings of the city wall were as sure as the rungs of a ladder. Up and over we went with practiced skill, and once more there was a drop, and the fingers sank the second joint in mud. Still the hand was not stopped. The fingers spread out, then curled, squeezing mud, then spread out in a kind of swimming motion until the fingertips reached more solid ground. This gave way to a paved street, and the filthy fingers padded silently along the cobblestones, remaining always in the deepest shadows.

"Sight" was a confusing thing. At times I seemed to view the five fingers working, as if I were a tiny observer seated on the back, just behind the knuckles, and at other times the hand would stop, raise the index finger like an eyestalk, and I would get a sweeping view through that.

My waking self, Julian, the man who had been duped, had no idea where we/the hand intended to go, but there was a definite mission in the motion of the fingers. The hand came to certain intersections, and the index finger would scout about, then I would be going down a particular street, to a specific destination.

At last there was a wretched hovel propped between two brick buildings. A board was missing from the door, so the hand could enter without difficulty.

Within, the pattering which was definitely not a rat crossed the floor, steering a wide curve around the glowing coals of the firepit in the middle of the floor. Moonlight streamed through the smoke hole in the roof, and I could clearly discern a person asleep on a heap of straw on the far side of the room. It was the old woman who had carried the sticks.

Stealthily the hand made its way through the straw, then began to climb the tattered blanket she had wrapped herself in. The hand began to climb the blanket onto her shoulder. The index finger stood straight up, again the "eye" of the creature, while the second and third fingers pinched cloth between them, as did the little finger and thumb. With these two grips the hand inched its way on top of her, then crept across her rising and falling body. I could feel her heartbeat beneath my fingertips as I moved down onto her breast, over the collarbone—

It was obvious what was intended. I desperately wanted to stop, to curl the fingers into a fist and drop into the straw, to shout a warning with all my breath. But I had no breath. My voice and lungs were back at the castle. I had no will, no control as the fingers slipped around the helpless crone's thin throat. Blood throbbed in her neck, but the skin felt like parchment.

Suddenly, with furious strength, the hand closed on her

windpipe. She awoke, sat up wide-eyed in terror, let out a single gurgling cry, and then could utter nothing more. For a minute she writhed in the straw, flailing wildly after her unseen assailant and meeting only empty air, and then she lay still. The horror of the thing was not merely the death, or even my inability to prevent it, but that *I had done the deed*. As the hand strangled her I felt the muscles of a phantom arm, my arm, the arm of my body back at the castle, straining with the work. I felt the weight of my whole body pressed on the woman, pushing her down until her neck snapped like one of the sticks she had been carrying.

Someone stirred in another part of the room.

"Grandmother? Is that you?" Bare footsteps moved near the firepit, and a handful of rushes was lighted, then carried in my direction. I could see the face of a young girl as she bent over her grandmother, and the contortions of revulsion and mad terror at the sight of the thing still perched on the corpse. The light went out again as the rushes were dropped to the floor. The granddaughter screamed and was answered by shouts from without.

Instantly the hand knew what to do. With unbelievable agility it scrambled up the wall and was out another hole in the rotted wood. Then followed a drop into the muddy back street, and a scramble across to another house, and up a wall. From atop the neighboring roof it watched and gloated—yes, there was a definite feeling of that emotion in the second mind, joined to my own, which I could not escape.

"It has happened again! Grandmother!" the girl tried to explain to others through hysterical tears. *"Nekatu!"*

It was then that I came to understand some of the peculiar things about this town.

III

It was no surprise, but a dreadful, sickening certainty when I awoke the next morning on the table and there was mud on my left hand.

Revenge, the King had said. In this way he wrought revenge on those who had overthrown him. No wonder there were no men-at-

arms on his battlements. He had an army of *Nekatu* which was
far more deadly.

I lurched to my feet and instantly fell. My legs would not
support me. I was sick, exhausted, as if I had just completed a
vast labor, and I realized that, as the King had said, the hand
was beginning to absorb my vitality into itself. I dropped to my
knees, grasping the edge of the table with my right hand. I left
the other arm hanging limp. The thing seemed asleep. Now, by
daylight, my body was my own.

Apparently there were limits. I had to stay alive long enough
for the thing to steal my life away. It would take a while. I
would have to be kept for a long time. The tray set down by the
hands the night before was still there. On it were cold meat,
bread, and cheese. A cup of wine stood beside it. This had *not*
been there before.

My breakfast was laid out for me.

I spent the day exploring the castle. I could not go into the
town, where I would be killed on sight. If I fled over the
countryside, making my way down one of the cliffs with only
one hand I could trust, I had no doubt the hand could bring me
back, or at the very least deal with me the same way it had with
the old woman. I could, at last resort, cast myself from the
walls, or simply refuse to eat until I starved, but these were
indeed last resorts. It is not like a warrior, *any* warrior, be he
Christian knight or pagan savage, to surrender before the battle is
joined. The enemy must be met, no matter how hopeless the
odds.

So all day I wandered through the ruined halls of the castle. I
found a library filled with books written in strange scripts. There
were also a few in Latin, and these I glanced through. Most were
treatises on magic, of vast age. One was dedicated: *To my Lord
Nero, who taught me how to begin.* The same Nero who reigned
shortly after Christ, and slew the apostles Peter and Paul. How
long had it been since King Tikos lost his natural hands? Surely
the folk of this town were not his subjects, but their remote
descendants.

When twilight was drawing near, I knew my efforts were over
for the day. Another night of helpless horror was to follow. But

efore anything happened I dragged an iron brazier I had found
to the room where the wooden table was, then gathered up
me dry rushes, bits of wood, and scraps of the fallen tapestries.
meant to keep the place lighted so I could see Tikos when he
ame to put the spell on me, and slay him if I could. I still had
y sword.

Supper had been set in my absence. I ate while the familiar
attering passed back and forth behind the walls. Long shadows
ossed the floor.

There was a footstep behind me.

"Ah, now that you've dined, it's time for another errand,"
id King Tikos.

Before I could even turn around, the cold blast overwhelmed
e.

Many more died that night, but not in the town below. The
ission was far stranger. I was in the company of a whole
rigade of *Nekatu*, perhaps as many as fifty. Together we climbed
the outside of the castle, to the top of a tower. There a flock
f black hawks were waiting, as still as carven gargoyles. Each
and climbed on the back of a bird, the thumb and forefinger
oked around the neck, the rest grasping the body. The feel was
ery familiar. I've handled falcons often.

There was a more terrifying drop than before as the bird I was
ding fell into the abyss, heavy with its burden, struggling for
ight. It flapped desperately, then caught the air and rose clum-
ly to join the others, all of them lurching in an equally heavy
anner. Below, the fields and hills rolled. Moonlight gleamed
the two rivers. We followed one of them to its source in the
ountains beyond a forest, then over the mountains until we
me to the manor of some lord. The birds waited patiently on
alls and window ledges while the passengers dismounted and
ent about their business. The hands worked in pairs this time,
ot necessarily left and right, but always in pairs. I was with a
ge black member—answering my question about Negroes.
ogether we came to a chamber in which a man and a woman
ept. Now the black hand did something which I had witnessed
e first night, but had never been able to imitate. It floated in
e air, as if attached to an invisible body, as those bringing the

tray had done. I▸ slid a sword from the scabbard which hur
from the bedpost. All this while my own hand was climbing t
the side of the bed, inching up a blanket. "A more advance
stage," the King had said. A *Nekatu* which still had a huma
body, a newcomer like myself, had not yet all the powers give
to that fiendish brotherhood. I could not yet rise and float. I ha
to crawl.

The murder was done. I/the hand in which my self wა
trapped crept to the face of the man, then clamped tightly ove
his mouth while the black hand slit his throat from ear to e
with the sword. The lady slept through the whole deed, s
swiftly and silently was it performed. Again I felt the weight ·
my whole body leaning over the bed, gagging my victim whi
my accomplice slew him.

The sword was placed gently on the floor and the two of ▸
returned to the windowsill, there mounting our bewitched steed
As if at a signal, the whole flock took off at once, bearing tʰ
army of *Nekatu* back to the castle of King Tikos. I was not tol
but I knew that what I had participated in was not unique tʰ
night. In twenty-five rooms wives would wake up, soaked wiʰ
blood, and scream as they found themselves sharing beds wiʰ
still warm corpses. Could King Tikos hear the screams? Was ▸
somehow nourished by the terror and death?

Once more I found myself in that room by the table, and
breakfast had been prepared for me. Where did he get the foo
No stores could keep fresh all that time. Did he send *Nekatu* ▸
rob butchers and bakers? Well, that was the most innocuoʷ
thing they would ever do.

I hated myself as I ate. It was all I could do not to vomit asⁱ
remembered what had happened. It was time, I told myself,
leap to an easy death, before more innocents perished. *I* was nᵉ
innocent. I had many times longed for death. But then tʰ
familiar terror came. . . . After death—damnation, the eterⁿ
torments I could escape only for that brief time I lived. Like a
men, I am ultimately selfish. I would sacrifice the whole wor
to escape Hell even for a short while. I could kill myself only ᵒ
a sudden, saving impulse swifter than thought. If I reasonᵉ

what was right, just, and the moral thing to do, I would forget all about rightness, justice, and morality, and be paralyzed.

That day I continued to search the castle, hoping to find some secret thing by which I could justify myself.

And I was rewarded. There was a small door beneath what had once been a long bench. I made a torch out of wood, weeds from a courtyard garden, and scraps of cloth, lit it with flint and steel from the pouch on my belt, and descended into a vault. There I found twelve stone coffins, each of them with, curiously, an opening of about a span cut into the top.

No, not curious at all. A span is measured by the spread of a man's fingers.

Within were *Nekatu* of "a more advanced stage of development." When I slid the lid off the first coffin, I grew faint at the sight, but quickly gathered my courage. There lay an ancient, withered corpse, little more than skin stretched tight over bones, save that on one of the arms the shrunken skin blossomed out into a perfect living hand.

The fury of loathing gave me strength. I hacked at the thing with my sword, severing the hand, cutting again and again until the fingers were scattered and the whole body was a ruin. The skull splintered; the ribcage collapsed into slivers and chips. Only when nothing remained recognizable did I stop, sweat-covered for all the dampness of the vault, breathing heavily from my labor. After a pause I went on to the next one and destroyed it as thoroughly, but more methodically.

I was encouraged that my left hand was *my* left hand as I did this work. It did as my muscles commanded, and aided me in my task.

That night, however, the King again appeared from nowhere—I still had no idea how he did it—and more evil work was done. The army of *Nekatu* was abroad once more, and I noticed, and despaired as I saw, that some of them were crisscrossed with imperfectly healed scars. One or two even "limped" as they crawled on broken fingers. But they did what their master bade them. This time we came to a monastery, and, after stealing candles from the chapel altar, each of the *Nekatu* crept into a cell and burned out the eyes of the monk therein.

IV

When next I awoke, my vital essence was so drained I coul not rise. I was getting rapidly weaker. My flesh was wastin away. Already I was as gaunt as a starving beggar, increasingl like the shrivelled corpse of the *Nekatu* in the coffins. Doubtles before long I would be unable to move at all, and many hand would carry me to those same or similar coffins, and place me i one of them. Only with utmost effort could I crawl to the chai eat, and live for another day. Now I knew I could never flin myself from a parapet. I'd never reach the wall. So I sat ther throughout the day, as sunlight shifted from window to windov along the south side of the room.

I was very cold. Somehow I found the strength to rise after while and light the brazier. I could think of nothing but warmth For warmth, in my wretched condition, I would sell my soul But my soul was already spoken for, so I had to provide fo myself.

Thus I sat as evening fell, leaning against the back of th chair, my sword before me on the table, both hands in my lap right on top of left in vain hope of restraining it. Beside me, th brazier sputtered and crackled, The smell of smoke was com forting—my single tie to earthly things? Whenever the flame burned low I fed them bits of straw, cloth, and splinters of rotte wood. A heap of fuel was within arm's reach.

King Tikos arrived. He did not come into the room; he wa merely *there*. I thought the white spot in the air was a trick o my tired eyes, but it grew and took shape, and he was in th room with me. His slippers padded softly on the floor as h walked. All but soundless, a horde of *Nekatu* kept pace with hir on extended fingers. There were more of them than I had eve imagined. They poured from the cracks and holes until the floc was covered. There were easily a thousand of them. How foolis to think my tiny group made up the whole army!

"It is time," said the King, "that our brother be brought full into our fellowship. No waiting in the vaults for him. The Maste is coming this night to claim and transform him."

He was speaking to the hands, not to me. I was merely a object to be dealt with. He paced back and forth as he spoke, th

Nekatu scurrying this way and that after him like thousands of crabs come out of the sea just long enough to devour a drowned sailor the waves had washed up.

"We must wait, brothers. Have patience. The Master will come when the Master feels it is time. In the Master's world, beyond our own, time is not as we know it. I have been there as none of you have, and have seen, so believe me. Shapes and sounds and colors are all wondrously transformed, unrecognizably different. Senses are confused. One *hears* the color white, tastes the sweet tang of terror. A scream is like a soft caress *within* the body. Space, and time, and distance? These do not exist where the Master dwells, any more than depths exist in the world of a drawing on a page of parchment. Can one of those figures stand up, and walk out of the book? The Master can. You and I shall be able to also, in the end, when this world likewise belongs to the Master. That is why I worship him. That is why he is greater even than the God who created this universe. The Master walks between many universes. *Whence comest thou? From walking to and fro in the sum of cosmoses, and up and down in it, between the planes and angles.* That is why the Master is the Master.

"And yet," said the King, pacing back and forth in the semidarkness amid the thousand disembodied hands, "and yet I do not fear the Master where I now stand, for he needs me, to become material in our world. To take on solid substance. *And the word was made flesh, and screamed among us.* He is not as powerful here as he is in the void between the voids."

I listened to all this with the dull incomprehension of a pig in the slaughterhouse overhearing the talk of two butchers. Surely Tikos was mad to talk of anything beyond the sphere of the Earth, the moon and sun moving around it, and the fixed stars in the spheres of the firmament beyond, but then I was surely mad to be dreaming this nightmare in which I now existed, and the whole world was mad to allow such thoughts to come to be, and God was mad, as I knew well, for having created it that way. *And the Earth was without shape and form, and darkness was on the face of the deep.* Ah! If only the Father had been truly wise, and not meddled!

*　　*　　*

"The Master comes!" There was a rippling of the air, like foam on the sea an instant before a great whale leaps from the depths. For the first time Tikos spoke to me: "Watch! Watch, Sir Knight, and listen, and observe the last thing you shall ever observe with mortal eyes and ears. Tonight on this night of nights, the last of the harvest moon, the Master comes into his chamber, and you will be within our grip. *Ours.* I am part of the Master. This is the ultimate secret. Now, as I have promised, you truly know the meaning of the word *Nekatu.* A messenger, a servant of the Master, a finger of his hand."

Literally. As I watched the whiteness in the air returned and surrounded the King. He stood still. A thousand hands paused on five thousand fingertips. Four columns of whiteness began to materialize around him, and as they did he lost his own shape. He was flowing together, arms melting into his body, his two legs become one. Like wax. A candle. *Lighted.* Fire. Dimly the association anchored in my mind.

A finger of the Master. Exactly. That was what he had become. The four other fingers appeared beside him, and he—the index finger—was lifted off the floor as the Master reared up. The Master was a huge hand, that of a giant as tall as the castle if any body had been present. Something reaching through the air out of an invisible world coexistent with our own.

The hand climbed up on the table. It was the size of a horse. The wood creaked under its weight.

All time seemed suspended, and in my abstraction, I noticed a curious thing. The finger which had been King Tikos had a red welt around it. Was the Master a kind of *Nekatu* of a larger world, not complete without the animate finger which was the king, or which he had become? Was this the ultimate bargain to which the maimed and outcast king had agreed so long ago, through which he gained his continual revenge?

Joined together, a voice in the back of my mind chanted. Candle. Wax. Melting. Fire. Wax. *Fire.*

Now my left hand, that which was *Nekatu,* had come alive. The rest of my body was too weak to obey any commands, so the hand was on the table, crawling toward the far end where the Master stood on fingertips a foot across, dragging me with it.

Now my awareness was entirely in my head. The hand didn't need me, and moved of itself.

So I was pulled forward, across the table, toward the grasp of the Master.

I leaned forward. My chin touched the hilt of my sword, which was still on the table in front of me. With impossible strength the *Nekatu* hand was dragging me up out of the chair, onto the table. It passed the overturned oil lamp from the first night.

Fire. Wax. Melting.

In the remote regions of my mind, where thoughts were still my own, the idea came. I laughed at the brilliance of it. I was completely detached, my awareness floating. What was happening was not *really* happening. It was an intellectual exercise. I had always been good at things like chess. There was all the time in the world to carefully consider. Soon, someday, I would try—

I lost myself wholly for an instant, and *was* in the *Nekatu* hand, unheeded, but feeling the attraction of the Master, the call to union, a kind of lust—

—and was again myself, and in less than a split second the thoughts, the little voices, melted and turned and twisted upon themselves: Fire. Wax. Fire. Candle. Fire. Fire. *Fire. . . .*

The unexpected: a convoluted stratagem—again I slipped into blackness, was in the hand for a longer interval, and the call was far, far stronger—and flashed back, perhaps for the last time, into the body and mind of the man Julian—the convoluted stratagem: while all attention was on my left hand, the *Nekatu*, the right hand was doing something.

In the realm of philosophical abstraction, detached from time and space, as an interesting exercise, the fingers of my *right* hand, my human hand, curled around the hilt of my sword as it lay there on the table.

With a sudden *thwunk!* the right hand brought the sword up and around and down, crashing into the tabletop, aimed at the *Nekatu* hand, but clumsily. It missed by less than the width of the blade.

The hand stopped, startled. The master stood there impassively. The thousand *Nekatu* on the floor remained motionless.

The grip on my left arm was relaxed for an instant. I was free.

My body fell backwards into the chair, and with desperate effort I thrust the left hand into the flaming brazier.

The *Nekatu* hand recoiled. The Master stumbled backwards, and toppled off the end of the table, landing with a heavy thud on the floor, crushing those beneath him. Now a lifeless hand hacked apart during the day feels nothing, but a living one at night is different—and the Master directs all his hands, feeling as they feel.

Feeling as I feel. The hand did not go for my throat. The Master now writhed with the agonies of those he had crushed in his fall, and I, linked to them as a *Nekatu*, felt the same. It was in the fury of this pain that I was able to put my left hand back on the tabletop, then with my right, with the sword I still held, strike the mightiest blow ever struck in all the battles of mankind. I could have felled whole cities with it. The blade crashed down, through the wrist, just above the place where it joined the *Nekatu* hand. Honest agony followed. I was severed from the Master—it was mortal blood that flowed now from the stump. Only my own body.

I screamed, and in screaming woke fully into myself. Thick in the midst of the fight, instinct took over. The Master stood up once more, trembling on his pale, flabby fingers, and began to crawl back up onto the table. I hurled the brazier at him, and again he retreated from the flames. I lifted the table with my bleeding stump, and the hand that still held the sword, and flipped it over on top of him. I sheathed the sword, and hurled handfuls of kindling onto the heap. There was some oil left in the lamp which now poured out and kept the fire going until it could catch on the wood.

All this while the *Nekatu* stood motionless on the floor, waiting for commands. I trampled them with my iron shoes.

All this while blood was gushing from my left arm. It was only as I fell forward, to the very edge of the flames now licking over the upside-down table, that I realized my death was moments away. To this day I am amazed that I was able to do anything as rational as reaching forward with the bleeding arm, forcing the wound into the fire, and closing the wound. This new pain somehow gave me strength enough to rise from my feet and

agger down the winding stair, through the door, and out of the
astle.

I was mad. I screamed. I howled. I laughed. I was as far from
ayself as I had been on the midnight missions of the *Nekatu*.
here was that remote part of me which knew what was going
n, but the rest raged in a frenzy of pain, fear, and sub-bestial
ary.

Do you believe in miracles? *Speak not!* Any words are lies!
ou know!

Was it not a miracle that when I came to the bottom of the
ountain road, with the castle burning fiercely behind me, the
eople of the town opened their gates and let me pass? "He is
ead," I said, not knowing if the Master even *could* die. I think
ey feared me more than King Tikos. I think they took me for
ome new demon more terrible than the old. They opened the
ate before I could blast it with a thunderbolt. They brought my
orse to me. To appease my wrath? To get rid of a dread savior
elicately before his unknown will be known? They saw my
ounded wrist and knew I was no longer *Nekatu*, and they saw
e glare from the castle above. Was this not a miracle?

Was it not a miracle that I found myself, when for the first
me in a very long while I could think coherently, riding across
meadow far to the west of the city, beyond the mountains, a
ace I had once spied from the air, it seemed, in a dream?

And what else could it have been but a miracle which brought
e at last to a monastery of blind monks, who discovered by feel
e wound on my arm, and said, "Look, brothers, he is afflicted
en as us," while carrying me to a bed and stumbling to fetch
edicines?

Later, when again I was reduced to beggary, I refrained from
lling stories, lest I somehow forget myself and accidentally
late how I lost my left hand twice.

THE RELUCTANT DRAGON

by Kenneth Grahame

Raised by relatives, Kenneth Grahame (1859–1932) wrote children's stories while pursuing a career with the Bank of England. His first two fantasy books were Pagan Papers *(1894) and* The Golden Age *(1895). But* The Wind in the Willows *(1908) and the section "The Reluctant Dragon" in* Dream Days *(1899) are his most famous works—having both been turned into Disney cartoons. The first recounts the episodic adventures of an irresponsible Toad and his friends the Badger, the Mole, and the Rat. The second concerns a young boy's attempts to dissuade St. George from confronting a friendly dragon.*

ong ago—might have been hundreds of years ago—in a cottage lf-way between this village and yonder shoulder of the Downs there, a shepherd lived with his wife and their little son. Now e shepherd spent his days—and at certain times of the year his ghts too—up on the wide ocean-bosom of the Downs, with ily the sun and the stars and the sheep for company, and the iendly chattering world of men and women far out of sight and earing. But his little son, when he wasn't helping his father, d often when he was as well, spent much of his time buried in

big volumes that he borrowed from the affable gentry and inter
ested parsons of the country round about. And his parents wer
very fond of him, and rather proud of him too, though the
didn't let on in his hearing, so he was left to go his own way an
read as much as he liked; and instead of frequently getting a cu
on the side of the head, as might very well have happened t
him, he was treated more or less as an equal by his parents, wh
sensibly thought it a very fair division of labour that they shoul
supply the practical knowledge, and he the book-learning. The
knew that book-learning often came in useful at a pinch, in spit
of what their neighbours said. What the Boy chiefly dabbled i
was natural history and fairy-tales, and he just took them as the
came, in a sandwichy sort of way, without making any distinction
and really his course of reading strikes one as rather sensible.

One evening the shepherd, who for some nights past had bee
disturbed and preoccupied, and off his usual mental balanc
came home all of a tremble, and, sitting down at the table wher
his wife and son were peacefully employed, she with her seam
he in following out the adventures of the Giant with no Heart i
his Body, exclaimed with much agitation:

"It's all up with me, Maria! Never no more can I go up o
them there Downs, was it ever so!"

"Now don't you take on like that," said his wife, who was
very sensible woman: "but tell us all about it first, whatever it
as has given you this shake-up, and then me and you and the so
here, between us, we ought to be able to get to the bottom o
it!"

"It began some nights ago," said the shepherd. "You kno
that cave up there—I never liked it, somehow, and the shee
never liked it neither, and when sheep don't like a thing there
generally some reason for it. Well, for some time past there
been faint noises coming from that cave—noises like heav
sighings, with grunts mixed up in them; and sometimes a snorin
far away down—*real* snoring, yet somehow not *honest* snorin
like you and me o' nights, you know!"

"*I* know," remarked the Boy quietly.

"Of course I was terrible frightened," the shepherd went o
"yet somehow I couldn't keep away. So this very evenin
before I come down, I took a cast round by the cave, quietl

And there—O Lord! there I saw him at last, as plain as I see you!"

"Saw *who*?" said his wife, beginning to share in her husband's nervous terror.

"Why *him*, I'm a-telling you!" said the shepherd. "He was sticking half-way out of the cave, and seemed to be enjoying of the cool of the evening in a poetical sort of way. He was as big as four cart-horses, and all covered with shiny scales—deep-blue scales at the top of him, shading off to a tender sort o' green below. As he breathed, there was a sort of flicker over his nostrils that you see over our chalk roads on a baking windless day in summer. He had his chin on his paws, and I should say he was meditating about things. Oh, yes, a peaceable sort o' beast enough, and not ramping or carrying on or doing anything but what was quite right and proper. I admit all that. And yet, what am I to do? Scales, you know, and claws, and a tail for certain, though I didn't see that end of him—I ain't *used* to 'em, and I don't *hold* with 'em, and that's a fact!"

The Boy, who had apparently been absorbed in his book during his father's recital, now closed the volume, yawned, clasped his hands behind his head, and said sleepily:

"It's all right, father. Don't you worry. It's only a dragon."

"Only a dragon?" cried his father. "What do you mean, sitting there, you and your dragons? *Only* a dragon indeed! And what do *you* know about it?"

" 'Cos it *is*, and 'cos I *do* know," replied the Boy quietly. "Look here, father, you know we've each of us got our line. *You* know about sheep, and weather, and things; *I* know about dragons. I always said, you know, that that cave up there was a dragon-cave. I always said it must have belonged to a dragon some time, and ought to belong to a dragon now, if rules count for anything. Well, now you tell me it *has* got a dragon, and so *that's* all right. I'm not half as much surprised as when you told me it *hadn't* got a dragon. Rules always come right if you wait quietly. Now, please, just leave this all to me. And I'll stroll up to-morrow morning—no, in the morning I can't, I've got a whole heap of things to do—well, perhaps in the evening, if I'm quite free, I'll go up and have a talk to him, and you'll find it'll be all right. Only please, don't you go worrying round there without me. You don't understand 'em a bit, and they're very sensitive, you know!"

"He's quite right, father," said the sensible mother. "As he says, dragons is his line and not ours. He's wonderful knowing about book-beasts, as every one allows. And to tell the truth, I'm not half happy in my own mind, thinking of that poor animal lying alone up there, without a bit o' hot supper or anyone to change the news with; and maybe we'll be able to do something for him; and if he ain't quite respectable our Boy'll find it out quick enough. He's got a pleasant sort o' way with him that makes everybody tell him everything."

Next day, after he'd had his tea, the Boy strolled up the chalky track that led to the summit of the Downs; and there, sure enough, he found the dragon, stretched lazily on the sward in front of his cave. The view from the point was a magnificent one. To the right and left, the bare and billowy leagues of Downs; in front, the vale, with its clustered homesteads, its threads of white roads running through orchards and well-tilled acreage, and, far away, a hint of grey old cities on the horizon. A cool breeze played over the surface of the grass, and the silver shoulder of a large moon was showing above distant junipers. No wonder the dragon seemed in a peaceful and contented mood; indeed, as the Boy approached he could hear the beast purring with a happy regularity. "Well, we live and learn!" he said to himself. "None of my books ever told me that dragons purred!"

"Hullo, dragon!" said the Boy quietly, when he had got up to him.

The dragon, on hearing the approaching footsteps, made the beginning of a courteous effort to rise. But when he saw it was a Boy, he set his eyebrows severely.

"Now don't you hit me," he said; "or bung stones, or squirt water, or anything. I won't have it, I tell you!"

"Not goin' to hit you," said the Boy wearily, dropping on the grass beside the beast: "and don't, for goodness' sake, keep on saying " 'Don't' "; I hear so much of it, and it's monotonous, and makes me tired. I've simply looked in to ask you how you were and all that sort of thing; but if I'm in the way I can easily clear out. I've lots of friends, and no one can say I'm in the habit of shoving myself in where I'm not wanted!"

"No, no, don't go off in a huff," said the dragon hastily; "fact is—I'm as happy up here as the day's long; never without an occupation, dear fellow, never without an occupation! And yet, between ourselves, it *is* a trifle dull at times."

The Boy bit off a stalk of grass and chewed it. "Going to make a long stay here?" he asked politely.

"Can't hardly say at present," replied the dragon. "It seems a nice place enough—but I've only been here a short time, and one must look about and reflect and consider before settling down. It's rather a serious thing, settling down. Besides—now I'm going to tell you something! You'd never guess it if you tried ever so!—fact is, I'm such a confoundedly lazy beggar!"

"You surprise me," said the Boy civilly.

"It's the sad truth," the dragon went on, settling down between his paws and evidently delighted to have found a listener at last: "and I fancy that's really how I came to be here. You see all the other fellows were so active and *earnest* and all that sort of thing—always rampaging, and skirmishing, and scouring the desert sands, and pacing the margin of the sea, and chasing knights all over the place, and devouring damsels, and going on generally—whereas I liked to get my meals regular and then to prop my back against a bit of rock and snooze a bit, and wake up and think of things going on and how they kept going on just the same, you know! So when it happened I got fairly caught."

"When *what* happened, please?" asked the Boy.

"That's just what I don't precisely know," said the dragon. "I suppose the earth sneezed, or shook itself, or the bottom dropped out of something. Anyhow there was a shake and a roar and a general stramash, and I found myself miles away underground and wedged in as tight as tight. Well, thank goodness, my wants are few, and at any rate I had peace and quietness and wasn't always being asked to come along and *do* something. And I've got such an active mind—always occupied, I assure you! But time went on, and there was a certain sameness about the life, and at last I began to think it would be fun to work my way upstairs and see what you other fellows were doing. So I scratched and burrowed, and worked this way and that way and at last I came out through this cave here. And I like the country, and the view, and the people—what I've seen of 'em—and on the whole I feel inclined to settle down here."

"What's your mind always occupied about?" asked the Boy. "That's what I want to know."

The dragon coloured slightly and looked away. Presently he said bashfully:

"Did you ever—just for fun—try to make up poetry—verses, you know?"

" 'Course I have," said the Boy. "Heaps of it. And some of it's quite good, I feel sure, only there's no one here cares about it. Mother's very kind and all that, when I read it to her, and so's father for that matter. But somehow they don't seem to—"

"Exactly," cried the dragon; "my own case exactly. They don't seem to, and you can't argue with 'em about it. Now you've got culture, you have, I could tell it on you at once, and I should just like your candid opinion about some little things I threw off lightly, when I was down there. I'm awfully pleased to have met you, and I'm hoping the other neighbours will be equally agreeable. There was a very nice old gentleman up here only last night, but he didn't seem to want to intrude."

"That was my father," said the Boy, "and he *is* a nice old gentleman, and I'll introduce you some day if you like."

"Can't you two come up here and dine or something to-morrow?" asked the dragon eagerly. "Only, of course, if you've got nothing better to do," he added politely.

"Thanks awfully," said the Boy, "but we don't go out anywhere without my mother, and, to tell you the truth, I'm afraid she mightn't quite approve of you. You see there's no getting over the hard fact that you're a dragon, is there? And when you talk of settling down, and the neighbours, and so on, I can't help feeling that you don't quite realize your position. You're an enemy of the human race, you see!"

"Haven't got an enemy in the world," said the dragon cheerfully. "Too lazy to make 'em, to begin with. And if I *do* read other fellows my poetry, I'm always ready to listen to theirs!"

"Oh, dear!" cried the Boy, "I wish you'd try and grasp the situation properly. When the other people find you out, they'll come after you with spears and swords and all sorts of things.

'ou'll have to be exterminated, according to their way of look-
ig at it! You're a scourge, and a pest, and a baneful monster!''

"Not a word of truth in it," said the dragon, wagging his head
)lemnly. "Character'll bear the strictest investigation. And now,
ere's a little sonnet-thing I was working on when you appeared
n the scene—"

"Oh, if you *won't* be sensible," cried the Boy, getting up,
I'm going off home. No, I can't stop for sonnets; my mother's
tting up. I'll look you up to-morrow, sometime or other, and
) for goodness' sake try and realize that you're a pestilential
:ourge, or you'll find yourself in a most awful fix. Good
ght!''

The Boy found it an easy matter to set the mind of his parents
ease about his new friend. They had always left that branch to
m, and they took his word without a murmur. The shepherd
as formally introduced and many compliments and kind en-
iiries were exchanged. His wife, however, though expressing her
illingness to do anything she could—to mend things, or set the
ive to rights, or cook a little something when the dragon had
en poring over sonnets and forgotten his meals, as male things
ill do, could not be brought to recognize him formally. The fact
at he was a dragon and "they didn't know who he was"
emed to count for everything with her. She made no objection,
)wever, to her little son spending his evenings with the dragon
iietly, so long as he was home by nine o'clock: and many a
easant night they had, sitting on the sward, while the dragon
ld stories of old, old times, when dragons were quite plentiful
d the world was a livelier place than it is now, and life was
ll of thrills and jumps and surprises.

What the Boy had feared, however, soon came to pass. The
ost modest and retiring dragon in the world, if he's as big as
ur cart-horses and covered with blue scales, cannot keep al-
gether out of the public view. And so in the village tavern of
ghts the fact that a real live dragon sat brooding in the cave on
e Downs was naturally a subject for talk. Though the villagers
ere extremely frightened, they were rather proud as well. It
as a distinction to have a dragon of your own, and it was felt to
a feather in the cap of the village. Still, all were agreed that
is sort of thing couldn't be allowed to go on. The dreadful

beast must be exterminated, the country-side must be freed from
this pest, this terror, this destroying scourge. The fact that no
even a hen-roost was the worse for the dragon's arrival wasn'
allowed to have anything to do with it. He was a dragon, and h
couldn't deny it, and if he didn't choose to behave as such tha
was his own look-out. But in spite of much valiant talk no her
was found willing to take sword and spear and free the sufferin
village and win deathless fame; and each night's heated discus
sion always ended in nothing. Meanwhile the dragon lolled o
the turf, enjoyed the sunsets, told antediluvian anecdotes to th
Boy, and polished his old verses while meditating on fresh ones

One day the Boy, on walking into the village, found every
thing wearing a festal appearance which was not to be accounte
for in the calendar. Carpets and gay-coloured stuffs were hun
out of the windows, the church bells clamoured noisily, the litt
street was flower-strewn, and the whole population jostled eac
other along either side of it, chattering, shoving, and orderir
each other to stand back. The Boy saw a friend of his own age
the crowd and hailed him.

"What's up?" he cried. "Is it the players, or bears, or
circus, or what?"

"It's all right," his friend hailed back. "He's a-coming."

"*Who's* a-coming?" demanded the Boy, thrusting into th
throng.

"Why, St. George, of course," replied his friend. "He
heard tell of our dragon, and he's comin' on purpose to slay th
deadly beast, and free us from his horrid yoke. O my! won
there be a jolly fight!"

Here was news indeed! The Boy felt that he ought to mal
quite sure for himself, and he wriggled himself in between th
legs of his good-natured elders, abusing them all the time f
their unmannerly habit of shoving. Once in the front rank, I
breathlessly awaited the arrival.

Presently from the far-away end of the line came the sound
great cheering. Next, the measured tramp of a great war-hor
made his heart beat quicker, and then he found himself cheerir
with the rest, as, amidst welcoming shouts, shrill cries
women, uplifting of babies, and waving of handkerchiefs, S
George paced slowly up the street. The Boy's heart stood st

nd he breathed with sobs, the beauty and the grace of the hero
vere so far beyond anything he had yet seen. His fluted armour
vas inlaid with gold, his plumed helmet hung at his saddle-bow,
nd his thick fair hair framed a face gracious and gentle beyond
xpression till you caught the sternness in his eyes. He drew rein
n front of the little inn, and the villagers crowded round with
reetings and thanks and voluble statements of their wrongs and
rievances and oppressions. The Boy heard the grave gentle
oice of the Saint, assuring them that all would be well now, and
hat he would stand by them and see them righted and free them
rom their foe; then he dismounted and passed through the
oorway and the crowd poured in after him. But the Boy made
ff up the hill as fast as he could lay his legs to the ground.

"It's all up, dragon!" he shouted as soon as he was within
ight of the beast. "He's coming! He's here now! You'll have to
ull yourself together and *do* something at last!"

The dragon was licking his scales and rubbing them with a bit
f house-flannel the Boy's mother had lent him, till he shone
ke a great turquoise.

"Don't be *violent*, Boy," he said without looking round. "Sit
own and get your breath, and try and remember that the noun
overns the verb, and then perhaps you'll be good enough to tell
ne *who's* coming?"

"That's right, take it coolly," said the Boy. "Hope you'll be
alf as cool when I've got through with my news. It's only St.
ieorge who's coming, that's all; he rode into the village half an
our ago. Of course you can lick him—a great big fellow like
ou! But I thought I'd warn you, 'cos he's sure to be round
arly, and he's got the longest, wickedest-looking spear you ever
id see!" And the Boy got up and began to jump round in sheer
elight at the prospect of the battle.

"O deary, deary me," moaned the dragon; "this is too awful.
won't see him, and that's flat. I don't want to know the fellow
t all. I'm sure he's not nice. You must tell him to go away at
nce, please. Say he can write if he likes, but I can't give him an
nterview. I'm not seeing anybody at present."

"Now, dragon, dragon," said the Boy imploringly, "don't be
erverse and wrongheaded. You've *got* to fight him some time
r other, you know, 'cos he's St. George and you're the dragon.

Better get it over and then we can go on with the sonnets. An
you ought to consider other people a little, too. If it's been du'
up here for you, think how dull it's been for me!''

"My dear little man," said the dragon solemnly, "jus
understand, once for all, that I can't fight and I won't fight. I'v
never fought in my life, and I'm not going to begin now, just t
give you a Roman holiday. In old days I always let the othe
fellows—the *earnest* fellows—do all the fighting, and no doul
that's why I have the pleasure of being here now."

"But if you don't fight he'll cut your head off!" gasped th
Boy, miserable at the prospect of losing both his fight and hi
friend.

"Oh, I think not," said the dragon in his lazy way. "You'
be able to arrange something. I've every confidence in you
you're such a *manager*. Just run down, there's a dear chap, an
make it all right. I leave it entirely to you."

The Boy made his way back to the village in a state of grea
despondency. First of all, there wasn't going to be any figh
next, his dear and honoured friend the dragon hadn't shown u
in quite such a heroic light as he would have liked; and lastl
whether the dragon was a hero at heart or not, it made n
difference, for St. George would most undoubtedly cut his hea
off. "Arrange things indeed!" he said bitterly to himself. "Th
dragon treats the whole affair as if it was an invitation to tea an
croquet."

The villagers were straggling homewards as he passed up th
street, all of them in the highest spirits, and gleefully discussin
the splendid fight that was in store. The Boy pursued his way
the inn, and passed into the principal chamber, where St. Georg
now sat alone, musing over the chances of the fight, and the sa
stories of wrong that had so lately been poured into his symp.
thetic ears.

"May I come in, St. George?" said the Boy politely, as I
paused at the door. "I want to talk to you about this little matt
of the dragon, if you're not tired of it by this time."

"Yes, come in, Boy," said the Saint kindly. "Another tale
misery and wrong, I fear me. Is it a kind parent, then, of who
the tyrant has bereft you? Or some tender sister or brother? Wel
it shall soon be avenged."

"Nothing of the sort," said the Boy. "There's a misunderstanding somewhere, and I want to put it right. The fact is, this is a *good* dragon."

"Exactly," said St. George, smiling pleasantly, "I quite understand. A good *dragon*. Believe me, I do not in the least regret that he is an adversary worthy of my steel, and no feeble specimen of his noxious tribe."

"But he's *not* a noxious tribe," cried the Boy distressedly. "Oh dear, oh dear, how *stupid* men are when they get an idea into their heads! I tell you he's a *good* dragon, and a friend of mine, and tells me the most beautiful stories you ever heard, all about old times and when he was little. And he's been so kind to mother, and mother'd do anything for him. And father likes him too, though father doesn't hold with art and poetry much, and always falls asleep when the dragon starts talking about *style*. But the fact is, nobody can help liking him when once they know him. He's so engaging and so trustful, and as simple as a child!"

"Sit down, and draw your chair up," said St. George. "I like a fellow who sticks up for his friends, and I'm sure the dragon has his good points, if he's got a friend like you. But that's not the question. All this evening I've been listening, with grief and anguish unspeakable, to tales of murder, theft, and wrong; rather too highly coloured, perhaps, not always quite convincing, but forming in the main a most serious roll of crime. History teaches us that the greatest rascals often possess all the domestic virtues; and I fear that your cultivated friend, in spite of the qualities which have won (and rightly) your regard, has got to be speedily exterminated."

"Oh, you've been taking in all the yarns those fellows have been telling you," said the Boy impatiently. "Why, our villagers are the biggest story-tellers in all the country round. It's a known fact. You're a stranger in these parts, or else you'd have heard it already. All they want is a *fight*. They're the most awful beggars for getting up fights—it's meat and drink to them. Dogs, bulls, dragons—anything so long as it's a fight. Why, they've got a poor innocent badger in the stable behind here, at this moment. They were going to have some fun with him to-day, but they're saving him up now till *your* little affair's over. And I've no doubt they've been telling you what a hero you were, and how you were bound to win, in the cause of right and justice, and so on; but let me tell you, I came down the street just now, and they were betting six to four on the dragon freely!''

"Six to four on the dragon!" murmured St. George sadly, resting his cheek on his hand. "This is an evil world, and sometimes I begin to think that all the wickedness in it is not entirely bottled up inside the dragons. And yet—may not this wily beast have misled you as to his real character, in order that your good report of him may serve as a cloak for his evil deeds? Nay, may there not be, at this very moment, some hapless Princess immured within yonder gloomy cavern?''

The moment he had spoken, St. George was sorry for what he had said, the Boy looked so genuinely distressed.

"I assure you, St. George," he said earnestly, "there's nothing of the sort in the cave at all. The dragon's a real gentleman, every inch of him, and I may say that no one would be more shocked and grieved than he would, at hearing you talk in that—that *loose* way about matters on which he has very strong views!''

"Well, perhaps I've been over-credulous," said St. George. "Perhaps I've misjudged the animal. But what are we to do? Here are the dragon and I, almost face to face, each supposed to be thirsting for each other's blood. I don't see any way out of it exactly. What do you suggest? Can't you arrange things somehow?''

"That's just what the dragon said," replied the Boy, rather nettled. "Really, the way you two seem to leave everything to me—I suppose you couldn't be persuaded to go away quietly, could you?''

"Impossible, I fear," said the Saint. "Quite against the rules. *You* know that as well as I do.''

"Well, then, look here," said the Boy, "it's early yet—would you mind strolling up with me and seeing the dragon and talking it over? It's not far, and any friend of mine will be most welcome.''

"Well, it's *irregular*," said St. George, rising, "but really it seems about the most sensible thing to do. You're taking a lot of trouble on your friend's account," he added good-naturedly, as they passed out through the door together. "But cheer up! Perhaps there won't have to be any fight after all."

"Oh, but I hope there will, though!" replied the little fellow wistfully.

"I've brought a friend to see you, dragon," said the Boy rather loud.

The dragon woke up with a start. "I was just—er—thinking about things," he said in his simple way. "Very pleased to make your acquaintance, sir. Charming weather we're having!"

"This is St. George," said the Boy, shortly. "St. George, let me introduce you to the dragon. We've come up to talk things over quietly, dragon, and now for goodness' sake do let us have a little straight common sense, and come to some practical business-ike arrangement, for I'm sick of views and theories of life and personal tendencies, and all that sort of thing. I may perhaps add that my mother's sitting up."

"So glad to meet you, St. George," began the dragon rather nervously, "because you've been a great traveller, I hear, and 've always been rather a stay-at-home. But I can show you many antiquities, many interesting features of our countryside, if you're stopping here any time—"

"I think," said St. George in his frank, pleasant way, "that we'd really better take the advice of our young friend here, and try to come to some understanding, on a business footing, about this little affair of ours. Now don't you think that after all the simplest plan would be just to fight it out, according to the rules, and let the best man win? They're betting on you, I may tell you, down in the village, but I don't mind that!"

"Oh, yes, do, dragon," said the Boy delightedly; "it'll save such a lot of bother!"

"My young friend, you shut up," said the dragon severely. "Believe me, St. George," he went on, "there's nobody in the world I'd sooner oblige than you and this young gentleman here. But the whole thing's nonsense, and conventionality, and popular thick-headedness. There's absolutely nothing to fight about, from beginning to end. And anyhow I'm not going to, so that settles it!"

"But supposing I make you?" said St. George, rather nettled.

"You can't," said the dragon triumphantly. "I should only go into my cave and retire for a time down the hole I came up. You'd soon get heartily sick of sitting outside and waiting for me to come out and fight you. And as soon as you'd really gone away, why, I'd come up again gaily, for I tell you frankly, I like this place, and I'm going to stay here!"

St. George gazed for a while on the fair landscape around them. "But this would be a beautiful place for a fight," he began again persuasively. "These great bare rolling Downs for the arena—and me in my golden armour showing up against your big blue scaly coils! Think what a picture it would make!"

"Now you're trying to get at me through my artistic sensibilities," said the dragon. "But it won't work. Not but what it would make a very pretty picture, as you say," he added, wavering a little.

"We seem to be getting rather nearer to *business*," put in the Boy. "You must see, dragon, that there's got to be a fight of some sort, 'cos you can't want to have to go down that dirty old hole again and stop there till goodness knows when."

"It might be arranged," said St. George thoughtfully. "I *must* spear you somewhere, of course, but I'm not bound to hurt you very much. There's such a lot of you that there must be a few *spare* places somewhere. Here, for instance, just behind your foreleg. It couldn't hurt you much, just here!"

"Now you're tickling, George," said the dragon coyly. "No, that place won't do at all. Even if it didn't hurt—and I'm sure it would, awfully—it would make me laugh, and that would spoil everything."

"Let's try somewhere else, then," said St. George patiently. "Under your neck, for instance—all these folds of thick skin—if I speared you here you'd never even know I'd done it!"

"Yes, but are you sure you can hit off the right place?" asked the dragon anxiously.

"Of course I am," said George, with confidence. "You leave that to me!"

"It's just because I've *got* to leave it to you that I'm asking," replied the dragon rather testily. "No doubt you would deeply regret any error you might make in the hurry of the moment; but you wouldn't regret it half as much as I should! However, suppose we've got to trust somebody, as we go through life, and your plan seems, on the whole, as good a one as any."

"Look here, dragon," interrupted the Boy, a little jealous on behalf of his friend, who seemed to be getting all the worst of the bargain: "I don't quite see where *you* come in! There's to be a fight, apparently, and you're to be licked; and what I want to know is, what are *you* going to get out of it?"

"St. George," said the dragon, "just tell him, please—what will happen after I'm vanquished in the deadly combat?"

"Well, according to the rules I suppose I shall lead you in triumph down to the marketplace or whatever answers to it," said St. George.

"Precisely," said the dragon. "And then—?"

"And then there'll be shoutings and speeches and things," continued St. George. "And I shall explain that you're converted, and see the error of your ways, and so on."

"Quite so," said the dragon. "And then—?"

"Oh, and then—" said St. George, "why, and then there will be the usual banquet, I suppose."

"Exactly," said the dragon; "and that's where *I* come in. Look here," he continued, addressing the Boy, "I'm bored to death up here, and no one really appreciates me. I'm going into Society, I am, through the kindly aid of our friend here, who's taking such a lot of trouble on my account; and you'll find I've got all the qualities to endear me to people who entertain! So now that's all settled, and if you don't mind—I'm an old-fashioned fellow—don't want to turn you out, but—"

"Remember, you'll have to do your proper share of the fighting, dragon!" said St. George, as he took the hint and rose to go; "I mean ramping, and breathing fire, and so on!"

"I can *ramp* all right," replied the dragon confidently; "as to breathing fire, it's surprising how easily one gets out of practice; but I'll do the best I can. Good night!"

They had descended the hill and were almost back in the village again, when St. George stopped short. "*Knew* I had forgotten something," he said. "There ought to be a Princess. Terror-stricken and chained to a rock, and all that sort of thing. Boy, can't you arrange a Princess?"

The Boy was in the middle of a tremendous yawn. "I'm tired

to death," he wailed, "and I *can't* arrange a Princess, or any-thing more, at this time of night. And my mother's sitting up, and *do* stop asking me to arrange more things till to-morrow!''

Next morning the people began streaming up to the Downs at quite an early hour, in their Sunday clothes and carrying baskets with bottle-necks sticking out of them, every one intent on securing good places for the combat. This was not exactly a simple matter, for of course it was quite possible that the dragon might win, and in that case even those who had put their money on him felt they could hardly expect him to deal with his backers on a different footing to the rest. Places were chosen, therefore, with circumspection and with a view to a speedy retreat in case of emergency; and the front rank was mostly composed of boys who had escaped from parental control and now sprawled and rolled about on the grass, regardless of the shrill threats and warnings discharged at them by their anxious mothers behind.

The Boy had secured a good front place, well up towards the cave, and was feeling as anxious as a stage-manager on a first night. Could the dragon be depended upon? He might change his mind and vote the whole performance rot; or else, seeing that the affair had been so hastily planned without even a rehearsal, he might be too nervous to show up. The Boy looked narrowly at the cave, but it showed no sign of life or occupation. Could the dragon have made a moonlight flitting?

The higher portions of the ground were now black with sightseers, and presently a sound of cheering and a waving of handkerchiefs told that something was visible to them which the Boy, far up towards the dragon-end of the line as he was, could not yet see. A minute more and St. George's red plumes topped the hill, as the Saint rode slowly forth on the great level space which stretched up to the grim mouth of the cave. Very gallant and beautiful he looked on his tall war-horse, his golden armour glancing in the sun, his great spear held erect, the little white pennon, crimson-crossed, fluttering at its point. He drew rein and remained motionless. The lines of spectators began to give back a little, nervously; and even the boys in front stopped pulling hair and cuffing each other, and leaned forward expectant.

"Now then, dragon!" muttered the Boy impatiently, fidgeting where he sat. He need not have distressed himself, had he only

known. The dramatic possibilities of the thing had tickled the
dragon immensely, and he had been up from an early hour,
preparing for his first public appearance with as much heartiness
as if the years had run backwards, and he had been again a little
dragonlet, playing with his sisters on the floor of their mother's
cave, at the game of saints-and-dragons, in which the dragon
was bound to win.

A low muttering, mingled with snorts, now made itself heard;
rising to a bellowing roar that seemed to fill the plain. Then a
cloud of smoke obscured the mouth of the cave, and out of the
midst of it the dragon himself, shining, sea-blue, magnificent,
pranced splendidly forth; and everybody said, "Oo-oo-oo!" as if
he had been a mighty rocket! His scales were glittering, his long
spiky tail lashed his sides, his claws tore up the turf and sent it
flying high over his back, and smoke and fire incessantly jetted
from his angry nostrils. "Oh, well done, dragon!" cried the Boy
excitedly. "Didn't think he had it in him!" he added to himself.

St. George lowered his spear, bent his head, dug his heels into
his horse's sides, and came thundering over the turf. The dragon
charged with a roar and a squeal—a great blue whirling combination of coils and snorts and clashing jaws and spikes and fire.

"Missed!" yelled the crowd. There was a moment's entangle-
ment of golden armour and blue-green coils and spiky tail, and
then the great horse, tearing at his bit, carried the Saint, his spear
swung high in the air, almost up to the mouth of the cave.

The dragon sat down and barked viciously, while St. George
with difficulty pulled his horse round into position.

"End of Round One!" thought the Boy. "How well they
managed it! But I hope the Saint won't get excited. I can trust
the dragon all right. What a regular play-actor the fellow is!"

St. George had at last prevailed on his horse to stand steady,
and was looking round him as he wiped his brow. Catching sight
of the Boy, he smiled and nodded, and held up three fingers for
an instant.

"It seems to be all planned out," said the Boy to himself.
"Round Three is to be the finishing one, evidently. Wish it
could have lasted a bit longer. Whatever's that old fool of a
dragon up to now?"

The dragon was employing the interval in giving a ramping

performance for the benefit of the crowd. Ramping, it should be explained, consists in running round and round in a wide circle, and sending waves and ripples of movement along the whole length of your spine, from your pointed ears right down to the spike at the end of your long tail. When you are covered with blue scales, the effect is particularly pleasing; and the Boy recollected the dragon's recently expressed wish to become a social success.

St. George now gathered up his reins and began to move forward, dropping the point of his spear and settling himself firmly in the saddle.

"Time!" yelled everybody excitedly; and the dragon, leaving off his ramping, sat up on end, and began to leap from one side to the other with huge ungainly bounds, whopping like a Red Indian. This naturally disconcerted the horse, who swerved violently, the Saint only just saving himself by the mane; and as they shot past the dragon delivered a vicious snap at the horse's tail which sent the poor beast careering madly far over the Downs, so that the language of the Saint, who had lost a stirrup, was fortunately inaudible to the general assemblage.

Round Two evoked audible evidence of friendly feeling towards the dragon. The spectators were not slow to appreciate a combatant who could hold his own so well and clearly wanted to show good sport; and many encouraging remarks reached the ears of our friend as he strutted to and fro, his chest thrust out and his tail in the air, hugely enjoying his new popularity.

St. George had dismounted and was tightening his girths, and telling his horse, with quite an Oriental flow of imagery, exactly what he thought of him, and his relations, and his conduct on the present occasion; so the Boy made his way down to the Saint's end of the line, and held his spear for him.

"It's been a jolly fight, St. George!" he said, with a sigh. "Can't you let it last a bit longer?"

"Well, I think I'd better not," replied the Saint. "The fact is, your simple-minded old friend's getting conceited, now they've begun cheering him, and he'll forget all about the arrangement and take to playing the fool, and there's no telling where he would stop. I'll just finish him off this round."

He swung himself into the saddle and took his spear from the

Boy. "Now don't you be afraid," he added kindly. "I've marked my spot exactly, and *he's* sure to give me all the assistance in his power, because he knows it's his only chance of being asked to the banquet!"

St. George now shortened his spear, bringing the butt well up under his arm; and, instead of galloping as before, he trotted smartly towards the dragon, who crouched at his approach, flicking his tail till it cracked in the air like a great cart-whip. The Saint wheeled as he neared his opponent and circled warily round him, keeping his eye on the spare place; while the dragon, adopting similar tactics, paced with caution round the same circle, occasionally feinting with his head. So the two sparred for an opening, while the spectators maintained a breathless silence.

Though the round lasted for some minutes, the end was so swift that all the Boy saw was a lightning movement of the Saint's arm, and then a whirl and a confusion of spines, claws, tail, and flying bits of turf. The dust cleared away, the spectators whooped and ran in cheering, and the Boy made out that the dragon was down, pinned to the earth by the spear, while St. George had dismounted, and stood astride of him.

It all seemed so genuine that the Boy ran in breathlessly, hoping the dear old dragon wasn't really hurt. As he approached, the dragon lifted one large eyelid, winked solemnly, and collapsed again. He was held fast to earth by the neck, but the Saint had hit him in the spare place agreed upon, and it didn't even seem to tickle.

"Bain't you goin' to cut 'is 'ed orf, master?" asked one of the applauding crowd. He had backed the dragon, and naturally felt a trifle sore.

"Well, not *to-day*, I think," replied St. George pleasantly. 'You see, that can be done at *any* time. There's no hurry at all. think we'll all go down to the village first, and have some refreshment, and then I'll give him a good talking-to, and you'll find he'll be a very different dragon!"

At that magic word *refreshment* the whole crowd formed up in procession and silently awaited the signal to start. The time for talking and cheering and betting was past, the hour for action had arrived. St. George, hauling on his spear with both hands, released the dragon, who rose and shook himself and ran his eye over his spikes and scales and things to see that they were all in order. Then the Saint mounted and led off the procession, the dragon following meekly in the company of the Boy, while the thirsty spectators kept at a respectful interval behind.

There were great doings when they got down to the village again, and had formed up in front of the inn. After refreshment St. George made a speech, in which he informed his audience that he had removed their direful scourge, at a great deal of trouble and inconvenience to himself, and now they weren't to go about grumbling and fancying they'd got grievances, because they hadn't. And they shouldn't be so fond of fights, because next time they might have to do the fighting themselves, which would not be the same thing at all. And there was a certain badger in the inn stables which had got to be released at once, and he'd come and see it done himself. Then he told them that the dragon had been thinking over things, and saw that there were two sides to every question, and he wasn't going to do it any more, and if they were good perhaps he'd stay and settle down there. So they must make friends, and not be prejudiced, and go about fancying they knew everything there was to be known, because they didn't, not by a long way. And he warned them against the sin of romancing, and making up stories and fancying other people would believe them just because they were plausible and highly-coloured. Then he sat down, amidst much repentant cheering, and the dragon nudged the Boy in the ribs and whispered that he could'nt have done it better himself. Then every one went off to get ready for the banquet.

Banquets are always pleasant things, consisting mostly, as they do, of eating and drinking; but the specially nice thing about a banquet is, that it comes when something's over, and there's nothing more to worry about, and to-morrow seems a long way off. St. George was happy because there had been a fight and he hadn't had to kill anybody; for he didn't really like killing, though he generally had to do it. The dragon was happy because there had been a fight, and so far from being hurt in it he had won popularity and a sure footing in Society. The Boy was happy because there had been a fight, and in spite of it all his two friends were on the best of terms. And all the others were happy because there had been a fight, and—well, they didn't require any other reasons for their happiness. The dragon exerted himself to say the right thing to everybody, and proved the life and soul of the evening; while the Saint and the Boy, as they looked on, felt that they were only assisting at a feast of which the honour and the glory were entirely the dragon's. But they didn't mind that, being good fellows, and the dragon was not in the least proud or forgetful. On the contrary, every ten minutes or so he leant over towards the Boy and said impressively: "Look here! You *will* see me home afterwards, won't you?" And the Boy always nodded, though he had promised his mother not to be out late.

At last the banquet was over, the guests had dropped away with many good nights and congratulations and invitations, and the dragon, who had seen the last of them off the premises, emerged into the street followed by the Boy, wiped his brow, sighed, sat down in the road and gazed at the stars. "Jolly night it's been!" he murmured. "Jolly stars! Jolly little place this. Think I shall just stop here. Don't feel like climbing up any beastly hill. Boy's promised to see me home. Boy had better do it then! No responsibility on my part. Responsibility all Boy's!" And his chin sank on his broad chest and he slumbered peacefully.

"Oh, *get* up, dragon," cried the Boy piteously. "You *know* my mother's sitting up, and I'm so tired, and you made me promise to see you home, and I never knew what it meant or I wouldn't have done it!" And the Boy sat down in the road by the side of the sleeping dragon, and cried.

The door behind them opened, a stream of light illumined the road, and St. George, who had come out for a stroll in the cool night air, caught sight of the two figures sitting there—the great motionless dragon and the tearful little Boy.

"What's the matter, Boy?" he inquired kindly, stepping to his side.

"Oh, it's this great lumbering *pig* of a dragon!" sobbed the Boy. "First he makes me promise to see him home, and then he says I'd better do it, and goes to sleep! Might as well try to see a *haystack* home! And I'm so tired, and mother's—" Here he broke down again.

"Now don't take on," said St. George. "I'll stand by you,

and we'll *both* see him home. Wake up, dragon!'' he said sharply, shaking the beast by the elbow.

The dragon looked up sleepily. ''What a night, George!'' he murmured; ''what a—''

''Now look here, dragon,'' said the Saint firmly. ''Here's this little fellow waiting to see you home, and you *know* he ought to have been in bed these two hours, and what his mother'll say *I* don't know, and anybody but a selfish pig would have *made* him go to bed long ago—''

''And he *shall* go to bed!'' cried the dragon, starting up. ''Poor little chap, only fancy his being up at this hour! It's a shame, that's what it is, and I don't think, St. George, you've been very considerate—but come along at once, and don't let us have any more arguing or shilly-shallying. You give me hold of your hand, Boy— thank you, George, an arm up the hill is just what I wanted!''

So they set off up the hill arm-in-arm, the Saint, the dragon, and the Boy. The lights in the little village began to go out; but there were stars, and a late moon, as they climbed to the Downs together. And, as they turned the last corner and disappeared from view, snatches of an old song were borne back on the night breeze. I can't be certain which of them was singing, but I *think* it was the Dragon!

THE IMMORTAL GAME

by Poul Anderson

    A freelance writer for over thirty-five years, Poul Ander-
son (1926-   ) has won the Tolkien Memorial, Nebula, and
Hugo awards. He is a superior and prolific writer of more
than fifty novels and two hundred shorter stories. Notable
works include Brain Wave *(1954),* The High Crusade *(1960),*
Three Hearts and Three Lions *(1961), and* Tau Zero *(1970)*
as well as "Call Me Joe" (1957), "The Longest Voyage"
(1960), "No Truce With Kings" (1962), "The Sharing of
Flesh" (1968), and "The Queen of Air and Darkness" (1971).
    The following story, as you will discover, is derived from a
classical source.

The first trumpet sounded far and clear and brazen cold, and
Rogard the Bishop stirred to wakefulness with it. Lifting his
eyes, he looked through the suddenly rustling, murmuring line of
soldiers, out across the broad plain of Cinnabar and the frontier,
and over to the realm of LEUKAS.

Away there, across the somehow unreal red-and-black dis-
tances of the steppe, he saw sunlight flash on armor and caught
the remote wild flutter of lifted banners. *So it is war,* he thought.
So we must fight again.

71

Again? He pulled his mind from the frightening dimness of that word. Had they ever fought before?

On his left, Sir Ocher laughed aloud and clanged down the vizard on his gay young face. It gave him a strange, inhuman look, he was suddenly a featureless thing of shining metal and nodding plumes, and the steel echoed in his voice: "Ha, a fight! Praise God, Bishop, for I had begun to fear I would rust here forever."

Slowly, Rogard's mind brought forth wonder. "Were you sitting and thinking—before now?" he asked.

"Why—" Sudden puzzlement in the reckless tones: "I think I was. . . . Was I?" Fear turning into defiance: "Who cares? I've got some LEUKANS to kill!" Ocher reared in his horse till the great metallic wings thundered.

On Rogard's right, Flambard the King stood, tall in crown and robes. He lifted an arm to shade his eyes against the blazing sunlight. "They are sending DIOMES, the royal guardsman, first," he murmured. "A good man." The coolness of his tone was not matched by the other hand, its nervous plucking at his beard.

Rogard turned back, facing over the lines of Cinnabar to the frontier. DIOMES, the LEUKAN King's own soldier, was running. The long spear flashed in his hand, his shield and helmet threw back the relentless light in a furious dazzle, and Rogard thought he could hear the clashing of iron. Then that noise was drowned in the trumpets and drums and yells from the ranks of Cinnabar, and he had only his eyes.

DIOMES leaped two squares before coming to a halt on the frontier. He stopped then, stamping and thrusting against the Barrier which suddenly held him, and cried challenge. A muttering rose among the cuirassed soldiers of Cinnabar, and spears lifted before the flowing banners.

King Flambard's voice was shrill as he leaned forward and touched his own guardsman with his scepter. "Go, Carlon! Go to stop him!"

"Aye, sire," Carlon's stocky form bowed, and then he wheeled about and ran, holding his spear aloft, until he reached the frontier. Now he and DIOMES stood face to face, snarling at each other across the Barrier, and for a sick moment Rogard wondered what those two had done, once in an evil and forgotten year, that there should be such hate between them.

"Let me go, sire!" Ocher's voice rang eerily from the slit-eyed mask of his helmet. The winged horse stamped on the hard red ground, and the long lance swept a flashing arc. "Let me go next."

"No, no, Sir Ocher." It was a woman's voice. "Not yet. There'll be enough for you and me to do, later in this day."

Looking beyond Flambard, the Bishop saw his Queen, Evyan the Fair, and there was something within him which stumbled and broke into fire. Very tall and lovely was the gray-eyed Queen of Cinnabar, where she stood in armor and looked out at the growing battle. Her sun-browned young face was coifed in steel, but one rebellious lock blew forth in the wind, and she brushed at it with a gauntleted hand while the other drew her sword snaking from its sheath. "Now may God strengthen our arms," she said, and her voice was low and sweet. Rogard drew his cope tighter about him and turned his mitered head away with a sigh. But there was a bitter envy in him for Columbard, the Queen's Bishop of Cinnabar.

Drums thumped from the LEUKAN ranks, and another soldier ran forth. Rogard sucked his breath hissingly in, for this man came till he stood on DIOMES' right. And the newcomer's face was sharp and pale with fear. There was no Barrier between him and Carlon.

"To his death," muttered Flambard between his teeth. "They sent that fellow to his death."

Carlon snarled and advanced on the LEUKAN. He had little choice—if he waited, he would be slain, and his King had not commanded him to wait. He leaped, his spear gleamed, and the LEUKAN soldier toppled and lay emptily sprawled in the black square.

"First blood!" cried Evyan, lifting her sword and hurling sunbeams from it. "First blood for us!"

Aye, so, thought Rogard bleakly. *But King* MIKILLATI *had a reason for sacrificing that man. Maybe we should have let Carlon die. Carlon the bold, Carlon the strong, Carlon the lover of laughter. Maybe we should have let him die.*

And now the Barrier was down for Bishop ASATOR of LEUKAS,

and he came gliding down the red squares, high and cold in his glistening white robes, until he stood on the frontier. Rogard thought he could see ASATOR's eyes as they swept over Cinnabar. The LEUKAN Bishop was poised to rush in with his great mace should Flambard, for safety, seek to change with Earl Ferric as the Law permitted.

Law?

There was no time to wonder what the Law was, or why it must be obeyed, or what had gone before this moment of battle. Queen Evyan had turned and shouted to the soldier Raddic, guardsman of her own Knight Sir Cupran: "Go! Halt him!" And Raddic cast her his own look of love, and ran, ponderous in his mail, up to the frontier. There he and ASATOR stood, no Barrier between them if either used a flanking move.

Good! Oh, good, my Queen! thought Rogard wildly. For even if ASATOR did not withdraw, but slew Raddic, he would be in Raddic's square, and his threat would be against a wall of spears. *He will retreat, he will retreat—*

Iron roared as ASATOR's mace crashed through helm and skull and felled Raddic the guardsman.

Evyan screamed, once only. "And I sent him! I sent him!" Then she began to run.

"Lady!" Rogard hurled himself against the Barrier. He could not move, he was chained here in his square, locked and barred by a Law he did not understand, while his lady ran toward death. "O Evyan, Evyan!"

Straight as a flying javelin ran the Queen of Cinnabar. Turning, straining after her, Rogard saw her leap the frontier and come to a halt by the Barrier which marked the left-hand bound of the kingdoms, beyond which lay only dimness to the frightful edge of the world. There she wheeled to face the dismayed ranks of LEUKAS, and her cry drifted back like the shriek of a stooping hawk: "MIKILLATI! Defend yourself!"

The thunder-crack of cheering from Cinnabar drowned all answer, but Rogard saw, at the very limits of his sight, how hastily King MIKILLATI stepped from the line of her attack, into the stronghold of Bishop ASATOR.

Now, thought Rogard fiercely, now the white-robed ruler

could never seek shelter from one of his Earls. Evyan had stolen his greatest shield.

"Hola, my Queen!" With a sob of laughter, Ocher struck spurs into his horse. Wings threshed, blowing Rogard's cope about him, as the Knight hurtled over the head of his own guardsman and came to rest two squares in front of the Bishop. Rogard fought down his own anger; he had wanted to be the one to follow Evyan. But Ocher was a better choice.

Oh, much better! Rogard gasped as his flittering eyes took in the broad battlefield. In the next leap, Ocher could cut down DIOMES, and then between them he and Evyan could trap MIKILLATI!

Briefly, that puzzlement nagged at the Bishop. Why should men die to catch someone else's King? What was there in the Law that said Kings should strive for mastery of the world and—

"Guard yourself, Queen!" Sir MERKON, King's Knight of LEUKAS, sprang in a move like Ocher's. Rogard's breath rattled in his throat with bitterness, and he thought there must be tears in Evyan's bright eyes. Slowly, then, the Queen withdrew two squares along the edge, until she stood in front of Earl Ferric's guardsman. It was still a good place to attack from, but not what the other had been.

BOAN, guardsman of the LEUKAN Queen DOLORA, moved one square forward, so that he protected great DIOMES from Ocher. Ocher snarled and sprang in front of Evyan, so that he stood between her and the frontier: clearing the way for her, and throwing his own protection over Carlon.

MERKON jumped likewise, landing to face Ocher with the frontier between them. Rogard clenched his mace and vision blurred for him; the LEUKANS were closing in on Evyan.

"Ulfar!" cried the King's Bishop. "Ulfar, can you help her?"

The stout old yeoman who was guardsman of the Queen's Bishop nodded wordlessly and ran one square forward. His spear menaced Bishop ASATOR, who growled at him—no Barrier between those two now!

MERKON of LEUKAS made another soaring leap, landing three squares in front of Rogard. "Guard yourself!" the voice belled from his faceless helmet. "Guard yourself, O Queen!"

No time now to let Ulfar slay ASATOR. Evyan's great eyes looked wildly about her; then, with swift decision, she stepped between MERKON and Ocher. Oh, a lovely move! Out of the fury in his breast, Rogard laughed.

The guardsman of the LEUKAN King's Knight clanked two squares ahead, lifting his spear against Ocher. It must have taken boldness thus to stand before Evyan herself; but the Queen of Cinnabar saw that if she cut him down, the Queen of LEUKAS could slay her. "Get free, Ocher!" she cried. "Get away!" Ocher cursed and leaped from danger, landing in front of Rogard's guardsman.

The King's Bishop bit his lip and tried to halt the trembling in his limbs. How the sun blazed! Its light was a cataract of dry white fire over the barren red and black squares. It hung immobile, enormous in the vague sky, and men gasped in their armor. The noise of bugles and iron, hoofs and wings and stamping feet, was loud under the small wind that blew across the world. There had never been anything but this meaningless war, there would never be aught else, and when Rogard tried to think beyond the moment when the fight had begun, or the moment when it would end, there was only an abyss of darkness.

Earl RAFAEON of LEUKAS took one ponderous step toward his King, a towering figure of iron readying for combat. Evyan whooped. "Ulfar!" she yelled. "Ulfar, your chance!"

Columbard's guardsman laughed aloud. Raising his spear, he stepped over into the square held by ASATOR. The white-robed Bishop lifted his mace, futile and feeble, and then he rolled in the dust at Ulfar's feet. The men of Cinnabar howled and clanged sword on shield.

Rogard held aloof from triumph. ASATOR, he thought grimly, had been expendable ányway. King MIKILLATI had something else in mind.

It was like a blow when he saw Earl RAFAEON's guardsman run forward two squares and shout to Evyan to guard herself. Raging, the Queen of Cinnabar withdrew a square to her rearward. Rogard saw sickly how unprotected King Flambard was now, the soldiers scattered over the field and the hosts of LEUKAS marshaling. But Queen DOLORA, he thought with a wild clutching of hope, Queen DOLORA, her tall cold beauty was just as open to a strong attack.

The soldier who had driven Evyan back took a leap across the frontier. "Guard yourself, O Queen!" he cried again. He was a small, hard-bitten, unkempt warrior in dusty helm and corselet. Evyan cursed, a bouncing soldierly oath, and moved one square forward to put a Barrier between her and him. He grinned impudently in his beard.

It is ill for us, it is a bootless and evil day. Rogard tried once more to get out of his square and go to Evyan's aid, but his will would not carry him. The Barrier held, invisible and uncrossable, and the Law held, the cruel and senseless Law which said a man must stand by and watch his lady be slain, and he railed at the bitterness of it and lapsed into a gray waiting.

Trumpets lifted brazen throats, drums boomed, and Queen DOLORA of LEUKAS stalked forth into battle. She came high and white and icily fair, her face chiseled and immobile in its haughtiness under the crowned helmet, and stood two squares in front of her husband, looming over Carlon. Behind her, her own Bishop SORKAS poised in his stronghold, hefting his mace in armored hands. Carlon of Cinnabar spat at DOLORAS'S feet, and she looked at him from cool blue eyes and then looked away. The hot dry wind did not ruffle her long pale hair; she was like a statue, standing there and waiting.

"Ocher," said Evyan softly, "out of my way."

"I like not retreat, my lady," he answered in a thin tone.

"Nor I," said Evyan. "But I must have an escape route open. We will fight again."

Slowly, Ocher withdrew, back to his own home. Evyan chuckled once, and a wry grin twisted her young face.

Rogard was looking at her so tautly that he did not see what was happening until a great shout of iron slammed his head around. Then he saw Bishop SORKAS, standing in Carlon's square with a bloodied mace in his hands, and Carlon lay dead at his feet.

Carlon, your hands are empty, life has slipped from them and there is an unending darkness risen in you who loved the world. Goodnight, my Carlon, goodnight.

"Madame—" Bishop SORKAS spoke quietly, bowing a little, and there was a smile on his crafty face. "I regret, madame, that—ah—"

"Yes. I must leave you." Evyan shook her head, as if she

had been struck, and moved a square backwards and sideways. Then, turning, she threw the glance of an eagle down the black squares to LEUKAS' Earl ARACLES. He looked away nervously, as if he would crouch behind the three soldiers who warded him. Evyan drew a deep breath sobbing into her lungs.

Sir THEUTAS, DOLORA's Knight, sprang from his stronghold, to place himself between Evyan and the Earl. Rogard wondered dully if he meant to kill Ulfar the soldier; he could do it now. Ulfar looked at the Knight who sat crouched, and hefted his spear and waited for his own weird.

"Rogard!"

The Bishop leaped, and for a moment there was fire-streaked darkness before his eyes.

"Rogard, to me! To me, and help sweep them from the world!"

Evyan's voice.

She stood in her scarred and dinted armor, holding her sword aloft, and on that smitten field she was laughing with a new-born hope. Rogard could not shout his reply. There were no words. But he raised his mace and ran.

The black squares slid beneath his feet, footfalls pounding, jarring his teeth, muscles stretching with a resurgent glory and all the world singing. At the frontier, he stopped, knowing it was Evyan's will though he could not have said how he knew. Then he faced about, and with clearing eyes looked back over that field of iron and ruin. Save for one soldier, Cinnabar was now cleared of LEUKAN forces, Evyan was safe, a counterblow was readying like the first whistle of hurricane. Before him were the proud banners of LEUKAS—now to throw them into the dust! Now to ride with Evyan into the home of MIKILLATI!

"Go to it, sir," rumbled Ulfar, standing on the Bishop's right and looking boldly at the white Knight who could slay him. "Give 'em hell from us."

Wings beat in the sky, the THEUTAS soared down to land on Rogard's left. In the hot light, the blued metal of his armor was like running water. His horse snorted, curveting and flapping its wings; he sat it easily, the lance swaying in his grasp, the blanke helmet turned to Flambard. One more such leap, reckoned Rogard wildly, and he would be able to assail the King of Cinnabar. Or—

no—a single spring from here and he would spit Evyan on his lance.

And there is a Barrier between us!

"Watch yourself, Queen!" The arrogant LEUKAN voice boomed hollow out of the steel mask.

"Indeed I will, Sir Knight!" There was only laughter in Evyan's tone. Lightly, then, she sped up the row of black squares. She brushed by Rogard, smiling at him as she ran, and he tried to smile back but his face was stiffened. Evyan, Evyan, she was plunging alone into her enemy's homeland!

Iron belled and clamored. The white guardsman in her path toppled and sank at her feet. One fist lifted strengthlessly, and a dying shrillness was in the dust: "Curse you, curse you, MIKILLATI, curse you for a stupid fool, leaving me here to be slain—no, no, no—"

Evyan bestrode the body and laughed again in the very face of Earl ARACLES. He cowered back, licking his lips—he could not move against her, but she could annihilate him in one more step. Beside Rogard, Ulfar whooped, and the trumpets of Cinnabar howled in the rear.

Now the great attack was launched! Rogard cast a fleeting glance at Bishop SORKAS. The lean white-coped form was gliding forth, mace swinging loose in one hand, and there was a little sleepy smile on the pale face. No dismay—? SORKAS halted, facing Rogard, and smiled a little wider, skinning his teeth without humor. "You can kill me if you wish," he said softly. "But do you?"

For a moment Rogard wavered. To smash that head—!

"Rogard! Rogard, to me!"

Evyan's cry jerked the King's Bishop around. He saw now what her plan was, and it dazzled him so that he forgot all else. LEUKAS *is ours!*

Swiftly he ran. DIOMES and BOAN howled at him as he went between them, brushing impotent spears against the Barriers. He passed Queen DOLORA, and her lovely face was as if cast in steel, and her eyes followed him as he charged over the plain of LEUKAS. Then there was no time for thinking, Earl RAFAEON loomed before him, and he jumped the last boundary into the enemy's heartland.

The Earl lifted a meaningless ax. The Law read death for him, and Rogard brushed aside the feeble stroke. The blow of his mace shocked in his own body, slamming his jaws together. RAFAEON crumpled, falling slowly, his armor loud as he struck the ground. Briefly, his fingers clawed at the iron-hard black earth, and then he lay still.

They have slain Raddic and Carlon—we have three guardsmen, a Bishop, and an Earl—Now we need only be butchers! Evyan, Evyan, warrior Queen, this is your victory!

DIOMES of LEUKAS roared and jumped across the frontier. Futile, futile, he was doomed to darkness. Evyan's lithe form moved up against ARACLES, her sword flamed and the Earl crashed at her feet. Her voice was another leaping brand: "Defend yourself, King!"

Turning, Rogard grew aware that MIKILLATI himself had been right beside him. There was a Barrier between the two men—but MIKILLATI had to retreat from Evyan, and he took one step forward and sideways. Peering into his face, Rogard felt a sudden coldness. There was no defeat there, it was craft and knowledge and an unbending steel will—*what was LEUKAS planning?*

Evyan tossed her head, and the wind fluttered the lock of hair like a rebel banner. "We have them, Rogard!" she cried.

Far and faint, through the noise and confusion of battle, Cinnabar's bugles sounded and the command of her King. Peering into the haze, Rogard saw that Flambard was taking precautions. Sir THEUTAS was still a menace, where he stood beside SORKAS. Sir Cupran of Cinnabar flew heavily over to land in front of the Queen's Earl's guardsman, covering the route THEUTAS must follow to endanger Flambard.

Wise, but—Rogard looked again at MIKILLATI's chill white face, and it was as if a breath of cold blew through him. Suddenly he wondered why they fought. For victory, yes, for mastery over the world—but when the battle had been won, what then?

He couldn't think past that moment. His mind recoiled in horror he could not name. In that instant he knew icily that this was not the first war in the world, there had been others before, and there would be others again. *Victory is death.*

But Evyan, glorious Evyan, she could not die. She would reign over all the world and—

Steel blazed in Cinnabar, MERKON of LEUKAS came surging forth, one tigerish leap which brought him down on Ocher's guardsman. The soldier screamed, once, as he fell under the trampling, tearing hoofs, but it was lost in the shout of the LEUKAN Knight: "Defend yourself, Flambard! Defend yourself!"

Rogard gasped. It was like a blow in the belly. He had stood triumphant over the world, and now all in one swoop it was brought toppling about him. THEUTAS shook his lance, SORKAS his mace, DIOMES raised a bull's bellow—somehow, incredibly somehow, the warriors of LEUKAS had entered Cinnabar and were thundering at the King's own citadel.

"No, no—" Looking down the long empty row of squares, Rogard saw that Evyan was weeping. He wanted to run to her, hold her close and shield her against the falling world, but the Barriers were around him. He could not stir from his square, he could only watch.

Flambard cursed lividly and retreated into his Queen's home. His men gave a shout and clashed their arms—there was still a chance!

No, not while the Law bound men, thought Rogard, not while the Barriers held. Victory was ashen, and victory and defeat alike were darkness.

Beyond her thinly smiling husband, Queen DOLORA swept forward. Evyan cried out as the tall white woman halted before Rogard's terrified guardsman, turned to face Flambard where he crouched, and called to him: "Defend yourself, King!"

"No—no—you fool!" Rogard reached out, trying to break the Barrier, clawing at MIKILLATI. "Can't you see, none of us can win, it's death for us all if the war ends. Call her back!"

MIKILLATI ignored him. He seemed to be waiting.

And Ocher of Cinnabar raised a huge shout of laughter. It belled over the plain, dancing joyous mirth, and men lifted weary heads and turned to the young Knight where he sat in his own stronghold, for there was youth and triumph and glory in his laughing. Swiftly, then, a blur of steel, he sprang, and his winged horse rushed out of the sky on DOLORA herself. She turned to meet him, lifting her sword, and he knocked it from her hand

and stabbed with his own lance. Slowly, too haughty to scream,
the white Queen sank under his horse's hoofs.

And MIKILLATI smiled.

"I see," nodded the visitor. "Individual computers, each
controlling its own robot piece by a tight beam, and all the
computers on a given side linked to form a sort of group-mind
constrained to obey the rules of chess and make the best possible
moves. Very nice. And it's a pretty cute notion of yours, making
the robots look like medieval armies." His glance studied the
tiny figures where they moved on the oversized board under one
glaring floodlight.

"Oh, that's pure frippery," said the scientist. "This is really
a serious research project in multiple computer-linkages. By
letting them play game after game, I'm getting some valuable
data."

"It's a lovely setup," said the visitor admiringly. "Do you
realize that in this particular contest the two sides are reproduc-
ing one of the great classic games?"

"Why, no. Is that a fact?"

"Yes. It was a match between Anderssen and Kieseritsky,
back in—I forget the year, but it was quite some time ago. Chess
books often refer to it as the Immortal Game. . . . So your
computers must share many of the properties of a human brain."

"Well, they're complex things, all right," admitted the scientist.
"Not all their characteristics are known yet. Sometimes my
chessmen surprise even me."

"Hm." The visitor stooped over the board. "Notice how
they're jumping around inside their squares, waving their arms,
batting at each other with their weapons?" He paused, then
murmured slowly: "I wonder—I wonder if your computers may
not have consciousness. If they might not have—minds."

"Don't get fantastic," snorted the scientist.

"But how do you know?" persisted the visitor. "Look, your
feedback arrangement is closely analogous to a human nervous
system. How do you know that your individual computers, even if
they are constrained by the group linkage, don't have individual
personalities? How do you know that their electronic senses
don't interpret the game as, oh, as an interplay of free will and

necessity; how do you know they don't receive the data of the moves as their own equivalent of blood, sweat and tears?" He shuddered a little.

"Nonsense," grunted the scientist. "They're only robots. Now—Hey! Look there! Look at that move!"

Bishop sorkas took one step ahead, into the black square adjoining Flambard's. He bowed and smiled. "The war is ended," he said.

Slowly, very slowly, Flambard looked about him. sorkas, merkon, theutas, they were crouched to leap on him wherever he turned; his own men raged helpless against the Barriers; there was no place for him to go.

He bowed his head. "I surrender," he whispered.

Rogard looked across the red and black to Evyan. Their eyes met, and they stretched out their arms to each other.

"Checkmate," said the scientist. "That game's over."
He crossed the room to the switchboard and turned off the computers.

THE STAINLESS-STEEL KNIGHT

by John T. Phillifent

The author of more than twenty science fiction novels and fifty shorter works, John T. Phillifent (1916-1976) was an Englishman who wrote primarily under the pen name of John Rackham. Most of his shorter stories have appeared in England only, and the majority of his novels are parts of the Ace Double Novel series. His works are highly readable exercises in light adventure; they include Beanstalk *(1973),* Hierarchies *(1973), and* King of Argent *(1973).*

Life with Lancelot (1973) offers an expanded series of adventures with the cybernetic fusion of Maxwell Smart and Don Quixote who first appeared in the following tale.

I

When the twisted and radioactive wreckage screamed down out of space onto their dark planet, the Shogleet were instantly intrigued. To that incredibly ancient race, evolved to the point where energy, matter and form had no more secrets to hide and only curiosity remained, anything new was an occasion for rejoicing. And this was new.

Metals, plastics, physical and chemical combinations—they were familiar enough. But this strange mass had been formed into a particular shape. They probed at once, and at once found that there was something more.

Something lived, but only just.

Using their combined talents, they caught at the fragile remnant, preserved it, studied it, reconstructed it. From the still viable patterns of intelligence, they deduced the whole. They remade a man. They went further, discovering his history and, from that, something of the history of the whole species. They were unwilling to admit that such a monstrosity could be genuine, yet their probings could not be argued. So they remade his ship, which had obviously been only a small part of the whole tangled wreckage, and they sent it back whence it had come. And they appointed one of their number to go with it, and him, to investigate.

The Shogleet crouched by Lancelot's beautiful boots, and purred. The purr was not a sign of pleasure, but the by-product of producing an outline-blurring vibration and curiosity-damping field. The corridor outside the Agent-Director's office was a busy place, and the Shogleet had no wish to be observed.

Yet it was pleased. These things called Men were even more fantastically odd than it had at first imagined. With its perceptors extended, it was listening to the conversation on the other side of the wall. Voices were discussing Lancelot.

"—not only made us a laughing-stock, but he's getting to be a damned pest! Hanging about outside my office, demanding to be sent on a mission. I wouldn't trust him to empty my waste-basket. What the hell am I going to do with him?"

"Perhaps we might cook up a mission for him, Chief."

"Don't be obscene, Peters. That moron, on a mission? Don't forget, this is the blasted idiot who tried to rescue a disabled star-ship with a one-man raft!'"

"Just the same, Chief, we could pick out something."

"But I can't send a Prime G-man on a routine call, damn it! Not that he is a Prime, except on paper. But you know what I mean."

"Ah, but wait until you hear what I've dug up. It's from a vivarium planet. We don't usually handle those. What generally happens is that the local man goes in, disguised, and re-sets the alarm, then smoothes out the fuss. Doesn't affect us unless it's a case of external invasion, you know."

"All right, all right. I know all that. But what's it to me? Some inside problem on a viv planet. So?"

"Yes. But this planet is called Avalon. It's static in the 'pseudo-feudal' stage, with a culture based on Arthurian legend. Get it?"

The Shogleet, recording all this avidly, heard a gasp. Putting mental query marks against the new terms, it went on listening.

"Arthurian!" Hugard breathed. "Peasants. Knights in armor. Sword and shield stuff. Go on."

"I thought we could play it up big, and let him have it. Make it sound a desperate emergency. Give him something to do."

"Yes. Quite harmless, of course. But I like the sound of it. Where is this Avalon?"

"That's the best part, Chief. It's in the Omega Centaurus cluster. That's twenty thousand lights away!"

"That settles it for me. It will take him a month, real time, just to get there. I'll be shut of him for a while. Sure we're not treading on any private toes with this?"

"Absolutely. Strictly a routine call, on a waiting list."

"Fine. Fine! Get me the data so I can blow it up big, and then shoot him in here. Peters, I won't forget this. To think that I'm going to be rid of that moron, for a while at least—"

The Shogleet crept to Lancelot's shoulder, shivering gently with anticipation. When the summons came, it rode into the office with him and saw him stiffen into a stern salute before the Director's desk.

"Ah, Lake," Hugard nodded portentously. "At last I have a mission for you. Something I cannot pass on to anyone else. It will tax your powers to the utmost. I am not asking you to volunteer; I am *ordering* you to go. That is how serious it is. You understand?"

"I do, sir," Lancelot said, sternly. "Rely on me!"

"Good man! I was counting on that. Now, you'll take full details with you to study en route, of course, but I can give you the gist. The planet is Avalon. The alarm is urgent. Avalon is a closed culture. No one, not even we of Galactopol, can intervene

in a closed culture, unless the situation is desperately critical."
The Shogleet felt Lancelot stiffen, saw the swell of his chest and
the fire in his eyes, and wondered anew at these strange creatures
who thrilled to the prospect of imminent danger.

"Most importantly"—Hugard hushed his voice—"as this is a
closed culture, I can only send one man. You will be alone.
Single-handed. You will be equipped, of course, as fully as
possible, compatible with the culture. But everything else will be
up to you. You're on your own."

"I understand, sir," Lancelot said simply. "Rely on me. If
it's called for, I'll stake my life, rather than let down the
Service." Huggard turned his face away, obviously overcome by
some strong emotion. Then, coughing, he handed a form to
Lancelot and stood up.

"That's your authorization. You'll pick up the rest of the
documents at the front office. How soon can you leave?"

"At once!" Lancelot snapped, saluting crisply. Hugard put
out a hand.

"Good luck, my boy. You'll need it."

"Thank you, sir." Lancelot took the hand with an enthusiasm
that made the Director wince. "Don't worry about me. I'll come
through!" He spun on his heel and marched from the office.

"You know," he confided to the Shogleet, "Hugard isn't
such a bad old guy, after all. I thought he was neglecting me.
But I can see his point, now. I've misjudged him."

"Lancelot," the Shogleet whispered, "do something for me.
Get a stock of visio-tapes on feudal cultures, vivarium planets
and the Arthurian legend."

"All right. Anything to oblige. But you pick the queerest
things to be curious about. Arthurian legends, is it? My Dad
used to be interested in them."

This the Shogleet already knew, as well as much more. It had
learned, for one thing, the truer version of how Lancelot Lake
came to be cast away in the first place. This it had picked up
from various sources, in and about Galactopol headquarters.

Lancelot Lake had been a humble technician in the lowest
grades of Galactopol, serving his time in a spaceways emergency-
and-observation station, and passing his time in dreams of

glamour and glory. He shared the simple faith of his equally simple parents, that it was just a matter of time before he had his big "break." And Fate had been very obliging.

The star-class liner *Orion*, carrying wealthy passengers but very little else, had developed a major defect in her main drive. Her skipper, in angry calm, warped out of hyper-drive, gave the order "Abandon Ship!" and pointed his lifeboat cluster toward the nearest E-and-O station. It had not been an emergency. There had not been the least danger—only nuisance, and the loss of a valuable ship. The lifeboat signals had plainly said so.

But Lancelot had read his own special brand of understanding into those signals. On the run, fired with holy zeal, he had broken out his one-man raft, designed purely for short-range forays about the surface of his planetoid-station. Linking in to the powerful, all-wave, sub-etheric emergency radio of the station and giving a blow-by-blow account of his effort, he had stormed off to rescue the *Orion* single-handed.

No one could hear the lifeboat signals, after that. The *Orion* company reached the E-and-O station quite safely. There, in company with every other open planet in the Galaxy, they had listened, fascinated, to the classic broadcast that Lancelot was pouring out.

Dedicated, always brave, heedless of personal safety, washed with the radiation from a rapidly disintegrating nuclear drive, he kept on to the inevitable, hopeless, gallant end. Like a gnat grappling a runaway elephant, he went spiralling down into the great gravity sink of Antares, until the thermal radiation from that giant sun overwhelmed his transmission.

The rest was silence.

Now, a stupid, gloriously gallant, *dead* hero is one thing. Posthumous awards are a matter of little consequence. It was nothing—the least they could do—to make the deceased Lancelot a Prime G-man. But the same hero returned from the dead was something else again, as the Shogleet had learned.

Perhaps, it pondered, they had done too good a job of the reconstruction. They had made him strictly according to the images in his own brain. Consequently, he was big, brawny, blue-eyed, golden-haired, handsome, and well-nigh indestructible . . . translating literally the concept "You can't keep a good man down." Had

Lancelot known Hamlet, he would have agreed with his description:
"What a piece of work is Man; how noble in reason; how infinite in
faculties; in form and moving, how express and admirable; in action
how like an angel; in apprehension how like a god!" But Hamlet was
insane, whereas Lancelot was sincere, simple, and assured of the
reality of his dream. Hence—as Hugard had said—a damned pest.

II

Lancelot's happy glow lasted well into the second week. Then
he grew bored. The ship, though small, was comfortable and
almost self-directive. There was nothing to do.

He decided to check his equipment. The Shogleet, engrossed
in the tortuous language of Malory, was interrupted by its ward,
who came bearing a long and shining rod tipped with a razor-
edged blade.

"This thing," he said. "It's a lance, isn't it? And there's
another thing, like a big blade with a cross-bar and a hand-grip.
A sword?"

"I would think so. There should be armor, also. I gather you
are to masquerade as a knight. From the literature, it seems there
actually was a knight named Sir Lancelot."

"That's so. My dad used to tell about him. Oh, Hugard knew
what he was doing when he picked me for this mission! Fate,
that's what it is." The Shogleet had other views, but kept
discreetly silent about them.

"The concept of a vivarium culture interests me," it said,
"Apparently not all men seek change, only a small percentage?"

"That's so," Lancelot nodded, sagely. "The happy man is
the adjusted man. Knows what he's good at and where he
belongs, and gets on with it. Like me, for instance. Natural-born
adventurer—and here I am."

"But you were originally a station-keeper. A mistake?"

"Oh, no. Psycho-dynamics is infallible. That station-keeper
job was just a starter, so that I could work up."

The Shogleet, knowing full well that Lancelot knew nothing at
all about the science of psycho-dynamics, wished it had asked
for a tape on that. It was curious to see how the technique would
work out on a whole planet seeded with one psycho-type.

Eventually, warning bells gave tongue and their little ship went down, on a guide beacon, over a green and peaceful world, dotted with islands, laced with blue sea, into a small glade ringed with rugged hills. It was just on sunrise, on a glorious spring morning.

Lancelot breathed deep of unfiltered air and the sweet scent of growing things, and found an immediate complaint to make.

"We're about a hundred miles away from the chief city, Camlan," he said, as he frowned at a map. "And no transport. I mean, that kit I have to wear, it's a weight. It's not going to be easy just getting it on, much less walking."

"According to the accounts," the Shogleet said, "a knight rode something. A steed, I believe, or horse. What is a horse, Lancelot?"

"Damned if I know. I vaguely recall drawings, when I was a kid. Sort of big animal, four legs, head at one end, tail at the other. But stop a bit, that explains something—" and he lugged out some massive pieces of metal-work. "These had me baffled, but they must be horse-armor. And this thing is a seat, to go on its back, I guess."

"I shall have to approximate," the Shogleet decided. "From your memories, and what I have read, I will transform myself into a horse."

"All right, but give me a hand with this hardware first. I can't get it on alone. In fact, I don't see how it *can* all go on one man!"

But, with patience and struggling, trial and error, they got the pieces that a skilled synthesist had fabricated from the patterns of museum relics buckled, strapped and locked about Lancelot.

His guess had been good. He could hardly hold upright under the load of metal.

"How the hell does anybody hop about," he complained, making a few labored steps, "and swing a sword in this lot? It's not possible!"

The Shogleet paid no attention. It was busy on its own account. Swallowing great quantities of air and energy, and speeding its metabolism to a great rate, it was converting its mass to a something that would fit that armor. Lancelot, shambling round, gave advice according to his blurred memories. Then, struggling mightily, he hoisted up the pieces one at a time, and then the saddle. Sweat was dribbling into his boots by the time he was done.

"Hell! This is a day's work by itself," he groaned, bashing his helmet in a vain attempt to wipe away the sweat from his brow. "There must be an easier way."

"I imagine," the Shogleet-horse guessed, "that this is why the knight had a squire, as it says in the tapes." Lancelot grunted his heartfelt agreement at this, hung the blank shield on a saddle-hook, the sword and sheath on the opposite side, stood the long lance by a handy tree, and eased his visor down past his nose, which was already raw from the first, light-hearted try.

Then he eyed the stirrups.

"You'll have to kneel," he said. "I'll never make it up there."

He climbed aboard gingerly, and they left the glade at a sedate walk. "First thing," he said firmly, "we get a squire. I'll never make it to Camlan at this rate."

"Very well," the Shogleet agreed, trying to work out a method of progress that would not unseat Lancelot. It compromised on a rubber-legged shamble which carried them at a smooth glide through what it assumed was a "woody glen." Half an hour of this brought them to a clearing, laid out in a chessboard of little fields, with a huddle of timber shacks in the center. Their arrival was the signal for a bedlam of shouts, screams and frantic barking from a horde of half-wild dogs.

The uproar lasted only a second or two. Then all was silent, apart from furtive rustlings in the nearby bushes.

"Where did everybody go?" Lancelot demanded, grabbing the saddle-horn. "How am I going to round up a squire, if they all run off like that? No, wait—there's one, over by that tree."

He was an old man, grizzle-haired and cramped with rheumatic stiffness. In his simple brown smock, he clung to the tree and trembled at their gliding approach. Lancelot let go the saddle-horn and tried to sit up, impressively.

"Ho, there!" he called. "Why did everyone run away?"

"Marry, fair sir," the oldster mumbled, cringing. "It would

have been at sight of the strange beast thou ridest. No mortal eye ever saw such a mount before.''

"What's wrong with me?" the Shogleet demanded curiously. "Isn't a horse like this?"

"Now strike me dead!" the peasant blanched, clutching the tree. "It spoke like a Christian. I heard it!"

"Naturally," Lancelot said grandly. " 'Tis a magic steed, just as I am a holy knight. I have need of a squire. Call the others, that I may choose."

"Nay, noble sir, we are but humble peasants. Wilt find no squire here."

"Oh, blast!" Lancelot relapsed into Galactic in his irritation. Then, with strained patience, "Where then shall a knight find himself a squire?"

"The Baron Deorham has many such," the old man offered. "Steeds, too, though none such as thou ridest. But he is a wonderly wroth man, and a great warrior. He will surely attack thee, an thou come near him."

"Fear not for me, old man. I am Sir Lancelot. I will to Deorham."

"Lancelot! Now am I dead and in hell, forsooth. Lancelot is legend!"

"Never mind that. Just point the way, you old fool." The old man cringed again, and wobbled a shaky arm in the direction of a rough track. The Shogleet went into its gliding run again.

"A pity I couldn't get him to put me right on this shape," it said. "I must study a real horse at the first opportunity."

"This feels all right," Lancelot argued. "Still, I suppose you're right. It won't do to scare the locals out of their wits all the time. . . . Say, that looks a likely place."

They had broken clear of trees, and before them the grass went away in a slow rise to a hill, where there was a massive gray building. "Just let me do the talking. Apparently horses aren't supposed to talk." He clutched the saddle-horn valiantly, and they went on at a fair speed.

Suddenly the Shogleet sensed life and movement nearby, and swung round.

"What did you do that for?" Lancelot demanded, clinging desperately. Then he saw what the Shogleet had detected. About seventy yards away, just rounding an outflung clump of trees, came three riders. On either side the figures were slight, but the man in the center was gross, his steed huge, his armor bright in the sun. His shield bore the device of a mailed fist, and his lance carried a fluttering blue plume at its tip.

"That's what I want," Lancelot muttered. "A picture on my shield and a flag on my stick. Then they'll know who I am."

"So that," the Shogleet murmured, interestedly, "is what a horse is like." And it discreetly began modifying its shape. "We should keep still," it advised. "Let him come to us. I want to see that creature move."

As if in answer to the thought the big man put up a mailed fist. They distinctly heard the click of his visor as it snapped into place. Then he applied his heels to his mount and began thundering at them over the turf.

"Look at him go!" Lancelot said, admiringly. "I must learn to ride like that." The mighty figure thundered nearer, and Lancelot grew uneasy. "He'll never be able to stop in time," he muttered. "Not at that clip. Now what's the fool up to?"—for the stranger had dropped his lance to the horizontal, and the point was aimed straight at Lancelot. The Shogleet, ever curious, stood quite still.

"Hey! You lunatic! Point that thing the other way!" Lancelot yelled. But it was obvious even to him that the other had no intention of doing any such thing. At the last minute, he managed to fumble up his shield. There was a rending crash as the point met shield, fair and square. Lancelot shot backwards over the Shogleet's cruppers, to land with a jarring thud on the ground. The Shogleet spun round, to watch as the young man groaned, sat up and then struggled to his feet.

"Art unhorsed!" the stranger roared. "Dost yield?"

"Yield nothing," Lancelot gasped, indignantly. "I wasn't even fighting. You want to give a bit of notice, next time you do something like that. Charging up like that without so much as a word . . ." and that was as far as he got. The strange knight, backing up and tossing away his shattered lance, had yanked out his sword. Putting heels to his horse again, he tore up to where Lancelot stood. His blade rose and fell mightily, and a clang echoed across the meadow. Lancelot went down on his knees,

ung there a moment and then kneeled over, groaning. The
Shogleet trotted to where he lay and nuzzled him.

"You must get up and fight," it murmured. "I believe you
re liable to be taken captive otherwise."

"Fight!" Lancelot mumbled. "I'm half-killed already. That
damned lunatic should be put away." He sat up and banged his
nailed fist on his helmet to clear his head. The knight backed off
. yard or two, waiting.

"Get up, quickly," the Shogleet encouraged, and knelt. This
ent the knight's horse into a rearing frenzy, giving Lancelot
ime to mount—and time to get annoyed, also.

"All right," he growled. "Wants a fight, does he? We'll see
bout that." He unsheathed his sword with an effort. The strange
night crouched, setting his horse into another gallop. At the
ritical moment, he stood up in his saddle to give more power to
is sword-arm. Lancelot heaved his shield up, the shock numb-
ng his arm, then swung blindly in riposte.

"Turn round," he ordered, as the knight charged past. "Let
e have another bash at him. I only nicked him that time."

"You may kill him, you know."

"And what d'you fancy he's been trying to do to me? I'm
lack and blue all over. Let me have another crack at him, I
aid!"

"Wouldn't it be wiser to ask him to yield? In that way, we
might get some information, which we sadly need." Lancelot
rumbled under his breath, but when he saw that his casual
wipe had sheared the knight's helmet-spike, and split his shield
1 half, he agreed reluctantly.

"Ho, knight," he called, and waved his sword. "Wilt yield?"

"To a foul fiend from the pit?" the knight roared, tossing
way his ruined shield and bent sword. "Never! Pit thy sorcery
gainst this!" And he unhooked from his saddle a short length of
eavy chain, ending in an iron ball studded with vicious spikes.
Once again, he came thundering forward.

"There!" Lancelot gasped. "I said the man was raving. If he
atches me with that thing, I'm a dead duck."

He put up his shield and peered round it warily. The spiked
all flailed through the air and crashed full on the shield, slam-
ing the young man over to an extreme angle. In sudden, blind

rage, he swung back, lashed out with the sword, felt it bite int
something. Then, as the Shogleet bridled off, he looked back
and his stomach squirmed.

The super-hard, razor-keen blade had sliced through armo
and knight, from shoulder to groin. There was blood everywhere

III

"The fool would have it," he muttered. "Now there'll b
trouble."

But the body was hardly flópped to rest before the two attend
ants rode up, slid from their mounts and went down, each on
knee, heads bowed.

"Spare me, Sir Knight," they said in unison. "I am th
servant."

"They're only kids," Lancelot said, surprised. "What ar
your names?"

"I am hight Alaric," said the ginger one, on the left.

"And I, Ector," the other added, shaking his long yellov
locks. "How shall we call thee, Lord?" The Shogleet felt Lancelo
brace up and stiffen.

"I am Sir Lancelot!" he announced. They promptly fell fla
on their faces. "Oh, get up!" he said, irritably. "I'm not goin
to eat you. Now, one's to be my squire, and the other to loo
after my horse. Which way do you want it?"

"The horse!" they said, together and at once.

"That won't be necessary," the Shogleet said, forgetting. "
can look after myself quite well." Again the two youths fell t
the ground, shaking and white.

"Get up!" Lancelot shouted. "How can I get anything done i
you keep passing out, all the time? Now, what happens abou
him?"

"Thy liege-men will attend to it, Lord," said Alaric, in
shaky voice.

"*My* liege-men?"

"But certainly. Hast slain Deorham. That which was his i
now thine."

"Oh!" Lancelot looked round. "Castle and all? Well, that
handy. And that was Deorham, was it? All right, one of you ni

ff and tell the gang the boss is coming home, hungry . . . and
ruised, too!''

"I will, Lord!" Alaric fled for his horse and raced on ahead.

The Shogleet contented itself with a modest canter, finding the
ew movement intriguing. Lancelot was not impressed.

"You're shaking me to a jelly," he groaned. "Can't we go
ack to the other way?''

"This is more accurate. You had better learn. You may have
) ride a real horse someday." Lancelot forgot to grumble as
ney reached the courtyard of the castle, and he could appreciate
ne size of the place. He slid off, and stood agape at high
ough-stone walls and towers, their slit-windows innocent of
lass, but with gay cloths trailing from every vantage point.
:ctor approached, unwillingly, to take the Shogleet's bridle.
.ancelot objected at once.

"You can't go off and leave me, not now. What'll I do? I
nean, you know more than me about all the customs and things.''

"It will be quite all right," the Shogleet consoled him in
;alactic, ignoring the flabbergasted stares of the men-at-arms
vho had drawn near. "Just give orders. Tell them what you
vant. I will join you as soon as I can.''

It went with Ector to a great low stable, where there were
nany half-wild horses and a great smell. As soon as it could be
lone, it cast off the horse-shape. It had given a degree of
nought to this, and decided it was best to assume some human-
ke form. So, on its rapid transit through the stables, courtyard
nd into the great hall, it settled into a small, dark-hued, manikin
nape, thinking to be less impressive and thus less frightening in
nat guise.

Trotting through the serfs who were busy scattering fresh
ashes on the stone-slab floor, it found Lancelot seated at the
ead of a long, rude table, on which more serfs were arranging
1atters heaped with hot food. He was deep in conversation with
n old, rugged-looking, gray-bearded man, but looked up as the
hogleet came close and scrambled on to the arm of his chair.

"This is Gildas," he said. "Calls himself a seneschal. Sort of
ead-man. Been telling me all about the property.''

Gildas backed off warily.

"Now, sooth," he muttered. "I do believe thou *art* Lancelot, and this thy familiar. What is it, a troll?"

"Lancelot," the Shogleet said, in Galactic. "Have you forgotten? We are on a mission. You should be asking Gildas for news of the emergency."

"Say, that's right. I'd forgotten. It's not every day a man gets a barony." He turned in his chair. "Draw near, Gildas. There is nothing to fear."

"Thou sayest it well, Lord," Gildas growled, "but I like it not. A troll that stands and parleys like a man. Still, it is but part and parcel with the strange things that have come on this land but lately."

"Ah, now, that's what I wanted to know about. What's going on? I have to know, because I'm here to stop it." Gildas stepped back, transformed from a sullen graybeard into an angry enemy.

"I knew it!" he roared. "I knew thou wert false! I will hail the men-at-arms, that they may cut thee down. Nay, strike me dead an thou canst, but I will say it."

"Oh, lord!" Lancelot muttered. "What now? For heaven's sake, man, I'm not going to strike anybody dead. Not again. I've had enough of that for one day. Just get a grip on yourself and tell me what it's all about."

"Methinks yon troll doth already know, and the question is but a trap. Natheless, I will tell. Ye wit well there is but one great sin in this land. It is hight 'Change.' The wise ones tell us this is the best of all worlds, and that it is sin to think otherwise. So all say, where it can be heard. But who can say what a man thinketh in his heart? To labor and sweat and garner the fruits of the land is the old way, the honest way. But who will labor and sweat when his fields may be ploughed, sown, aye, and garnered into his barn, without he turn a hand? This be a change that many welcome."

"I haven't the foggiest idea what you're going on about," Lancelot confessed. "Don't tell me the sky is going to fall over a few ploughed fields? I was thinking of gathering some of those lads out there to ride with me to Camlan—"

"Camlan!" Gildas leaped back again, surprisingly spry for one of his age. "Again I say ye are false!" And he had his mouth open to shout as Lancelot jumped up and seized him.

"Stop it!" he yelled. "I'm getting sick of this doubletalk. Why the hell can't you come right out and say what you mean?" He turned to the Shogleet, with Gildas dangling chokingly from his mailed fists. "Can you make any sense out of it? I think they're *all* stark raving mad here."

The Shogleet eyed Gildas.

"Put him down," it said. "Now, what land is this, and who is your king?"

"This is Brython," Gildas said, squeakily, "and our king hight Cadman. Soon to be Cadman of the Fiery Dragon, in sooth. He dwells in Alban, twenty miles south. If ye be the wise troll, advise this your master to ride to Cadman and plead to aid, on our side!"

"I'm beginning to get it," Lancelot sighed. "What's Camlan then?"

"Camlan is for Bors, King of the Kellat, and our deadly foe. Even now doth he call an army of knights, to invade our land and seize our dragon. To destroy it, he claims, but many suspect it is but to capture it for his own use."

"Oh, come now. A real dragon?"

"It is sooth, Lord. I myself have seen it, and my eyes were weak for a day after. It is truly a fearsome thing for an enemy. But for us it be great good. It is strange, and we all fear it, but who can argue against a full barn and tilled fields, all without labor?"

"A dragon which labors in the field? That would be something really worth seeing, Lancelot. The tapes said nothing of this."

"A dragon!" Lancelot murmured, dreamily. "That would be right up my street. All right, Gildas, we'll leave the question of politics for a bit. Shove some of that grub my way, would you? And pass some tools." Gildas frowned at this.

"There are no eating implements in this culture, Lancelot," the Shogleet advised, drawing on its studies. "Dagger and fingers only."

Before Lancelot could voice his grumble, Gildas said, "Wilt permit thy wives now, Lord?"

"My what? How do I come to have wives?"

"They were Deorham's, are now thine. They wait thy leave to come to table."

"Good grief! Now I have a couple of wives."

"Nay, Lord. Six."

Lancelot shrank into his glittering armor. He cast an appealing eye on the Shogleet. "What do I do now? Six wives! One would be too many."

"Ask Gildas," the Shogleet advised. "He will know. There was nothing in the tapes about such a situation, so I cannot help you."

"Here a minute," Lancelot gulped. "I have been long in the grave and forget many customs of this land. What shall I do with these—women? What are they all for, anyway? And why six?"

"Marry, Lord, but I understand thee not. A man may take as many wives as he needs and can support, if he be a knight. And what would a wife be for, but to serve? Still, it matters not, now. If thou art truly for our cause, then must eat and depart forthwith. All is to hand. We can fetch Alban by nightfall."

"What, right away?"

"All is to hand," Gildas repeated firmly. "Even this day did Deorham make ready for the journey, to join Cadman and all the other great knights of this land, against the Kellat. Else thou wouldst not have found him in the meadow, where he did but try out his armor and steed." Lancelot groaned and looked about feverishly. The Shogleet, watching, saw him shudder.

"I'm up a tree this time. I can't face a twenty-mile drag, not after what I've just had from the Baron. I ache, I tell you. But I don't fancy all these women hanging about either. I'm caught both ways."

"The Lady Phillipa hath the healing touch," Gildas offered. "If thou wilt shed thy mail, Lord, she will attend thee." And he clapped his hands before Lancelot could stop him.

They came in at once. The Shogleet suspected they had been close at hand, listening. At any rate, there was no need to warn the Lady Phillipa that her services were needed. A large and robust woman of some thirty years, she made at once for the hapless knight and, with Gildas assisting, had him out of his mail as readily as a mother undresses a child, and with as little concern.

It was the Shogleet's first contact with women at close quarters and it was intensely interested in this new phenomenon. What it found particularly puzzling was Lancelot's obvious awkwardness, as if he was afraid the females might see the body that had been built for him. This was not the behavior-pattern that it had traced in Lancelot in the beginning. According to that, he was lordly and quietly compelling in the presence of the opposite sex. It began to suspect that this, too, had been part of the young man's fantasies. It was all very strange.

Half an hour later, on a real horse, into the saddle of which Lancelot had been hoisted by a primitive block-and-tackle arrangement and three sweating serfs, the young man led a great rout from the castle courtyard. On his arm, the Shogleet listened keenly to the chatter of the men around. A few were mounted, most were afoot, and they all were filled with enthusiasm for the battle ahead. But, of the dragon, there were divided opinions. Some thought it a blessing, a gift from the gods to a deserving country, but they were in a minority. The rest devoutly believed that it was evil. The right and proper thing for a man was to work or to fight, they declared. What man could do either, when a dragon did both so much better than any man? Not so, they said, and this legendary knight was come, for sure, to rid them of it.

Lancelot, jogging along in his armor, was acting and talking in anything but a knightly manner, but the Shogleet paid him little heed. Disguised under the ministrations of Lady Phillipa, it had managed to help him with doses of carefully tuned energy. The young man was as good as new, except in spirit, in which region he was badly bruised.

"I shall never keep this up for twenty miles," he groaned, as his teeth jarred and clicked at every pace. "I'm a nervous wreck, I tell you. If this is knight errantry, then I've had it." They made a good twenty miles an hour, and should have fetched Alban in two hours. But it was nearer five, and the sun lowering in the sky, before the roofs of the city came in sight. Then the Shogleet recalled, from its studies, the low level of education consistent with this culture. Few of these people could count as far as twenty. For them, forty was well-nigh an infinite number.

Over the bridge and into the narrow streets of Alban, Lancelot was pushed into the lead. The Shogleet sharpened its senses for more information about the dragon. There were whispers on all sides about the "knight with the naked shield" and "how his armor doth glitter, like silver," but not a mention of the mysterious beast. In the center of the city they came to the castle. The crowd of idle sightseers gave way to a great throng of men-at-arms, knights, squires.

They came to the foot of a great flight of steps.

"That's it," Lancelot said, with resigned conviction. "Just let me fall off right here. I'm through."

But Alaric had spurred his mount forward, just as a tall, gray-headed man, with a heavily lined, strong face, came to the head of the steps.

"Your Majesty," the squire cried in a high but quite audible voice. "I am squire to this knight. This day hath he slain Deorham in a great battle. Whereupon, and without stay for rest, hath he ridden right speedily, with this great company, to offer service with thee against thine enemy. Your Majesty this is Sir Lancelot!"

The Shogleet could hear the great gasp which ran through the crowd at this awesome name. Even the King himself seemed to shrink a little.

"It is, indeed, a great honor," he said uneasily, "to have such a great one return from the shades to serve in our cause. Dismount, Sir Lancelot. Approach and be welcomed to our presence." Lancelot crawled wearily from the saddle. He stood on shaky legs, looked up the steps and began to climb.

But the Shogleet, with its razor-keen senses, had caught something highly irregular. Alaric had gone on, to keep one pace to the rear of Lancelot, while Ector stayed to hold the horse.

"Ector!" the Shogleet hissed, becoming part-visible for the purpose. "See you that man in the brown jerkin and the cap over his eyes, there close by the knight in the falcon shield?" Ector peered, and nodded.

"Mark him. Discover what you can. When the moment is ripe, have word with him, and say Lancelot has need of him. Have him come."

"And if he will not come, Lord?"

"Whisper in his ear this word. It is a great magic, so forget it not. The word is 'Galactopol.' Hearing it, he will come."

Ector repeated the word fearfully, and went off with the horse. The Shogleet scurried up the steps, its curiosity-damping field going full blast. Lancelot was wearily explaining to King Cadman that he had travelled far and fast, and that all he wanted to do, right then and there, was to rest.

"They must be made of steel and leather," he complained bitterly, in the chamber that had been assigned to him, as Alaric helped him unbuckle his armor. "Believe it or not, but that crowd down there are just getting set for an all-night session. Drinking, carousing and eating. Mountains of food. Entertainers standing by. Women all over the place. Don't they ever get tired?" The squire was sent off for bread and wine and a bowl of hot water, and the Shogleet soon had Lancelot easier in body. But his spirits were well down.

"I'm a flop at this game," he gloomed. "All right, I've turned up a dragon. But suppose I can't fight it? And suppose I do? I still don't know what the emergency is all about, and I've no idea how to start looking. I'm a duff, I tell you. Best thing I can do is go back to Director Hugard and turn in my badge."

"Patience," the Shogleet counseled. "I think Ector may have news for us. Ah, here he is now."

IV

Ector had found his man. Lancelot looked, indifferently.

"Who might you be?" he asked.

"That's a good question," the stranger replied crisply. "I was going to ask the same thing. Who the hell are you? And what's the big idea of riding around in that fake chrome-silicon-steel armor, hey?"

"That's it," the Shogleet nodded, shimmering into full visibility. "That's what I heard you say, down there by the steps." The man in brown stepped back carefully, blinked a time or two and swallowed.

"I don't believe it," he said. "I see it. I hear it. A little brown pixy, with red eyes, talking Galactic. But I don't believe it."

"Hey!" Lancelot sat up, painfully. "That's a point, too. You're talking Galactic. Who *are* you, anyway?"

"He is obviously a Galactopol agent," the Shogleet said patiently. "The real point is, why is he here? Why would they send two agents?"

"Two agents?" The stranger stared, then pushed his cap back. "I'm beginning to get it, I think. Heard of you, haven't I? Lancelot Lake?"

"That's right. And you?"

"Oh, I'm just a third-level sector man. Name's Alfred North. Pass myself off as a journeyman blacksmith here. It's a living with all the armor about. That's how I could spot your stuff. Nothing here to even scratch that. You'd be a pay-off bet in a tourney."

"No fear!" Lancelot said, hastily. "I've had all I want of that. But what is this all about? What's the emergency?"

"It's a dilly, all right." North fished out a case, offered it. "Smoke?"

"Thanks!" Lancelot's eyes shone, until he recalled the squires. "How about them, then? Won't they mind?"

"It'll scare them, but they'll write it off as magic. That's a handy way to cover up anything you don't understand. That's why they can take the dragon so easily."

"There really is a dragon, then?"

"But surely. You mean you didn't know? It's had me stopped, I can tell you. I was thinking of screaming for special aid. How come you're here, if you don't know about it?"

"I guess I'm your special aid. I only got here this morning and I can't seem to keep still long enough to find out anything that makes sense."

North frowned, then shrugged resignedly. "I suppose you special boys have your own methods. Anyway, I'd say you have the right approach in this case. We usually work under cover but this one isn't like that at all. When the alarm went off, wasn't bothered—"

"That alarm," the Shogleet interrupted. "I am curious about that. Is it some form of automatic device?"

North sighed. "I was hoping you'd go away, if I didn't pay any attention. Ah, well." He inhaled thoughtfully. "You see when these planets are colonized, they implant the compatible beliefs as a dogma. But, just to take care of any sports, there's a ritual, a form of exorcism, that is triggered off by any major change. And that fires the alarm. Doesn't happen very often. It's usually a gene-twist. Some kid gets curious about the stars up there, or begins to fiddle about with experiments in steam-pressure. That kind of thing. But this one is different.''

"A real dragon?" Lancelot asked, wide-eyed.

"That would be the day." North grinned. Then he sneaked a look at the Shogleet, and his grin slipped a little. "No," he said, stubbing out his smoke-tube. "If you think back a couple of hundred years, when they were terraforming this planet, they used machinery. Big stuff. One gadget was a combined cultivator-harvester. Thorium-powered, and just about everlasting. They used hundreds of 'em. And somebody goofed. One got left behind, in a cave they were using for storage space. Now, after all these years, one of the local boys has found it. He's using it.''

"Hold on," Lancelot objected. "He wouldn't know how."

"That's the hell of it. He wouldn't have to; I've checked. The thing is run from a mentrol—a sort of headband, with trimmings. You put it on, and think your orders, like 'stop,' 'go,' 'right,' 'left,' 'fast,' and 'slow.' And what more do you want? The way I figure it, somebody must have found the mentrol and tried it on for size, and that started the whole thing off.''

"Yeeow!" Lancelot gasped. "He must have had the hell of a fright when it came rumbling out of its cave. But it all fits. The way they lap up magic here, it wouldn't be any trouble for them to spot that whoever wears the mentrol controls the beast. Which is right, anyway. Who owns it now?"

"That's Sir Brian de Boyce. Next to old Cadman, he's the big boy in these parts. The way I heard it, one of his freemen found the mentrol, so Sir Brian eliminated him, and took charge. And it's ruining the economy. There isn't a peasant in miles who's put his back into his job in months. I'm stymied. I'm only a freeman here. I can't just charge in and tell Sir Brian what to do. But you can. You're a knight.''

"That's all right," Lancelot mused, "but how do I get it from him?"

"You'll fight him for it, of course." Lancelot fell back.

"Oh, no! I'm not having any more of that," he groaned. "You didn't see what Deorham did to me. I can show you the bruises—"

"Come off it." North was curt. "If you took a stroll down to the main hall right now, you'd find that they're working out the list for the big fight, in the morning. No, not against Bors and his boys. Against each other."

"Eh? What for?"

"It's the culture pattern. Trial by combat. Knights fight for rank, prestige. Cadman wouldn't dream of leading a field of knights unless they had all been graded by prowess. That's how it's done. The winners qualify; the losers flunk out. I'll bet you there's a dozen down there right now, just aching to have a crack at you. You can *call* yourself Sir Lancelot. But they'll want you to prove it. And you can't refuse, either; if you chicken out, your name will smell. Even a serf will spit on you."

"Oh lord!" Lancelot sat up, and put his head in his hands. "I wish I'd never seen this place. What the hell am I going to do?"

"Your best bet is to lash out with a challenge to Sir Brian right away. If you're lucky, and he's free to take you on, then all you have to do is chop him down, and you're top man—and the mentrol is yours. You'd better be quick. The competition is fierce."

Masquerading as a horse again, the Shogleet carried Lancelot through the busy streets, early the next morning. It was of the opinion that Lancelot had been reasonably fortunate. He had drawn one strange knight from the far west, called Gnut, an unknown about whom fantastic stories were rife.

"Discounting the tales," it argued, "for these people have only the vaguest ideas of accuracy, you are fortunate. You will defeat Gnut, then Sir Brian, and the mentrol will be yours."

Lancelot refused to be cheered. "I'm sick of this knight business," he muttered. "I spend all my time in this blasted metal straightjacket, jogging my guts out on a horse, people bashing me about. Now I've got to fight a couple of guys I've never seen before. And if I win what happens? Every knight for miles around will be waiting to have a bash at me to show how good he is. And they talk about competition in a dynamic culture! They don't know what they're talking about."

They were turning the corner, by a high-roofed house. The Shogleet was pondering on the unspoken implication in Lancelot's words. He was actually so low in spirit as to entertain the thought that he might not win! Then there came a gentle hail from the balcony, and a gay-colored scrap of silk fluttered through the sunlight, to catch on the tip of Lancelot's lance.

" 'Tis a troth, Lord," Alaric said. "Wouldst have me seek out its owner?" Then he explained, as Lancelot was completely fogged. He would enter the house, find out who had tossed the silk, ask for her glove, and Lancelot would carry it into battle. "An thou art victorious, Lord, the hand which fits the glove is thine. It is the custom."

"But I've got six wives, now!"

"What of that?" Alaric demanded. "Who knoweth what treasures may hap, today? I know not of Gnut, but Sir Brian is a wonderly rich man—and all can be thine."

"Good grief!" Lancelot shuddered. "Doesn't a man ever settle down with just one wife here?"

"To wed, thou meanest? Marry, that is a different matter. That is the way of a man who is old, and would put an end to glory and adventure."

"Precious few of these lads will live so long," Lancelot mumbled. "The way they go at it. What do you call 'old'?"

Alaric frowned. "I can but guess, sire. A great many years certainly. As many as thirty."

The Shogleet was amused by Lancelot's sudden silence. It knew he was thirty-three. But there was food for thought, too. If it was rare for a knight to live longer than thirty years, then this would be a self-control mechanism to keep down the numbers of the nonproductive to within the capacity of an agricultural community. Knighthood, it seemed, served the multiple function of entertainment, hazard, prestige and the skimming off of the restless few.

But the wives were an enigma. The Shogleet determined to question North at the first opportunity.

*   *   *

The tournament field was a riot of color. Gay streamers flirted with the breeze from the pavilions at either end. Each pennant was a knight. Tabarded heralds carried rosters. The chattering populace was accommodated on rude plank seats along either length of the field. In the privileged center of one side was the royal stand, thick with drapes.

Alaric was kept busy pointing out the various celebrities, reeling off their reputations, their possessions, their pedigrees, until even the Shogleet marvelled a little at such a memory. Then the boy saw Sir Brian's pennant. He indicated it.

"His lands are the most spacious in Brython, second only to the King. Vast herds, great forests and three castles."

"How many wives?"

"As I heard it last, sire, eleven."

"Oh, great!" Lancelot sagged. "That's a hell of an incentive to win. But if I don't kill him, then he'll kill me!"

Bugles rent the chatter, and set the pennants rising and falling. The contest began. Lancelot watched gloomily.

"Look at that!" he muttered to the Shogleet. "Ton and a half of raving insanity, travelling at about thirty miles an hour. Double it, because the other lunatic is doing the same. No wonder they count you out if you fall. By the time you stop that with your belly and fall about five feet onto hard ground, plus all the hardware, it's no wonder they don't get up to argue."

The pennants rose and fell. Trumpets blared. Brass-lunged heralds told the tally of victor and vanquished. Then up went a barred black pennant, with a gold spot. A herald roared.

"Sir Gnut, of the Westland . . . to meet Sir Lancelot!"

Alaric broke out a pure white pennant, and the challenge was shouted back.

"Sir Lancelot to meet Sir Gnut!"

The great surf-roar of the crowd was stilled as that fabulous name spread from lip to lip. Lancelot settled himself in the saddle, and put out a hand for the lance which Alaric held ready. But the Shogleet had already spotted Gnut, at the other end. A smallish man, in all-black mail, on a small, wiry stallion, he looked fast.

"Leave the lance," it ordered. "Prepare to use your sword." It cantered on to the field before Lancelot could argue "Now sit firm. Fend off his point with your shield, then cut him down with your sword."

"Who, me?" Lancelot chattered. "How the blazes can I, with you bouncing me about like that?" A great yell went up from the crowd as the gallant knight flung his arms about the neck of his steed to keep from falling off.

The Shogleet halted. The warden's flag fell. Sir Gnut went into his gallop at once, head well down, crouching over his crouched lance. Lancelot fumbled for his sword. The Shogleet braced itself. Lance met shield with a rending crash, and splintered into matchwood. The Shogleet pranced backward and round, to keep Lancelot in the saddle. Gnut was equally nimble, tossing away the ruined lance and whipping out his blade. In and out like a snake, he battered Lancelot, again and again, rocking him in his saddle until he was good and angry.

"All right!" he roared. "You asked for it!" And he stood in his stirrups, waiting for the black knight to charge in just once more. Then the Shogleet felt him slash down, viciously . . . and there was a shocked *Aaah!* from the crowd.

"Serve him right," Lancelot growled as they trotted from the field, and the serfs ran on to carry off the sliced remains of Sir Gnut. "Let's hope that made Sir Brian stop and think a bit."

V

Back in his tent there was a surprise waiting for Lancelot.

The Shogleet, poking its horse-head through the tent flap, saw a slim, girlish figure, with her glossy gold hair done in gleaming braids about her head. This was the youngest female it had seen. It studied her with great interest. Her complexion was curiously translucent, so that the flush of blood in her cheek was clearly visible. And her voice was soft and low, as she greeted Lancelot. Alaric, as usual, was on hand with explanations.

"This is the Lady Jessica, sire. She who threw thee the silk which thou accepted."

"I pray," she said, softly, "that thou'rt willing to accept my glove as a gage, Sir Knight." Timidly she held out a slim hand. Lancelot took it as if it was an eggshell. The Shogleet was completely baffled by his beet-red face and the glazed look in his eye. This was a side to Lancelot that it had not seen before.

The Lady Jessica had to stand on tiptoe to put her face to Lancelot's. Then she went even more red in the face, and whispered, "I pray that thou wilt be triumphant, Sir Knight—for my sake!"

Then she was gone, leaving Lancelot staring into vacancy and rubbing his cheek. North pushed his way into the tent, grinning.

"Nice work, Lake," he said. "Not much style, but you chopped him down quick."

"Here—" Lancelot said, abstractedly. "Something I wanted to ask you. This business about wives. I mean, I won six from Deorham. Lord knows how many Gnut had, but Sir Brian has eleven. What do I do with all them?"

"Ah!" North chuckled. "You're a bit mixed, there. The word should rightly be 'housewives.' They're a kind of high-class servant. When you think about it, there isn't much else a high-born lady can do, except run the domestic side, while the menfolk are busy battling. They have their duties, you see, like keeping track of the hired help, tending to the kitchen, the bedchamber, the linen—that sort of thing. They tend to the man of the house, too, of course, and entertain his guests. But they're strictly property. No need to be bothered, if that's what you're worried about."

Lancelot's face went red again. "So there isn't any regular getting married and settling down, then?"

"Oh, sure, but that's a different thing. For the knight who is past his prime and wants to settle down. Retire. You know. He usually selects some old place out in the sticks, turns in the rest of his property to the King, to be a prize for some contender, and settles in to raise a family. More squires and ladies, and the whole thing starts all over again. Not many get that far. It's too dull for them. Why?"

Lancelot was saved his stammering explanation by the sound of a herald from the field. Sir Brian's pennant had gone up.

"Take the lance this time," the Shogleet decided, studying Sir Brian.

"Good grief!" Lancelot had been looking, too. "See the size

f him! No wonder he's the top man in these parts. He's going to ake a bit of knocking out."

The Shogleet pricked up its ears at the sudden change in Lancelot's tone, but it had more urgent matters to consider. "Couch your lance firmly," it advised. "Aim for his midriff." The flag fell. They began to go forward, from a canter into a gallop, Lancelot manfully sitting forward and forgetting to complain. The mighty Sir Brian thundered toward them, his lance glittering in the sun. At the very moment of impact, the Shogleet stiffened, rearing on its haunches to keep Lancelot in the saddle. There was a deafening double clang from the shields, a wheeze from Lancelot as the wind was punched out of him, the screech of tortured metal and a gruesome gargle from Sir Brian.

Then, despite all the Shogleet could do, it felt Lancelot lifted and dragged from the saddle.

Skidding furiously to a stop, it wheeled to look. There was Lancelot, on foot, dazedly clutching the haft of the lance. The other end, with its razor tip, had stabbed through Sir Brian's shield, his armor and Sir Brian himself, and stuck out a hand's breadth on the far side.

With a grunting effort, Lancelot tore the lance free. He staggered back as the Shogleet cantered up, to kneel so that he could mount. The crowd was stunned into momentary silence. Then it went wild.

Even King Cadman looked shaken, as they cantered past the royal stand for the salute and accolade. Back in the tent, Lancelot eased himself out of his helmet and sat.

"That's me," he said flatly. "I'm through, done, finished." North pushed through the tent-flap just in time to disagree with the last word.

"There's still the dragon," he said. "That shouldn't be too hard, now that you've won the mentrol. Nice bout, that was. Just as well you're not staying in these parts. The rest of the boys won't stand a chance against you."

"It's the superior metal, of course," the Shogleet commented, poking its horsehead into the tent. North jumped a clear foot off the ground, knocking his head on the wooden spar of the tent.

"Talking horses, now," he breathed. "Is this routine equipment for you Prime G-men?"

"Forget that," Lancelot snapped. "What about this dragon? Let's get it over with, and we'll see whether I'm staying here or not."

North eyed him thoughtfully. "I suggest you play it this way. There should be a coffee break, soon. You get an audience with Cadman. Tell him this dragon is a great evil. You've come to kill it and, once done, you'll return to the shades. That way everybody'll be shut up. All right?"

"Sounds simple enough. But *can* I kill the thing?"

"I'll fix that," North said briskly, "once I have the mentrol." He glanced out of the tent and chuckled. "Here they come now."

"Who?"

"Sir Brian's crowd. His lieges, turning themselves in. You want the lad with the gadget. Never mind the rest."

"Suppose . . ." said Lancelot, in a tone that made the Shogleet prick up its ears at once. "Suppose I was staying here, and didn't want all these retainers hanging about—what's the routine procedure?"

"Nothing to it." North gave him that thoughtful look again. "You just manumit them. Give 'em their freedom. They'll just go off and sign up with somebody else. It's not wise, though, because you couldn't run an estate without staff, and they work for their keep."

"That's a point," Lancelot admitted. He went to receive his spoils with a pensive air.

Late that afternoon, with the awed populace keeping a safe distance, the Shogleet bore Lancelot, following North, who was on foot, to the meadow where the monster "slept." North had the mentrol in his hand.

"This shouldn't be any trouble," he said. "A bit of expert sabotage, and it will be all over. There she is, folks."

It was easy to see why the peasants had dubbed it a dragon. A sectioned body, all of fifty feet long, hugged the ground, rising to a twenty-foot-high hump in front. There a single head-lamp gave it a one-eyed, evil look.

"That front scoop," North explained, "can be set to any level
u like, and there are controls which can be adjusted so that the
iff is processed, inside. Got a rudimentary 'brain'—enough to
entify and reject organic matter that's still alive. It wouldn't
uch a man, even if you tried to make it. Not that any of the
cals would have the nerve to chance it. Nor do I blame them.
cidentally, it processes wastes and makes its own bags and
rtilizer, all in one operation. That's not doing the economy any
od, either, believe me. I've been stuck because I couldn't lay
y hands on this little gadget. But now I have it, I know that it's
mobile. Nothing can happen until I put it on my head. Come
."

But the Shogleet had other ideas.

"Lancelot," it said. "You had better go back. Warn the
dience not to come too near. And there is someone you would
sh to see, I think?"

"That's right." Lancelot slid down eagerly, and went clank-
g back.

"You're a smart animal," North said, shrewdly. "What's on
ur mind?"

"Answer me a question, first. I gather that there is a sort of
rsonal polarity, an attraction and an attachment between hu-
ins of opposite sexes, if certain other factors are favorable. It
olves such activities as marrying, settling down, raising a
nily—all of which are concepts which I do not quite understand.
t I believe such relationships are not amenable to reason.
s?"

"If you mean that there's neither sense nor reason in a guy
o's in love, that's dead right," North chuckled. "Love makes
ool of a man. There's never been a cure for it yet."

"That is what I thought. Thank you. Now, it is not enough
t the dragon be destroyed. It must be *seen* to be destroyed.
pressively."

"It's a good point. What's on your mind?"

The Shogleet proceeded to tell him, in rapid, explicit detail.
rth's eyes widened.

"I can do it, sure, if that's the way you want it. I hope you
w what you're doing, that's all."

He hurried off across the meadow, to disappear into the

gaping jaws of the cultivator. Lancelot came clanking back. H had already mounted by the time North returned.

"Let's get it over with," he said impatiently, dropping h visor. "I might as well tell you that as soon as I've finished wi this thing, I'm retiring from Galactopol. I'm through. Now, wh do I do?"

"It's all fixed," North said dryly. "I'll get well clear, th I'll put this on and make it look as if you two are battling. Wh you've had enough, you bash it with your sword."

"Fat lot of good that's going to do!"

"I told you, it's all fixed. Keep an eye out for a yellc danger-plate. It's marked 'DRIVE-UNIT SAFETY COVER Just hit that. That's all."

The Shogleet broke into a gentle canter. Lancelot drew h sword. The long, gleaming machine suddenly broke into lo and grumbling life, its great jaws agape. With a growl of gea it moved and swung its great head round, like a humped serpe seeking prey. Then the headlight lit up, sending out a brig beam.

"You know," Lancelot jerked, as the Shogleet swerved chase the lumbering machine, "this isn't such a bad place, af all. I mean, once you get away from this armor-plated busine: I think I'll retire. I own all Sir Brian's lands now. I could set down, take life easy—"

"But you are a Prime G-man, Lancelot. It is your duty return to Headquarters and report the successful completion of yc mission."

"North will take care of that for me."

"But you don't really belong here."

"What's that got to do with it? It's a free country, isn't it Lancelot waved his sword valiantly, and the Shogleet swerv suddenly, so that the tip of the blade struck the yellow panel.

The bang was enough to impress even the Shogleet.

It was very busy, for a few fractionated seconds, warding blast, radiation and chunks of flying debris. Then there wa: ringing silence. In a thick haze of settling dust, it turned, scra bled up out of the hole and crept over the torn and ruptured ea to where North was peering, open-mouthed, from a shelter bankside. Of the Brythons there was nothing to be seen but the puffs of dust from their flying heels.

"You look all right," North gasped, "but what about him?"

"He is stunned, and in temporary fugue. It will pass. If you would hang the mentrol on my saddle, we will be leaving. You can clear up the odd details?"

"Sure, I can handle those. You're leaving right now?"

"I think it would be wise. Lancelot seems to have formed one of those attachments, for a certain young lady. He intended to remain here permanently. That would have been unwise, I understand?"

"Dead right," North grinned, but there were grim undertones. "With what he's got, and you along, he would be 'Change' in a big way. That wouldn't do. I'd have to interfere. And that might be nasty."

"Yes, that is what I thought. It is better this way."

"Just what are you, anyway—a sort of guardian angel?"

"You might say that, yes," the Shogleet nodded, and set off to gallop the long trail, back to the ship.

But it was still curious. It wondered just what Director Hugard would say when Lancelot got back.

DIPLOMAT-AT-ARMS

by Keith Laumer

A *former diplomat and Air Force captain, Keith Laumer (1925-   ) began writing science fiction in the late 1950s. Much of his work consists of satirical depictions of interstellar diplomacy (*Envoy to New Worlds, *1963;* Galactic Diplomat; *1965,* Retief and the Warlords, *1968;* Retief, Ambassador to Space, *1969;* Retief of the CDT, *1971;* Retief's Ransom, *1971;* Retief, Emissary to the Stars, *1975; and* Retief at Large, *1979), but he is also noted for fast-paced action stories such as* Worlds of the Imperium *(1962) and* Dinosaur Beach *(1971).*

"Diplomat-at-Arms" offers a fusion of both trends as well as a rare view of an aging Retief.

The cold white sun of Northroyal glared on pale dust and vivid colors in the narrow raucous street. Retief rode slowly, unconscious of the huckster's shouts, the kaleidoscope of smells, the noisy milling crowd. His thoughts were on events of long ago on distant worlds; thoughts that set his features in narrow-eyed grimness. His bony, powerful horse, unguided, picked his way carefully, with flaring nostrils, wary eyes alert in the turmoil.

The mount sidestepped a darting gamin and Retief leaned

forward, patted the sleek neck. The job had some compensations, he thought; it was good to sit on a fine horse again, to shed the gray business suit—

A dirty-faced man pushed a fruit cart almost under the animal's head; the horse shied, knocked over the cart. At once a muttering crowd began to gather around the heavy-shouldered gray-haired man. He reined in and sat scowling, an ancient brown cape over his shoulders, a covered buckler slung at the side of the worn saddle, a scarred silver-worked claymore strapped across his back in the old cavalier fashion.

Retief hadn't liked this job when he had first heard of it. He had gone alone on madman's errands before, but that had been long ago—a phase of his career that should have been finished. And the information he had turned up in his background research had broken his professional detachment. Now the locals were trying an old tourist game on him; ease the outlander into a spot, then demand money. . . .

Well, Retief thought, this was as good a time as any to start playing the role; there was a hell of a lot here in the quaint city of Fragonard that needed straightening out.

"Make way, you rabble!" he roared suddenly. "Or by the chains of the sea-god I'll make a path through you!" He spurred the horse; neck arching, the mount stepped daintily forward.

The crowd made way reluctantly before him. "Pay for the merchandise you've destroyed," called a voice.

"Let peddlers keep a wary eye for their betters," snorted the man loudly, his eye roving over the faces before him. A tall fellow with long yellow hair stepped squarely into his path.

"There are no rabble or peddlers here," he said angrily. "Only true cavaliers of the Clan Imperial. . . ."

The mounted man leaned from his saddle to stare into the eyes of the other. His seamed brown face radiated scorn. "When did a true Cavalier turn to commerce? If you were trained to the Code you'd know a gentleman doesn't soil his hands with penny-grubbing, and that the Emperor's highroad belongs to the mounted knight. So clear your rubbish out of my path, if you'd save it."

"Climb down off that nag," shouted the tall young man,

eaching for the bridle. "I'll show you some practical knowledge
f the Code. I challenge you to stand and defend yourself."

In an instant the thick barrel of an antique Imperial Guards
ower gun was in the gray-haired man's hand. He leaned negli-
ently on the high pommel of his saddle with his left elbow, the
istol laid across his forearm pointing unwaveringly at the man
efore him.

The hard old face smiled grimly. "I don't soil my hands in
reet brawling with new-hatched nobodies," he said. He nodded
)ward the arch spanning the street ahead. "Follow me through
ie arch, if you call yourself a man and a Cavalier." He moved
n then; no one hindered him. He rode in silence through the
rowd, pulled up at the gate barring the street. This would be the
rst real test of his cover identity. The papers which had gotten
im through Customs and Immigration at Fragonard Spaceport
ie day before had been burned along with the civilian clothes.
rom here on he'd be getting by on the uniform and a cast-iron
erve.

A purse-mouthed fellow wearing the uniform of a Lieutenant-
nsign in the Household Escort Regiment looked him over,
quinted his eyes, smiled sourly.

"What can I do for you, Uncle?" He spoke carelessly, lean-
g against the engraved buttress mounting the wrought-iron
ite. Yellow and green sunlight filtered down through the leaves
the giant linden trees bordering the cobbled street.

The gray-haired man stared down at him. "The first thing you
n do, Lieutenant-Ensign," he said in a voice of cold steel, "is
me to a position of attention."

The thin man straightened, frowning. "What's that?" His
pression hardened. "Get down off that beast and let's have a
ok at your papers—if you've got any."

The mounted man didn't move. "I'm making allowances for
e fact that your regiment is made up of idlers who've never
arned to soldier," he said quietly. "But having had your
ention called to it, even you should recognize the insignia of a
attle Commander."

The officer stared, glancing over the drab figure of the old
an. Then he saw the tarnished gold thread worked into the

design of a dragon rampant, almost invisible against the faded
color of the heavy velvet cape.

He licked his lips, cleared his throat, hesitated. What in name
of the Tormented One would a top-ranking battle officer be
doing on this thin old horse, dressed in plain worn clothing?
"Let me see your papers—Commander," he said.

The Commander flipped back the cape to expose the ornate
butt of the power pistol.

"Here are my credentials," he said. "Open the gate."

"Here," the Ensign spluttered, "What's this . . ."

"For a man who's taken the Emperor's commission," the old
man said, "you're criminally ignorant of the courtesies due a
general officer. Open the gate or I'll blow it open. You'll not
deny the way to an Imperial Battle officer." He drew the pistol.

The Ensign gulped, thought fleetingly of sounding the alarm
signal, of insisting on seeing papers . . . then as the pistol
came up, he closed the switch, and the gate swung open. The
heavy hooves of the gaunt horse clattered past him; he caught
a glimpse of a small brand on the lean flank. Then he was
staring after the retreating back of the terrible old man.
Battle Commander indeed! The old fool was wearing a fortune
in valuable antiques, and the animal bore the brand of a
thoroughbred battle-horse. He'd better report this. . . . He picked
up the communicator, as a tall young man with an angry face
came up to the gate.

Retief rode slowly down the narrow street lined with the stalls
of suttlers, metalsmiths, weapons technicians, free-lance squires.
The first obstacle was behind him. He hadn't played it very
suavely, but he had been in no mood for bandying words. He
had been angry ever since he had started this job; and that, he
told himself, wouldn't do. He was beginning to regret his high-
handedness with the crowd outside the gate. He should save the
temper for those responsible, not the bystanders; and in any
event, an agent of the Corps should stay cool at all times. That
was essentially the same criticism that Magnan had handed him
along with the assignment, three months ago.

"The trouble with you, Retief," Magnan had said, "is that
you are unwillng to accept the traditional restraints of the Service

you conduct yourself too haughtily, too much in the manner of a
free agent. . . ."

His reaction, he knew, had only proved the accuracy of his
superior's complaint. He should have nodded penitent agreement,
indicated that improvement would be striven for earnestly; instead,
he had sat expressionless, in a silence which inevitably appeared
antagonistic.

He remembered how Magnan had moved uncomfortably, cleared
his throat, and frowned at the papers before him. "Now, in the
matter of your next assignment," he said, "we have a serious
situation to deal with in an area that could be critical."

Retief almost smiled at the recollection. The man had placed
himself in an amusing dilemma. It was necessary to emphasize
the great importance of the job at hand, and simultaneously to
avoid letting Retief have the satisfaction of feeling that he was to
be intrusted with anything vital; to express the lack of confidence
the Corps felt in him while at the same time invoking his
awareness of the great trust he was receiving. It was strange how
Magnan could rationalize his personal dislike into a righteous
concern for the best interests of the Corps.

Magnan had broached the nature of the assignment obliquely,
mentioning his visit as a tourist to Northroyal, a charming,
backward little planet settled by Cavaliers, refugees from the
breakup of the Empire of the Lily.

Retief knew the history behind Northroyal's tidy, proud,
tradition-bound society. When the Old Confederation broke up,
dozens of smaller governments had grown up among the civi-
lized worlds. For a time, the Lily Empire had been among the
most vigorous of them, comprising twenty-one worlds, and supporting an excellent military force under the protection of which
the Lilyan merchant fleet had carried trade to a thousand far-
flung worlds.

When the Concordiat had come along, organizing the previously sovereign states into a new Galactic jurisdiction, the
Empire of the Lily had resisted, and had for a time held the
massive Concordiat fleets at bay. In the end, of course, the
gallant but outnumbered Lilyan forces had been driven back to
the gates of the home world. The planet of Lily had been saved
catastrophic bombardment only by a belated truce which guaran-

teed self-determination to Lily on the cessation of hostilities
disbandment of the Lilyan fleet, and the exile of the entir
membership of the Imperial Suite, which, under the Lilyan cla
tradition, had numbered over ten thousand individuals. Ever
man, woman, and child who could claim even the most distan
blood relationship to the Emperor, together with their servants
dependents, retainers, and protégés, were included. The mov
took weeks to complete, but at the end of it the Cavaliers, a
they were known, had been transported to an uninhabited, col
sea-world, which they named Northroyal. A popular bit of lor
in connection with the exodus had it that the ship bearing th
Emperor himself had slipped away en route to exile, and that th
ruler had sworn that he would not return until the day he coul
come with an army of liberation. He had never been heard fror
again.

The land area of the new world, made up of innumerab
islands, totaled half a million square miles. Well stocked wit
basic supplies and equipment, the Cavaliers had set to work ar
turned their rocky fief into a snug, well-integrated—if tradition
ridden—society, and today exported seafoods, fine machiner
and tourist literature.

It was in the last department that Northroyal was best know
Tales of the pomp and color, the quaint inns and good food, th
beautiful girls, the brave display of royal cavalry, and the fab
lous annual Tournament of the Lily attracted a goodly number
sightseers, and the Cavalier Line was now one of the planet
biggest foreign-exchange earners.

Magnan had spoken of Northroyal's high industrial potentia
and her well-trained civilian corps of space navigators.

"The job of the Corps," Retief interrupted, "is to seek o
and eliminate threats to the peace of the Galaxy. How does
little story-book world like Northroyal get into the act?"

"More easily than you might imagine," Magnan said. "He
you have a close-knit society, proud, conscious of a tradition
military power, empire. A clever rabble-rouser using the rig
appeal would step into a ready-made situation there. It wou
take only an order on the part of the planetary government

turn the factories to war production, and convert the merchant fleet into a war fleet—and we'd be faced with a serious power imbalance—a storm center.''

"I think you're talking nonsense, Mr. Minister," Retief said bluntly. "They've got more sense than that. They're not so far gone on tradition as to destroy themselves. They're a practical people.''

Magnan drummed his fingers on the desk top. "There's one factor I haven't covered yet," he said. "There has been what amounts to a news blackout from Northroyal during the last six months. . . ."

Retief snorted. "What news?"

Magnan had been enjoying the suspense. "Tourists have been having great difficulty getting to Northroyal," he said. "Fragonard, the capital, is completely closed to outsiders. We managed, however, to get an agent in." He paused, gazing at Retief. "It seems," he went on, "that the rightful Emperor has turned up."

Retief narrowed his eyes. "What's that?" he said sharply.

Magnan drew back, intimidated by the power of Retief's tone, annoyed by his own reaction. In his own mind, Magnan was candid enough to know that this was the real basis for his intense dislike for his senior agent. It was an instinctive primitive fear of physical violence. Not that Retief had ever assaulted anyone; but he had an air of mastery that made Magnan feel trivial.

"The Emperor," Magnan repeated. "The traditional story is that he was lost on the voyage to Northroyal. There was a legend that he had slipped out of the hands of the Concordiat in order to gather new support for a counteroffensive, hurl back the invader, all that sort of thing."

"The Concordiat collapsed of its own weight within a century," Retief said. "There's no invader to hurl back. Northroyal is free and independent, like every other world."

"Of course, of course," Magnan said. "But you're missing the emotional angle, Retief. It's all very well to be independent; but what about the dreams of empire, the vanished glory, destiny, et cetera?"

"What about them?"

"That's all our agent heard; it's everywhere. The news strips are full of it. Video is playing it up; everybody's talking it. The returned Emperor seems to be a clever propagandist; the next step will be a full-scale mobilization. And we're not equipped to handle that.''

"What am I supposed to do about all this?"

"Your orders are, and I quote, to proceed to Fragonard and there employ such measures as shall be appropriate to negate the present trend toward an expansionist sentiment among the populace." Magnan passed a document across the desk to Retief for his inspection.

The orders were brief, and wasted no wordage on details. As an officer of the Corps with the rank of Counselor, Retief enjoyed wide latitude, and broad powers—and corresponding responsibility in the event of failure. Retief wondered how this assignment had devolved on him, among the thousands of Corps agents scattered through the Galaxy. Why was one man being handed a case which on the face of it should call for a full mission?

"This looks like quite an undertaking for a single agent, Mr. Minister," Retief said.

"Well, of course, if you don't feel you can handle it . . .'' Magnan looked solemn.

Retief looked at him, smiling faintly. Magnan's tactics had been rather obvious. Here was one of those nasty jobs which could easily pass in reports as routine if all went well; but even a slight mistake could mean complete failure, and failure meant war; and the agent who had let it happen would be finished in the Corps.

There was danger in the scheme for Magnan, too. The blame might reflect back on him. Probably he had plans for averting disaster after Retief had given up. He was too shrewd to leave himself out in the open. And for that matter, Retief reflected, too good an agent to let the situation get out of hand.

No, it was merely an excellent opportunity to let Retief discredit himself, with little risk of any great credit accruing to him in the remote event of success.

Retief could, of course, refuse the assignment, but that would be the end of his career. He would never be advanced to the rank of Minister, and age limitations would force his retirement in a year or two. That would be an easy victory for Magnan.

Retief liked his work as an officer-agent of the Diplomatic Corps, that ancient supranational organization dedicated to the controvention of war. He had made his decision long ago, and he had learned to accept his life as it was, with all its imperfections. It was easy enough to complain about the petty intrigues, the tyranies of rank, the small inequities. But these were merely a part of the game, another challenge to be met and dealt with. The overcoming of obstacles was Jame Retief's specialty. Some of the obstacles were out in the open, the recognized difficulties inherent in any tough assignment. Others were concealed behind a smoke-screen of personalities and efficiency reports; and both were equally important. You did your job in the field, and then you threaded your way through the maze of Corps politics. And if you couldn't handle the job—any part of it—you'd better find something else to do.

He had accepted the assignment, of course, after letting Magnan wonder for a few minutes; and then for two months he had buried himself in research, gathering every scrap of information, direct and indirect, that the massive files of the Corps would yield. He had soon found himself immersed in the task, warming to its challenge, fired with emotions ranging from grief to rage as he ferreted out the hidden pages in the history of the exiled Cavaliers.

He had made his plan, gathered a potent selection of ancient documents and curious objects; a broken chain of gold, a tiny key, a small silver box. And now he was here, inside the compound of the Grand Corrida.

Everything here in these ways surrounding and radiating from the Field of the Emerald Crown—the arena itself—was devoted to the servicing and supplying of the thousands of First Day contenders in the Tournament of the Lily, and the housing and tending of the dwindling number of winners who stayed on for the following days. There were tiny eating places, taverns, inns; all consciously antique in style, built in imitation of their counterparts left behind long ago on far-off Lily.

"Here you are, Pop, first-class squire," called a thin red-haired fellow.

"Double up and save credits," called a short dark man. "First Day contract . . ."

Shouts rang back and forth across the alleylike street as the stall keepers scented a customer. Retief ignored them, moved on toward the looming wall of the arena. Ahead, a slender youth stood with folded arms before his stall, looking toward the approaching figure on the black horse. He leaned forward, watching Retief intently, then straightened, turned and grabbed up a tall narrow body shield from behind him. He raised the shield over his head, and as Retief came abreast, called "Battle officer!"

Retief reined in the horse, looked down at the youth.

"At your service, sir," the young man said. He stood straight and looked Retief in the eye. Retief looked back. The horse minced, tossed his head.

"What is your name, boy?" Retief asked.

"Fitzraven, sir."

"Do you know the Code?"

"I know the Code, sir."

Retief stared at him, studying his face, his neatly cut uniform of traditional Imperial green, the old but well-oiled leather of his belt and boots.

"Lower your shield, Fitzraven," he said. "You're engaged." He swung down from his horse. "The first thing I want is care for my mount. His name is Danger-by-Night. And then I want an inn for myself."

"I'll care for the horse myself, Commander," Fitzraven said. "And the Commander will find good lodging at the sign of the Phoenix-in-Dexter-Chief; quarters are held ready for my client." The squire took the bridle, pointing toward the inn a few doors away.

Two hours later, Retief came back to the stall, a thirty-two-ounce steak and a bottle of Nouveau Beaujolais having satisfied a monumental appetite induced by the long ride down from the spaceport north of Fragonard. The plain banner he had carried in his saddlebag fluttered now from the staff above the stall. He moved through the narrow room to a courtyard behind, and stood in the doorway watching as Fitzraven curried the dusty hide of the lean black horse. The saddle and fittings were laid out on a heavy table, ready for cleaning. There was clean straw in the stall where the horse stood, and an empty grain bin and water bucket indicated the animal had been well fed and watered.

Retief nodded to the squire, and strolled around the courtyard staring up at the deep blue sky of early evening above the irregular line of roofs and chimneys, noting the other squires, the variegated mounts stabled here, listening to the hubbub of talk, the clatter of crockery from the kitchen of the inn. Fitzraven finished his work and came over to his new employer.

"Would the Commander like to sample the night life in the Grand Corrida?"

"Not tonight," Retief said. "Let's go up to my quarters; I want to learn a little more about what to expect."

Retief's room, close under the rafters on the fourth floor of the inn, was small but adequate, with a roomy wardrobe and a wide bed. The contents of his saddlebags were already in place in the room.

Retief looked around. "Who gave you permission to open my saddlebags?"

Fitzraven flushed slightly. "I thought the Commander would wish to have them unpacked," he said stiffly.

"I looked at the job the other squires were doing on their horses," Retief said. "You were the only one who was doing a proper job of tending the animal. Why the special service?"

"I was trained by my father," Fitzraven said. "I serve only true knights, and I perform my duties honorably. If the Commander is dissatisfied . . ."

"How do you know I'm a true knight?"

"The Commander wears the uniform and weapons of one of the oldest Imperial Guards Battle Units, the Iron Dragon," Fitzraven said. "And the Commander rides a battle horse, true-bred."

"How do you know I didn't steal them?"

Fitzraven grinned suddenly. "They fit the Commander too well."

Retief smiled. "All right, son, you'll do," he said. "Now brief me on the First Day. I don't want to miss anything. And you may employ the personal pronoun."

For an hour Fitzraven discussed the order of events for the

elimination contests of the First Day of the Tournament of the
Lily, the strategies that a clever contender could employ to husband
his strength, the pitfalls into which the unwary might fall.

The tournament was the culmination of a year of smaller
contests held throughout the equatorial chain of populated islands.
The Northroyalans had substituted various forms of armed combat for the sports practiced on most worlds; a compensation for
the lost empire, doubtless, a primitive harking-back to an earlier,
more glorious day.

Out of a thousand First Day entrants, less than one in ten
would come through to face the Second Day. Of course, the
First Day events were less lethal than those to be encountered
farther along in the three-day tourney, Retief learned; there
would be few serious injuries in the course of the opening day,
and those would be largely due to clumsiness or ineptitude on the
part of the entrants.

*   *   *

There were no formal entrance requirements, Fitzraven said,
other than proof of minimum age and status in the Empire. Not
all the entrants were natives of Northroyal; many came from
distant worlds, long-scattered descendants of the citizens of the
shattered Lily Empire. But all competed for the same prizes;
status in the Imperial peerage, the honors of the Field of the
Emerald crown, and Imperial grants of land, wealth to the
successful.

"Will you enter the First Day events, sir," Fitzraven asked,
"or do you have a Second or Third Day certification?"

"Neither," Retief said. "We'll sit on the sidelines and watch."

Fitzraven looked surprised. It had somehow not occurred to
him that the old man was not to be a combatant. And it was too
late to get seats. . . .

"How . . ." Fitzraven began, after a pause.

"Don't worry," Retief said. "We'll have a place to sit."

Fitzraven fell silent, tilted his head to one side, listening.
Loud voices, muffled by walls, the thump of heavy feet.

"Something is up," Fitzraven said. "Police." He looked at
Retief.

"I wouldn't be surprised," Retief said, "if they were looking
for me. Let's go find out."

"We need not meet them," the squire said. "There is another ay . . ."

"Never mind," Retief said. "As well now as later." He inked at Fitzraven and turned to the door.

Retief stepped off the lift into the crowded common room, itzraven at his heels. Half a dozen men in dark blue tunics and ll shakos moved among the patrons, staring at faces. By the oor Retief saw the thin-mouthed Ensign he had overawed at the ate. The fellow saw him at the same moment and plucked at the eeve of the nearest policeman, pointing.

The man dropped a hand to his belt, and at once the other oliceman turned, followed his glance to Retief. They moved ward him with one accord. Retief stood waiting.

The first cop planted himself before Retief, looking him up nd down. "Your papers!" he snapped.

Retief smiled easily. "I am a peer of the Lily and a battle fficer of the Imperial forces," he said. "On what pretext are ou demanding papers of me, Captain?"

The cop raised his eyebrows.

"Let's say you are charged with unauthorized entry into the ontrolled area of the Grand Corrida, and with impersonating an nperial officer," he said. "You didn't expect to get away with did you, Grandpa?" The fellow smiled sardonically.

"Under the provisions of the Code," Retief said, "the status a peer may not be questioned, nor his actions interfered with cept by Imperial Warrant. Let me see yours, Captain. And I ggest you assume a more courteous tone when addressing your perior officer." Retief's voice hardened to a whip crack with e last words.

The policeman stiffened, scowled. His hand dropped to the ghtstick at his belt.

"None of your insolence, old man," he snarled. "Papers! ow!"

Retief's hand shot out, gripped the officer's hand over the ck. "Raise that stick," he said quietly, "and I'll assuredly at out your brains with it." He smiled calmly into the captain's lging eyes. The captain was a strong man. He threw every nce of his strength into the effort to bring up his arm, to pull free of the old man's grasp. The crowd of customers, the squad of police, stood silently, staring, uncertain of what was going on. Retief stood steady; the officer strained, reddened. The old man's arm was like cast steel.

"I see you are using your head, Captain," Retief said. "Your decision not to attempt to employ force against a peer was an intelligent one."

The cop understood. He was being offered an opportunity to save a little face. He relaxed slowly.

"Very well, uh, sir," he said stiffly. "I will assume you can establish your identity properly; kindly call at the commandant's office in the morning."

Retief released his hold and the officer hustled his men out, shoving the complaining Ensign ahead. Fitzraven caught Retief's eye and grinned.

"Empty pride is a blade with no hilt," he said. "A humble man would have yelled for help."

Retief turned to the barman. "Drinks for all," he called. A happy shout greeted this announcement. They had all enjoyed seeing the police outfaced.

"The cops don't seem to be popular here," the old man said.

Fitzraven sniffed. "A law-abiding subject parks illegally for five minutes, and they are on him like flies after dead meat; but let his car be stolen by lawless hoodlums—they are nowhere to be seen."

"That has a familiar sound," Retief said. He poured out a tumbler of vodka, looked at Fitzraven.

"Tomorrow," he said. "A big day."

A tall blond young man near the door looked after him with bitter eyes.

"All right, old man," he muttered. "We'll see then."

The noise of the crowd came to Retief's ears as a muted rumble through the massive pile of the amphitheater above. A dim light filtered from the low-ceilinged corridor into the cramped office of the assistant Master of the Games.

"If you know your charter," Retief said, "you will recall that a Battle Commander enjoys the right to observe the progress of the games from the official box. I claim that privilege."

"I know nothing of this," the cadaverous official replied.

impatiently. "You must obtain an order from the Master of the Games before I can listen to you." He turned to another flunkey, opened his mouth to speak. A hand seized him by the shoulder, lifted him bodily from his seat. The man's mouth remained open in shock.

Retief held the stricken man at arm's length, then drew him closer. His eyes blazed into the gaping eyes of the other. His face was white with fury.

"Little man," he said in a strange, harsh voice, "I go now with my groom to take my place in the official box. Read your Charter well before you interfere with me—and your Holy Book as well." He dropped the fellow with a crash, saw him slide under the desk. No one made a sound. Even Fitzraven looked pale. The force of the old man's rage had been like a lethal radiation crackling in the room.

The squire followed as Retief strode off down the corridor. He breathed deeply, wiping his forehead. This was some old man he had met this year, for sure!

Retief slowed, turning to wait for Fitzraven. He smiled ruefully. 'I was rough on the old goat," he said. "But officious pip-squeaks sting me like deerflies."

They emerged from the gloom of the passage into a well-situated box, to the best seats in the first row. Retief stared at the white glare and roiled dust of the arena, the banked thousands of faces looming above, and a sky of palest blue with one tiny white cloud. The gladiators stood in little groups, waiting. A strange scene, Retief thought. A scene from dim antiquity, but real, complete with the odors of fear and excitement, the hot wind that ruffled his hair, the rumbling animal sound from the thousand throats of the many-headed monster. He wondered what it was they really wanted to see here today. A triumph of skill and courage, a reaffirmation of ancient virtues, the spectacle of men who laid life on the gaming table and played for a prize called glory—or was it merely blood and death they wanted?

It was strange that this archaic ritual of the blood tournament, combining the features of the Circus of Caesar, the joust of Medieval Terran Europe, the Olympic Games, a rodeo, and a six-day bicycle race should have come to hold such an important place in a modern culture Retief thought. In its present form it

was a much-distorted version of the traditional Tournament of
the Lily, through whose gauntlet the nobiliy of the old Empire
had come. It had been a device of harsh enlightenment to insure
and guarantee to every man, once each year, the opportunity to
prove himself against others whom society called his betters.
Through its discipline, the humblest farm lad could rise by
degrees to the highest levels in the Empire. For the original
Games had tested every facet of a man, from his raw courage to
his finesse in strategy, from his depths of endurance under
mortal stress to the quickness of his intellect, from his instinc
for truth to his wiliness in eluding a complex trap of violence.

In the two centuries since the fall of the Empire, the Games
had gradually become a tourist spectacle, a free-for-all, a
celebration—with the added spice of danger for those who did
not shrink back, and fat prizes to a few determined finalists. The
Imperial Charter was still invoked at the opening of the Games
the old Code reaffirmed; but there were few who knew or cared
what the Charter and Code actually said, what terms existed
there. The popular mind left such details to the regents of the
tourney. And in recent months, with the once sought-after tour
ists suddenly and inexplicably turned away, it seemed the Game
were being perverted to a purpose even less admirable. . . .

Well, thought Retief, perhaps I'll bring some of the fine prin
into play, before I'm done.

Bugle blasts sounded beyond the high bronze gate. Then with
a heavy clang it swung wide and a nervous official stepped ou
nodding jerkily to the front rank of today's contenders.

The column moved straight out across the field, came togethe
with other columns to form a square before the Imperial box
High above, Retief saw banners fluttering, a splash of color from
the uniforms of ranked honor guards. The Emperor himself wa
here briefly to open the Tournament.

Across the field the bugles rang out again; Retief recognize
the Call to Arms and the Imperial Salute. Then an amplifie
voice began the ritual reading of the Terms of the Day.

". . . by the clement dispensation of his Imperial Majesty, t
be conducted under the convention of Fragonard, and there b
none dissenting . ." The voice droned on.

It finished at last, and referees moved to their positions. Retief looked at Fitzraven. "The excitement's about to begin."

Referees handed out heavy whips, gauntlets and face shields. The first event would be an unusual one.

Retief watched as the yellow-haired combatant just below the box drew on the heavy leather glove which covered and protected the left hand and forearm, accepted the fifteen-foot lash of braided oxhide. He flipped it tentatively, laying the length out along the ground and recalling it with an effortless turn of the wrist, the frayed tip snapping like a pistol shot. The thing was heavy, Retief noted, and clumsy; the leather had no life to it.

The box had filled now; no one bothered Retief and the squire. The noisy crowd laughed and chattered, called to acquaintances in the stands and on the field below.

A bugle blasted peremptorily nearby, and white-suited referees darted among the milling entrants, shaping them into groups of five. Retief watched the blond youth, a tall frowning man, and three others of undistinguished appearance.

Fitzraven leaned toward him. "The cleverest will hang back and let the others eliminate each other," he said in a low voice, "so that his first encounter will be for the set."

Retief nodded. A man's task here was to win his way as high as possible; every stratagem was important. He saw the blond fellow inconspicuously edge back as a hurrying referee paired off the other four, called to him to stand by, and led the others to rings marked off on the dusty turf. A whistle blew suddenly, and over the arena the roar of sound changed tone. The watching crowd leaned forward as the hundreds of keyed-up gladiators laid on their lashes in frenzied effort. Whips cracked, men howled, feet shuffled; here the crowd laughed as some clumsy fellow sprawled, yelping; there they gasped in excitement as two surly brutes flogged each other in all-out offense.

Retief saw the tip of one man's whip curl around his opponent's ankle, snatch him abruptly off his feet. The other pair circled warily, rippling their lashes uncertainly. One backed over the line unnoticing and was led away expostulating, no blow having been struck.

The number on the field dwindled away to half within moments. Only a few dogged pairs, now bleeding from cuts, still contested

the issue. A minute longer and the whistle blew as the last was
settled.

The two survivors of the group below paired off now, and as
the whistle blasted again, the tall fellow, still frowning, brought
the other to the ground with a single sharp flick of the lash.
Retief looked him over. This was a man to watch.

More whistles, and a field now almost cleared; only two men
left out of each original five; the blond moved out into the circle,
stared across at the other. Retief recognized him suddenly as the
fellow who had challenged him outside the gate, over the spilled
fruit. So he had followed through the arch.

The final whistle sounded and a hush fell over the watchers.
Now the shuffle of feet could be heard clearly, the hissing breath
of the weary fighters, the creak and slap of leather.

The blond youth flipped his lash out lightly, saw it easily
evaded, stepped aside from a sharp counterblow. He feinted,
reversed the direction of his cast, and caught the other high on
the chest as he dodged aside. A welt showed instantly. He saw a
lightning-fast riposte on the way, sprang back. The gauntlet
came up barely in time. The lash wrapped around the gauntlet,
and the young fellow seized the leather, hauled sharply. The
other stumbled forward. The blond brought his whip across the
fellow's back in a tremendous slamming blow that sent a great
fragment of torn shirt flying. Somehow the man stayed on his
feet, backed off, circled. His opponent followed up, laying down
one whistling whipcrack after another, trying to drive the other
over the line. He had hurt the man with the cut across the back
and now was attempting to finish him easily.

He leaned away from a sluggish pass, and then Retief saw
agony explode in his face as a vicious cut struck home. The
blond youth reeled in a drunken circle, out on his feet.

Slow to follow up, the enemy's lash crashed across the circle
the youth, steadying quickly, slipped under it, struck at the
other's stomach. The leather cannoned against the man, sent the
remainder of his shirt fluttering in a spatter of blood. With a
surge of shoulder and wrist that made the muscles creak, the
blond reversed the stroke, brought the lash back in a vicious cut
aimed at the same spot. It struck, smacking with a wet explosive

crack. And he struck again, again, as the fellow tottered back, fell over the line.

The winner went limp suddenly, staring across at the man who lay in the dust, pale now, moving feebly for a moment, then slackly still. There was a great deal of blood, and more blood. Retief saw with sudden shock that the man was disemboweled. That boy, thought Retief, plays for keeps.

The next two events constituting the First Day trials were undistinguished exhibitions of a two-handed version of an old American Indian wrestling and a brief bout of fencing with blunt-tipped weapons. Eighty men were certified for the Second Day before noon, and Retief and Fitzraven were back in the inn room a few minutes later. "Take some time off now while I catch up on my rest," Retief said. "Have some solid food ready when I wake." Then he retired for the night.

With his master breathing heavily in a profound sleep, the squire went down to the common room and found a table at the back, ordered a mug of strong ale, and sat alone, thinking.

This was a strange one he had met this year. He had seen at once that he was no idler from some high-pressure world, trying to lose himself in a fantasy of the old days. And no more was he a Northroyalan; there was a grim force in him, a time-engraved stamp of power that was alien to the neat well-ordered little world. And yet there was no doubt that there was more in him of the true Cavalier than in a Fragonard-born courtier. He was like some ancient warrior noble from the days of the greatness of the Empire. By the two heads, the old man was strange, and terrible in anger!

Fitzraven listened to the talk around him.

"I was just above," a blacksmith at the next table was saying. "He gutted the fellow with the lash! It was monstrous! I'm glad I'm not one of the fools who want to play at warrior. Imagine having your insides drawn out by a rope of dirty leather!"

"The games have to be tougher now," said another. "We've lain dormant here for two centuries, waiting for something to come—some thing to set us on our way again to power and wealth. . . ."

"Thanks, I'd rather go on living quietly as a smith and

enjoying a few of the simple pleasures—there was no glory in that fellow lying in the dirt with his belly torn open, you can be sure of that.''

"There'll be more than torn bellies to think about, when we mount a battle fleet for Grimwold and Tania," said another.

"The Emperor has returned," snapped the warlike one. "Shall we hang back where he leads?"

The smith muttered. "His is a tortured genealogy, by my judgment. I myself trace my ancestry by three lines into the old Palace at Lily."

"So do we all. All the more reason we should support our Emperor."

"We live well here; we have no quarrel with other worlds. Why not leave the past to itself?"

"Our Emperor leads; we will follow. If you disapprove, enter the Lily Tournament next year and win a high place; then your advice will be respected."

"No thanks. I like my insides to stay on the inside."

Fitzraven thought of Retief. The old man had said that he held his rank in his own right, citing no genealogy. That was strange indeed. The Emperor had turned up only a year ago, presenting the Robe, the Ring, the Seal, the crown jewels, and the Imperial Book which traced his descent through five generations from the last reigning Emperor of the Old Empire.

How could it be that Retief held a commission in his own right, dated no more than thirty years ago? And the rank of Battle Commander. That was a special rank, Fitzraven remembered, a detached rank for a distinguished noble and officer of proven greatness, assigned to no one unit, but dictating his own activities.

Either Retief was a fraud . . . but Fitzraven pictured the old man, his chiseled features that time had not disguised, his soldier's bearing, his fantastic strength, his undoubtedly authentic equipage. Whatever the explanation, he was a true knight. That was enough.

Retief awoke refreshed, and ravenous. A great rare steak and a giant tankard of autumn ale were ready on the table. He ate, ordered more and ate again. Then he stretched, shook himself, no trace of yesterday's fatigue remaining. His temper was better, too, he realized. He was getting too old to exhaust himself.

"It's getting late, Fitzraven," he said. "Let's be going."

They arrived at the arena and took their places in the official box in time to watch the first event, a cautious engagement with swords.

After four more events and three teams of determined but colorless competition, only a dozen men were left on the field awaiting the next event, including the tall blond youth whom Retief had been watching since he had recognized him. He himself, he reflected, was the reason for the man's presence here; and he had acquitted himself well.

Retief saw a burly warrior carrying a two-handed sword paired off now against the blond youth. The fellow grinned as he moved up to face the other.

This would be a little different, the agent thought, watching; this fellow was dangerous. Yellow-hair moved in, his weapon held level across his chest. The big man lashed out suddenly with the great sword, and the other jumped back, then struck backhanded at his opponent's shoulder, nicked him lightly, sliding back barely in time to avoid a return swing. The still grinning man moved in, the blade chopping the air before him in a whistling figure-eight. He pressed his man back, the blade never pausing.

There was no more room; the blond fellow jumped sideways, dropping the point of his sword in time to intercept a vicious cut. He backstepped; he couldn't let that happen again. The big man was very strong.

The blade was moving again now, the grin having faded a little. He'll have to keep away from him, keep circling, Retief thought. The big fellow's pattern is to push his man back to the edge, then pick him off as he tries to sidestep. He'll have to keep space between them.

The fair-haired man backed, watching for an opening. He jumped to the right, and as the other shifted to face him, leaped back to the left and catching the big man at the end of his reach to the other side, slashed him across the ribs and kept moving. The man roared, twisting around in vicious cuts at the figure that darted sideways, just out of range. Then the blond brought his claymore across in a low swing that struck soldily across the back of the other's legs, with a noise like a butcher separating ribs with a cleaver.

Like a marionette with his strings cut, the man folded to his knees, sprawled. The other man stepped back, as surgeons' men swarmed up to tend the fallen fighter. There were plenty of them available now; so far the casualties had been twice normal. On the other mounds in view, men were falling. The faint-hearted had been eliminated; the men who were still on their feet were determined, or desperate. There would be no more push-overs.

"Only about six left," Fitzraven called.

"This has been a rather unusual tournament so far," Retief said. "That young fellow with the light hair seems to be playing rough, forcing the pace."

"I have never seen such a businsslike affair," Fitzraven said. "The weak-disposed have been frightened out, and the fighters cut down with record speed. At this rate there will be none left for the Third Day."

There was delay on the field, as referees and other officials hurried back and forth; then an announcement boomed out. The Second Day was officially concluded. The six survivors would be awarded Second Day certificates, and would be eligible for the Third and Last Day tomorrow.

Retief and Fitzraven left the box, made their way through the crowd back to the inn.

"See that Danger-by-Night is well fed and exercised," Retief said to the squire. "And check over all of my gear thoroughly. I wish to put on my best appearance tomorrow; it will doubtless be my last outing of the kind for some time."

Fitzraven hurried away to tend his chores, while Retief ascended to his room to pore over the contents of his dispatch case far into the night.

The Third Day had dawned gray and chill, and an icy wind whipped across the arena. The weather had not discouraged the crowd, however. The stands were packed and the overflow of people stood in the aisles, perched high on the back walls, crowding every available space. Banners flying from the Imperial box indicated the presence of the royal party. This was the climactic day. The field, by contrast, was almost empty; two of the Second Day winners had not reentered for today's events, having apparently decided that they had had enough honor for one year. They would receive handsome prizes, and respectable titles; that was enough.

The four who had come to the arena today to stake their winning and their lives on their skill at arms would be worth watching, Retief thought. There was the blond young fellow, still unmarked; a great swarthy ruffian; a tall broad man of perhaps thirty; and a squat bowlegged fellow with enormous shoulders and long arms. They were here to win or die.

From the officials' box Retief and Fitzraven had an excellent view of the arena, where a large circle had been marked out. The officials seated nearby had given them cold glances as they entered, but no one had attempted to interfere. Apparently, they had accepted the situation. Possibly, Retief thought, they had actually studied the Charter. He hoped they had studied it carefully. It would make things easier.

Announcements boomed, officials moved about, fanfares blasted, while Retief sat absorbed in thought. The scene reminded him of things he had long forgotten, days long gone, of his youth, when he had studied the martial skills, serving a long apprenticeship under his world's greatest masters. It had been his father's conviction that nothing so trained the eye and mind and body as fencing, judo, savate, and the disciplines of the arts of offense, and defense.

He had abandoned a priceless education when he had left his home to seek his fortune in the mainstream of galactic culture, but it had stood him in good stead on more than one occasion. An agent of the Corps could not afford to let himself decline into physical helplessness, and Retief had maintained his skills as well as possible. He leaned forward now, adjusting his binoculars as the bugles rang out. Few in the crowd were better qualified than Retief to judge today's performance. It would be interesting to see how the champions handled themselves on the field.

*   *   *

The first event was about to begin, as the blond warrior was paired off with the bowlegged man. The two had been issued slender foils, and now faced each other, blades crossed. A final whistle blew, and blade clashed on blade. The squat man was fast on his feet, bouncing around in a semicircle before his taller antagonist, probing his defense with great energy. The blond man backed away slowly, fending off the rain of blows with slight motions of his foil. He jumped back suddenly, and Retief saw a red spot grow on his thigh. The apelike fellow was more dangerous than he had appeared.

Now the blond man launched his attack, beating aside the weapon of the other and striking in for the throat, only to have his point deflected at the last instant. The short man backed now, giving ground reluctantly. Suddenly he dropped into a grotesque crouch, and lunged under the other's defense in a desperate try for a quick kill. It was a mistake; the taller man whirled aside; and his blade flicked delicately once. The bowlegged man slid out flat on his face.

"What happened?" Fitzraven said, puzzled. "I didn't see the stroke that nailed him."

"It was very pretty," Retief said thoughtfully, lowering the glasses. "Under the fifth rib and into the heart."

Now the big dark man and the tall broad fellow took their places. The bugles and whistles sounded, and the two launched a furious exchange, first one and then the other forcing his enemy back before losing ground in turn. The crowd roared its approval as the two stamped and thrust, parried and lunged.

"They can't keep up this pace forever," Fitzraven said. "They'll have to slow down."

"They're both good," Retief said. "And evenly matched."

Now the swarthy fellow leaped back, switched the foil to his left hand, then moved quickly in to the attack. Thrown off his pace, the other man faltered, let the blade nick him on the chest, again in the arm. Desperate, he backpedaled, fighting defensively now. The dark man followed up his advantage, pressing savagely, and a moment later Retief saw a foot of bright steel projecting startlingly from the tall man's back. He took two steps, then folded, as the foil was wrenched from the dark man's hand.

Wave upon wave of sound rolled across the packed stands. Never had they seen such an exhibition as this! It was like the legendary battle of the heroes of the Empire, the fighters who had carried the Lily banner half across the galaxy.

"I'm afraid that's all," Fitzraven said. "These two can elect either to share the victory of the Tourney now, or to contend for sole honors, and in the history of the Tournament on Northroyal, there have never been fewer than three to share the day."

"It looks as though this is going to be the first time, then," Retief said. "They're getting ready to square off."

Below on the field, a mass of officials surrounded the dark man and the fair one, while the crowd outdid itself. Then a bugle sounded in an elaborate salute.

"That's it," Fitzraven said excitedly. "Heroes' Salute. They're going to do it."

"You don't know how glad I am to hear that," Retief said.

"What will the weapon be?" the squire wondered aloud.

"My guess is, something less deadly than the foil," Retief replied.

Moments later the announcement came. The two champions of the day would settle the issue with bare hands. This, thought Retief, would be something to see.

The fanfares and whistles rang out again, and the two men moved cautiously together. The dark man swung an open-handed blow, which smacked harmlessly against the other's shoulder. An instant later the blond youth feinted a kick, instead drove a hard left to the dark man's chin, staggering him. He followed up, smashing two blows to the stomach, then another to the head. The dark man moved back, suddenly reached for the blond man's wrist as he missed a jab, whirled, and attempted to throw his opponent. The blond man slipped aside, and locked his right arm over the dark man's head, seizing his own right wrist with his left hand. The dark man twisted, fell heavily on the other man, reaching for a headlock of his own.

The two rolled in the dust, then broke apart and were on their feet again. The dark man moved in, swung an open-handed slap which popped loudly against the blond man's face. It was a device, Retief saw, to enrage the man, dull the edge of his skill.

The blond man refused to be rattled, however; he landed
blows against the dark man's head, evaded another attempt t
grapple. It was plain that he preferred to avoid the other'
bearlike embrace. He boxed carefully, giving ground, landing
blow as the opportunity offered. The dark man followed doggedly
seemingly unaffected by the pounding. Suddenly he leaped, too
two smashing blows full in the face, and crashed against th
blond man, knocking him to the ground. There was a flying blu
of flailing arms and legs as the two rolled across the turf, and a
they came to rest, Retief saw that the dark man had gotten hi
break. Kneeling behind the other, he held him in a rigi
stranglehold, his back and shoulder muscles bulging with th
effort of holding his powerful adversary immobilized.

"It's all over," Fitzraven said tensely.

"Maybe not," Retief replied. "Not if he plays it right, an
doesn't panic."

The blond man strained at the arm locked at his throa
twisting it fruitlessly. Instinct drove him to tear at the throttlin
grip, throw off the smothering weight. But the dark man's gri
was solid, his position unshakable. Then the blond stoppe
struggling abruptly and the two seemed as still as an image i
stone. The crowd fell silent, fascinated.

"He's given up," Fitzraven said.

"No; watch," Retief said. "He's starting to use his head."

The blond man's arms reached up now, his hands moving ove
the other's head, seeking a grip. The dark man pulled his hea
in, pressing against his victim's back, trying to elude his grip
Then the hands found a hold, and the blond man bent suddenl
forward, heaving with a tremendous surge. The dark man cam
up, flipped high, his grip slipping. The blond rose as the othe
went over his head, shifted his grip in midair, and as the dar
man fell heavily in front of him, the snap of the spine could b
heard loud in the stillness. The battle was over, and the blon
victor rose to his feet amid a roar of applause.

Retief turned to Fitzraven. "Time for us to be going, Fitz,
he said.

The squire jumped up. "As you command, sir; but the cere
mony is quite interesting. . . ."

"Never mind that; let's go." Retief moved off, Fitzraven following, puzzled.

* * *

Retief descended the steps inside the stands, turned and started down the corridor.

"This way, sir," Fitzraven called. "That leads to the arena."

"I know it," Retief said. "That's where I'm headed."

Fitzraven hurried up alongside. What was the old man going to do now? "Sir," he said, "no one may enter the arena until the tourney has been closed, except the gladiators and the officials. I know this to be an unbreakable law."

"That's right, Fitz," Retief said. "You'll have to stop at the grooms' enclosure."

"But you, sir," Fitzraven gasped . . .

"Everything's under control," Retief said. "I'm going to challenge the champion."

In the Imperial box, the Emperor Rolan leaned forward, fixing his binoculars on a group of figures at the officials' gate. There seemed to be some sort of disturbance there. This was a piece of damned impudence, just as the moment had arrived for the imperial presentation of the Honors of the Day. The Emperor turned to an aide.

"What the devil's going on down there?" he snapped.

The courtier murmured into a communicator, listened.

"A madman, Imperial Majesty," he said smoothly. "He wished to challenge the champion."

"A drunk, more likely," Rolan said sharply. "Let him be removed at once. And tell the Master of the Games to get on with the ceremony!"

The Emperor turned to the slim dark girl at his side.

"Have you have found the Games entertaining, Monica?"

"Yes, sire," she replied unemotionally.

"Don't call me that, Monica," he said testily. "Between us here is no need of formalities."

"Yes, Uncle," the girl said.

"Damn it, that's worse," he said. "To you I am simply Rolan." He placed his hand firmly on her silken knee. "And now if they'll get on with this tedious ceremony, I should like to be on the way. I'm looking forward with great pleasure to showing you my estates at Snowdahl."

The Emperor drummed his fingers, stared down at the field, raised the glasses only to see the commotion again.

"Get that fool off the field," he shouted, dropping the glasses. "Am I to wait while they haggle with this idiot? It's insufferable. . . ."

Courtiers scurried, while Rolan glared down from his seat.

Below, Retief faced a cluster of irate referees. One, who had attempted to haul Retief bodily backward, was slumped on a bench, attended by two surgeons.

"I claim the right to challenge, under the Charter," Retief repeated. "Nobody here will be so foolish, I hope, as to attempt to deprive me of that right, now that I have reminded you of the justice of my demand."

From the control cage directly below the Emperor's high box, a tall seam-faced man in black breeches and jacket emerged, followed by two armed men. The officials darted ahead, stringing out between the two, calling out. Behind Retief, on the other side of the barrier, Fitzraven watched anxiously. The old man was full of surprises, and had a way of getting what he wanted, but even if he had the right to challenge the Champion of the Games, what purpose could he have in doing so? He was as strong as a bull, but no man his age could be a match for the youthful power of the blond fighter. Fitzraven was worried; he was fond of this old warrior. He would hate to see him locked behind the steel walls of Fragonard Keep for thus disturbing the order of the Lily Tournament. He moved closer to the barrier, watching.

The tall man in black strode through the chattering officials, stopped before Retief, motioned his two guards forward.

He made a dismissing motion toward Retief. "Take him off the field," he said brusquely. The guards stepped up, laid hands on Retief's arms. He let them get a grip, then suddenly stepped back and brought his arms together. The two men cracked heads, stumbled back. Retief looked at the black-clad man.

"If you are the Master of the Games," he said clearly, "you are well aware that a decorated battle officer has the right challenge, under the Imperial Charter. I invoke that prerogative now, to enter the lists against the man who holds the field."

"Get out, you fool," the official hissed, white with fury. "The Emperor himself has commanded—"

"Not even the Emperor can override the Charter, which predates his authority by four hundred years," Retief said coldly. "Now do your duty."

"There'll be no more babble of duties and citing of technicalities while the Emperor waits," the official snapped. He turned to one of the two guards, who hung back now, eyeing Retief. "You have a pistol; draw it. If I give the command, shoot him between the eyes."

Retief reached up and adjusted a tiny stud set in the stiff collar of his tunic. He tapped his finger lightly against the cloth. The sound boomed across the arena. A command microphone of the type authorized a Battle Commander was a very efficient device.

"I have claimed the right to challenge the champion," he said slowly. The words rolled out like thunder. "This right is guaranteed under the Charter to any Imperial battle officer who wears the Silver Star."

The Master of the Games stared at him aghast. This was getting out of control. Where the devil had the old man gotten a microphone and a PA system? The crowd was roaring now like a gigantic surf. This was something new!

Far above in the Imperial box the tall gray-eyed man was rising, turning toward the exit. "The effrontery," he said in a voice choked with rage. "That I should sit awaiting the pleasure . . ."

The girl at his side hesitated, hearing the amplified voice booming across the arena.

"Wait, Rolan," she said. "Something is happening. . . ."

The man looked back. "A trifle late," he snapped.

"One of the contestants is disputing something," she said. "There was an announcement—something about an Imperial officer challenging the champion."

The Emperor Rolan turned to an aide hovering nearby.

"What is this nonsense?"

The courtier bowed. "It is merely a technicality, Majesty. A formality lingering on from earlier times."

"Be specific," the Emperor snapped.

The aide lost some of his aplomb. "Why, it means, ah, tha an officer of the Imperial forces holding a battle commission an certain high decorations may enter the lists at any point, withou other qualifying conditions. A provision never invoked unde modern . . ."

The Emperor turned to the girl. "It appears that someon seeks to turn the entire performance into a farcical affair, at m expense," he said bitterly. "We shall see just how far—"

"I call on you, Rolan," Retief's voice boomed, "to enforc the Code."

"What impertinence is this?" Rolan growled. "Who is th fool at the microphone?"

The aide spoke into his communicator, listened.

"An old man from the crowd, sire. He wears the insignia of Battle Commander, and a number of decorations, including th Silver Star. According to the Archivist, he has the legal right t challenge."

"I won't have it," Rolan snapped. "A fine reflection on m that would be. Have them take the fellow away; he's doubtles crazed." He left the box, followed by his entourage.

"Rolan," the girl said, "wasn't that the way the Tourney were, back in the days of the Empire?"

"*These* are the days of the Empire, Monica. And I am nc interested in what used to be done. This is today. Am I t present the spectacle of a doddering old fool being hacked t bits, in my name? I don't want the timid to be shocked b butchery. It might have unfortunate results for my propagand program. I'm currently emphasizing the glorious aspects of th coming war, not the sordid ones. There has already been to much bloodshed today; an inauspicious omen for my expansio plan."

On the field below, the Master of the Games stepped closer t Retief. He felt the cold eyes of the Emperor himself boring int his back. This old devil could bring about his ruin. . . .

"I know all about you," he snarled. "I've checked on you

since you forced your way into an official area; I interviewed
two officers . . . you overawed them with glib talk and this
threadbare finery you've decked yourself in. Now you attempt to
ride rough-shod over me. Well, I'm not so easily thrust aside. If
you resist arrest any further, I'll have you shot where you
stand!''

Retief drew his sword.

"In the name of the Code you are sworn to serve," he said,
his voice ringing across the arena, "I will defend my position."
He reached up and flipped the stud at his throat to full pick-up.

"To the Pit with your infernal Code!" bellowed the Master,
and blanched in horror as his words boomed sharp and clear
across the field to the ears of a hundred thousand people. He
stared around, then whirled back to Retief. "Fire," he screamed.

A pistol cracked, and the guard spun, dropped. Fitzraven held
the tiny power gun leveled across the barrier at the other guard.
"What next, sir?" he asked brightly.

The sound of the shot, amplified, smashed deafeningly across
the arena, followed by a mob roar of excitement, bewilderment,
shock. The group around Retief stood frozen, staring at the dead
man. The Master of the Games made a croaking sound, eyes
bulging. The remaining guard cast a glance at the pistol, then
turned and ran.

There were calls from across the field; then a troop of brown-
uniformed men emerged from an entry, trotted toward the
group. The officer at their head carried a rapid-fire shock gun
in his hand. He waved his squad to a halt as he reached the fringe
of the group. He stared at Retief's drab uniform, glanced at the
corpse. Retief saw that the officer was young, determined-looking,
wearing the simple insignia of a Battle Ensign.

The Master of the Games found his voice. "Arrest this villain!"
he screeched, pointing at Retief. "Shoot the murderer!"

The ensign drew himself to attention, saluted crisply.

"Your orders, sir," he said.

"I've told you!" the Master howled. "Seize this malefactor!"

The ensign turned to the black-clad official. "Silence, sir, or I
shall be forced to remove you," he said sharply. He looked at
Retief. "I await the Commander's orders."

Retief smiled, returned the young officer's salute with a wave of his sword, then sheathed it. "I'm glad to see a little sense displayed here, at last, Battle Ensign," he said. "I was beginning to fear I'd fallen among Concordiatists."

The outraged Master began an harangue which was abruptly silenced by two riot police. He was led away, protesting. The other officials disappeared like a morning mist, carrying the dead guard.

"I've issued my challenge, Ensign," Retief said. "I wish it to be conveyed to the champion-apparent at once." He smiled. "And I'd like you to keep your men around to see that nothing interferes with the orderly progress of the Tourney in accordance with the Charter in its original form."

The ensign's eyes sparkled. Now here was a battle officer who sounded like a fighting man; not a windbag like the commandant of the Household Regiment from whom the ensign took his orders. He didn't know where the old man came from, but any battle officer outranked any civilian or flabby barracks soldier, and this was a Battle Commander, a general officer, and of the Dragon Corps!

Minutes later, a chastened Master of the Games announced that a challenge had been issued. It was the privilege of the champion to accept, or to refuse the challenge if he wished. In the latter event, the challenge would automatically be met the following year.

"I don't know what your boys said to the man," Retief remarked, as he walked out to the combat circle, the ensign at his left side and slightly to the rear, "but they seem to have him educated quickly."

"They can be very persuasive, sir," the young officer replied.

They reached the circle, stood waiting. Now, thought Retief, I've got myself in the position I've been working toward. The question now is whether I'm still man enough to put it over.

He looked up at the massed stands, listening to the mighty roar of the crowd. There would be no easy out for him now. Of course, the new champion might refuse to fight; he had every right to do so, feeling he had earned his year's rest and enjoyment of his winnings. But that would be a defeat for Retief as final as death on the dusty ground of the arena. He had come this far by bluff, threat, and surprise. He would never come this close again.

It was luck that he had clashed with this young man outside the gate, challenged him to enter the lists. That might give the challenge the personal quality that would elicit an angry acceptance.

The champion was walking toward Retief now, surrounded by referees. He stared at the old man, eyes narrowed. Retief returned the look calmly.

"Is this dodderer the challenger?" the blond youth asked scathingly. "It seems to me I have met his large mouth before?"

"Never mind my mouth, merchant," Retief said loudly. "It is not talk I offer you, but the bite of steel."

The yellow-haired man reddened, then laughed shortly. "Small glory I'd win out of skewering you, old graybeard."

"You'd get even less out of showing your heels," Retief said.

"You will not provoke me into satisfying your perverted ambition to die here," the other retorted.

"It's interesting to note," Retief said, "how a peasant peddler wags his tongue to avoid a fight. Such rabble should not be permitted on honorable ground." He studied the other's face to judge how this line of taunting was going on. It was distasteful to have to embarrass the young fellow; he seemed a decent sort. But he had to enrage him to the point that he would discard his wisdom and throw his new-won prize on the table for yet another cast of the dice. And his sore point seemed to be mention of commerce.

"Back to your cabbages, then, fellow," Retief said harshly, "before I whip you there with the flat of my sword."

The young fellow looked at him, studying him. His face was grim. "All right," he said quietly. "I'll meet you in the circle."

Another point gained, Retief thought, as he moved to his position at the edge of the circle. Now, if I can get him to agree to fight on horseback . . .

He turned to a referee. "I wish to suggest that this contest be conducted on horseback—if the peddler owns a horse and is not afraid.''

The point was discussed between the referee and the champion's attendants, with many glances at Retief, and much waving of arms. The official returned. ''The champion agrees to meet you by day or by night, in heat or cold, on foot or on horseback.''

''Good,'' said Retief. ''Tell my groom to bring out my mount.''

It was no idle impulse which prompted this move. Retief had no illusions as to what it would take to win a victory over the champion. He knew that his legs, while good enough for most of the business of daily life, were his weakest point. They were no longer the nimble tireless limbs that had once carried him up to meet the outlaw Mal de Di alone in Bifrost Pass. Nine hours later he had brought the bandit's two-hundred-and-ten-pound body down into the village on his back, his own arm broken. He had been a mere boy then, younger than this man he was now to meet. He had taken up Mal de Di's standing challenge to any unarmed man who would come alone to the high pass, to prove that he was not too young to play a man's part. Perhaps now he was trying to prove he was not too old. . . .

An official approached leading Danger-by-Night. It took an expert to appreciate the true worth of the great gaunt animal, Retief knew. To the uninitiated eye, he presented a sorry appearance, but Retief would rather have had this mount with the imperial brand on his side than a paddock full of show horses.

A fat white charger was led out to the blond champion. It looked like a strong animal, Retief thought, but slow. His chances were looking better, things were going well.

A ringing blast of massed trumpets cut through the clamor of the crowd. Retief mounted, watching his opponent. A referee came to his side, handed up a heavy club, studded with long projecting spikes. ''Your weapon, sir,'' he said.

Retief took the thing. It was massive, clumsy; he had never before handled such a weapon. He knew no subtleties of technique with this primitive bludgeon. The blond youth had surprised him, he admitted to himself, smiling slightly. As the challenged party, he had the choice of weapons, of course. He had picked an unusual one.

Retief glanced across at Fitzraven, standing behind the inner barrier, jaw set, a grim expression on his face. That boy, thought Retief, doesn't have much confidence in my old bones holding out.

The whistle blew. Retief moved toward the other man at a trot, the club level at his side. He had decided to handle it like a shortsword, so long as that seemed practical. He would have to learn by experience.

The white horse cantered past him swerving, and the blond fellow whirled his club at Retief's head. Automatically, Retief raised his club, fended off the blow, cut at the other's back, missed. This thing is too short, Retief thought, whirling his horse. I've got to get in closer. He charged at the champion as the white horse was still in midturn, slammed a heavy blow against his upraised club, rocking the boy; then he was past, turning again. He caught the white horse shorter this time, barely into his turn, and aimed a swing at the man, who first twisted to face him, then spurred, leaped away. Retief pursued him, yelping loudly. Get him rattled, he thought. Get him good and mad!

The champion veered suddenly, veered again, then reared his horse high, whirling, to bring both forefeet down in a chopping attack. Retief reined in, and Danger-by-Night sidestepped disdainfully, as the heavy horse crashed down facing him.

That was a pretty maneuver, Retief thought; but slow, too slow.

His club swung in an overhand cut; the white horse tossed his head suddenly, and the club smashed down across the animal's skull. With a shuddering exhalation, the beast collapsed, and the blond man sprang clear.

Retief reined back, dismayed. He hadn't wanted to kill the animal. He had the right, now, to ride the man down from the safety of the saddle. When gladiators met in mortal combat, there were no rules except those a man made for himself. If he dismounted, met his opponent on equal terms, the advantage his horse had given him would be lost. He looked at the man standing now, facing him, waiting, blood on his face from the fall. He thought of the job he had set himself, the plan that hinged on his victory here. He reminded himself that he was old, too old to meet youth on equal terms; but even as he did so, he was reining the lean battle stallion back, swinging down from the saddle. There were some things a man had to do, whether logic was served or not. He couldn't club the man down like a mad dog from the saddle.

There was a strange expression on the champion's face. He sketched a salute with the club he held. "All honor to you, old man," he said. "Now I will kill you." He moved in confidently.

Retief stood his ground, raising his club to deflect a blow, shifting an instant ahead of the pattern of the blond man's assault. There was a hot exchange as the younger man pressed him, took a glancing blow on the temple, stepped back breathing heavily. This wasn't going as he had planned. The old man stood like a wall of stone, not giving an inch; and when their weapons met, it was like flailing at a granite boulder. The young fellow's shoulder ached from the shock. He moved sideways, circling cautiously.

Retief moved to face him. It was risky business, standing up to the attack, but his legs were not up to any fancy footwork. He had no desire to show his opponent how stiff his movements were, or to tire himself with skipping about. His arms were still as good as any man's, or better. They would have to carry the battle.

The blond jumped in, swung a vicious cut; Retief leaned back, hit out in a one-handed blow, felt the club smack solidly against the other's jaw. He moved now, followed up, landed again on the shoulder. The younger man backed, shaking his head. Retief stopped, waited. It was too bad he couldn't follow up his advantage, but he couldn't chase the fellow all over the arena. He had to save his energy for an emergency. He lowered his club, leaned on it. The crowd noises waxed and waned, unnoticed. The sun beat down in unshielded whiteness, and fitful wind moved dust across the field.

"Come back, peddler," he called. "I want you to sample more of my wares." If he could keep the man angry, he would be careless; and Retief needed the advantage.

The yellow-haired man charged suddenly, whirling the club. Retief raised his, felt the shock of the other's weapon against his. He whirled as the blond darted around him, shifted the club to his left hand in time to ward off a wild swing. Then the fingers of his left hand exploded in fiery agony, and the club flew from his grasp. His head whirled, vision darkening, at the pain from his smashed fingers. He tottered, kept his feet, managed to blink away the faintness, to stare at this hand. Two fingers were missing, pulped, unrecognizable. He had lost his weapon; he was helpless now before the assault of the other.

His head hummed harshly, and his breath came like hot sand across an open wound. He could feel a tremor start and stop in his leg, and his whole left arm felt as though it had been stripped of flesh in a shredding machine. He had not thought it would be as bad as this. His ego, he realized, hadn't aged gracefully.

Now is the hour, old man, he thought. There's no help for you to call on, no easy way out. You'll have to look within yourself for some hidden reserve of strength and endurance and will; and you must think well now, wisely, with a keen eye and a quick hand, or lose your venture. With a moment stiffened by the racking pain-shock, he drew his ceremonial dagger, a jewel-encrusted blade ten inches long. At the least he would die with a weapon in his hand and his face to the enemy.

The blond youth moved closer, tossed the club aside.

"Shall a peddler be less capable of the *beau geste* than the arrogant knight?" He laughed, drawing a knife from his belt. "Is your head clear, old man?" he asked. "Are you ready?"

"A gesture . . . you can . . . ill afford," Retief managed. Even breathing hurt. His nerves were shrieking their message of shock at the crushing of living flesh and bone. His forehead was pale, wet with cold sweat.

The young fellow closed, struck out, and Retief evaded the point by an inch, stepped back. His body couldn't stand pain as once it had, he was realizing. He had grown soft, sensitive. For too many years he had been a Diplomat, an operator by manipulation, by subtlety and finesse. Now, when it was man to man, brute strength against brute strength, he was failing.

But he had known when he started that strength was not enough, not without agility; it was subtlety he should be relying on now, his skill at trickery, his devious wit.

Retief caught a glimpse of staring faces at the edge of the

field, heard for a moment the mob roar, and then he was again wholly concentrated on the business at hand.

He breathed deeply, struggling for clear-headedness. He had to inveigle the boy into a contest in which he stood a chance. If he could put him on his mettle, make him give up his advantage of tireless energy, quickness . . .

"Are you an honest peddler, or a dancing master?" Retief managed to growl. "Stand and meet me face to face."

The blond man said nothing, feinting rapidly, then striking out. Retief was ready, nicked the other's wrist.

"Gutter fighting is one thing," Retief said. "But you are afraid to face the old man's steel, right arm against right arm." If he went for that, Retief thought, he was even younger than he looked.

"I have heard of the practice," the blond man said, striking at Retief, moving aside from a return cut. "It was devised for old men who did not wish to be made ridiculous by more agile men. I understand that you think you can hoodwink me, but I can beat you at your own game. . . ."

"My point awaits your pleasure," Retief said.

The younger man moved closer, knife held before him. Just a little closer, Retief thought. Just a little closer.

The blond man's eyes were on Retief's. Without warning, Retief dropped his knife and in a lightning motion caught the other's wrist.

"Now struggle, little fish," he said. "I have you fast."

The two men stood chest to chest, staring into each other's eyes. Retief's breath came hard, his heart pounded almost painfully. His left arm was a great pulsating weight of pain. Sweat ran down his dusty face into his eyes. But his grip was locked solidly. The blond youth strained in vain.

With a twist of his wrist Retief turned the blade, then forced the youth's arm up. The fellow struggled to prevent it, throwing all his weight into his effort, fruitlessly. Retief smiled.

"I won't kill you," he said, "but I will have to break your arm. That way you cannot be expected to continue the fight."

"I want no favors from you, old man," the youth panted.

"You won't consider this a favor until the bones knit," Retief said. "Consider this a fair return for my hand."

He pushed the arm up, then suddenly turned it back, levered the upper arm over his forearm, and yanked the tortured member down behind the blond man's back. The bones snapped audibly, and the white-faced youth gasped, staggered as Retief released him.

There were minutes of confusion as referees rushed in, announcements rang out, medics hovered, and the crowd roared its satisfaction, after the fickle nature of crowds. They were satisfied.

An official pushed through to Retief. He wore the vivid colors of the Review regiment. Retief reached up and set the control on the command mike.

"I have the honor to advise you, sir, that you have won the field, and the honors of the day." He paused, startled at the booming echoes, then went on. The bystanders watched curiously, as Retief tried to hold his concentration on the man, to stand easily, while blackness threatened to move in over him. The pain from the crushed hand swelled and focused, then faded, came again. The great dry lungfuls of air he drew in failed to dispel the sensation of suffocation. He struggled to understand the words that seemed to echo from a great distance.

"And now in the name of the Emperor, for crimes against the peace and order of the Empire, I place you under arrest for trial before the High Court at Fragonard."

Retief drew a deep breath, gathered his thoughts to speak.

"Nothing," he said, "could possibly please me more."

The room was vast and ornate, and packed with dignitaries, high officials, peers of the Lily. Here in the great chamber known as the Blue Vault, the High Court sat in silent ranks, waiting.

The charges had been read, the evidence presented. The prisoner, impersonating a peer of the Lily and an officer of an ancient and honored Corps, had flaunted the law of Northroyal and the authority of the Emperor, capping his audacity with murder, done by the hand of his servant sworn. Had the prisoner anything to say?

Retief, alone in the prisoner's box in the center of the room, his arm heavily bandaged and deadened with dope, faced the court. This would be the moment when all his preparations would be put to the ultimate test. He had laid long plans toward this hour. The archives of the Corps were beyond comparison in the galaxy, and he had spent weeks there, absorbing every detail of the facts that had been recorded on the world of Northroyal, and on the Old Empire which had preceded it. And to the lore of the archives, he had added facts known to himself, data from his own wide experience. But would those tenuous threads of tradition, hearsay, rumor, and archaic record hold true now? That was the gamble on which his mission was staked. The rabbits had better be in the hat.

He looked at the dignitaries arrayed before him. It had been a devious route, but so far he had succeeded; he had before him the highest officials of the world, the High Justices, the Imperial Archivist, the official keepers of the Charter and the Code, and of the protocols and rituals of the tradition on which this society was based. He had risked everything on his assault on the sacred stasis of the Tournament, but how else could he have gained the ears of this select audience, with all Northroyal tuned in to hear the end of the drama that a hundred thousand had watched build to its shattering climax?

Now it was his turn to speak. It had better be good.

"Peers of the realm," Retief said, speaking clearly and slowly, "the basis of the charges laid against me is the assumption that I have falsified my identity. Throughout, I have done no more than exercise the traditional rights of a general officer and of a Lilyan peer, and, as befits a Cavalier, I have resisted all attempts to deprive me of those honored prerogatives. While it is regrettable that the low echelon of officials appears to be ignorant of the status of a Lilyan Battle Commander, it is my confident assumption that here, before the ranking nobles of the Northroyalan peerage, the justice of my position will be recognized."

As Retief paused, a dour graybeard spoke up from the Justices bench.

"Your claims are incoherent to this court. You are known to none of us; and if by chance you claim descent from some renegade who deserted his fellow Cavaliers at the time of the

Exile, you will find scant honor among honest men here. From this, it is obvious that you delude yourself in imagining that you can foist your masquerade on this court successfully."

"I am not native to Northroyal," Retief said, "nor do I claim to be. Nor am I a descendant of renegades. Are you gentlemen not overlooking the fact that there was one ship which did not accompany the Cavaliers into exile, but escaped Concordiat surveillance and retired to rally further opposition to the invasion?"

There was a flurry of muttered comment, putting together of heads, and shuffling of papers. The High Justice spoke.

"This would appear to be a reference to the vessel bearing the person of the Emperor Roquelle and his personal suite. . . ."

"That is correct," Retief said.

"You stray farther than ever from the credible," a justice snapped. "The entire royal household accompanied the Emperor Rolan on the happy occasion of his rejoining his subjects here at Northroyal a year ago."

"About that event, I will have more to say later," Retief said coolly. "For the present, suffice it to say that I am a legitimate descendant—"

"It does indeed *not* suffice to say!" barked the High Justice. 'Do you intend to instruct this court as to what evidence will be acceptable?"

"A figure of speech, Milord," Retief said. "I am quite able to prove my statement."

"Very well," said the High Justice. "Let us see your proof, though I confess I cannot conceive of a satisfactory one."

Retief reached down, unsnapped the flat dispatch case at his belt, drew out a document.

"This is my proof of my bona fides," he said. "I present it in evidence that I have committed no fraud. I am sure that you will recognize an authentic commission-in-patent of the Emperor Roquelle. Please note that the seals are unbroken." He passed the paper over.

A page took the heavy paper, looped with faded red ribbon and plastered with saucer-sized seals, trotted over to the Justices' bench and handed it up to the High Justice. He took it, gazed at it, turning it over, then broke the crumbling seals. The nearby Justices leaned over to see this strange exhibit. It was a heavily embossed document of the Old Empire type, setting forth genealogy and honors, and signed in sprawling letters with the name of an emperor two centuries dead, sealed with his tarnished golden seal. The Justices stared in amazement. The document was worth a fortune.

"I ask that the lowermost paragraph be read aloud," Retief said. "The amendment of thirty years ago."

The High Justice hesitated, then waved a page to him, handed down the document. "Read the lowermost paragraph aloud," he said.

The page read in a clear, well-trained voice.

"KNOW ALL MEN BY THESE PRESENTS THAT WHEREAS: THIS OUR LOYAL SUBJECT AND PEER OF THE IMPERIAL LILY JAME JARL FREELORD OF THE RETIEF; OFFICER IMPERIAL OF THE GUARD; OFFICER OF BATTLE; HEREDITARY LEGIONNAIRE OF HONOR; CAVALIER OF THE LILY; DEFENDER OF SALIENT WEST; BY IMPERIAL GRACE OFFICER OF THE SILVER STAR; HAS BY HIS GALLANTRY, FIDELITY AND SKILL BROUGHT HONOR TO THE IMPERIAL LILY AND WHEREAS WE PLACE SPECIAL CONFIDENCE AND ESTEEM IN THIS SUBJECT AND PEER: WE DO THEREFORE APPOINT AND COMMAND THAT HE SHALL FORTH WITH ASSUME AND HENCEFORTH BEAR THE HONORABLE RANK OF BATTLE COMMANDER: AND THAT HE SHALL BEAR THE OBLIGATIONS AND ENJOY THE PRIVILEGES APPERTAINING THEREUNTO: AS SHALL HIS HEIRS FOREVER."

There was a silence in the chamber as the page finished reading. All eyes turned to Retief, who stood in the box, a strange expression on his face.

The page handed the paper back up to the High Justice, who resumed his perusal.

"I ask that my retinal patterns now be examined, and matched to those coded on the amendment," Retief said. The High Justice beckoned to a Messenger, and the court waited a restless five minutes until the arrival of an expert who quickly made the necessary check. He went to the Justice's bench, handed up a report form, and left the courtroom. The magistrate glanced at the form, turned again to the document. Below Roquelle's seal

were a number of amendments, each in turn signed and sealed.
The justices spelled out the unfamiliar names.

"Where did you get this?" the High Justice demanded
uncertainly.

"It has been the property of my family for nine generations,"
Retief replied.

Heads nodded over the document, gray beards wagged.

"How is it," asked a Justice, "that you offer in evidence a
document bearing amendments validated by signatures and seals
completely unknown to us? In order to impress this court, such a
warrant might well bear the names of actual former emperors,
rather than of fictitious ones. I note the lowermost amendment,
purporting to be a certification of high military rank dated only
thirty years ago, is signed 'Ronare.' "

"I was at that time attached to the Imperial Suite-in-Exile,"
Retief said. "I commanded the forces of the Emperor Ronare."

The High Justice and a number of other members of the court
snorted openly.

"This impertinence will not further your case," the old magistrate said sharply. "Ronare, indeed. You cite a nonexistent
authority. At the alleged time of issue of this warrant, the father
of our present monarch held the Imperial fief at Trallend."

"At the time of the issue of this document," Retief said in
ringing tones, "the father of your present ruler held the bridle
when the Emperor mounted!"

An uproar broke out from all sides. The Master-at-arms pounded
in vain for silence. At length a measure of order was restored by
a gangly official who rose and shouted for the floor. The roar
died down, and the stringy fellow, clad in russet velvet with the
gold chain of the Master of the Seal about his neck, called out,
"Let the court find the traitor guilty summarily and put an end to
this insupportable insolence. . . ."

"Northroyal has been the victim of fraud," Retief said loudly
in the comparative lull. "But not on my part. The man Rolan is
an impostor."

*   *   *

A tremendous pounding of gavels and staffs eventually brought
the outraged dignitaries to grim silence. The Presiding Justice

peered down at Retief with doom in his lensed eyes. "Your knowledge of the Lilyan tongue and of the forms of court practice as well as the identity of your retinal patterns with those of the warrant tend to substantiate your origin in the Empire. Accordingly, this court is now disposed to recognize in you that basest of offenders, a renegade of the peerage." He raised his voice. "Let it be recorded that one Jame Jarl, a freelord of the Imperial Lily and officer Imperial of the Guard has by his own words disavowed his oath and his lineage." The fiery old man glared around at his fellow jurists. "Now let the dog of a broken officer be sentenced!"

"I have proof of what I say," Retief called out. "Nothing has been proven against me. I have acted by the Code, and by the Code I demand my hearing!"

"You have spurned the Code," said a fat dignitary.

"I have told you that a usurper sits on the Lily throne," Retief said. "If I can't prove it, execute me."

There was an icy silence.

"Very well," said the High Justice. "Present your proof."

"When the man, Rolan, appeared," Retief said, "he presented the Imperial seal and ring, the ceremonial robe, the major portion of the crown jewels, and the Imperial Genealogy."

"That is correct."

"Was it noted, by any chance, that the seal was without its chain, that the robe was stained, that the most important of the jewels, the ancient Napoleon Emerald, was missing, that the ring bore deep scratches, and that the lock on the book had been forced?"

A murmur grew along the high benches of the court. Intent eyes glared down at Retief.

"And was it not considered strange that the Imperial signet was not presented by this would-be Emperor, when that signet alone constitutes the true symbol of the Empire?" Retief's voice had risen to a thunderous loudness.

The High Justice stared now with a different emotion in his eyes.

"What do you know of these matters?" he demanded, but without assurance.

Retief reached into a tiny leather bag at his side, drew out something which he held out for inspection.

"This is a broken chain," he said. "It was cut when the seal was stolen from its place in Suite-in-Exile." He placed the heavy links on the narrow wainscot before him. "This," he said, "is the Napoleon Emerald, once worn by the legendary Bonaparte in a ring. It is unique in the galaxy, and easily proved genuine." There was utter stillness now. Retief placed a small key beside the chain and the gem. "This key will open the forced lock of the Imperial Genealogical Record."

Retief brought out an ornately wrought small silver casket and held it in view.

"The stains on the robe are the blood of the Emperor Ronare, shed by the knife of a murderer. The ring is scratched by the same knife, used to sever the finger in order to remove the ring." A murmur of horrified comment ran round the room now. Retief waited, letting all eyes focus on the silver box in his hand. It contained a really superb copy of the Imperial Signet; like the chain, the key and the emerald, the best that the science of the Corps could produce, accurate even in its internal molecular structure. It had to be, if it were to have a chance of acceptance. It would be put to the test without delay, matched to an electronic matrix with which it would, if acceptable, resonate perfectly. The copy had been assembled on the basis of some excellent graphic records; the original signet, as Retief knew, had been lost irretrievably in a catastrophic palace fire, a century and a half ago.

He opened the box, showed the magnificent wine-red crystal set in platinum. Now was the moment. "This is the talisman which alone would prove the falseness of the impostor Rolan," Retief said. "I call upon the honorable High Court to match it to the matrix; and while that is being done, I ask that the honorable Justices study carefully the genealogy included in the Imperial patent which I have presented to the court."

A messenger was dispatched to bring in the matrix while the Justices adjusted the focus of their corrective lenses and clustered over the document. The chamber buzzed with tense excitement. This was a fantastic development indeed!

The High Justice looked up as the massive matrix device was

wheeled into the room. He stared at Retief. "This genealogy—"
he began.

A Justice plucked at his sleeve, indicated the machine, whispering something. The High Justice nodded.

Retief handed the silver box down carefully to a page, watched as the chamber of the machine was opened, the great crystal placed in position. He held his breath as technicians twiddled controls, studied dials, then closed a switch. There was a sonorous musical tone from the machine.

The technician looked up. "The crystal," he said, "does match the matrix."

Amid a burst of exclamations which died as he faced the High Justice, Retief spoke.

"My lords, peers of the Imperial Lily," he said in a ringing voice, "know by this signet that we, Retief, by the grace of God Emperor, do now claim our rightful throne."

And just as quickly as the exclamations had died, they rose once more—a mixture of surprise and awe.

EPILOGUE

"A brilliant piece of work, Mr. Minister, and congratulations on your promotion," the Ambassador-at-large said warmly. "You've shown what individualism and the unorthodox approach can accomplish where the academic viewpoint would consider the situation hopeless."

"Thank you, Mr. Ambassador," Retief replied, smiling. "I was surprised myself when it was all over, that my gamble paid off. Frankly, I hope I won't ever be in a position again to be quite so inventive."

"I don't mind telling you now," the Ambassador said, "that when I saw Magnan's report of your solo assignment to the case, I seriously attempted to recall you, but it was too late. It was a nasty piece of business sending a single agent in on a job with the wide implications of this one. Mr. Magnan had been under a strain, I'm afraid. He is having a long rest now. . . ."

Retief understood perfectly. His former chief had gotten the axe, and he himself had emerged clothed in virtue. That was the

ne compensation of desperate ventures; if you won, they paid
vell. In his new rank, he had a long tenure ahead. He hoped the
ext job would be something complex and far removed from
Northroyal. He thought back over the crowded weeks of his brief
eign there as Emperor. It had been a stormy scene when the
itterly resisting Rolan had been brought to face the High Court.
The man had been hanged an hour before sunrise on the follow-
ng day, still protesting his authenticity. That, at least, was a lie.
Retief was grateful that he had proof that Rolan was a fraud,
ecause he would have sent him to the gallows on false evidence
ven had he been the true heir.

His first act after his formal enthronement had been the aboli-
on in perpetuity of the rite of the tourney, and the formal
ancellation of all genealogical requirements for appointments
ublic or private. He had ordered the release and promotion of
he Battle Ensign who had ignored Rolan's arrest order and had
een himself imprisoned for his pains. Fitzraven he had seen
ppointed to the Imperial War College—his future assured.

Retief smiled as he remembered the embarrassment of the
oung fellow who had been his fellow-finalist in the tourney. He
ad offered him satisfaction on the field of honor as soon as his
rm healed, and had been asked in return for forgetfulness of
oor judgment. He had made him a Captain of the Guard and a
eer of the realm. He had the spirit for it.

There had been much more to do, and Retief's days had been
rowded with the fantastically complex details of disengaging a
ocial structure from the crippling reactionary restraints of ossi-
ed custom and hallowed tradition. In the end, he had produced
a fresh and workable new constitution for the kingdom which he
oped would set the world on an enlightened and dynamic path
o a productive future.

The memory of Princess Monica lingered pleasantly; a true
rincess of the Lily, in the old tradition. Retief had abdicated in
er favor; her genealogy had been studded with enough Imperial
rebears to satisfy the crustiest of the Old Guard peerage; of
ourse, it could not compare with the handsome document he
ad displayed showing his own descent in the direct line through
ven—or was it eight—generations of Emperors-in-exile from

the lost monarch of the beleaguered Lily Empire, but it wa
enough to justify his choice. Rolan's abortive usurpation had a
least had the effect of making the Northroyalans appreciate a
enlightened ruler.

At the last, it had not been easy to turn away forever from th
seat of Empire which he so easily sat. It had not been lightly tha
he had said good-by to the lovely Monica, who had reminde
him of another dark beauty of long ago.

A few weeks in a modern hospital had remedied the harshe
after-effects of his short career as a gladiator, and he was read
now for the next episode that fate and the Corps might have i
store. But he would not soon forget Northroyal. . . .

". . . magnificent ingenuity," someone was saying. "Yo
must have assimilated your indoctrination on the background ur
usually thoroughly to have been able to prepare in advance ju:
those artifacts and documents which would prove most essentia
And the technical skill in the production itself. Remarkable. T
think that you were able to hoodwink the high priests of the cu
in the very sanctum sanctorum."

"Merely the result of careful research," Retief said modestly
"I found all I needed on late developments, buried in our file:
The making of the Signet was quite a piece of work; but cred
for that goes to our own technicians."

"I was even more impressed by that document," a youn
counselor said. "What a knowledge of their psychology and c
technical detail that required."

Retief smiled faintly. The others had all gone into the ha
now, amid a babble of conversation. It was time to be going. H
glanced at the eager junior agent.

"No," he said, "I can't claim much credit there. I've had th
document for many years; it, at least, was perfectly genuine."

DREAM DAMSEL

by Evan Hunter

> *In the early 1950s, Evan Hunter (1926-   ), William P. McGivern, and John D. MacDonald all wrote science fiction and fantasy before veering into lives of crime. And while we enjoy their subsequent triumphs, we can't help wishing they'd stayed. Ghosts (1980) provides a recent return of Hunter within the context of his "Ed McBain" 87th Precinct series. But earlier works worth reading include* Find the Feathered Serpent *(1952), a novel of time travel, "Malice in Wonderland" (1954), a preview of drug cultures, "The Fallen Angel," a deal-with-the-devil tale, and "Dream Damsel," a story of wishes and reality.*

I went first to the lady Eloise, since I was her champion, and it was only fair and knightly that she should be the first to know.

There was a fair sky overhead that day, with scudding clouds beyond the bannered towers of Camelot, and below their stately ramparts the rich green curve of the earth bending to meet the eggshell blue of the sky. We sat in the stone courtyard while an attendant played the lute, plucking gently at the strings, and I did not bid him cease because music seemed somehow fitting for the sorrow of the occasion. The lady Eloise sat with her hands

165

folded demurely in her lap, awaiting my pleasure. I raised my visored helmet and said, "Elly . . ."

She lifted incredibly long lashes, tilting her amber eyes to mine. The bodice of her gown rose and fell with her gentle breathing. "Yes, my Lord Larimar," she said.

"I've something on my mind," I told her, "and it behooves me to give tongue to it."

"Give it tongue, then," Eloise said. "Trippingly, I pray you."

I rose and began pacing the courtyard. I had recently jousted with Sir Mordred, and a few of my armor joints were loose, and I'm afraid I made a bit of noise as I paced. I lifted my voice above the noise and said, "As you know, I've been your champion for, lo, these many months."

"Yes, m'lord," she said.

"Many a dragon have I slain for you," I said. I gave heed to the lute music, and corrected it to "for thee," waxing flowery to befit the occasion.

"That's true," Eloise said. "Most true, Larry."

"Yes." I nodded my head, and my helmet rattled. "And many an ogre have I sent to a dishonorable death, Elly, many a vile demon have I decapitated in thy name, wearing thy favor, charging forth to do battle upon my courageous steed, rushing over hill and dale, down valley, across stream . . ."

"Yes, m'lord," Eloise said.

"Yes. And all for thy love, Elly, all for thy undying love."

"Yes, Larry?" she said, puzzled.

"Arthur himself has seen fit to honor me for my undaunting courage, my unwavering valor. I carry now, among others, the Medal of the Sainted Slayer, the *Croix de Tête de Dragon*, and even . . ."

"Yes?" Eloise asked excitedly.

"Even," I said modestly, "the much coveted Clustered Blueberry Sprig."

"You are very brave," Eloise said, lowering her lashes, "and a most true knight, m'lord."

"Fie," I shouted over the music of the lute, "I come not to speak of bravery. For what is bravery?" I snapped my gauntleted fingers. "Bravery is naught!"

"Naught, m'lord?"

"Naught. I come because I must speak my mind, else I cannot live with honor or keep my peace with mine ownself."

"Thine ownself? Speak then, m'lord," Eloise said, "and trippingly, pray you."

"I desire," I said, "to call it quits."

"Sir?"

"Quits. Finis. *Pftt*."

"*Pftt*, m'lord?"

"Pfttt, Elly."

"I see."

"It is not that I do not love thee, Elly," I said. "Perish the thought."

"Perish it," she said.

"For you are lovely and fair and true and constant and a rarity among women. And I am truly nothing when compared to thee."

"True," Eloise said, nodding her head. "That's true."

"So it is not that I do not love thee. It is that . . ."

I paused because my visor fell over my face.

"Yes?"

I lifted the visor. "It is that I love another better than thee."

"Oh."

"Yes."

"Guinevere?" she asked. "Has that wench . . ."

"Nay, not Guinevere, our beloved queen."

"Elaine then? Elaine the fair, Elaine the . . ."

"Nay, nor is it Elaine."

"Pray who then, pray?"

"The lady Agatha."

"The lady who?"

"Agatha."

"I know of no maiden named Agatha. Are you jesting with me, my Lord Larimar? Do you pull my maidenly leg?"

"Nay. There is an Agatha, Elly, and I do love her, and she doth love me, and we do intend to join our plights in holy matrimony."

"I see," Eloise said.

"I have therefore petitioned Arthur to release me from my

vows concerning thee, Eloise. I tell you this now because it would not be fair if I am to marry Agatha, which I fully intend doing, to maintain me as a champion when my heart would elsewhere be.''

"I see," Eloise said again.

"Yes. I hope you understand, Elly. I hope we can still be friends."

"Of course," Eloise said, smiling weakly. "And I suppose you'll want your Alpha Beta Tau pin back."

"Keep it," I said magnanimously. And then, to show how magnanimous I really was, I reached into my tunic and said, "Ho, lute player! Here are a pair of dragon ears for thee, for thy fine music!"

The lute player dropped to the stones and kissed both my feet, and I smiled graciously.

I killed two small dragons that day, catching the second one with my mace before he'd even had a chance to breathe any fire upon me. I cut off their heads and slung them over my jeweled saddle and then rode back to the shining spires of Camelot. Launcelot and Guinevere were just leaving for their afternoon constitutional, so I waved at them and then took my gallant steed to the stables, where I left him with my squire, a young boy named Gawain.

I wandered about a bit, watching Merlin playing pinochle with some unsuspecting knight trainees, and then stopping to pass the time of day with Galahad, a fellow I've never enjoyed talking to because his white armor and helmet are so blinding in the sun. Besides, he is a bit of a braggart, and I soon tired of his talk and went to eat a small lunch of roast pheasant, lamb mutton, cheese, bread, wine, nuts, apples, and grapes, topping it off with one of Arthur's best cigars.

I went back to the stables after lunch to get my gallant steed and then I rode in the jousting exercises, knocking Mordred for a row of beer barrels, and being in turn knocked head over teacups by Launcelot, whose ride with Guinivere seemed to have done him well.

I gathered myself together afterwards, and was leading my horse back to the stables when Arthur caught up with me.

"Larry!" he called. "Ho there, Larry! Wait up!"

I stopped and waited for Arthur to come alongside, and I said, "What's up, beloved king?"

"Just what I wanted to ask you, Larry," he said, blowing out a tremendous cloud of cigar smoke. "What *is* all this nonsense?"

"What nonsense, my liege?"

"About wanting to break your champion vows. Now, hell, Larry, that just isn't done, and you know it."

"It's the only honorable thing to do, Art," I said.

"Honor, shmonor," Arthur answered. "I'm thinking of the paper work involved. These dispensations are a pain in the neck, Larry. After all, you should have thought of this when you took the vows. Any knight . . ."

"I'm sorry, Art," I said, "but it's the only way. I've given it a lot of thought, believe me."

"But I don't understand," Arthur said, blowing some more smoke at me. "What's wrong between you and Elly? Now, she's a damn fine kid, Larry, and I hope . . ."

"She *is* a damn fine kid," I agreed, "but it's all off between us."

"Why?"

"I've found another damsel."

"This Agatha? Now look, Larry, this is old Artie you're talking to, and not some kid still wet behind the ears. Now you know as well as I do that there's no Agatha in my court, so now . . ."

"I know that, Art. I never said she was in your court."

"But you call her the Lady Agatha!" Arthur said.

"I know."

"A foreign broad?" Arthur asked.

"No. A dream damsel."

"A *what?*"

"A dream damsel. I dream her."

"Now, what was that again, Larry?"

"I dream her. I dream the Lady Agatha."

"That's what I thought you . . . say, Larry, did Launcelot hurt you today during the joust? He plays rough, that fellow, and I've been meaning to . . ."

"No, he didn't hurt me at all. Few ribs, but nothing serious. I really do dream my lady, Art."

"You mean at night? When you're asleep?"

"Aye."

"You mean you just think her up?"

"Aye."

"Yes you. Do you think her up?"

"That's what I'm trying to tell you."

"Then she isn't real?" Arthur asked.

"Oh, she's real all right. Not during the day, of course, but when I dream her up at night, she's real as can be."

"Foo," Arthur said. "This is all nonsense. Now you get back to Elly and tell her . . ."

"No, my liege," I said. "I intend to marry the lady Agatha."

"But she's only a dream!" Arthur protested.

"Not *only* a dream, noble king. Much more than a dream to me. A woman of flesh and blood. A woman who loves me truly, and whom I do truly love."

"Fie," Arthur said. "You're being absurd. I'll send Merlin around to say a few incantations over you. You're probably bewitched."

"Nay, my lord, I'm not bewitched. I dream the lady Agatha of my own accord. There's no enchantment whatever attached to it."

"No enchantment, eh? Perhaps you've been taking to the grape then, Larry? Perhaps the enchantment is all in a cup?"

"Nay, that neither. I tell you I dream her of my own accord."

Arthur puffed on his cigar again.

"How on earth do you do that?"

"It's really quite simple," I said. "I set me down on my couch, and I close my eyes, and I visualize a damsel with blond hair and blue eyes, and lips like the blushing rose, and skin like Oriental ivory. Carmine nails, like pointed drops of blood, and an hourglass waist. A voice like the brush of velvet, flanks like a good horse in joust, a wit as sharp as any pike, a magic as potent as Merlin's. That is my lady Agatha, Art. I visualize her and then I fall asleep, and she materializes."

"She . . . materializes," Arthur said, stroking his beard.

"Aye. And she loves me."

"You?" Arthur asked, examining me with scrutiny.

"Yes, me." I paused. "What's wrong with that?"

"Nothing, nothing," Arthur said hastily. "But tell me, Larry, how do you plan on marrying her? I mean, a dream, after all. . ."

"Look at it this way, Art," I said. "During the daytime, I go to work anyway. There's always another dragon to kill, or some giant to fell, and ogres by the dozen, Lord knows, not to mention other assorted monsters of various sizes and shapes, and maidens in distress, and sea serpents, and . . . oh, you know. You've been in the business much longer than I."

"So?"

"So what does a man need a wife for during the daytime? He'd never get to see her anyway. Do you follow me?"

"Yes," Arthur said, "but . . ."

"Therefore, I'll marry the lady Agatha and see her at night, when most knights see their wives anyway. Why, I wouldn't be surprised if that's why they're called knights, Art."

"But how do you propose to marry her? Who will . . ."

"I shall dream a friar, and he shall marry us."

"I do believe you've been slaying too many dragons, my Lord Larimar," Arthur said. "After all, your dream girl—in all fairness—doesn't sound any lovelier than the fair Eloise."

I poked the king in the ribs and said, "Art, you're just getting old, that's all."

"Maybe so, boy," he reflected, "but I think I'll send Merlin around, anyway. Few incantations never hurt anyone."

"Art, please . . ."

"He's salaried," Arthur said, and so I conceded. . . .

Merlin and Eloise came to me together, he looking very wise and very magical in his pointed hat and flowing robes; she looking very sad and very lovely, though not as lovely as my lady Agatha.

"Tell me," Merlin said, "all about your dream damsel."

"What is there to tell?"

"Well, what does she look like?"

"She's blond . . ."

"Um-huh, then we shall need some condor livers," Merlin said.

"And blue-eyed," I went on.

"Then we'll need a few dragon eggs, pastel-hued."

"And . . . oh, she's very lovely."

"I see," Merlin said wisely. "And do you love her?"

"I do indeed."

"And she you?" he asked, cocking an eyebrow.

"Verily."

"She truthfully loves thee?"

"Of course."

"She is lovely you say, and she loves—forgive me—*thee?*"

"Why, yes," I said.

"She loves . . . *thee?*"

"Three times already has she loved me, and still you do not hear? Turn up your hearing aid, wizard," I said.

"Forgive me," Merlin said, shaking his head. "I just . . ."

"She has told me upon many an occasion that I am just what she has been waiting for," I said. "Tall, manly, bold, courageous and very handsome!"

"She said these things about *you?*" Merlin asked.

"Yes, of course."

"That you were the man she waited for? That you were . . . tall?"

"Yes."

"And . . . and manly?"

"Yes."

Merlin coughed, perhaps first realizing how tall and manly I really was. "And . . . and . . ." He coughed again. ". . . handsome?"

"All those," I said.

Merlin continued coughing until I thought he would choke. "And all those she waited for, and all those she found in . . ." He coughed again. ". . . *you?*"

"And why not, wizard?" I asked.

"You are truly bewitched, Lord Larimar," he said, "truly."

He pulled back the sleeve of his robe, and spread his fingers wide, and then he said, "*Alla-bah-roo-muh-jig-bah-roo, zing, zatch, zootch!*"

I listened to the incantation and I yawned. But apparently Eloise was taking all this nonsense to heart because she stared at

Merlin wide-eyed, looking lovely but not so lovely as my lady Agatha, and then she looked at me, and her eyes got wider and wider and wider. . . .

Oh, there was so much to do in preparation. My dispensation from Arthur came through the next week, and I went about busily making plans for my wedding to Agatha. I wanted to dream up something really special, something that would never be forgotten as long as England had a history. I wanted a big wedding, and so I had to plan beforehand so that I could dream it all up in one night, which was no easy task.

I wanted to dream up the entire court on white stallions, their shields blazing, their swords held high to catch the gleaming rays of the sun, the gallery packed with damsels in pink and white and the palest blue. I wanted to dream the banners of Camelot fluttering in green and yellow and orange over the towers, with a pale sky beyond, and a mild breeze blowing. I wanted to dream a friar who would be droll and yet serious, chucklingly fat, but piously religious.

And most of all, I wanted to dream the lady Agatha in her wedding gown, a fine thing of lace and pearls, with a low bodice and a hip-hugging waist. All these things I wanted to dream, and they had to be planned beforehand. So what with slaying dragons and ogres and planning for the wedding, I was a fairly busy young knight, and I didn't get around to visiting Eloise again until the night before the wedding.

Her lady-in-waiting was most cordial.

"My mistress is asleep," she said.

"Asleep?" I glanced at my hourglass. "Why, it's only four minutes past six."

"She has been retiring early of late," the woman said.

"Poor child," I said, wagging my head. "Her heart is doubtless breaking. Ah well, *c'est la guerre*."

"*C'est*," the woman said.

"When she awakes on the morrow, tell her I am going to dream her a seat of honor at the wedding. Tell her. She will be pleased."

"Sir?"

"Just tell her. She'll understand."

"Yes, sir."

"Matter of fact," I said, "I'd better get to bed myself. Want to practice up. I've got a lot to dream tomorrow night."

"Sir?"

"Never mind," I said. I reached into my tunic and said, "Here's a dragon's tooth for lending a kind ear."

I ripped the tooth from my hourglass fob and deposited it in her excitedly overwhelmed, shaking, grateful palm.

Then I went home and to bed and to dream of my lady Agatha.

I went first to the lady Eloise on the morrow, since it was only fair and knightly that she should be the first to know. I did no raise my visor for I did not desire her to see my face.

"Elly," I said, "I've got something on my mind, and i behooves me to give tongue to it."

"Give it tongue, then," Eloise said. "Trippingly, pray you."

"It's all off," I told her. "The lady Agatha and me. We're through. She called it quits."

"Quits?" Eloise said. "Finis? *Pfttt?*"

"Even so," I said.

"Really now," Eloise said, smiling.

"There's someone else, Elly. My lady Agatha has someone else. Someone taller, manlier, handsomer. I know it's hard to believe. But there is someone else, someone who just came along . . . suddenly."

"How terrible for you," Eloise said happily.

"Yes. I can't understand it. He just popped up, just like that right there beside her. I . . . I saw him, Elly, a big handsom knight on a white horse. Right there in my dream, I saw him."

"Did you really?" Eloise asked sadly, clapping her hand together.

"Yes," I said. "So she wants him, and not me. So I thought if you'll still have me, Elly, if you'll still take me as you champion . . ."

"Well . . ."

". . . and perhaps someday as your husband, then . . ."

Eloise stepped forward, and there was a twinkle in her ey when she lifted my visor.

"You're tall and manly and handsome enough for me, you goof," she said. I looked at her and suddenly remembered that she'd been doing an awful lot of sleeping lately, and I started to say, "Hey!"

But she wrapped her arms around my armor and kissed me soundly on the mouth, and all I could do was stare at her in wonder and murmur, "Eloise! I never dreamed!"

Eloise smiled secretly and said, "*I* did."

THE LAST DEFENDER
OF CAMELOT

by Roger Zelazny

A master of shorter works, Roger Zelazny (1937–   ) has won the Prix Apollo as well as the Hugo, Nebula, and American Library Association awards. Notable stories include "A Rose for Ecclesiastes" (1963), "The Doors of His Face, the Lamps of His Mouth" (1965), "For a Breath I Tarry" (1966), Lord of Light (1968), and "Home Is the Hangman" (1975). Character depiction and style are perhaps his greatest strengths, and, as illustrated by the following Arthurian tale, much of his material is developed from myths, occult belief systems, or religions.

The three muggers who stopped him that October night in San Francisco did not anticipate much resistance from the old man, despite his size. He was well-dressed, and that was sufficient.

The first approached him with his hand extended. The other two hung back a few paces.

"Just give me your wallet and your watch," the mugger said. "You'll save yourself a lot of trouble."

The old man's grip shifted on his walking stick. His shoulders straightened. His shock of white hair tossed as he turned his head to regard the other.

"Why don't you come and take them?"

The mugger began another step but he never completed it. The stick was almost invisible in the speed of its swinging. It struck him on the left temple and he fell.

Without pausing, the old man caught the stick by its middle with his left hand, advanced and drove it into the belly of the next nearest man. Then, with an upward hook as the man doubled, he caught him in the softness beneath the jaw, behind the chin, with its point. As the man fell, he clubbed him with its butt on the back of the neck.

The third man had reached out and caught the old man's upper arm by then. Dropping the stick, the old man seized the mugger shirtfront with his left hand, his belt with his right, raised him from the ground until he held him at arm's length above his head and slammed him against the side of the building to his right, releasing him as he did so.

He adjusted his apparel, ran a hand through his hair and retrieved his walking stick. For a moment he regarded the three fallen forms, then shrugged and continued on his way.

There were sounds of traffic from somewhere off to his left. He turned right at the next corner. The moon appeared above tall buildings as he walked. The smell of the ocean was on the air. It had rained earlier and the pavement still shone beneath streetlamps. He moved slowly, pausing occasionally to examine the contents of darkened shop windows.

After perhaps ten minutes, he came upon a side street showing more activity than any of the others he had passed. There was a drugstore, still open, on the corner, a diner farther up the block and several well-lighted storefronts. A number of people were walking along the far side of the street. A boy coasted by on a bicycle. He turned there, his pale eyes regarding everything he passed.

Halfway up the block, he came to a dirty window on which was painted the word READINGS. Beneath it were displayed the outline of a hand and a scattering of playing cards. As he passed the open door, he glanced inside. A brightly garbed woman, her hair bound back in a green kerchief, sat smoking at the rear of the room. She smiled as their eyes met and crooked an index finger toward herself. He smiled back and turned away, but . .

He looked at her again. What was it? He glanced at his watch.

Turning, he entered the shop and moved to stand before her. She rose. She was small, barely over five feet in height.

"Your eyes," he remarked, "are green. Most gypsies I know have dark eyes."

She shrugged.

"You take what you get in life. Have you a problem?"

"Give me a moment and I'll think of one," he said. "I just came in here because you remind me of someone and it bothers me—I can't think who."

"Come into the back," she said, "and sit down. We'll talk."

He nodded and followed her into a small room to the rear. A threadbare oriental rug covered the floor near the small table at which they seated themselves. Zodiacal prints and faded psychedelic posters of a semireligious nature covered the walls. A crystal ball stood on a small stand in the far corner beside a vase of cut flowers. A dark, long-haired cat slept on a sofa to the right of it. A door to another room stood slightly ajar beyond the sofa. The only illumination came from a cheap lamp on the table before him and from a small candle in a plaster base atop the shawl-covered coffee table.

He leaned forward and studied her face, then shook his head and leaned back.

She flicked an ash onto the floor.

"Your problem?" she suggested.

He sighed.

"Oh, I don't really have a problem anyone can help me with. Look, I think I made a mistake coming in here. I'll pay you for your trouble, though, just as if you'd given me a reading. How much is it?"

He began to reach for his wallet, but she raised her hand.

"Is it that you do not believe in such things?" she asked, her eyes scrutinizing his face.

"No, quite the contrary," he replied. "I am willing to believe in magic, divination and all manner of spells and sendings, angelic and demonic. But—"

"But not from someone in a dump like this?"

He smiled.

"No offense," he said.

A whistling sound filled the air. It seemed to come from the next room back.

"That's all right," she said, "but my water is boiling. I'd forgotten it was on. Have some tea with me? I do wash the cups. No charge. Things are slow."

"All right."

She rose and departed.

He glanced at the door to the front but eased himself back into his chair, resting his large, blue-veined hands on its padded arms. He sniffed then, nostrils flaring, and cocked his head as at some half-familiar aroma.

After a time, she returned with a tray, set it on the coffee table. The cat stirred, raised her head, blinked at it, stretched, closed her eyes again.

"Cream and sugar?"

"Please. One lump."

She placed two cups on the table before him.

"Take either one," she said.

He smiled and drew the one on his left toward him. She placed an ashtray in the middle of the table and returned to her own seat, moving the other cup to her place.

"That wasn't necessary," he said, placing his hands on the table.

She shrugged.

"You don't know me. Why should you trust me? Probably got a lot of money on you."

He looked at her face again. She had apparently removed some of the heavier makeup while in the back room. The jawline, the brow . . . He looked away. He took a sip of tea.

"Good tea. Not instant," he said. "Thanks."

"So you believe in all sorts of magic?" she asked, sipping her own.

"Some," he said.

"Any special reason why?"

"Some of it works."

"For example?"

He gestured aimlessly with his left hand.

"I've traveled a lot. I've seen some strange things."

"And you have no problems?"

He chuckled.

"Still determined to give me a reading? All right. I'll tell you a little about myself and what I want right now, and you can tell me whether I'll get it. Okay?"

"I'm listening."

"I am a buyer for a large gallery in the East. I am something of an authority on ancient work in precious metals. I am in town to attend an auction of such items from the estate of a private collector. I will go to inspect the pieces tomorrow. Naturally, I hope to find something good. What do you think my chances are?"

"Give me your hands."

He extended them, palms upward. She leaned forward and regarded them. She looked back up at him immediately.

"Your wrists have more rascettes than I can count!"

"Yours seem to have quite a few, also."

She met his eyes for only a moment and returned her attention to his hands. He noted that she had paled beneath what remained of her makeup, and her breathing was now irregular.

"No," she finally said, drawing back, "you are not going to find here what you are looking for."

Her hand trembled slightly as she raised her teacup. He frowned.

"I asked only in jest," he said. "Nothing to get upset about. I doubted I would find what I am really looking for, anyway."

She shook her head.

"Tell me your name."

"I've lost my accent," he said, "but I'm French. The name is DuLac."

She stared into his eyes and began to blink rapidly.

"No . . ." she said. "No."

"I'm afraid so. What's yours?"

"Madam LeFay," she said. "I just repainted that sign. It's still drying."

He began to laugh, but it froze in his throat.

"Now—I know—who—you remind me of. . . ."

"You reminded me of someone, also. Now I, too, know."

Her eyes brimmed, her mascara ran.

"It couldn't be," he said. "Not here. . . . Not in a place like this. . . ."

"You dear man," she said softly, and she raised his right hand to her lips. She seemed to choke for a moment, then said, "I had thought that I was the last, and yourself buried at Joyous Gard. I never dreamed . . ." Then, "This?" gesturing about the room. "Only because it amuses me, helps to pass the time. The waiting—"

She stopped. She lowered his hand.

"Tell me about it," she said.

"The waiting?" he said. "For what do you wait?"

"Peace," she said. "I am here by the power of my arts, through all the long years. But you—how did you manage it?"

"I—" He took another drink of tea. He looked about the room. "I do not know how to begin," he said. "I survived the final battles, saw the kingdom sundered, could do nothing—and at last departed England. I wandered, taking service at many courts, and after a time under many names, as I saw that I was not aging—or aging very, very slowly. I was in India, China—I fought in the Crusades. I've been everywhere. I've spoken with magicians and mystics—most of them charlatans, a few with the power, none so great as Merlin—and what had come to be my own belief was confirmed by one of them, a man more than half charlatan, yet . . ." He paused and finished his tea. "Are you certain you want to hear all this?" he asked.

"I want to hear it. Let me bring more tea first, though."

She returned with the tea. She lit a cigarette and leaned back. "Go on."

"I decided that it was—my sin," he said, "with . . . the Queen."

"I don't understand."

"I betrayed my Liege, who was also my friend, in the one thing which must have hurt him most. The love I felt was stronger than loyalty or friendship—and even today, to this day, it still is. I cannot repent, and so I cannot be forgiven. Those were strange and magical times. We lived in a land destined to become myth. Powers walked the realm in those days, forces which are now gone from the earth. How or why, I cannot say. But you know that it is true. I am somehow of a piece with those gone things, and the laws that rule my existence are not normal laws of the natural world. I believe that I cannot die; that it has fallen my lot, as punishment, to wander the world till I have completed the Quest. I believe I will only know rest the day I find the Holy Grail. Giuseppe Balsamo, before he became known as Cagliostro, somehow saw this and said it to me just as I had thought it, though I never said a word of it to him. And so I have traveled the world, searching. I go no more as knight, or soldier, but as an appraiser. I have been in nearly every museum on Earth, viewed all the great private collections. So far, it has eluded me."

"You *are* getting a little old for battle."

He snorted.

"I have never lost," he stated flatly. "Down ten centuries, I have never lost a personal contest. It is true that I have aged, yet whenever I am threatened all of my former strength returns to me. But, look where I may, fight where I may, it has never served me to discover that which I must find. I feel I am unforgiven and must wander like the Eternal Jew until the end of the world."

She lowered her head.

". . . And you say I will not find it tomorrow?"

"You will never find it," she said softly.

"You saw that in my hand?"

She shook her head.

"Your story is fascinating and your theory novel," she began, "but Cagliostro was a total charlatan. Something must have betrayed your thoughts, and he made a shrewd guess. But he was wrong. I say that you will never find it, not because you are unworthy or unforgiven. No, never that. A more loyal subject than yourself never drew breath. Don't you know that Arthur forgave you? It was an arranged marriage. The same thing happened constantly elsewhere, as you must know. You gave her something he could not. There was only tenderness there. He understood. The only forgiveness you require is that which has been withheld all these long years—your own. No, it is not a doom that has been laid upon you. It is your own feelings which led you to assume an impossible quest, something tantamount to total unforgiveness. But you have suffered all these centuries upon the wrong trail."

When she raised her eyes, she saw that his were hard, like ice or gemstones. But she met his gaze and continued: "There is not now, was not then, and probably never was, a Holy Grail."

"I saw it," he said, "that day it passed through the Hall of the Table. We all saw it."

"You thought you saw it," she corrected him. "I hate to shatter an illusion that has withstood all the other tests of time, but I fear I must. The kingdom, as you recall, was at that time in turmoil. The knights were growing restless and falling away from the fellowship. A year—six months, even—and all would have collapsed, all Arthur had striven so hard to put together. He knew that the longer Camelot stood, the longer its name would endure, the stronger its ideals would become. So he made a decision, a purely political one. Something was needed to hold things together. He called upon Merlin, already half-mad, yet still shrewd enough to see what was needed and able to provide it. The Quest was born. Merlin's powers created the illusion you saw that day. It was a lie, yes. A glorious lie, though. And it served for years after to bind you all in brotherhood, in the name of justice and love. It entered literature, it promoted mobility and the higher ends of culture. It served its purpose. But it was— never—really—there. You have been chasing a ghost. I am sorry Launcelot, but I have absolutely no reason to lie to you. I know magic when I see it. I saw it then. That is how it happened."

For a long while he was silent. Then he laughed.

"You have an answer for everything," he said. "I could almost believe you, if you could but answer me one thing more—Why am I here? For what reason? By what power? How is it I have been preserved for half the Christian era while other men grow old and die in a handful of years? Can you tell me now what Cagliostro could not?"

"Yes," she said, "I believe that I can."

He rose to his feet and began to pace. The cat, alarmed, sprang from the sofa and ran into the back room. He stooped and snatched up his walking stick. He started for the door.

"I suppose it was worth waiting a thousand years to see you afraid," she said.

He halted.

"That is unfair," he replied.

"I know. But now you will come back and sit down," she said.

He was smiling once more as he turned and returned.

"Tell me," he said. "How do you see it?"

"Yours was the last enchantment of Merlin, that is how I see it."

"Merlin? Me? Why?"

"Gossip had it the old goat took Nimue into the woods and she had to use one of his own spells on him in self-defense—a spell which caused him to sleep forever in some lost place. If it was the spell that I believe it was, then at least part of the rumor was incorrect. There was no known counterspell, but the effects of the enchantment would have caused him to sleep not forever but for a millennium or so, and then to awaken. My guess now is that his last conscious act before he dropped off was to lay this enchantment upon you, so that you would be on hand when he returned."

"I suppose it might be possible, but why would he want me or need me?"

"If I were journeying into a strange time, I would want an ally once I reached it. And if I had a choice, I would want it to be the greatest champion of the day."

"Merlin . . ." he mused. "I suppose that it could be as you say. Excuse me, but a long life has just been shaken up, from beginning to end. If this is true . . ."

"I am sure that it is."

"If this is true . . . A millennium, you say?"

"More or less."

"Well, it is almost that time now."

"I know. I do not believe that our meeting tonight was a matter of chance. You are destined to meet him upon his awakening, which should be soon. Something has ordained that you meet me first, however, to be warned."

"Warned? Warned of what?"

"He is mad, Launcelot. Many of us felt a great relief at his passing. If the realm had not been sundered finally by strife it would probably have been broken by his hand, anyway."

"That I find difficult to believe. He was always a strange man—for who can fully understand a sorcerer?—and in his later years he did seem at least partly daft. But he never struck me as evil.''

"Nor was he. His was the most dangerous morality of all. He was a misguided idealist. In a more primitive time and place and with a willing tool like Arthur, he was able to create a legend. Today, in an age of monstrous weapons, with the right leader as his catspaw, he could unleash something totally devastating. He would see a wrong and force his man to try righting it. He would do it in the name of the same high ideal he always served, but he would not appreciate the results until it was too late. How could he—even if he were sane? He has no conception of modern international relations.'' ·

"What is to be done? What is my part in all of this?''

"I believe you should go back, to England, to be present at his awakening, to find out exactly what he wants, to try to reason with him.''

"I don't know . . . How would I find him?''

"You found me. When the time is right, you will be in the proper place. I am certain of that. It was meant to be, probably even a part of his spell. Seek him. But do not trust him.''

"I don't know, Morgana." He looked at the wall, unseeing. "I don't know.''

"You have waited this long and you draw back now from finally finding out?''

"You are right—in that much, at least." He folded his hands, raised them and rested his chin upon them. "What I would do if he really returned, I do not know. Try to reason with him, yes. Have you any other advice?''

"Just that you be there.''

"You've looked at my hand. You have the power. What did you see?''

She turned away.

"It is uncertain," she said.

That night he dreamed, as he sometimes did, of times long gone. They sat about the great Table, as they had on that day. Gawain was there, and Percival. Galahad . . . He winced. This day was different from other days. There was a certain tension in the air, a before-the-storm feeling, an electrical thing. . . . Merlin stood at the far end of the room, hands in the sleeves of his long robe, hair and beard snowy and unkempt, pale eyes staring—at what, none could be certain. . . .

After some timeless time, a reddish glow appeared near the door. All eyes moved toward it. It grew brighter and advanced slowly into the room—a formless apparition of light. There were sweet odors and some few soft strains of music. Gradually, a form began to take shape at its center, resolving itself into the likeness of a chalice. . . .

He felt himself rising, moving slowly, following it in its course through the great chamber, advancing upon it, soundlessly and deliberately, as if moving underwater . . .

. . . Reaching for it.

His hand entered the circle of light, moved toward its center, neared the now blazing cup and passed through. . . .

Immediately, the light faded. The outline of the chalice wavered, and it collapsed in upon itself, fading, fading, gone. . . .

There came a sound, rolling, echoing about the hall. Laughter.

He turned and regarded the others. They sat about the table, watching him, laughing. Even Merlin managed a dry chuckle.

Suddenly, his great blade was in his hand, and he raised it as he strode toward the Table. The knights nearest him drew back as he brought the weapon crashing down.

The Table split in half and fell. The room shook.

The quaking continued. Stones were dislodged from the walls. A roof beam fell. He raised his arm.

The entire castle began to come apart, falling about him, and still the laughter continued.

He awoke damp with perspiration and lay still for a long while. In the morning, he bought a ticket for London.

Two of the three elemental sounds of the world were suddenly with him as he walked that evening, stick in hand. For a dozen days, he had hiked about Cornwall, finding no clues to that which he sought. He had allowed himself two more before giving up and departing.

Now the wind and the rain were upon him, and he increased his pace. The fresh-lit stars were smothered by a mass of cloud and wisps of fog grew like ghostly fungi on either hand. He moved among trees, paused, continued on.

"Shouldn't have stayed out this late," he muttered, and after several more pauses, *"Nel mezzo del cammin di nostra vita mi ritrovai per una selva oscura, che la diritta via era smarrita."* Then he chuckled, halting beneath a tree.

The rain was not heavy. It was more a fine mist now. A bright patch in the lower heavens showed where the moon hung veiled.

He wiped his face, turned up his collar. He studied the position of the moon. After a time, he struck off to his right. There was a faint rumble of thunder in the distance.

The fog continued to grow about him as he went. Soggy leaves made squishing noises beneath his boots. An animal of indeterminate size bolted from a clump of shrubbery beside a cluster of rocks and tore off through the darkness.

Five minutes . . . ten . . . He cursed softly. The rainfall had increased in intensity. Was that the same rock?

He turned in a complete circle. All directions were equally uninviting. Selecting one at random, he commenced walking once again.

Then, in the distance, he discerned a spark, a glow, a wavering light. It vanished and reappeared periodically, as though partly blocked, the line of sight a function of his movements. He headed toward it. After perhaps half a minute, it was gone again from sight, but he continued on in what he thought to be its direction. There came another roll of thunder, louder this time.

When it seemed that it might have been illusion or some short-lived natural phenomenon, something else occurred in that same direction. There was a movement, a shadow-within-shadow shuffling at the foot of a great tree. He slowed his pace, approaching the spot cautiously.

There!

A figure detached itself from a pool of darkness ahead and to the left. Manlike, it moved with a slow and heavy tread, creaking sounds emerging from the forest floor beneath it. A vagrant moonbeam touched it for a moment, and it appeared yellow and metallically slick beneath moisture.

He halted. It seemed that he had just regarded a knight in full armor in his path. How long since he had beheld such a sight? He shook his head and stared.

The figure had also halted. It raised its right arm in a beckoning gesture, then turned and began to walk away. He hesitated for only a moment, then followed.

It turned off to the left and pursued a treacherous path, rocky, slippery, heading slightly downward. He actually used his stick now, to assure his footing, as he tracked its deliberate progress. He gained on it, to the point where he could clearly hear the metallic scraping sounds of its passage.

Then it was gone, swallowed by a greater darkness.

He advanced to the place where he had last beheld it. He stood in the lee of a great mass of stone. He reached out and probed it with his stick.

He tapped steadily along its nearest surface, and then the stick moved past it. He followed.

There was an opening, a crevice. He had to turn sidewise to pass within it, but as he did the full glow of the light he had seen came into sight for several seconds.

The passage curved and widened, leading him back and down. Several times, he paused and listened, but there were no sounds other than his own breathing.

He withdrew his handkerchief and dried his face and hands carefully. He brushed moisture from his coat, turned down his collar. He scuffed the mud and leaves from his boots. He adjusted his apparel. Then he strode forward, rounding a final corner, into a chamber lit by a small oil lamp suspended by three delicate chains from some point in the darkness overhead. The yellow knight stood unmoving beside the far wall. On a fiber mat atop a stony pedestal directly beneath the lamp lay an old man in tattered garments. His bearded face was half-masked by shadows.

He moved to the old man's side. He saw then that those ancient dark eyes were open.

"Merlin . . . ?" he whispered.

There came a faint hissing sound, a soft croak. Realizing the source, he leaned nearer.

"Elixir . . . in earthen rock . . . on ledge . . . in back," came the gravelly whisper.

He turned and sought the ledge, the container.

"Do you know where it is?" he asked the yellow figure.

It neither stirred nor replied, but stood like a display piece. He turned away from it then and sought further. After a time, he located it. It was more a niche than a ledge, blending in with the wall, cloaked with shadow. He ran his fingertips over the container's contours, raised it gently. Something liquid stirred within it. He wiped its lip on his sleeve after he had returned to the lighted area. The wind whistled past the entranceway and he thought he felt the faint vibration of thunder.

Sliding one hand beneath his shoulders, he raised the ancient form. Merlin's eyes still seemed unfocused. He moistened Merlin's lips with the liquid. The old man licked them, and after several moments opened his mouth. He administered a sip, then another and another. . . .

Merlin signaled for him to lower him, and he did. He glanced again at the yellow armor, but it had remained motionless the entire while. He looked back at the sorcerer and saw that a new light had come into his eyes and he was studying him, smiling faintly.

"Feel better?"

Merlin nodded. A minute passed, and a touch of color appeared upon his cheeks. He elbowed himself into a sitting position and took the container into his hands. He raised it and drank deeply.

He sat still for several minutes after that. His thin hands which had appeared waxy in the flamelight, grew darker, fuller. His shoulders straightened. He placed the crock on the bed beside him and stretched his arms. His joints creaked the first time he did it, but not the second. He swung his legs over the edge of the bed and rose slowly to his feet. He was a full head shorter than Launcelot.

"It is done," he said, staring back into the shadows. "Much has happened, of course. . . ."

"Much has happened," Launcelot replied.

"You have lived through it all. Tell me, is the world a better place or is it worse than it was in those days?"

"Better in some ways, worse in others. It is different."

"How is it better?"

"There are many ways of making life easier, and the sum total of human knowledge has increased vastly."

"How has it worsened?"

"There are many more people in the world. Consequently, there are many more people suffering from poverty, disease, ignorance. The world itself has suffered great depredation, in the way of pollution and other assaults on the integrity of nature."

"Wars?"

"There is always someone fighting, somewhere."

"They need help."

"Maybe. Maybe not."

Merlin turned and looked into his eyes.

"What do you mean?"

"People haven't changed. They are as rational—and irrational—as they were in the old days. They are as moral and law-abiding—and not—as ever. Many new things have been learned, many new situations evolved, but I do not believe that the nature of man has altered significantly in the time you've slept. Nothing you do is going to change that. You may be able to alter a few features of the times, but would it really be proper to meddle? Everything is so interdependent today that even you would not be able to predict all the consequences of any actions you take. You might do more harm than good; and whatever you do, man's nature will remain the same."

"This isn't like you, Lance. You were never much given to philosophizing in the old days."

"I've had a long time to think about it."

"And I've had a long time to dream about it. War is your craft, Lance. Stay with that."

"I gave it up a long time ago."

"Then what are you now?"

"An appraiser."

Merlin turned away, took another drink. He seemed to radiate a fierce energy when he turned again.

"And your oath? To right wrongs, to punish the wicked . . . ?"

"The longer I lived the more difficult it became to determine what was a wrong and who was wicked. Make it clear to me again and I may go back into business."

"Galahad would never have addressed me so."

"Galahad was young, naive, trusting. Speak not to me of my son."

"Launcelot! Launcelot!" He placed a hand on his arm. "Why all this bitterness for an old friend who has done nothing for a thousand years?"

"I wished to make my position clear immediately. I feared you might contemplate some irreversible action which could alter the world balance of power fatally. I want you to know that I will not be party to it."

"Admit that you do not know what I might do, what I can do."

"Freely. That is why I fear you. What *do* you intend to do?"

"Nothing, at first. I wish merely to look about me, to see for myself some of these changes of which you have spoken. Then I will consider which wrongs need righting, who needs punishment, and who to choose as my champions. I will show you these things, and then you can go back into business, as you say."

Launcelot sighed.

"The burden of proof is on the moralist. Your judgment is no longer sufficient for me."

"Dear me," the other replied, "it is sad to have waited this long for an encounter of this sort, to find you have lost your faith in me. My powers are beginning to return already, Lance. Do you not feel magic in the air?"

"I feel something I have not felt in a long while."

"The sleep of ages was a restorative—an aid, actually. In a while, Lance, I am going to be stronger than I ever was before. And you doubt that I will be able to turn back the clock?"

"I doubt you can do it in a fashion to benefit anybody. Look, Merlin, I'm sorry. I do not like it that things have come to this either. But I have lived too long, seen too much, know too much of how the world works now to trust any one man's opinion concerning its salvation. Let it go. You are a mysterious, revered legend. I do not know what you really are. But forgo exercising your powers in any sort of crusade. Do something else this time around. Become a physician and fight pain. Take up painting. Be a professor of history, an antiquarian. Hell, be a social critic and point out what evils you see for people to correct themselves."

"Do you really believe I could be satisfied with any of those things?"

"Men find satisfaction in many things. It depends on the man, not on the things. I'm just saying that you should avoid using your powers in any attempt to effect social changes as we once did, by violence."

"Whatever changes have been wrought, time's greatest irony lies in its having transformed you into a pacifist."

"You are wrong."

"Admit it! You have finally come to fear the clash of arms! An appraiser! What kind of knight are you?"

"One who finds himself in the wrong time and the wrong place, Merlin."

The sorcerer shrugged and turned away.

"Let it be, then. It is good that you have chosen to tell me all these things immediately. Thank you for that, anyway. A moment."

Merlin walked to the rear of the cave, returned in moments attired in fresh garments. The effect was startling. His entire appearance was more kempt and cleanly. His hair and beard now appeared gray rather than white. His step more sure and steady. He held a staff in his right hand but did not lean upon it.

"Come walk with me," he said.

"It is a bad night."

"It is not the same night you left without. It is not even the same place."

As he passed the suit of yellow armor, he snapped his fingers near its visor. With a single creak, the figure moved and turned to follow him.

"Who is that?"

Merlin smiled.

"No one," he replied, and he reached back and raised the visor. The helmet was empty. "It is enchanted, animated by a spirit," he said. "A trifle clumsy, though, which is why I did not trust it to administer my draught. A perfect servant, however, unlike some. Incredibly strong and swift. Even in your prime you could not have beaten it. I fear nothing when it walks with me. Come, there is something I would have you see."

"Very well."

Launcelot followed Merlin and the hollow knight from the cave. The rain had stopped, and it was very still. They stood on an incredibly moonlit plain where mists drifted and grasses sparkled. Shadowy shapes stood in the distance.

"Excuse me," Launcelot said. "I left my walking stick inside." He turned and reentered the cave.

"Yes, fetch it, old man," Merlin replied. "Your strength is already on the wane."

When Launcelot returned, he leaned upon the stick and squinted across the plain.

"This way," Merlin said, "to where your questions will be answered. I will try not to move too quickly and tire you."

"Tire me?"

The sorcerer chuckled and began walking across the plain. Launcelot followed.

"Do you not feel a trifle weary?" he asked.

"Yes, as a matter of fact, I do. Do you know what is the matter with me?"

"Of course. I have withdrawn the enchantment which has protected you all these years. What you feel now are the first tentative touches of your true age. It will take some time to catch up with you, against your body's natural resistance, but it is beginning its advance."

"Why are you doing this to me?"

"Because I believed you when you said you were not a pacifist. And you spoke with sufficient vehemence for me to realize that you might even oppose me. I could not permit that for I knew that your old strength was still there for you to call upon. Even a sorcerer might fear that, so I did what had to be done. By my power was it maintained; without it, it now drains away. It would have been good for us to work together once again, but I saw that that could not be."

Launcelot stumbled, caught himself, limped on. The hollow knight walked at Merlin's right hand.

"You say that your ends are noble," Launcelot said, "but do not believe you. Perhaps in the old days they were. But more than the times have changed. You are different. Do you not feel it yourself?"

Merlin drew a deep breath and exhaled vapor.

"Perhaps it is my heritage," he said. Then, "I jest. Of course, I have changed. Everyone does. You yourself are a perfect example. What you consider a turn for the worse in me is but the tip of an irreducible conflict which has grown up between us in the course of our changes. I still hold with the true ideals of Camelot."

Launcelot's shoulders were bent forward now and his breathing had deepened. The shapes loomed larger before them.

"Why, I know this place," he gasped. "Yet, I do not know it. Stonehenge does not stand so today. Even in Arthur's time it lacked this perfection. How did you get here? What has happened?"

He paused to rest, and Merlin halted to accommodate him.

"This night we have walked between the worlds," the sorcerer said. "This is a piece of the land of Faërie and that is the true Stonehenge, a holy place. I have stretched the bounds of the worlds to bring it here. Were I unkind I could send you back with it and strand you there forever. But it is better that you know a sort of peace. Come!"

Launcelot staggered along behind him, heading for the great circle of stones. The faintest of breezes came out of the west, stirring the mists.

"What do you mean—know a sort of peace?"

"The complete restoration of my powers and their increase will require a sacrifice in this place."

"Then you planned this for me all along!"

"No. It was not to have been you, Lance. Anyone would have served, though you will serve superbly well. It need not have been so, had you elected to assist me. You could still change your mind."

"Would you want someone who did that at your side?"

"You have a point there."

"Then why ask—save as a petty cruelty?"

"It is just that, for you have annoyed me."

Launcelot halted again when they came to the circle's periphery. He regarded the massive stands of stone.

"If you will not enter willingly," Merlin stated, "my servant will be happy to assist you."

Launcelot spat, straightened a little and glared.

"Think you I fear an empty suit of armor, juggled by some Hell-born wight? Even now, Merlin, without the benefit of wizardly succor, I could take that thing apart."

The sorcerer laughed.

"It is good that you at least recall the boasts of knighthood when all else has left you. I've half a mind to give you the opportunity, for the manner of your passing here is not important. Only the preliminaries are essential."

"But you're afraid to risk your servant?"

"Think you so, old man? I doubt you could even bear the weight of a suit of armor, let alone lift a lance. But if you are willing to try, so be it!"

He rapped the butt of his staff three times upon the ground.

"Enter," he said then. "You will find all that you need within. And I am glad you have made this choice. You were insufferable, you know. Just once, I longed to see you beaten, knocked down to the level of lesser mortals. I only wish the Queen could be here, to witness her champion's final engagement."

"So do I," said Launcelot, and he walked past the monolith and entered the circle.

A black stallion waited, its reins held down beneath a rock. Pieces of armor, a lance, a blade and a shield leaned against the side of the dolmen. Across the circle's diameter, a white stallion awaited the advance of the hollow knight.

"I am sorry I could not arrange for a page or a squire to assist you," Merlin said, coming around the other side of the monolith. "I'll be glad to help you myself, though."

"I can manage," Launcelot replied.

"My champion is accoutered in exactly the same fashion," Merlin said, "and I have not given him any edge over you in weapons."

"I never liked your puns either."

Launcelot made friends with the horse, then removed a small strand of red from his wallet and tied it about the butt of the lance. He leaned his stick against the dolmen stone and began to don the armor. Merlin, whose hair and beard were now almost black, moved off several paces and began drawing a diagram in the dirt with the end of his staff.

"You used to favor a white charger," he commented, "but

thought it appropriate to equip you with one of another color, since you have abandoned the ideals of the Table Round, betraying the memory of Camelot.''

"On the contrary," Launcelot replied, glancing overhead at the passage of a sudden roll of thunder. "Any horse in a storm, and I am Camelot's last defender."

Merlin continued to elaborate upon the pattern he was drawing as Launcelot slowly equipped himself. The small wind continued to blow, stirring the mist. There came a flash of lightning, startling the horse. Launcelot calmed it.

Merlin stared at him for a moment and rubbed his eyes. Launcelot donned his helmet.

"For a moment," Merlin said, "you looked somehow different. . . ."

"Really? Magical withdrawal, do you think?" he asked, and he kicked the stone from the reins and mounted the stallion.

Merlin stepped back from the now-completed diagram, shaking his head, as the mounted man leaned over and grasped the lance.

"You still seem to move with some strength," he said.

"Really?"

Launcelot raised the lance and couched it. Before taking up the shield he had hung at the saddle's side, he opened his visor and turned and regarded Merlin.

"Your champion appears to be ready," he said. "So am I."

Seen in another flash of light, it was an unlined face that looked down at Merlin, clear-eyed, wisps of pale gold hair ringing the forehead.

"What magic have the years taught you?" Merlin asked.

"Not magic," Launcelot replied. "Caution. I anticipated you. So, when I returned to the cave for my stick, I drank the rest of your elixir."

He lowered the visor and turned away.

"You walked like an old man. . . ."

"I'd a lot of practice. Signal your champion!"

Merlin laughed.

"Good! It is better this way," he decided, "to see you go down in full strength! You still cannot hope to win against a spirit!"

Launcelot raised the shield and leaned forward.

"Then what are you waiting for?"

"Nothing!" Merlin said. Then he shouted, "Kill him, Raxas!"

A light rain began as they pounded across the field; and staring ahead, Launcelot realized that flames were flickering behind his opponent's visor. At the last possible moment, he shifted the point of his lance into line with the hollow knight' blazing helmet. There came more lightning and thunder.

His shield deflected the other's lance while his went on to strike the approaching head. It flew from the hollow knight' shoulders and bounced, smouldering, on the ground.

He continued on to the other end of the field and turned When he had, he saw that the hollow knight, now headless, wa doing the same. And beyond him, he saw two standing figures where moments before there had been but one.

Morgan Le Fay, clad in a white robe, red hair unbound an blowing in the wind, faced Merlin from across his pattern. I seemed they were speaking, but he could not hear the words Then she began to raise her hands, and they glowed like col fire. Merlin's staff was also gleaming, and he shifted it befor him. Then he saw no more, for the hollow knight was ready fc the second charge.

He couched his lance, raised the shield, leaned forward an gave his mount the signal. His arm felt like a bar of iron, hi strength like an endless current of electricity as he raced dow the field. The rain was falling more heavily now and the light ning began a constant flickering. A steady rolling of thunde smothered the sound of the hoofbeats, and the wind whistled pas his helm as he approached the other warrior, his lance centere on his shield.

They came together with an enormous crash. Both knight reeled and the hollow one fell, his shield and breastplate pierce by a broken lance. His left arm came away as he struck the eartl the lancepoint snapped and the shield fell beside him. But he bega to rise almost immediately, his right hand drawing his long sword

Launcelot dismounted, discarding his shield, drawing his ow great blade. He moved to meet his headless foe. The other struc first and he parried it, a mighty shock running down his arm He swung a blow of his own. It was parried.

They swaggered swords across the field, till finally Launcelot saw his opening and landed his heaviest blow. The hollow knight toppled into the mud, his breastplate cloven almost to the point where the spear's shaft protruded. At that moment, Morgan Le Fay screamed.

Launcelot turned and saw that she had fallen across the pattern Merlin had drawn. The sorcerer, now bathed in a bluish light, raised his staff and moved forward. Launcelot took a step toward them and felt a great pain in his left side.

Even as he turned toward the half-risen hollow knight who was drawing his blade back for another blow, Launcelot reversed his double-handed grip upon his own weapon and raised it high, point downward.

He hurled himself upon the other, and his blade pierced the cuirass entirely as he bore him back down, nailing him to the earth. A shriek arose from beneath him, echoing within the armor, and a gout of fire emerged from the neck hole, sped upward and away, dwindled in the rain, flickered out moments later.

Launcelot pushed himself into a kneeling position. Slowly then, he rose to his feet and turned toward the two figures who again faced one another. Both were now standing within the ruddied geometries of power, both were now bathed in the bluish light. Launcelot took a step toward them, then another.

"Merlin!" he called out, continuing to advance upon them. "I've done what I said I would! Now I'm coming to kill you!"

Morgan Le Fay turned toward him, eyes wide.

"No!" she cried. "Depart the circle! Hurry! I am holding him here! His power wanes! In moments, this place will be no more. Go!"

Launcelot hesitated but a moment, then turned and walked as rapidly as he was able toward the circle's perimeter. The sky seemed to boil as he passed among the monoliths.

He advanced another dozen paces, then had to pause to rest. He looked back to the place of battle, to the place where the two figures still stood locked in sorcerous embrace. Then the scene was imprinted upon his brain as the skies opened and a sheet of fire fell upon the far end of the circle.

Dazzled, he raised his hands to shield his eyes. When he

lowered it, he saw the stones falling, soundless, many of ther
fading from sight. The rain began to slow immediately. Sorcere
and sorceress had vanished along with much of the structure o
the still-fading place. The horses were nowhere to be seen
He looked about him and saw a good-sized stone. He heade
for it and seated himself. He unfastened his breastplate an
removed it, dropping it to the ground. His side throbbed, an
he held it tightly. He doubled forward and rested his face on hi
left hand.

The rains continued to slow and finally ceased. The win
died. The mists returned.

He breathed deeply and thought back upon the conflict. Thi
this was the thing for which he had remained after all the other
the thing for which he had waited, for so long. It was over now
and he could rest.

There was a gap in his consciousness. He was brought
awareness again by a light. A steady glow passed between h
fingers, pierced hs eyelids. He dropped his hand and raised h
head, opening his eyes.

It passed slowly before him in a halo of white light. H
removed his sticky fingers from his side and rose to h
feet to follow it. Solid, glowing, glorious and pure, not
all like the image in the chamber, it led him on out acro
the moonlit plain, from dimness to brightness to dimnes
until the mists enfolded him as he reached at last to embra
it.

HERE ENDETH THE BOOK OF LAUNCELOT,
LAST OF THE NOBLE KNIGHTS OF THE
ROUND TABLE, AND HIS ADVENTURES
WITH RAXAS, THE HOLLOW KNIGHT,
AND MERLIN AND MORGAN LE FAY,
LAST OF THE WISE FOLK OF CAMELOT,
IN HIS QUEST FOR THE SANGREAL.

QUO FAS ET GLORIA DUCUNT.

A KNYGHT THER WAS

by Robert F. Young

One of the most prolific short story writers in science fiction, Robert F. Young (1915–   ) is a (now retired) machinist with the heart of a poet. Almost everything he has done is well written, his major concern is romance, and the explanation of fairy tales and myths is a prominent theme. Outstanding works include "One Love Have I" (1955), "Flying Pan" (1956), "The Dandelion Girl" (1961), "When Time Was New" (1964), "L'Arc de Jeanne" (1966), and "Starscape with Frieze of Dreams" (1970).

Still, any "Best of" collection would have to include the following tale of a time thief who finds his life work attempting to steal the Holy Grail.

> *A Knyght ther was, and that a worthy man,*
> *That fro the tyme that he first bigan*
> *To ryden out, he loved chivalrye,*
> *Trouthe and honour, fredom and curteisye*
> $\qquad\qquad\qquad$ *The Canterbury Tales*

I

Mallory, who among other things was a time-thief, rematerialized the time-space boat *Yore* in the eastern section of a secluded valley in ancient Britain and typed CASTLE, EARLY SIXTH-CENTURY on the lumillusion panel. Then he stepped over to the control-room telewindow and studied the three-dimensional screen. The hour was 8:00 p.m.; the season, summer; the year 542 A.D.

Darkness was on hand, but there was a full moon rising and he could see trees not far away—oaks and beeches, mostly. Roving the eye of the camera, he saw more trees of the same species. The "castle of Yore" was safely ensconced in a forest. Satisfied, he turned away.

If his calculations were correct, the castle of Carbonek stood in the next valley to the south, and on a silver table in a chamber of the castle stood the object of his quest.

If his calculations were correct.

Mallory was not one to keep himself in suspense. Stepping into the supply room, he stripped down to his undergarments and proceeded to get into the custom-built suit of armor which he had purchased expressly for the operation. Fortunately, while duplication of early-sixth-century design had been mandatory, there had been no need to duplicate early-sixth-century materials, and sollerets, spurs, greaves, cuisses, breastplate, pauldrons, gorget, arm-coverings, gauntlets, helmet, and chain-mail vest had all been fashioned of light weight alloys that lent ten times as much protection at ten times less poundage. The helmet was his particular pride and joy: in keeping with the period piece after which it had been patterned, it looked like an upside-down metal wastepaper basket, but the one-way transparency of the special alloy that had gone into its construction gave him unrestricted vision, while two inbuilt audio-amplifiers performed a corresponding service for his hearing.

The outer surface of each piece had been burnished to a high degree, and he found himself a dazzling sight indeed when he looked into the supply-room mirror. This effect was enhanced no end when he buckled on his chrome-plated scabbard and red-hilted sword and hung his snow-white shield around his neck. His polished spear, when he stood it beside him, was almost anticlimatic. It shouldn't have been. It was a good three and one-half inches in diameter at the base, and it was as tall as a young flagpole.

As he stood there looking at his reflection, the red cross in the center of the shield took on the hue of freshly shed blood. The period-piece expert who had designed the shield had insisted on the illusion, saying that it made for greater authenticity, and Mallory hadn't argued with him. He was glad now that he hadn't. Raising the visor of his helmet, he winked at himself and said, "I hereby christen ye 'Sir Galahad.' "

Next, he bethought himself of his steed. Armor clanking, he left the supply room and walked down the short passage to the rec-hall. The rec-hall occupied the entire forward section of the TSB and had been designed solely for the benefit of the time-tourists whom Mallory regularly conducted on past-tours as a cover-up for the illegal activities which he pursued in between trips. In the present instance, however, the hall went quite well with the *Yore's* lumillusioned exterior, possessing, with its gallerylike mezzanine, its long snack table, and its imitation flagstone flooring, an early-sixth-century aspect of its own—an aspect marred only slightly by the "anachronistic" telewindows inset at regular intervals along the walls.

Mallory's steed stood in a stall-like enclosure that was formed by the tourist bar and one of the walls, and it was a splendid "beast" indeed—as splendid a one as the twenty-second-century robotics industry was capable of creating. Originally, Mallory had planned on bringing a real horse with him, but as this would have necessitated his having to learn how to ride, he had decided against it. The decision had been a wise one: Easy Money looked more like a horse than most real horses did, could travel twice as fast, and was as easy to ride and to maneuver as a golp jetney. It was light-brown in color with a white diamond on its forehead, it was equipped with a secret croup-compartment and an inbuilt saddle, and its fetlock-length trappings were made of genuine synthisilk threaded with gold. It wore no armor—it did not need to: weapons manufactured during the Age of Chivalry could no more penetrate its "hide" than a toothpick could.

Come on, Easy Money, Mallory encephalopathed. *You and I have a little job to do.*

The rohorse emitted several realistic whinnies, backed out of its "stall," trotted smartly over to his side, and nuzzled his right pauldron. Mallory mounted—not gracefully, it is true, but at least without the aid of the winch he would have needed if his armor had been manufactured in the sixth century—and inserted the red pommel of his spear in the stirrup socket. Then, activating the *Yore's* lock, he rode across the imaginary drawbridge that spanned the mirage-moat, and set forth into the forest. As the "portcullis" closed behind him, symbolically bringing phase one of Operation Sangraal to a close, he thought of Jason Perfidion.

Standing in front of the floor-to-ceiling, wall-to-wall fireplace in the big balconied room, Perfidion said, "Mallory, you're wasting your time. Worse, you're wasting mine."

The room climaxed a vertical series of slightly less sumptuous chambers known collectively as the Perfidion Tower, and the Perfidion Tower stood with a score of balconied brothers on a blacktop island in the exact center of Kansas' largest golp course. A short distance from the fraternal gathering stood yet another tower—the false tower into which Mallory had lumillusioned his TSB upon his arrival. On the Golp Terrace, as the blacktop island was called, everyone and everything conformed—or else.

The room itself was known to time-thieves as "Perfidion's Lair." And yet there was nothing about Jason Perfidion—nothing physical, that is—that suggested the predator. He was Mallory's age—thirty-three—tall, dark of hair, and strikingly handsome. He looked like—and was—a highly successful businessman with a triplex on Get-Rich-Quick Street, and he gave the impression that he was as honest as the day was long. Just the same, the predator was there, and if you were alert enough you could sometimes glimpse it peering out through the smoky windowpanes of his eyes.

It wasn't peering out now, though. It was sleeping. However, it was due to wake up any second. "Then you're not interested in fencing the Holy Grail?" Mallory asked.

Annoyance intensified the slight swarthiness of Perfidion's cheeks. "Mallory, you know as well as I do that the Grail never really existed, that it was nothing more than the mead-inspired daydream of a bunch of quixotic knights. So go and get your hair cut and forget about it."

"But suppose it *did* exist," Mallory insisted. "Suppose, tomorrow afternoon at this time, I were to come in here and set it down on this desk here? How much could you get for it?"

Perfidion laughed. "How much *couldn't* I get for it! Why, without even stopping to think I can name you a dozen collectors who'd give their right arm for it."

"I'm not interested in right arms," Mallory said. "I'm interested in dollars. How many Kennedees could you get for it?"

"A megamillion—maybe more. More than enough, certainly, to permit you to retire from time-lifting and to take up residence on Get-Rich-Quick Street. But it doesn't exist, and it never did, so get out of here, Mallory, and stop squandering my valuable time."

Mallory withdrew a small stereophoto from his breast pocket and tossed it on the desk. "Have a look at that first—then I'll go," he said.

Perfidion picked up the photo. "An ordinary enough yellow bowl," he began, and stopped. Suddenly he gasped, and jabbed one of the many buttons that patterned his desktop. Seconds later, a svelte blonde whom Mallory had never seen before stepped out of the lift tube. Like most general-purpose secretaries, she wore a maximum of makeup and a minimum of clothing, and moved in an aura of efficiency and sex. "Get me my photo-projector, Miss Tyler," Perfidion said.

When she returned with it, he set it on his desk and inserted the stereophoto. Instantly, a huge cube materialized in the center of the room. Inside the cube there was a realistic image of a resplendent silver table, and upon the image of the table stood an equally realistic image of a resplendent golden bowl. Perfidion gasped again.

"Unusual workmanship, wouldn't you say?" Mallory said.

Perfidion turned toward the blonde. "You may go, Miss Tyler."

She was staring at the contents of the cube and apparently did not hear him. "I said," he repeated, "that you may go, Miss Tyler."

"Oh. Yes . . . yes sir."

When the lift-tube door closed behind her, Perfidion turned to Mallory. For a fraction of a second the predator was visible behind the smoky windowpanes of his eyes; then, quickly, it ducked out of sight. "Where was this taken, Tom?"

"It's a distance shot," Mallory said. "I took it through one of the windows of the church Joseph of Arimathea built in Glastonbury."

"But how did you know—"

"That it was there? Because it *had* to be there. Sometime ago, while escorting a group of tourists around ancient Britain, I happened to witness Joseph of Arimathea's landing—and happened to catch a glimpse of what he brought with him. I used to think that the Grail was a pipe dream, too, but when I saw it with my own eyes, I knew that it couldn't have been. However, I knew I'd need evidence to convince you, so I jumped back to a later place-time and got a shot of it."

"But why a shot, Tom? Why didn't you lift it then and there?"

"You concede that it is the Grail then?"

"Of course it's the Grail—there's not the slightest question about it. Why didn't you lift it?"

"Well, for one thing, I wanted to make sure that lifting it would be worth my while, and for another, Glastonbury wasn't the logical place-time from which to lift it, because, assuming that the rest of the legend is also true, it was seen after that place-time. No time-thief ever bucked destiny yet and came out the winner, Jason; I play my percentages."

"I know you do, Tom. You're one of the best time-lift men in the business, and the Past Police would be the first to admit it. . . . I daresay you've already pinpointed the key place-time?"

Mallory grinned, showing his white teeth. "I certainly have, but if you think I'm going to divulge it, you're sadly mistaken, Jason. And stop looking at my hair—it won't tell you anything beyond the fact that I've been using Hair-haste. Shoulder-length hair was the rage in more eras than one."

Perfidion smiled warmly, and clapped Mallory on the back. "I'm not trying to ferret out your secret, Tom. I know better than that. Lifting is your line, fencing mine. You bring me the Grail, I'll sell it, take my cut, and everything will be fine. You know me, Tom."

"I sure do," Mallory said, taking the stereophoto out of the projector and returning it to his breast pocket.

Perfidion snapped his fingers. "A happy thought just occurred o me! I've got a golp date with Rowley of Puriproducts, so why don't you join us, Tom? You play a pretty good game, as I recall."

Mollified, Mallory said, "I'll have to borrow a set of your etsticks."

"I'll get them for you on the way down. Come on, Tom."

Mallory accompanied him across the room. "Keep mum about his to Rowley now," Perfidion said confidentially. "He's a potential customer, but we don't want to let the cat out of the bag yet, do we? Or should I say the 'Grail.' " He took time out to grin at his little joke, then, "By the way, Tom, I take it you're all set as regards costume, equipment and the like."

"I've got the sweetest little suit of armor you ever laid eyes on," Mallory said.

"Fine—no need for me to offer any advice in that respect then." Perfidion opened the lift door. "After you, Tom."

They plummeted down the tube together.

It had been a good game of golp—from Mallory's standpoint, anyway. He had trounced Rowley roundly, and he would have inflicted a similar ignominy upon Perfidion had not the latter been called away in the middle of the game and been unable to return till it was nearly over. Oh well, Mallory thought, encephalo-guiding his rohorse through the ancient forest, there'll be other chances. Aloud, he said, "Step lively now, Easy Money, and let's get this caper over with so we can return to civilization and start feeling what it's like to be rich."

In response to the encephalo-waves that had accompanied his words, Easy Money increased its pace, the infrared rays of its eye units illumining its way. In places, light from the rising noon seeped through the foliage, but otherwise darkness was the rule. The air was cool and damp—the sea was not far distant—and the sound of frogs and insects was omnipresent and now and then there was the rustling sound of some small and fleeing forest creature.

Presently the ground began to rise, and not long afterward the trees thinned out temporarily and rohorse and rider emerged on the moonlit crest of the ridge that separated the two valleys. In the distance Mallory made out the moon-gilt towers and turrets

of a large castle, and knew it to be Carbonek beyond a doubt. He
sighed with relief. He was all set now—provided his masquerade
went over. Conversely, if it didn't go over he was finished: his
sword and his spear were his only weapons, and his shield and
his armor his only protection. True, each article was superior in
quality and durability to its corresponding article in the Age of
Chivalry, but otherwise none of them was anything more than
what it seemed. Mallory might be a time-thief; but within the
framework of his profession he believed in playing fair.

In response to his encephalopathed directions, Easy Money
picked its way down the slope to the ridge and reentered the
forest. Not long afterward it stepped onto what was euphemisti-
cally referred to in that day and age as a "highway" but which
in reality was little more than a wide-hoof-trampled lane. As
Mallory's entire plan of action was based on boldness, he spurned
the shadows of the bordering oaks and beeches and encephalpathed
the rohorse to keep to the center of the lane. He met no one,
however, despite the earliness of the hour, nor had he really
expected to. It was highly improbable that any freemen would be
abroad after dark, and as for the knight-errants who happened to
be in the neighborhood, it was highly improbable that any of
them be abroad after dark either.

He grinned. To read *Le Morte d'Arthur*, you'd think that the
chivalry boys had been in business twenty-four hours a day,
slaying ogres, rescuing fair damosels, and searching for the
Sangraal; but not if you read between the lines. Mallory had read
Arthur only cursorily, but he had had a hunch all along that in
the majority of cases the quest for the Sangraal had served as an
out, and that the knights of the Table Round had spent more time
wenching and wassailing than they had conducting their so-
called dedicated search, and the hunch had played an important
role in the shaping of his strategy.

The highway turned this way and that, never pursuing a
straight course unless such a logical procedure was unavoidable.
Once, he thought he heard hoofbeats up ahead, but he met no
one, and not long afterward he saw the pale pile of Carbonek
looming above the trees to his left, and encephalo-guided Easy
Money into the lane that led to the entrance. There was no moat
but the portcullis was an imposing one. Flanking it on either side

was a huge stone lion, and framing it were flaming torches in regularly spaced niches. Warders in hauberk and helmet looked down from the lofty wall, their halberds gleaming in the dancing torchlight. Mallory swallowed: the moment of truth had arrived.

He halted Easy Money and canted his white shield so that the red cross in its center would be visible from above. Then he marshaled his smattering of Old English. "I hight Sir Galahad of the Table Round," he called out in as bold a voice as he could muster. "I would rest my eyes upon the Sangraal."

Instantly, confusion reigned upon the wall as the warders vied with one another for the privilege of operating the cumbersome windlass that raised and lowered the portcullis, and presently, to the accompaniment of a chorus of creaks and groans and scrapings, the ponderous iron grating began to rise. Mallory forced himself to wait until it had risen to a height befitting a knight of Sir Galahad's caliber, then he rode through the gateway and into the courtyard, congratulating himself on the effectiveness of his impersonation.

"Ye will come unto the chamber of the Sangraal sixty paces down the corridor to thy left eftsoon ye enter the chief fortress, sir knight," one of the warders called down. "And ye had arrived a little while afore, ye had encountered Sir Launcelot du Lake, the which did come unto the fortress and enter in, wherefrom he came out anon and departed."

Mallory would have wiped his forehead if his forehead had been accessible and if his hands had not been encased in metal gloves. Fooling the warders was one thing, but passing himself off as Sir Galahad to the man who was Sir Galahad's father would have been quite another. He had learned from the pages of his near-namesake's *Arthur* that Sir Launcelot had visited Carbonek before Sir Galahad had, but the pages had not revealed whether the time lapse had involved minutes, hours, or years, and for that matter, Mallory wasn't altogether certain whether the second visit they described had been the real Sir Galahad's which meant failure, or a romanticized version of his own, which meant success. His near-namesake was murky at best, and reading him you were never sure where anybody was, or when any given event was taking place.

The courtyard was empty, and after crossing it, Mallory dismounted, encephalopathed Easy Money to stay put, and climbed the series of stone steps that led to the castle proper. Entering the building unchallenged, he found himself at the junction of three corridors. The main one stretched straight ahead and debouched into a large hall. The other two led off at right angles, one to the left and one to the right. Boisterous laughter emanated from the hall, and he could see knights and other nobles sitting at a long banquet table. Scattered among them were gentlewomen in rich silks, and hovering behind them were servants bearing large demijohns. He grinned. Just as he had figured—King Pelles was throwing a wingding.

Quickly, Mallory turned down the left-hand corridor and started along it, counting his footsteps. Rushes rustled beneath his feet and the flickering light of wall torches gave him a series of grotesque shadows. He saw no one: all of the servants were in the banquet hall, pouring wine and mead. He laughed aloud.

Forty-eight paces sufficed to see him to the chamber door. It was a perfectly ordinary door. Opening it, he thought at first the room beyond was ordinary, too. Then he saw the burning candles arranged along the walls, and beneath them, standing in the center of the floor, the table of silver. The table of the Sangraal. . . .

There was no Sangraal on the table, however. There was no Sangraal in the room, for that matter. There was a girl, though. She was huddled forlornly in a corner, and she was crying.

II

Mallory laid his spear aside, strode across the room, and raised the girl to her feet. "The Sangraal," he said, forgetting in his agitation the few odds and ends of Old English he had memorized. "Where is it?"

She raised startled eyes that were as round, and almost as large, as plums. Her face was round, too, and faintly childlike. Her hair was dark-brown, and done up in a strange and indeterminate coiffeur that was as charming as it was disconcerting. Her ankle-length dress was white, and there was a bow on the bodice that matched the plum-blueness of her eyes. A few cosmetics properly applied, would have turned her into an attractive woman, and even without them, she rated a second look.

She stared at him for some time, then, "Surely ye be an advision, sir," she said. "I . . . I know ye not."

Mallory swung his shield around so that she could see the red cross. "Now do you know me?"

She gasped, and her eyes grew even rounder. "Sir . . . Sir Galahad! Oh, fair knight, wherefore did ye not say?"

Mallory ignored the question. "The Sangraal," he repeated. "Where is it?"

Her tears had ceased temporarily; now they began again. "Oh, fair sir!" she cried, "ye see tofore you a damosel at mischief, the which was given guardianship of the Holy Vessel at her own request, and bewrayed her trust, a damosel—"

"Never mind all that," Mallory said. "Where's the Sangraal?"

"I wot not, fair sir."

"But you must know if you were guarding it!"

"I wot not whither it was taken."

"But you must wot who took it."

"Wot I well, fair knight. Sir Launcelot, the which is thy father, bare it from the chamber."

Mallory was stunned. "But that's impossible! My fa—Sir Launcelot wouldn't steal the Sangraal!"

"Well I wot, fair sir; yet steal it he did. Came he unto the chamber and saith, I hight Sir Launcelot du Lake of the Table Round, whereat I did see his armor to be none other; so then took he the Vessel covered with the red samite and bare it with him from the chamber, whereat I—"

"How long ago?"

"But a little while afore eight of the clock. Sithen I have wept. I know now no good knight, nor no good man. And I now from thy holy shield and from thy good name that thou art good knight, and I beseech ye therefore to help me, for ye be a shining knight indeed, wherefore ye ought not to fail no damosel which is in distress, and she besought you of help."

Mallory only half heard her. Sir Launcelot was too much with him. It was inconceivable that a knight of such noble principles could even consider touching the Sangraal, to say nothing of making off with it. Maybe, though, his principles hadn't been

quite as noble as they had been made out to be. He had bee
Queen Guinevere's paramour, hadn't he? He had lain with th
fair Elaine, hadn't he? When you came right down to it, he coul
very well have been a scoundrel at heart all along—a scoundre
whose true nature had been toned down by writers like Malor
and poets like Tennyson. All of which, while it strongly sug
gested that he was capable of stealing the Sangraal, threw not th
slightest light on his reason for having done so. Mallory wa
right back where he had started from.

He turned to the girl. "You said something about needing m
help. What do you want me to do?"

Instantly, her tears stopped and she clasped her hands togethe
and looked at him with worshipful eyes. "Oh, fair sir, ye b
most kind indeed! Well I wot from thy shining armor that ye—'

"Knock it off," Mallory said.

"Knock it off? I wot not what—"

"Never mind. Just tell me what you want me to do."

"Ye must bear me from the castle, fair sir, or the king learns
have bewrayed my trust and wreaks his wrath upon me. An
then ye must help me regain the Holy Cup and return it to th
chamber."

"We'll worry about getting the Cup back after we're beyon
the walls," Mallory said, starting for the door. "Come on—
they're all in the banquet hall and as drunk as lords—they won
even see us go by."

She hung back. "But the warders, fair sir—they be not enchafe
And King Pelles, by my own wish, did forbid them to pass me.'

Mallory stared at her. "By your own wish! Well of all th
crazy—" Abruptly he dropped the subject. "All right then—
how *do* we get out of here?"

"There lieth beneath the fortress and the forest a parlo
passage wherein dwells the fiend, the which I have much discom
fit of. But with ye aside me, fair knight, there is naught
fear."

Mallory had read enough Malory to be able to take sixt
century fiends in his stride. "I'll have to take my horse along,
he said. "Is there room for it to pass?"

"Yea, fair sir. The tale saith that aforetime many knights d
ride out beneath the fortress and the forest and did smite th

Saxons, Saracens, and Pagans, the which did compass the castle about, from behind, whereupon the battle was won.''

Mallory stepped outside the chamber, the girl just behind him, and encephalophathed the necessary directions. After a moment, Easy Money came trotting down the corridor to his side. The girl gasped, and, to his astonishment, threw her arms around the rohorse's neck. ''He is a noble steed indeed, fair sir,'' she said, ''and worthy of a knight fitting to sit in the Siege Perilous.'' Presently she stepped back, frowning. ''He . . . he is most cold, fair sir.''

''All horses of that breed are,'' Mallory explained. ''Incidentally, his name is Easy Money.''

''La! such a strange name.''

''Not so strange.'' Mallory raised his visor, making a mental note to see to it that any and all suits of armor he might buy in the future were air-conditioned. He got his spear. ''Let's be on our way, shall we?''

''Ye . . . ye have blue eyes, fair sir.''

''Never mind the color of my eyes—let's get out of here.''

She seemed to make up her mind about something. ''An ye will follow me, sir knight,'' she said, and started down the corridor.

A ramp, the entrance of which was camouflaged by a rotating section of the inner castle wall, gave access to the subterranean passage. The passage itself, in the flickering light of the torch that the girl had brought along, appeared at first to be nothing more than a natural cave enlarged through the centuries by the stream that still flowed down its center. Presently, however, Mallory saw that in certain places the stone walls had been cut back in such a way that the space on either side of the stream never narrowed to a width of less than four feet. He saw other evidence of human handiwork too—dungeons. They were little more than shallow caves now, though, their iron gratings having rusted and fallen away.

After proceeding half a hundred yards, he paused. ''I don't know what we're walking for when we've got a perfectly good horse at our disposal,'' he told the girl. ''Come on, I'll help you into the saddle and I'll jump on behind.''

She shook her head. "No, fair knight, it is not fitting for a gentlewoman to ride tofore her champion. Ye will mount, and I will ride behind."

"Suit yourself," Mallory said. He climbed into the saddle with a clank and a clatter, and helped her up on Easy Money's croup. "By the way, you never did tell me your name."

"I hight the damosel Rowena."

"Pleased to meet you," Mallory said. *Giddy-ap, Easy Money*, he encephalopathed.

They rode in silence for a little while, the light from Rowena's torch dancing acappella rigadoons on bare walls and dripping ceilings, Easy Money's hoofbeats hardly audible above the purling of the stream. Presently Rowena said. "It were best that ye drew out thy sword, fair sir, for anon the fiend will beset us."

"He hasn't beset us yet," Mallory pointed out.

"La! fair sir, he will."

He saw no harm in humoring her, and did as she had suggested. "You mentioned something a while back about having been given guardianship for the Sangraal at your own request," he said. "How did that come about?"

"List, fair sir, and I will tell ye. But first I must tell ye of Sir Bors de Ganis, of which Sir Lionel is brother. It happed one day that Sir Bors did ride into a forest in the Kingdom of Mennes unto the hour of midday, and there befell him a marvelous adventure. So he met at the departing of the two ways two knights that led Lionel, his brother, all naked, bounden upon a strong hackney, and his hands bounden tofore his breast. And every each of them held in his hands thorns wherewith they went beating him so sore that the blood trailed down more than in an hundred places of his body, so that he was all blood tofore and behind, but he said never a word; as he which was great of heart he suffered all that ever they did to him as though he had felt none anguish.

"Anon Sir Bors dressed him to rescue him that was his brother; and so he looked upon the other side of him, and saw a knight which brought a fair gentlewoman, and would have set her in the thickest place of the forest for to have been the more surer out of the way from them that sought him. And she which was nothing assured cried with a high voice: 'Saint Mary, succor your maid.' And anon she espied where Sir Bors came riding. And when she came nigh him she deemed him a knight of the Round Table, whereof she hoped to have some comfort; and then she conjured him: By the faith that he ought unto him in whose service thou art entered in, and for the faith ye owe unto the high order of knighthood, and for the noble King Arthur's sake, that I suppose that made thee knight, that thou help me, and suffer me not to be shamed of this knight. When—''

"Just a minute," Mallory interrupted, thoroughly bewildered and simultaneously afflicted with an irrational sense of *déjà vu*. "This gentlewoman you speak of—would she by any chance be you?"

"Wit ye well, fair sir. When—''

"But if she's you, why don't you use the first person singular instead of the third?"

"I wot not what—''

"Why don't you use 'I' instead of 'she' when you refer to yourself directly?"

"It would not be fitting, fair knight. When Bors heard her say thus he had so much sorrow there he nyst not what to do. For if I let my brother be in adventure he must be slain, and that would I not for all the earth. And if I help not the maid she is shamed for ever, and also she shall lose her virginity the which she shall never get again. Then lift he up his eyes and said weeping: Fair sweet Lord, whose liege man I am, keep Lionel, my brother, that these knights slay him not, and for pity of you, and for Mary's sake, I shall succor this maid. Then dressed he him unto the knight the which had the gentlewoman, and then—''

*   *   *

"Hist!" Mallory whispered. "I heard something."

For a moment the light flared wildly as though she had nearly dropped the torch. "Wh . . . whence came the sound, fair knight?"

"From the other side of the stream." He peered into the vacillating shadows, but saw nothing but the darker shadows of one of the innumerable man-made caves. The sound he had heard had brought to mind the dull clang that metal makes when it collides with stone, and it had been so faint as to have been barely audible above the purling of the stream. Thinking back, he was not altogether certain that he had heard it at all. "My imagination's getting the best of me, I guess," he said presently. "There's no one there."

Her warm breath penetrated the crevices of his gorget and fanned the back of his neck. "Ye . . . ye ween not that it could have been the fiend prowling?"

"Of course I ween not! Relax, and finish your story. But get to the point, will you?"

"An . . . an it so please. . . . And then Sir Bors cried: Sir knight, let your hand off that maiden, or ye be but dead. And then he set down the maiden, and was armed at all pieces save he lacked his spear. Then he dressed his shield, and drew out his sword, and Bors smote him so hard that it went through his shield and habergeon on the left shoulder. And through great strength he beat him down to the earth, and at the pulling out of Bors' spear there he swooned. Then came Bors to the maid and said: How seemeth it to you of this knight ye be delivered at this time? Now sir, said she, I pray you lead me there as this knight had me. So shall I do gladly: and took the horse of the wounded knight, and set the gentlewoman upon him, and so brought her as she desired. Sir knight, said she, ye have better sped than ye weened, for an I had lost my maidenhead, five hundred men should have died for it. What knight was he that had you in the forest? By my faith, said she, he is my cousin. So wot I never with what engyn the fiend enchafed him, for yesterday he took me from my father privily; for I nor none of my father's men mistrusted him not, and if he had my maidenhead he should have died for the sin, and his body shamed and dishonored for ever. Thus as—"

"*Shhh!*"

This time, Mallory was certain that he had heard something. The sound had had much in common with the previous sound, except that it had suggested metal scraping against, rather than colliding with, stone. Directly across the stream was another cave, this one shallow enough to permit the torchlight to penetrate its deeper shadows, and looking into those shadows, he caught a faint gleam of reflected light.

Rowena must have caught it, too, for he heard her gasp behind him. "It were best that I thanked ye now for thy great kindness, fair knight," she said, "for anon we be no longer on live."

"Nonsense!" Mallory said. "If this fiend of yours is any-where in the vicinity, he's probably more afraid of us than we are of him."

The cave was behind them now. "Per . . . peradventure he hath already had meat," Rowena said hopefully. "The tale saith that and the fiend be filled, he becomes aweary and besets not them the which do pass him by in peace."

"I'll keep my sword handy just in case he changes his mind," Mallory said. "Meanwhile, get on with your autobiography—only for Pete's sake, cut it short, will you?"

"An it please, fair sir. Thus as the fair gentlewoman stood talking with Sir Bors there came twelve knights seeking after her, and anon she told them all how Bors had delivered her; then they made great joy, and besought him to come to her father, a great lord, and he should be right welcome. Truly, said Bors, that may not be at this time, for I have a great adventure to do in this country. So he commended them unto God and departed. The fair gentlewoman did grieve mickle to see him leave, and she saith, sir knights, noble was the service that brave knight did render unto thy liege's daughter in the saving of her maidenhead the which she could never get again, for that be none other than his own brother the which he fauted. Therefore, noble must be both his king and his cause, wherefore it be befitting that a gentlewoman of thy liege's daughter's nature leave the castle of her father betimes that she may render fitting service to her succor's cause and be worthy of his deed. Thus spake this fair gentlewoman, whereat she did mount upon her palfrey and so departed her from thence and did ride as fast as her palfrey might bear her, whereupon after many days she came to the castle of Carbonek and did seek out King Pelles and did beseech him that she might be made guardian of the Sangraal, whereat he did graciously consent to her request and did consent also that she be made prisoner in the fortress by her own wish. And now she was bewrayed her trust, fair sir, and the table of silver whereon the Sangraal stood stands empty."

For some time after she finished talking, Mallory was silent. Was she trying to pull his leg? he wondered. Or were the gentlewomen of her day and age really as high-minded and as

feathered-brained as she would have him believe? He decided
not to go into the matter for the moment. "Tell me, Rowena,"
he said, "if the Sangraal is visible only to those who are worthy
of it, as I have been led to believe, how are any of those
wassailers whooping it up back there in that banquet hall going
to know whether it's gone or not?"

"It be ofttimes averred that all cannot see the Holy Cup, as ye
say, fair knight. Natheless, all that have come unto the chamber
sithen my trust began, they did see it, and Sir Launcelot, the
which is much with sin, he did see it—and did take it."

"He's not going to get very far with it, though," Mallory
said. And then, "How long is the tunnel anyway?"

"Anon we shall see the stars, fair sir."

She was right, and a few minutes later, after rounding a turn
in the passage, they emerged upon the bank of a small river. The
subterranean stream that had kept them company emerged, too,
and joined its larger sister on the way to the sea. On either hand,
cliffs rose up, and the susurrus of waves breaking on sand could
be heard in the distance.

Mallory guided Easy Money upstream to where the cliffs
dwindled down to thickly forested slopes. It took him but a
moment to orient himself, and presently rohorse and riders were
headed in the direction of the highway. "Now," said he, "if
you'll tell me where you want to be dropped off, I'll see what I
can do about getting the Grail back."

There was a brief silence. Then, "An . . . an ye wish, ye may
leave me here."

He halted Easy Money, dismounted, and lifted her down to
the ground. He looked around, expecting to see a habitation of
some sort. He saw nothing but trees. He faced the girl again.
"Don't you have any friends or relatives you can stay with?"

An argent shaft of moonlight slanting down through the foliage illumined her face. "There be none nigh, fair sir, nor
none nearer than an hundred miles. I shall abide your again-
coming here in the forest."

Mallory stared at her. She didn't look—or act either, for that
matter—as though she knew enough to get in out of the rain.
"Abide here in the forest! Why, you wouldn't last a week!"

"But ye will return hither with the Sangraal long afore that, whereupon we two together shall return the Holy Vessel to the chamber and I shall not be made to suffer the severing of my two hands."

He was aghast. "They wouldn't dare cut off your hands!"

"They dare much fair knight. Know ye naught of the customs of the land?"

He was silent. What in the world was he going to do about her? She would probably wait here for him until she starved to death or, equally as distressing, until she was apprehended. Abruptly he shrugged his shoulders—to the extent that his pauldrons permitted—and remounted the rohorse. Why should it matter to him what became of her? He'd returned to the Age of Chivalry to steal the Sangraal, not to play nursemaid to damosels in distress. "Don't take any wooden nickels now," he said.

Two tiny stars appeared in the pale regions of her eyes and twinkled down her cheeks. "May the good Lord speed ye upon thy quest, fair knight, and may He guard ye well."

"Oh, for Pete's sake!" Mallory said, and reaching down, pulled her up onto Easy Money's croup. "I have a castle not far from here. I'll drop you off, then I'll go after the Sangraal."

Her breath was a warm little wind seeping through the crevices of his gorget. "Oh, fair, sir, ye be the noblest of all the knights in all the land, and I shall serve thee faithfully for the rest of my days!"

The rohorse whinnied. *Giddy-up, Easy Money,* Mallory encephalopathed, and they started out.

III

Rowena fell for the *Yore* hook, line, and sinker. Not even the modern interior gave her pause. Those objects which happened to be beyond her ken—and there were many of them—she interpreted as "appointments befitting a noble knight," and as for the rooms themselves, she merely identified them with the rooms out of her own experience that they most closely resembled. Thus, the rec-hall became "the banquet hall," the supply room became "the kitchen," the control room became "the sorcerer's tower," the tourist compartments became "the sleeping tower," Mallory's bedroom-office became "the lord's quarters," the lavatory became "the chapel," and the generator room became "the dungeon." Only two things disconcerted her: the absence of servants and the fact that Easy Money was stabled in the banquet hall. Mallory got around the first by telling her that he had given the servants a leave of absence, and she herself got around the second by declaring it to be no more than fitting for such a splendid stead to be accorded special treatment. Certainly, Mallory reflected, she was nothing if she was not cooperative.

After showing her around he wasted no time in getting down to the business on hand, and stepping into the control room, he punched out the data necessary to take the *Yore* back to 7:15 p.m. of the same day, and to rematerialize it one half mile west of its present position, as an overlap was bound to occur. There was a barely noticeable tremor as the transition took place, and simultaneously the darkness showing on the control-room telewindow transmuted to dusk.

Turning away from the jump board, he saw Rowena regarding him with large eyes from the doorway. "We're now back to a point in time that preceded the theft of the Sangraal," he told her, "and we're relocated farther down the valley. But don't let it throw you. None other than Merlin himself built the magic apparatus you see before you in this room, and you know yourself that once he makes up his mind to it, Merlin can do anything."

She blinked once, but evinced no other sign of surprise. "Yes, fair sir," she said, "I am ware of the magic of Merlin."

"However," Mallory went on, "magic such as this isn't something for a gentlewoman such as yourself to fool around with, so I must forbid you to enter this room during my absence from the castle. Also, while we're on the subject, I must also forbid you to leave the castle during my absence. Merlin would be upset no end if there were two damosels that hight Rowena gallivanting around the countryside at the same time."

She blinked again. "By my troth, fair sir," she said, "I would lever die than disobey thy two commands." And then "Have ye ate any meat late?"

This time, Mallory blinked. "Meat?"

"It is fitting that ye should eat meat afore ye ride out."

"Oh, you mean food. I'll eat when I get back. But there's no need for you to wait." He took her into the supply room and showed her where the vacuum tins were stored. "You open them like this," he explained, pulling one out and activating the desealer. "Then, as soon as the contents cool off a little, you sit down to dinner."

"But this be not meat," she objected.

"Maybe not, but it's a good substitute, and a lot better for you." A thought struck him, and he took her into the lavatory and showed her how to operate the hot and cold-water dispenser, ascribing the setup to more of Merlin's magic. He debated on whether to explain the function and purpose of the adjacent shower, decided not to. There was a limit to all things, and an apparatus for washing one's whole body was simply too far-fetched for anyone living in the sixth century to take seriously.

Back in the rec-hall, he donned his helmet and gauntlets, reset the gauntlet timepiece, picked up his spear and encephalopathed Easy Money to his side. Mounting, he set the spear in the stirrup socket. Rowena gazed up at him, plum-blue eyes round with awe and admiration—and concern. "Wit ye well, fair sir," she said, "that Sir Launcelot, the which is thy father, is a knight of many victories, and therefore ye must take care."

Mallory grinned. "Dismay you not, fair damsel, I'll smite him from his steed before he can say 'Queen Guinevere.' " He straightened his sword belt, activated the *Yore's* lock, and rode across the mirage-moat and entered the forest. The "portcullis" closed behind him.

Dusk had become darkness by the time he reached the highway. Approximately half an hour later he would reach the highway again. However, the seeming paradox did not disconcert him in the least: this was far from being the first time he had backtraced himself on a job.

As "before," he spurned the shadows of the bordering oaks and beeches and encephalopathed Easy Money to keep to the center of the lane. And, as "before," no one was abroad. Probably King Pelles' wassail was already in progress, or, if not, the goodly knights and gentlewomen were still at evensong. In any event, he reached the lane that led to the castle of Carbonek without mishap.

After entering the lane, he encephalopathed Easy Money into
the concealment of the shadows of the bordering trees and settled
back in the saddle to wait. Rowena's placing the time of the theft
at "a little while afore eight of the clock" had been a general
estimate at best; hence he had allowed himself plenty of leeway
and had arrived on the scene a little early. It was well that he
had, for hardly a minute passed before he heard hoofbeats approaching from the south, and presently he saw a tall knight
astride a resplendent steed turn into the lane. His armor gleamed
in the moonlight and bespoke a quality and class that only a
knight of Sir Launcelot's statue would be able to afford.

Mallory watched him ride down the lane to the lion-flanked
entrance and heard him announce himself as Sir Launcelot. The
portcullis was raised without delay, and the knight rode through
the gateway and disappeared from view.

Mallory frowned in the darkness. Something about the incident had failed to jibe. He thought back, but he could isolate
nothing that, in retrospect anyway, seemed in the least incongruous
He tried again, with the same result, and at length he concluded
that the note of discord had originated in his imagination.

Again, he settled back to wait. He wasn't particularly worried
about the outcome of the forthcoming encounter—the superiorit
of his weapons and armor should be more than enough to se
him through—but just the same he wished there was some way
to avoid it. There wasn't, of course. Sir Launcelot's theft of the
Sangraal was already incorporated in fact, and, as a *fait accompli*
could not be obviated by a previous theft. All Mallory could d
was to make his move after the *fait accompli* in the hope that tha
was when he *had* made his move. A time-thief didn't hav
nearly as much leeway as his seeming freedom of movemen
might lead the uninitiated to believe. About all he could do wa
to play along with destiny and await his opportunities. If destin
smiled, he succeeded; if destiny frowned, he did not. However
Mallory was optimistic about his forthcoming bid for the Grai
for if it wasn't in the books for him to wrest the Cup from S
Launcelot, the chances were he wouldn't have gotten as far as h
had.

He estimated that it would take the man five minutes to ente
the castle, proceed to the chamber, seize the Sangraal, return

the courtyard and come riding back to the portcullis. Seven
minutes proved to be nearer the mark. In response to a hail from
within the wall, several of the warders bent to the windlass,
whereupon the portcullis scraped and groaned aloft, and the tall
knight came riding out just as the hands of Mallory's time-piece
registered 7:43 p.m.

Mallory let him pass, straining his eyes in vain for a glimpse
of the Sangraal. He waited till Sir Launcelot was half a hundred
yards from the highway before he encephalopathed Easy Money
to follow, and he waited till a bend in the road hid the castle of
Carbonek from view before encephalopathing the command to
charge. At this point, Sir Launcelot became aware that he was no
longer alone, and wheeled his steed around. Without an instant's
hesitation, he dressed his spear and launched a countercharge.
All Mallory could think of was a twentieth-century steam loco-
motive bearing down upon him.

He swallowed grimly, "aventred" his own spear, and upped
Easy Money's pace. Two could play at being locomotives. The
approaching knight and steed loomed larger; the sound of hoofbeats crescendoed into staccato thunder. The spear pointing straight
toward Mallory's breastplate had something of the aspect of a
jetpropelled flagpole. Hurriedly, he got his shield into position.
Maybe the man would spot the red cross, realize its significance,
and slow down.

If he spotted it, he gave no sign, and only came the faster.
Mallory braced himself for the forthcoming impact. However,
the impact never occurred. At the last moment his antagonist
directed the spearpoint at Mallory's helmet, did something that
made it separate itself from the shaft to the accompaniment of a
gout of incandescence and came streaking through the air like a
little comet. Mallory tried to dodge, but he would have been
equally as successful if he had tried to dodge a real comet. There
was a deafening *clang!* in the region of his left audio-amplifier,
and the whole left side of his face went numb. Just before he
blacked out he saw the oncoming knight veer his steed, wheel it
around, and ride off. A peal of all-too-familiar laughter drifted
back over the man's shoulder.

*   *   *

"Now," said the rent-a-robogogue, "you will try again: A is for Atom, B is for Bomb, C is for Conform, D is for Dollar, E is for Economy, and F is for Fun. What comes after F?"

The boy Mallory squirmed in his ABC chair. "I don't know what comes next and I don't care!"

"I'll box your ears," the rent-a-robogogue threatened.

"You wouldn't dare!"

"Yes I would—I'm a physical-chastisement model, you know. Now, we'll try once more: A is for Atom, B is for Bomb, C is for Conform, D is for Dollar, E is for Economy, and F is for Fun. What comes after F?"

"I told you that I didn't know and that I didn't care!"

"I warned you," said the rent-a-robogogue.

"Ow!" the boy Mallory cried.

"Ow!" the man Mallory groaned, sitting up in the weeds beside the early-sixth-century highway.

All was silence around him, if you discounted the stridulations of insects and the *be-ke korak-korak-korak* of frogs. A few yards away, Easy Money stood immobile in the moonlight. Mallory raised his hand to his helmet and felt the sizable dent that the spearpoint had made. Gingerly, he took the helmet off. Who in the world would have dreamed that they had jet rifles in this day and age!

The absurdity of the thought snapped him back to full awareness. A moment later he remembered the peal of familiar laughter.

Perfidion!

The man must have wanted the Grail desperately to have come after it himself, which meant that it was probably worth much more than he had let on. But how had he known when and where to essay the lift? More specifically, how had he found out when and where to essay the lift on such short notice?

Mallory thought back. He was reasonably certain that he had made no slips of the tongue during his visit to the Perfidion Tower and during the ensuing game of golp, and he was equally certain that he had let fall no revealing references to the place-time he had so carefully pinpointed. Where, then, had he gone astray?

Suddenly, way back in his mind, Perfidion said, "By the way,

Tom, I take it you're all set as regards costume, equipment and the like.''

"I've got the sweetest little suit of armor you ever laid eyes on," Mallory heard himself answer.

He swore. So that was it! All Perfidion had needed to do was to make the rounds of the costumers who specialized in armor, and to shell out a few Kennedees to the one Mallory had patronized last. Then, in possession of the knowledge that Mallory was embarking into the past as Sir Galahad, all Perfidion had had to do was to consult one of the many experts he kept at his beck and call. The expert had undoubtedly told him where Sir Galahad was supposed to have found the Grail before taking it to Sarras, and, equally as important, approximately when the event was supposed to have taken place. Further questions could not have failed to elicit the additional information that Sir Launcelot had come to the chamber of the Sangraal before Sir Galahad had, and from this Perfidion had undoubtedly deduced that Sir Launcelot could very well have been a time-thief in disguise, too, and that the man, having arrived on the scene first, could very well have been responsible for the Grail's so-called return to Heaven, despite what legend said to the contrary. Certainly it had been a gamble worth taking, and obviously Perfidion had taken it.

And won the jackpot.

But that didn't mean he was going to keep the jackpot. Not by a long shot. Mallory encephalopathed Easy Money to his side and pulled himself to his feet with the help of the left stirrup and hung his helmet on the pommel. Then he picked up his spear and clambered into the saddle. "We're not beat yet, Easy Money," he said. *Gidd-yap!*

Easy Money whinnied, stamped his feet, and started back toward the *Yore*. A short while later they passed the lane that led to the castle of Carbonek. Presently Mallory heard the *clip-clop* of approaching hoofbeats, and not wanting to risk an encounter in his weakened condition, he encephalo-guided the rohorse off the highway and into the deep shadows of a big oak. There was something tantalizingly familiar about the horse and rider coming down the highway. Small wonder: the "horse" was Easy Money and the rider was himself. He was on his way to the castle of Carbonek to lift the Holy Grail.

Mallory gazed after his retreating figure disgustedly. "Sucker!"
he said.

IV

Rowena nearly threw a fit when Mallory rode into the rec-hall.
"Oh, fair knight, ye be sorely wounded indeed!" she cried,
helping him down from his rohorse. "Certes, an ye bleed so
much ye may die!"

Mallory's head was throbbing, and he saw two damosels that
hight Rowena instead of only one. "I'll be all right after I lie
down for a while," he said. "And don't worry about the
bleeding—it's almost stopped."

He took a step in the direction of his bedroom office, staggered and would have fallen if she hadn't caught his arm. Her
strength astonished him: for all the lightness of his armor, it still
lent him an overall weight of some two hundred and ten pounds;
and yet the shoulder which she provided for him to lean on did
not give once all the way to his bedside. She had his pauldrons,
breastplate, and arm-coverings off in no time flat. His cuisses,
greaves, and sollerets followed. The last he remembered was
lying there in his undergarments and his chainmail vest with
three faces swimming in the misted sea of his vision, each of
them invested with the peculiar beauty that concern, and concern
alone, can grant.

"How is mammakin's little man now?" the rent-a-mammakin
asked, applying soothing sedasalve to the boy Mallory's swollen
ear.

"He hit me, mammakin," the boy Mallory sobbed. "Just
because I wouldn't tell him that G stands for Geography. I hate
geography! I hate it, hate it, hate it!"

"Nasty old rent-a-robogogue! Mammakin sent him away. He
was an old model that got rented out by mistake. Is mammakin's
little man's ear all right now?"

The boy Mallory sat up. "I want my real—" he began.

The man Mallory sat up. "I want my real—" he began.

"I have great joy of thy swift recovery, fair sir," Rowena
said.

She was perched on the edge of his bed, applying a cool and

oothing ointment to his ear. On the table by the bed lay a basin f water, and on her lap lay a pink tube. He grabbed the tube, ooked at the label. *Sedasalve.* He sighed with relief. "Where id you find it?" he asked.

"La! fair sir, when ye did seem no longer on live I did run oth toward and forward in the castle seeking a magical salve vhereby I might succor ye, whereupon I did come to a white box the chapel wherein lay magical tubes of diverse colors and atures whereof I did choose one and—"

Mallory was incredulous. "You chose a tube at random?" he emanded. "Good Lord, it might have contained a counteragent at could have killed me!"

"The . . . the letters thereon seemed of a magical nature, fair night. And . . . and the color was seemly."

"Well, anyway it was the right one." He looked at her. Could he read? he wondered. He was tempted to ask her, but refrained or fear of embarrassing her. "In that same white box," he said, you will find a big bottle filled with round red pellets. Would ou get it for me?"

When she returned with it, he took two of the pills, then he aid his head back on the pillow. "They'll restore the blood I ost," he explained, "but in order for them to do the job roperly I've got to lie perfectly still for at least one hour."

She sat down on the edge of the bed. "Marry! the magic of Merlin is marvelous, albeit not as marvelous as the magic of oseph of Arimathea."

"What did he do that was so marvelous?"

The plum-blue eyes were fixed full upon his face. "Ye wit aught of the tale of the white shield ye bear, fair sir? List, and I ill tell ye:

"It befell after the passion of our Lord thirty-two year, that oseph of Arimathea, the gentle knight, the which took down our ord off the holy Cross, at that time departed from Jerusalem ith a great party of his kindred with him. And so he labored till at they came to a city that hight Sarras. And at that same hour at Joseph came to Sarras there was a king that hight Evelake, at had great war against the Saracens, and in especially against he Saracen, the which was King Evelake's cousin, a rich king d a mighty, which marched nigh this land, and his name was

called Tolleme la Feintes. So on a day these two met to d
battle. Then Joseph, the son of Joseph of Arimathea, went t
King Evelake and told him he should be discomfit and slain, b
if he left his belief of the old law and believed upon the new law
And then there he showed him the right belief of the Hol
Trinity, to the which he agreed unto with all his heart; and the
this shield was made for King Evelake, in the name of Him th
died upon the Cross. And then—''

"Hold it a minute," Mallory said. "This shield you've finall
got around to mentioning—is it the same one you set out to te
me about?"

"Wit ye well, fair sir. And then through King Evelake's goo
belief he had the better of King Tolleme. For when Evelake wa
in the battle there was a cloth set afore the shield, and when l
was in the greatest peril he left put away the cloth, and then h
enemies saw a figure of a man on the Cross, wherethrough the
all were discomfit. And so it befell that a man of King Evelake
was smitten his hand off, and bare that hand in his other han
and Joseph called that man unto him and bade him go with goo
devotion touch the Cross. And as soon as that man had touche
the Cross with his hand it was as whole as ever it was tofor
Then soon after there fell a great marvel, that the cross of th
shield at one time vanished away that no man wist where
became. And then King Evelake was baptized, and for the mo
part all the people of that city. So, soon after Joseph wou
depart, and King Evelake would go with him whether he wou
or nold. And so by fortune they came into this land, that at th
time was called Great Britain: and there they found a great felo
paynim, that put Joseph into prison. And so—''

"A great *what?*" Mallory asked. In one sense the story w
familiar to him, but what bothered him was the fact that it w
familiar in another sense too—a sense he couldn't put his fing
on.

"A wicked unbeliever in our Lord. And so by fortune tidin
came unto a worthy man that hight Mondrames, and he asse
bled all his people for the great renown he had heard of Josep
and so he came into the land of Great Britain and disinherit
this felon paynim and consumed him; and therewith deliver

oseph out of prison. And after that all the people were turned to
ıe Christian faith.

"Not long after that Joseph was laid in his deadly bed. And
ᵛhen King Evelake saw that he made much sorrow, and said:
ᵒr thy love I have left my country, and sith ye shall depart out
f this world, leave me some token of yours that I may think on
ᵒu. Joseph said: That will I do full gladly; now bring me your
ıield that I took you when ye went into battle against King
ᵒlleme. Then Joseph bled at the nose, so that he might not by
ᵒ means be staunched. And there upon that shield be made a
ross of his own blood. Now may ye see a remembrance that I
ᵒve you, for ye shall never see this shield but ye shall think on
ıe, and it shall be always as fresh as it is now. And never shall
ıan bear this shield about his neck but he shall repent it, unto
ıe time that Galahad, the good knight, bare it; and the last of
ıy lineage shall have it about his neck, that shall do many
ıarvelous deeds. Now, said King Evelake, where shall I put this
ıield, that this worthy knight may have it? Ye shall leave it
ıere as Nacien, the hermit, shall be put after his death; for
ıither shall that good knight come the fifteenth day after that he
ıall receive the order of knighthood: and so . . ."

When Mallory awoke Rowena's head was resting on his chest,
ıd she was breathing the soft and even breaths of untroubled
ᵉep. Her hair, viewed thus closely, was not as dark as he had at
rst believed it to be. It was brown, really, rather than dark-
rown. And astonishingly lustrous. Without thinking, he rested
ıs hand lightly upon her head. She stirred then, and sat up,
ıbbing her plum-blue eyes. For a moment she stared at him
ıcomprehendingly, then, "Prithee forgive me, fair sir," she
ıid.

Mallory sat up, too. "Forgive you for what? Go open a couple
f vacuum tins while I get into my armor—I'm going to bring
ıis caper to a close."

"Thy . . . thy strength has returned?"

"I never felt better in my life."

In the rec-hall he said, sitting down at the table before one of
ıe two vacuum tins she had opened, "You never did ask me
hat happened."

"Ye will tell me of thy own will an ye wish me to know."

Mallory took a mouthful of simulsteak, chewed and swallowed. "Your Sir Launcelot turned out to be a phony, and pulled a rabbit out of his helmet the nature of which I'd better not try to describe to you."

Eyes round as plums, she regarded him across the table. "A . . . a phony, fair sir?"

Mallory nodded. "That's a sort of felon paynim who plays golp."

"But with my own eyes I did see his armor, fair knight."

"That's right—you saw his armor. But you didn't see him. A certain character by the name of Perfidion was residing behind that hardware—not the good Sir Launcelot."

"Perfidion?"

Mallory grinned. "Sir Jason Perfidion—a knight errant ye wot not of. But the tournament's not over yet, and this time *I've* got the rabbit: he think's I'm dead."

"He . . . he left ye for dead, fair sir?"

"That he did, and if that little brain-buster of his had struck just one inch to the right, I'd have been just that." He shoved his empty vacuum tin away and stood up. "Excuse me a minute— I've got to visit the sorcerer's tower again."

In the control room, he took the *Yore* back to 7:20 p.m. of the same day and rematerialized it half a mile farther down the valley. Turning, he saw that Rowena had followed him and was watching him from the doorway. "Whereabouts may I find oat that I may feed thy horse, fair knight?" she asked.

"Easy Money doesn't eat. He—" Mallory paused astonished as two of the largest tears he had ever seen coalesced in her eye and went tumbling down her cheeks. "Oh, it's not that he' sick," he rushed on. "It's just that horses like him don't require food to keep them going. Why, Easy Money's guaranteed for . . . he'll live another thirty years."

The sun came up beyond the plum-blue horizons of her eyes. "It pleaseth me mickle to hear ye speak thus, fair knight. I . . . have great joy of him."

Back in the rec-hall, Mallory pulled on his gauntlets, reset his timepiece, and donned his helmet. The left audio-amplifier was shot, but otherwise the piece was in good condition—aside from

the dent, of course. He encephalopathed Easy Money to his side,
hung his shield around his neck, and mounted. "Hand me my
spear, will you, Rowena?" he asked.

She did so. "Ye be a most noble knight indeed, fair sir," she
said, "for to set so little store by thine own life in the service of
a damosel the which is undeserving of thy deeds. I . . . . I would
lever that ye forsook the Sangraal than that ye be fordone."

Her concern touched him, and he removed his helmet and
leaned down and kissed her on the forehead. "Keep the home
fires burning," he said; then, setting his helmet back in place, he
activated the lock, rode across the mirage-moat, and set forth
into the forest once again.

V

This time when he reached the crest of the ridge that separated
the two valleys, Mallory took an azimuth on the towers of
Carbonek, encephalo-fed the direction to Easy Money, and pro-
grammed the "animal" to proceed in as straight a course as
possible.

In the east, the moon was just beginning to rise; in the west,
traces of the sunset lingered blood-red just above the horizon. On
the highway below, a knight sitting astride a brown rohorse and
bearing a white shield with a red cross in the center was riding
toward Carbonek to challenge a twenty-second-century "felon
paynim" in imitation Age-of-Chivalry armor. In the valley Mallory
had just left behind him there were two castles named *Yore*, and
soon, a third would pop into existence and yet another Mallory
come riding out. Mallory grinned. It was a little bit like playing
chess.

The forest which Easy Money presently entered was parklike
in places, and sometimes the trees thinned out into wide, moonlit
meadows. Crossing one of the meadows, Mallory saw the first
star, and when at length Easy Money emerged on the highway,
the heavens were decked out in typical midsummer panoply. The
rohorse had followed its programming almost perfectly and had
emerged at a point just south of the lane leading to the castle of
Carbonek. All Mallory had to do was to encephalo-guide it
farther down the highway to a point beyond the site of the

forthcoming joust. While doing so, he kept well within the
concealing shadows of the bordering oaks and beeches where the
ground was soft and could give forth no tellale *clip-clop* of
hoofbeats. His circumspection proved wise—as in one sense, of
course, it already had—and when the false Sir Launcelot came
riding by on his way to the castle and the chamber of the
Sangraal, he was no more aware of Mallory III's presence by the
roadside than he would presently be aware of Mallory II's presence in the shadows of the trees that bordered the lane.

Mallory III grinned again and brought Easy Money to a halt
just beyond the next bend. "Wit ye well, Sir Jason, that thy
hours be numbered," he said.

He remained seated in the saddle, feeling pretty good about
the world. In no time at all, if his one-man ambuscade came off,
he would be on his way back to the *Yore*, and thence to the
twenty-second century and a haircut. Selling the Sangraal without the aid of a professional time-fence like Perfidion would be
difficult, of course, but it could be done, and once it was done,
he, Mallory, could take his place on Get-Rich-Quick Street with
the best of them, and no questions would be asked. There was,
to be sure, the problem of what to do about a certain damosel
that hight Rowena, but he would face that when he came to it.
Maybe he could drop her off a dozen years in the future in a
region far enough removed from Carbonek to ensure her safety.
He would see.

At this point in his reflections he was jolted into alertness by
the sound of approaching hoofbeats. A moment later he heard a
second set of hoofbeats and knew that Mallory II had made his
presence known. Presently both sets crescendoed into staccato
thunder as the two "knights" came pounding toward each other,
and not long afterward there was a clank and a clatter as Mallory
II went tumbling out of his saddle and into the roadside weeds.
Finally the single set of hoofbeats took over again, and Mallory
III saw a horse and rider coming around the bend in the highway.
He braced himself.

Before making his play, he waited till horse and rider were
directly opposite him; then he encephalopathed Easy Money to
charge. "Sir Launcelot" managed to get his shield up in time,
but the maneuver did him no good. Mallory's spearhead struck

the shield dead center, and "Sir Launcelot" went sailing out of his saddle to land with an awesome clatter flat on his back on the highway. He did not get up.

Dismounting, Mallory removed the man's helmet. It was Perfidion all right. There was a large bruise on the side of his head and he was out cold, but he was still breathing. Next, Mallory looked for the Sangraal. Perfidion had concealed it somewhere, and apparently he had done the job well. Since the armor could not have accommodated an object of that size, the hiding place had to be somewhere on the body of his horse. The horse was standing quietly beside Easy Money in the middle of the highway. It was jet-black and its fetlock-length trappings were blue, threaded with silver; otherwise, the two steeds were identical. Mallory tumbled to the truth then, went over to where the black "horse" was standing, raised its trappings, found the tiny activator button, and depressed it. The croup-hood rose up, and there in the secret compartment, wrapped in red samite, lay the cause of the mounting absentee rate in King Arthur's court.

Always the skeptic, Mallory raised a corner of the samite in order to make certain that he was not being cheated. Instantly, a reflected ray of moonlight stabbed upward into his eyes, and for a moment he was blinded. Exorcising the thought that sneaked into his mind, he closed the croup-hood, rearranged the trappings, and returned to Perfidion's side. Dragging the armor-encumbered man over to the black rohorse and slinging him over the saddle was no easy matter, but Mallory managed; then he picked up Perfidion's helmet and spear and set the former on the pommel and wedged the latter in one of the stirrups. Finally he mounted Easy Money and, encephalopathing the black rohorse to follow, set out down the highway away from the castle of Carbonek.

Make-believe castles could fool the hadbeens, but they couldn't fool a professional. He spotted the phony towers of Perfidion's TSB rising above the trees before he had proceeded half a mile. After raising the "portcullis," he got the man down from the black rohorse, dragged him inside, and propped him against the rec-hall bar. Then he got the man's helmet and spear and laid them beside him. After considerable reflection, he went into the control room, set the time-dial for June 10, 1964, the space-dial for a busy intersection in downtown Los Angeles, and punched out HOT DOG STAND on the lumillusion panel. Satisfied, he went into the generator room and short-circuited the automatic throwout unit so that when rematerialization took place, the generator would burn up. Finding a ball of heavy-duty twine, he returned to the control room, tied one end to the master switch, and began backing out of the TSB, unwinding the twine as he went.

In the rec-hall, he paused, and grinned down at the still-unconscious Perfidion. "It's a better break than you meant to give me, Jason," he said. "And don't worry—once you explain to the authorities what you're doing in a suit of sixth-century armor and how you happened to open a giant hotdog stand in the middle of a traffic-clogged crossroads, you'll be all right. As a matter of fact, with your knowledge of things to come, you'll probably wind up a richer man than you are now—if the smog doesn't get you first." He stepped through the lock, jerked the twine, and the "castle" vanished into thin air.

Remounting Easy Money and encephalopathing the black rohorse to follow, he started back toward the *Yore*, taking a direct route through the forest. He was halfway to his destination and had just emerged into a wide meadow when he saw the knight with the white shield riding toward him in the bright moonlight. In the center of the shield there was a vivid blood-red cross.

When the knight saw Mallory, he brought his steed to a halt. Moonlight glimmered eerily on his shield, turned his helmet to silver. His armor seemed to emit an unearthly light—a light that was at once terrifying and transcendent. The hilt of his sword was as blood-red as the cross on his shield; so was the pommel of his spear. Here was righteousness incarnate. Here in the form of an armored man on horseback was the quintessence of the Age of Chivalry—not the Age of Chivalry as exemplified by the vain and boasting nobles who had constituted nine-tenths of the knight-errantry profession and who had used the quest of the Holy Grail as an excuse to seek after mead and maidens, but the Age of Chivalry as it might have been if the ideal behind it had been shared by the many instead of by the few; the Age of Chivalry, in short, as it had come down to posterity through the pages of Malory's *Le Morte d'Arthur*.

At length the knight spoke: "I hight Sir Galahad of the Table Round."

Reluctantly, Mallory encephalopathed his two rohorses to halt, and said the only thing he had left to say: "I hight St. Thomas of the castle *Yore*."

"By whose leave bear ye likenesses of the red arms and the white shield whereon shines the red cross the which was put here by Joseph of Armathea whilst he lay dying in his deadly bed?"

Mallory did not answer.

There was a silence. Then, "I would joust with ye," Sir Galahad said.

There it was, laid right on the line. The challenge—

The death sentence.

Nonsense! Mallory told himself. He's nothing but a nineteen-year-old kid. With your rohorse and your superior weapons you can unseat him in two seconds flat, and once he's down, that glorified junk pile he's wearing will glue him to the ground so fast he won't be able to lift a finger!

Aloud, he said, "Have at me then!"

Instantly, Sir Galahad wheeled his horse around and rode to the far side of the meadow. There, he wheeled the horse around again and dressed his spear. Moonlight danced a silvery saraband on his white shield, and the blood-red cross blurred and seemed to run.

Mallory dressed his own spear. Immediately, Sir Galahad charged. *Full speed ahead, Easy Money!* Mallory encephalopathed, and the rohorse took off like a rocket.

All he had to do was to hang on tight, and the joust would be in the bag, he reassured himself. Sir Galahad's spear would break like a matchstick, while his own superior spear would penetrate Sir Galahad's shield as though the shield was made of tissue paper, as in a sense it really was when you compared the metal that constituted it to modern alloys. No matter how you looked at the situation, the kid was in for a big letdown. Mallory almost felt sorry for him.

The hoofbeats of horse and rohorse crescendoed; there was the resounding *clang!* of steel coming into violent contact with steel. Mallory's spear struck Sir Galahad's shield dead center—and snapped in two. Sir Galahad's spear struck Mallory's shield dead center—and Mallory sailed over Easy Money's croup and crashed to the ground.

He was stunned, both mentally and physically. Staggering to his feet, he drew his sword and raised his shield. Sir Galahad had wheeled his horse around, and now he came riding back. Several yards from Mallory, he tossed his spear aside, dismounted as lightly as though he wore no armor at all, drew his sword, and advanced. Mallory stepped forward, his confidence returning. His spear had been defective—that was it. But his sword and his shield weren't and now that the kid had elected to give him a sporting chance, he would teach the young upstart a lesson that he would never forget.

Again, the two men came together. Down came Sir Galahad's sixth century sword; up went Mallory's twenty-second-century shield. There was an ear-piercing *clang*, and the shield parted down the middle.

Aghast, Mallory stepped back. Sir Galahad moved in, sword upraised again. Mallory raised his own sword, caught the full force of the terrific down-rushing blow on the blade. His sword was cut cleanly in two, his left pauldron was cleanly cleaved, and a great numbness afflicted his left shoulder. He went down.

He stayed down.

Sir Galahad leaned over him, unbroken sword uplifted. The cross in the center of the snow-white shield was a bright and burning red. "Ye must yield you as an overcome man, or else I may slay you."

"I yield," Mallory said.

Sir Galahad sheathed his sword. "Ye be not sorely wounded, and sithen I desire not neither of thy two steeds, as belike they be as unworthy as thy pieces, ye can return to thy castle unholpen."

Mallory blacked out for a moment, and when he came to, the shining knight was gone.

He lay there in the moonlight for some time, looking up at the stars. At length he fought his way to his feet and encephalopathed the two rohorses to his side. Mounting Easy Money, he encephalopathed it to return to the westernmost "castle of Yore" and encephalopathed the other rohorse to follow. He left his broken weapons where they lay.

What had gone out of the world during the last sixteen hundred years that had left sophisticated twenty-second-century steel inferior in quality to naive sixth-century wrought iron? What did Sir Galahad have that he, Mallory, lacked? Mallory shook his head. He did not know.

The moonlit "towers" of the *Yore* had become visible through the trees before it occurred to him that before riding away the man just might have removed the Sangraal from the black rohorse's croup. At first thought, such a possibility was too absurd to be entertained, but not on second thought. According to *Le Morte d'Arthur*, the fellowship of Sir Galahad, Sir Percivale, and Sir Bors had taken both the table of silver and the Sangraal to Sarras where, some time later, the Sangraal had been "borne up to heaven," never to be seen again. Whether they had taken the table of silver did not concern Mallory, but what did concern him was the fact that if they had taken the Sangraal they could have done so only if it had fallen into Sir Galahad's hands this very night. Tomorrow would be too late—now was too late, in fact—provided, of course, that Mallory was destined to return with it to the twenty-second century. Here, then, was the crossroads, the real moment of truth: was he destined to succeed, or wasn't he?

Hurriedly, he encephalopathed the two rohorses to halt, dismounted, and raised the black rohorse's trappings. He was dizzy from the loss of blood, but he did not let his dizziness dissuade him from his purpose, and he had the croup-hood raised in a matter of a few seconds. He held his breath when he looked within, expelled it with relief. The Sangraal had not been disturbed.

He lifted it out of the croup-compartment, straightened its red samite covering, and cradled it in his arms. Too weak to remount Easy Money, he encephalopathed the two rohorses to follow and began walking toward the *Yore*. Rowena must have seen him coming on one of the telewindows, for she had the lock open when he arrived. Her face went white when she looked at him, and when she saw the Grail, her eyes grew even larger than plums. He went over and set it gently down on the rec-hall table, then he collapsed into a nearby chair. He had just enough presence of mind left to send her for the bottle of blood-restorer pills, and just enough strength left to swallow several of them

when she brought it. Then he boarded the phantom ship that had
mysteriously appeared beside him and set sail upon the soundless
sea of night.

VI

"No," said the rent-a-mammakin, "you cannot see her. She is
displeased with your score in the get-rich-quick race."

"I did my best," the boy Mallory sobbed. "But when it came
to stepping on all those faces, I just couldn't do it!"

The rent-a-mammakin arranged its features into a severe frown
and strengthened its grip on the boy Mallory's arm. "You knew
that they were only painted on the game floor to symbolize
the Competitive Spirit," it said. "Why couldn't you step on
them?"

The boy Mallory made a final desperate effort to gain the
bedroom door which his mother had just slammed and before
which the rent-a-mammakin stood, then he sank defeated to the
floor. "I don't know why—I just couldn't, that's all," he sobbed.
He raised his voice. "But I *will* step on them! I'll step on real
faces too—just you wait and see. I'll be a bigger get-rich-quickman
than my father ever dreamed of being. I'll show her!"

"I'll show her," the man Mallory murmured, "just you wait
and see."

He opened his eyes. Save for himself, the bedroom-office was
empty. "Rowena!"

No answer.

He raised his voice. "Rowena!"

Again, no answer.

He frowned. The door to the bedroom-office was open, and
the "castle" certainly wasn't so large that his voice couldn't
carry from one end of it to the other.

His shoulder throbbed faintly, but otherwise he was unaware
of his wound. Rowena had bound it neatly—it was said that Age
of Chivalry gentlewomen were quite proficient in such matters—
and apparently she had once again got hold of the right
counteragent.

He sat up and swung his feet to the floor. So far, so good.
Tentatively, he stood up. A wave of vertigo broke over him

After it passed, he was as good as new. The blood-restorer pills had done their work well.

Nevertheless, everything was not as it should be. Something was very definitely wrong. "Rowena!" he called again.

Still no answer.

She had removed his armor and piled it neatly at the foot of the bed. He stared at the various pieces, trying desperately to think. Something had awakened him—that was it. The slamming of a door . . . or a lock.

He took a deep breath. He smelled green things. Dampness. A forest at eventide . . .

He knew then what was wrong. The lock of the *Yore* had been opened and had been left open long enough for the evening air to permeate the interior of the TSB; long enough, in other words, to have permitted someone to ride across the imaginary drawbridge that spanned the mirage-moat. Afterward, the lock had slammed back into place of its own accord.

He hurried into the rec-hall. Easy Money stood all alone behind the tourist-bar. The black rohorse was gone.

His eyes leaped to the rec-hall table. The Sangraal was gone, too.

He groaned. The little idiot was taking it back! And after he had forbidden her to leave the "castle" too! Well, no, he hadn't forbidden her, exactly: he had forbidden her to leave it *during his absence*.

He walked over to the telewindow nearest the lock and scrutinized the screen. She was nowhere in sight, but night was on hand and the range of his vision, while considerably abetted by the light of the rising moon, was limited to the nearer trees.

Presently he frowned. Was it still the same night, or had he been unconscious for almost twenty-four hours?

It *couldn't* be the same night—the position of the moon disproved that. And yet he could swear that he had been unconscious for no more than a few hours.

Belatedly, he remembered his gauntlet timepiece, and returned to the bedroom-office. The timepiece registered 10:32. But that didn't make any sense either: the moon was still low in the sky.

He knew then that there could be but one answer, and he

headed for the control room posthaste. Sure enough, the jump-
board timedial had been set for 8:00 p.m. of the same day. He
looked at the space-dial. That had been set to rematerialize the
Yore one half mile farther west.

He wiped his forehead. Good Lord, she might have sent the
TSB all the way back to the Age of Reptiles! Even worse, she
might have plunked it right down in the middle of WWIII!

She hadn't though. In point of fact, she had done exactly what
she had set out to do—taken the *Yore* back to a point in time
from which the Sangraal could be returned to the castle of
Carbonek less than an hour after it had been stolen.

Suddenly he remembered how she had watched him from the
doorway of the control room each time he had reset the time- and
space-dials. Technologically speaking, she was little more than a
child, but jump-boards were as uncomplicated as modern technol-
ogy could make them, and a person needed to be but little more
than a child to operate them.

Grimly, Mallory returned to his bedroom-office and got into
his armor; then, ignoring the throbbing of his reawakened wound,
he mounted Easy Money and set out. He had no weapons, but it
could not be helped. With a little luck, he would have need of
none. He was about due for a little luck, if you asked him.

He gambled that Rowena would use the same route back to the
chamber of the Sangraal that they had used in leaving it—actually,
she had no other choice—and he encephalo-guided Easy Money
at a fast trot in the direction of the river in the hope of overtaking
her before she reached the entrance to the subterranean passage.
However, the hope did not materialize, and he saw no sign of
her till he reached the entrance himself. Strictly speaking, he saw
no sign of her then either, but he did discern several dislodged
stones that could have been thrown up by the black rohorse's
hoofs.

Entering the passage, he frowned. Until that moment, the
incongruity of a sixth-century damosel encephalo-guiding a twenty-
second-century rohorse had not struck him. After a moment,
though, he had to admit that the incongruity was not as glaring as
it had at first seemed. "Encephalopathing" was merely a glorified term for "thinking," and Rowena, shortly after mounting
Perfidion's steed, must have made the discovery that she had

only to think where she wanted to go in order for the rohorse to take her there.

He had not remembered to bring a light, nor did he need one. The infrared rays of Easy Money's eye units were more than sufficient for the task on hand, and overtaking the girl would have been as easy as rolling off a log—if she hadn't been riding a rohorse, too. Overtaking her wasn't of paramount importance anyway: he could confiscate the Sangraal after she returned it just as easily as he could before.

The odd part about the whole thing was that Mallory never once thought of the inevitable overlap till he saw the flicker of torchlight up ahead. An instant later he heard the sound of a woman's voice, and instinctively he encephalo-guided Easy Money into a nearby shallow cave.

The flickering light grew gradually brighter, and presently hoofbeats became audible. The woman's voice was loud and clear now, and Mallory made out her words above the purling of the underground stream: ". . . And then he set down the maiden, and was armed at all pieces save he lacked his spear. Then he dressed his shield, and drew out his sword, and Bors smote him so hard that it went through his shield and habergeon on the left shoulder. And through great strength he beat him down to the earth, and at the pulling of Bors' spear there he swooned. Then came Bors to the maid and said: How seemeth it to you of this knight ye be delivered at this time? Now sir, said she, I pray you lead me there as this knight had me. So shall I do gladly: and took the horse of the wounded knight, and set the gentlewoman upon him, and so brought her as she desired. Sir knight, said she, ye have better sped than ye weened, for an I had lost my maidenhead, five hundred men should have died for it. What knight was he that had you in the forest? By my faith, said she, he is my cousin. So wot I never with what engyn the fiend enchafed him, for yesterday he took me from my father privily; for I nor none of my father's men mistrusted him not, and if he had had my maidenhead he should have died for the sin, and his body shamed and dishonored for ever. Thus as . . ."

At this point, the truth behind the sense of *déjà vu* that Mallory had experienced the first time he had heard the tale hit him so hard between the eyes that he jerked back his head. When he did so, his helmet came into contact with the cave wall and scraped against the stone. The rohorse and its two riders were directly across the stream now. *"Shhh!"* Mallory I whispered.

Rowena I gasped. "It were best that I thanked ye now for thy great kindness, fair knight," she said, "for anon we be no longer on live."

"Nonsense!" Mallory I said. "If this fiend of yours is anywhere in the vicinity, he's probably more afraid of us than we are of him."

"Per . . . peradventure he hath already had meat," Rowena I said hopefully. "The tale saith that an the fiend be filled he becomes aweary and besets not them the which do pass him by in peace."

"I'll keep my sword handly just in case he changes his mind," Mallory I said. "Meanwhile, get on with your autobiography—only for Pete's sake, cut it short, will you?"

"An it please, fair sir. Thus as the fair gentlewoman stood talking with Sir Bors there came twelve knights seeking after her, and anon . . ."

For a long while after the voices faded away, Mallory IV could not move. Hearing the story the second time and, more important, hearing it from the standpoint of an observer, he had been able to identify it for what it really was—an excerpt from *Le Morte d'Arthur*. The Joseph of Arimathea bit had been an excerpt, too, he realized now, probably lifted word for word from the text. It was odd indeed that a sixth-century damosel who presumably couldn't read could be on such familiar terms with a book that would not be published for another nine hundred and forty-three years.

But not so odd if she was a twenty-second-century blonde in a sixth-century damosel's clothing.

Remembering Perfidion's secretary, Mallory felt sick. No, there was no noticeable resemblance between her and the damosel that hight Rowena; but the removal of a girdle and a quarter of a pound of makeup, not to mention the application of a "luster-rich" brown hairdye and the insertion of a pair of plum-blue contact lenses, could very well have brought such a resemblance into being—and quite obviously had. The Past Police were noted for their impersonations, and most of them had eidetic memories.

Come on, Easy Money, Mallory encephalopathed. *You and I have got a little score to settle.*

When he entered the chamber of the Sangraal, Rowena IV was arranging the red samite cover around the Grail. She jumped when she saw him. "Marry! fair sir, ye did startle me. Methinketh ye be asleep in thy castle."

"Knock it off," Mallory said. "The masquerade's over."

She regarded him with round uncomprehending eyes. He got the impression that she had been crying. "The . . . the masquerade, fair knight?"

"That's right . . . the masquerade. You're no more the damosel Rowena than I'm the knight Sir Galahad."

She lowered her eyes to his breastplate. "I . . . I wot well ye be not Sir Galahad, fair sir. It . . . it happed that aforetime I did see Sir Galahad with my own eyes, and when ye did unlace thy unberere and I did see thy face, I knew ye could not be him of which ye spake." Abruptly she raised her head and looked at him defiantly. "But I knew from thy eyes that ye be most noble, fair sir, and therefore an ye did pretend to be him the which ye were not, ye did so for noble cause, and it were not for me to question."

"I said knock it off," Mallory said, but with considerably less conviction. "I'm on to you—don't you see? You're a time-fink."

"A . . . a time fink? I wot not what—"

"An agent of the Past Police. One of those do-gooders who run around history replacing stolen goods and turning in hardworking people like myself. You gave yourself away when you lifted that Sir Bors bit straight out of *Le Morte d'Arthur* and—"

"But I did say ye sooth, fair sir. Sir Bors did verily succor my maidenhead. I wot not how there can be two of ye and two of me and four hackneys when afore there were but two, and I wot not how by touching the magic board in thy castle in a certain fashion that I could make the hour earlier and I wot not how the magic steed I did bestride brought me hither—I wot not none of these matters, fair sir. I wot only that the magic of thy castle is marvelous indeed."

For a while, Mallory didn't say anything. He couldn't. In the plum-blue eyes fixed full upon his face, truth shone, and that same truth had invested her every word. The damosel Rowena despite all evidence to the contrary and despite the glaring paradox the admission gave rise to, was not a phony, never had been a phony, and never would be a phony. She was, as a matter of fact—with the exception of Sir Galahad—the only completely honest person he had known in all his life.

"Tell me," he said, at length, "weren't you afraid to come back through that passage alone? Weren't you afraid the fiend would get you?"

"La! fair sir—I had great fear. But it were not fitting that bethought me of myself at such a time." She paused. Then "What might be thy true name, sir knight?"

"Mallory," Mallory said. "Thomas Mallory."

"I have great joy of thy acquaintance, Sir Thomas."

Mallory only half heard her. He was looking at the samite-covered Sangraal. No more obstacles stood between him and his quest, and time was a-wasting. He started to take a step in the direction of the silver table.

His foot did not leave the floor.

He was acutely aware of Rowena's eyes. As a matter of fact he could almost feel them upon his face. It wasn't that they were any different than they had been before: it was just that he was suddenly and painfully cognizant of the trust and the admiration that shone in them. Despite himself, he had the feeling that he was standing in bright and blinding sunlight.

Again, he started to take a step in the direction of the silver table. Again, his foot did not leave the floor.

It wasn't so much the fact that she didn't believe he would take the Sangraal that bothered him: it was the fact that she couldn't conceive of him taking it. She could be convinced that black was white, perhaps, and that white was black, and that fiends hung out in empty caves and castles; but she could never be convinced that a "knight" of the qualities she imputed to Mallory could perform a dishonorable act.

And there it was, laid right on the line. For all the good the Grail was going to do Mallory, it might just as well have been at the bottom of the Mindanao Deep.

He sighed. His gamble hadn't paid off any more than Perfidion's had. The real Sir Galahad was the one who had inherited the Grail after all—not the false one. The false one grinned ruefully. "Well," he told the damosel Rowena, "it's been nice knowing you." He swallowed; for some reason his throat felt tight. "I . . I imagine you'll be all right now."

To his amazement, she broke into tears. "Oh, Sir Thomas!" she cried. "In my great haste to return the Sangraal to the chamber and to right the grievous wrong committed by the untrue knight Sir Jason, I did bewray my trust again. For when I espied ye and me and Easy Money in the passage I did suffer a great discomfit, and it so happed that when my steed did enter into a cave that the Sangraal came free from my hands and . . and—"

Mallory was staring at her. "You dropped it?"

Stepping over to the silver table, she lifted a corner of the red samite. The dent was not a deep one, but just the same you didn't have to look twice to see it. "I . . . I nyst not what to do," she said.

Suddenly Mallory remembered the first sound he had heard in the passage when he and Rowena were leaving the castle of Carbonek. "Well, how do you like that!" he said. He grinned. "I take it that this puts your hands in jeopardy all over again—right?"

"Yes, Sir Thomas, but I would lever die than beseech thee again to—"

"Which," Mallory continued happily, "makes it out of the question for a knight such as myself to leave you behind." He took her arm. "Come on," he said. "I don't know how I'm going to fit a sixth-century damosel into twenty-second-century society, but believe me, I'm going to try!"

"And . . . and will ye take Easy Money to this land whereof we speak, Sir Thomas?"

"Sir Thomas" grinned. "Wit ye well," he said, "and his buddy, too. Come on."

*   *   *

In the *Yore*, he tossed his helmet and gauntlets into a corner of the rec-hall and proceeded straight to the control room. There with Rowena standing at his elbow, he set the time-dial for June 21, 2178, and the space-dial for the Kansas City Time-Touris Port. Lord, it would be good to get home again and get a haircut "Here goes," he told Rowena, and threw the switch.

There was a faint tremor. "Brace yourself, Rowena," he said and took her over to the control-room telewindow.

Together, they gazed upon the screen. Mallory gasped. The vista of spiral suburban dwellings which he had been expecting was not in the offing. In its stead was a green, tree-stippled countryside. In the distance, a castle was clearly discernible.

He stared at it. It wasn't a sixth-century job like Carbonek—it was much more modern. But it was still a castle. Obviously, the jump-board had malfunctioned and thrown the *Yore* only a little ways into the future, the while leaving it in pretty much the same locale.

He returned to the jump-board to find out. Just as he reached it, its lights flickered and went out. The time-and space-dials however, remained illumined long enough for him to see when and where the TSB had rematerialized. The year was 1428 A.D. the locale, Warwickshire.

Mallory made tracks for the generator room. The generator was smoking and the room reeked with the stench of shorted wires.

He swore. Perfidion!

So that was why the man had broken with tradition and invited a common time-thief to a game of golp!

If he had been anyone but Perfidion he would have gimmicked the controls of the *Yore* so that Mallory would have wound up directly in the fifteenth century sans sojourn in the sixth. But being Perfidion, he had wanted Mallory to know how completely he was being outsmarted. The chances were, though, that if the man had anticipated the near-coincidence of the two visits to the chamber of the Sangraal he would have seen to it that Mallory had never gotten a chance to use his Sir Galahad suit.

Returning to the control room, Mallory saw that the lumillusion panel had been pre-programmed to materialize the *Yore* as a fifteenth-century English castle. Apparently it had been in the books all along for him to become a fifteenth-century knight, just as it had been in the books all along for Perfidion to become the proprietor of a misplaced hotdog stand.

Mallory laughed. He had gotten the best of the bargain after all. At least there was no smog in the fifteenth century.

Who was he supposed to be? he wondered. Had his name gone down in history by any chance?

Abruptly he gasped. Was *he* the Sir Thomas Malory with estates in Northhampshire and Warwickshire? Was *he* the Sir Thomas Malory who had compiled and translated and written *Le Morte d'Arthur?* Almost nothing about the man's life was known, and probably the little that was known had been assumed. He *could* have popped up from nowhere, made his fortune through foreknowledge, and been knighted. He *could* have been a reformed time-thief stranded in the fifteenth century.

But if he, Mallory, was Malory, how in the world was he going to get five hundred chapters of semihistorical data together and pass them off as *Le Morte d'Arthur?*

Suddenly he understood everything.

Going over to where Rowena was still standing in front of the telewindow, he said, "I'll bet you know no end of stories about the doings of the knights of the Table Round."

"La! Sir Thomas. Ever I saw day of my life I have heard naught else in the court of my father."

"Tell me," Mallory said, "how did this Round Table business begin? Or, better yet, how did the Grail business begin? We can take up the Round Table business later on."

She thought for a moment. Then, "List, fair sir, and I will say ye: At the vigil of Pentecost, when all the fellowship of the Round Table were come unto Camelot and there heard their service, and the tables were set ready to the meat, right so entered into the hall a full fair gentlewoman on horseback, that had ridden full fast, for her horse was all besweated. Then she there alit, and came before the king and saluted him; and he said: Damosel, God thee bless. Sir, said she, for God's sake say me where Sir Launcelot is. Yonder ye may see him, said the king. Then she went unto Launcelot and said: Sir Launcelot, I salute you on King Pelles' behalf, and I require you come on with me hereby into a forest. Then Sir Launcelot asked her with whom

she dwelled. I dwell, said she, with King Pelles. What will ye
with me? said Launcelot. Ye shall know, said she, when ye—"

"That'll do for now," Mallory interrupted. "We'll come back
to it as soon as I get stocked up on paper and ink. Scheherazade,"
he added.

"Scheherazade, Sir Thomas? I wot not—"

He leaned down and kissed her. "There's no need for you to
wot," he said. Probably, he reflected, he would have to do a
certain amount of research in order to record the happenings that
had ensued his and Rowena's departure, and undoubtedly said
research would result ironically in the recording of the true visits
of Sirs Galahad and Launcelot to the chamber of the Sangraal—
the "time-slots" on which he and Perfidion had gambled and
lost their shirts. The main body of the work, however, had been
deposited virtually on his lap, and its style and flavor had been
arbitrarily determined. Moreover, contrary to what history would
later maintain, the job could not be done in prison, but right here
in the "castle of Yore" with Rowena sitting—and dictating—
beside him. As for the impossibility of giving a sixth-century
damosel as his major source, that could be avoided—as in one
sense it already had been—by making frequent allusions to
imaginary French sources. And as for the main obstacle to the
endeavor—his twenty-second-century cynicism—that had been
obviated during his encounter with Sir Galahad.

The book wouldn't be published till 1485, but just the same,
he was keen to get started on it. Writing it should be fun. Which
reminded him: "I know we haven't known each other very long
in one sense, Rowena," he said, "but in another, we've known
each other for almost nine hundred years. Will you marry me?"

She blinked once. Then her plum-blue eyes showed how truly
blue they could become and she threw her arms around his
gorget. "Wit ye well, Sir Thomas," said she, "that there is
nothing in the world but I would lever do than be thy bride!"

Thus did the prose epic known
successively as "La Mort d'Arthury,"
THE MOST ANCIENT
AND FAMOUS HISTORY OF THE
RENOWNED PRINCE ARTHUR,

KING OF BRITAINE,
AS ALSO, ALL THE NOBLE ACTS,
AND HEROICKE DEEDS
OF HIS VALIANT KNIGHTS
OF THE ROUND TABLE,
and ''Le Morte d'Arthur''
come to be recorded.

DIVIDE AND RULE

by L. Sprague de Camp

The multitalented L. Sprague de Camp (1907–   ) has won the International Fantasy, Tolkien Fantasy, and Science Fiction Writers of America Grand Master awards. He is most noted for authoring Lest Darkness Fall *(1941), a classical story of time travel; coauthoring the zany Harold Shea fantasies (with Fletcher Pratt); and polishing, expanding, and ordering Robert E. Howard's Conan series. Virtually ignored, however, are a number of de Camp's most skillful works, such as* Genus Homo *(1950, coauthored with P. Schuyler Miller),* The Tritonian Ring *(1953), and* The Dragon of the Ishtar Gate *(1961). So we are especially pleased with being able to bring his delightful* Unknown *novella of alien occupation, "Divide and Rule," back into print once again.*

I

The broad Hudson, blue under spring skies, was dotted with sails. The orchards in the valley were aglow with white and purple blossoms. Beyond the river frowned Storm King, not much of a mountain by western standards, but impressive enough to a York Stater. The landscape blazed with the livid green of young leaves—and Sir Howard van Slyck, second son of the Duke of Poughkeepsie, wished to God he could get at the itch under his breastplate without going to the extreme of dismounting and removing half his armor.

As the huge black gelding plodded along the bypass that took the Albany Post Road around Peekskill, its rider reflected that he hadn't been too clever in starting out from Ossining fully accoutered. But how was he to know the weather would turn hot so suddenly? The sponge-rubber padding under the plates made the suit suffocatingly hot. Little drops of sweat crawled down his skin; and then, somewhere around Croton, the itch had begun. It seemed to be right under the Van Slyck trademark, which, inlaid in the plastron, was the only ornamentation on an otherwise plain suit. The trademark was a red maple leaf in a white circle, with the Van Slyck motto, "Give 'em the works," in a circle around it.

Twice he had absently reached up to scratch, to be recalled to the realities of the situation by the rasp of metal on metal. Maybe a smoke would help him forget it. He opened a compartment in his saddle, took out pipe, tobacco, and lighter, and lit up. (He really preferred cigarettes, but the ashes dribbled down inside his helmet.)

The bypass swung out over the New York Central tracks. Sir Howard pulled over to his own side to let a six-horse bus clatter past, then walked the gelding over to the edge and looked down. Up the tracks his eye was caught by the gleam of the brass rings on the ends of the tusks of an elephant pulling a string of little cars; the afternoon freight for New York, he thought. By the smallness of the animal's ears he knew it was the Indian species. Evidently the Central had decided against switching to African elephants. The Pennsylvania used them because they were bigger and faster, but they were also less docile. The Central had tried one out as an experiment the year before; the duke, who was a big stockholder in the Central, had told him about it. On the trial run the brakeman had been careless and let the lead car bump the elephant's hind legs, whereupon the animal had pulled two cars off the track and would have killed the chairman of the board if it had been able to catch him.

Sir Howard resumed his way north, relieved to note that the

itch had stopped. At the intersection of the bypass with the connecting road to the Bronx Parkway he drew rein again. Something was coming down the road in long, parabolic leaps. He knew what that meant. With a grunt of annoyance he heaved himself out of the saddle. As the thing drew near he took the pipe out of his mouth and flipped his right arm up in salute.

The thing, which looked rather like a kangaroo wearing a football helmet, shot by without apparently looking at them. Sir Howard had heard of sad cases of people who had neglected to salute hoppers because they thought they weren't looking at them. He felt no particular resentment at having to salute the creature. After all, he'd been doing it all his life. Such irritation as he felt was merely at the idea of having to hoist his own two hundred and ten pounds, plus forty pounds of chrome-nickel steel plate, back on his tall mount on a hot day.

Seven miles up the Post Road lay Castle Peekskill, and Sir Howard fully intended to sponge a dinner and a night's sleep off his neighbor. Halfway up the winding road he heard a musical toot. He pulled off the asphalt; a long black torpedo on wheels was swooping up the grade behind him. He unshipped the duralumin lance from its boot, and as the car whizzed past, the maple-leaf flag of the Van Slycks fluttered down in an arc. He got a glimpse of the occupants; four hoppers, their heads looking rather like those of giant rats under the inevitable helmets. Luckily you didn't have to dismount for hoppers in power vehicles; they went by too fast for such a rule to be practical. Sir Howard wondered—as had many others—what it would be like to travel in a power vehicle. Of course there was an easy way to find out; just break a hopper law. Unfortunately, the ride received in that way was a strictly one-way affair.

"Oh, well, no doubt God had known what He was about when He had made the rule allowing nobody but hoppers to have power vehicles and explosives and things. Man had been very wicked, so God had sent the hoppers to rule over him. At least that was what you learned in school. His brother Frank had doubts; had, very secretly, confided them to Sir Howard. Frank even said that once man had had his own power vehicles. He didn't know about that; the hoppers knew a terrible lot, and if that had been so they'd have had it so taught in the schools. Still,

Frank was smart, and what he said wasn't to be laughed off. Frank was a queer duck, always poking around old papers after useless bits of knowledge. Sir Howard wondered how it was that he got on so well with his skinny little elder brother, with whom he had so little in common. He certainly hoped nothing would happen to Frank before the old man was gathered unto his fathers. He'd hate to have the management of the duchy around his neck, at least just yet. He was having too much fun.

He swung off the road when Castle Peekskill appeared over the treetops, near the site of the old village of Garrison. He stopped before the gate and blew a whistle. The gatekeeper popped out of the tower with his usual singsong of: "Who are you and what do you seek?" Then he said: "Oh, it's you, Sir Howard. I'll tell Lord Peekskill you're here." And presently the gate—a huge slab of reinforced concrete hinged at the bottom—swung out from the wall and down.

John Kearton—Baron Peekskill—was in the courtyard as Sir Howard's horse went *plop-plop* over the concrete. He had evidently just come in from a try for a pheasant, as he wore an old leather jacket and very muddy boots and leaned on a light crossbow.

"Howard, my boy!" he shouted. He was a short man, rather stout, with reddish-brown hair and beard. "Get out of your tinware and into your store clothes. Here, Lloyd, take Sir Howard's duffel bag to the first guest room. You'll stay overnight with us, won't you? Of course you will! I want to hear about the war. WABC had an announcer at the Battle of Mount Kisco, but he saw a couple of the Connecticut horses coming toward him and pulled foot. After that all we could hear was the sound of his horse going hell-for-leather back to Ossining."

"I'll be glad to stay," said Sir Howard. "If I'm not putting you out—"

"No, no, not a bit of it. You've got that same horse still, I see. I like entires better for war horses myself."

"They may have more pep," admitted the knight, "but this old fellow does what I want him to, which is the main thing. Three years ago he took third in his class at the White Plains show. That was before he got those scars. But take a look at this saddle; it's a new and very special model. See: built-in radio compartments in the cantle for your things, and everything. Got it at a discount, too.''

Sir Howard clanked upstairs after his host. The transparent lucite visor of his burganet was already up; he unlatched the bib and pushed it up, too, then carefully wriggled his head out of the helmet. His square, craggy face bore the little beard and mustache affected by his class. His nose was not all that a nose should be, as the result of an encounter with the business end of a billhook. But he had refused to have it plasticized back into shape, on the ground that he could expect more than one broken nose in his life, and the surgery would, therefore, be a waste of money. His inky-black hair covered a highly developed brain, somewhat rusty from disuse. When you could knock any man in the duchy out of his saddle, and drink any man in the duchy under the table, and had a way with the girls, there were few stimuli to heavy thinking.

Peekskill remarked. ''That's a nice suit you have. What is it, a Packard?''

''Yeah,'' replied Sir Howard, pulling off a rerebrace. ''It's several years old; I suppose I'll have to trade it in for a new model one of these days. The only trouble is that new suits cost money. What do you think of the new Ford?''

''Hm-m-m—I dunno. I'm not sure I like that all-lucite helmet. It does give you vision in all directions. But if they make it thick enough to stop a poleax, it'll make you top-heavy, I think. And the lucite gets scratched and nicked up so quickly, especially in a fight.''

''Let's see your kicker, John,'' said Sir Howard, reaching for the crossbow. ''Marlin, isn't it?''

''No, Winchester, last year's. I had my armorer take off that damned windage adjustment, which I never used, anyway. That's why it looks different. But let's hear about the war. The papers gave us just the bare facts.''

''Oh, there wasn't much to it,'' said Sir Howard with exaggerated indifference. ''I killed a man. Funny: I've been in six fights, and that was the first time I really knew I'd gotten one of the enemy. I'm not counting that bandit fellow we caught up at Staatsburg. You know how it is in a fight: everybody's hitting at you and vice versa, and you don't have time to see what damage you've done.

"I shouldn't claim much credit for this killing, though. I signed up at Ossining because the city manager's a cousin of mine, and they pay well. The C. M. collected a couple of hundred heavy horses from lower Westchester, and he had the commons of Ossining and Tarrytown for pikes. He'd heard that Danbury was going to get a contingent of heavy horses from Torrington. So he put us in two groups, lances in the first only. I was in the second, so they made me leave my toothpick behind. That's a nice little sticker, by the way; Hamilton Standard made it.

"We found them just this side of Mount Kisco. Our scouts flushed an ambush, very neat; chevaux-de-frisse at the far end, horses on either side, crossbows behind every bush. The C. M. swung us south to smash one of their bodies of horses before the other could come up. When we shook out and charged, their left wing scattered without waiting for us as if six devils with green ears were after them. I couldn't see anything because of the lances in front of my group. But the ground's pretty rough, you know, and you can't keep a nicely dressed line. The first thing I knew was when something went *bong* on my helmet, and these red-shirted chaps with spiked helmets and shields were all around me, poking at the joints in my suit. They were Danbury's right wing. He hadn't been able to get any heavy horses, after all, but he seemed to have enlisted all the light horses in Connecticut. They were crab-suited, with chain pants hanging down from their cuirasses.

"I swung at a couple of them, but they were out of reach each time the ax got there. Then Paul Jones almost stepped on a couple of dismounted red-shirts. I chopped at one, but he got his shield up in time. And before I could recover, the other one, who didn't have a shield, grabbed the shaft in both hands and tried to take it away from me. I was afraid to let go for fear he'd kill my horse before I could get my sword out. And while we were having our tug-of-war, some crab on the other side of me—the left side—grabbed my ankle and shoved it up. Of course, I went out of the saddle as pretty as a pay check, right on top of this chap who wanted my ax.

"I couldn't see anything for a few minutes because I had my head in a bush. When I got up on my knees there weren't any more red-shirts in sight. They'd found us pretty hard nuts to crack, and when they saw the pikes coming they beat it. I found I still had hold of the ax. The Danburian was underneath me, and the spike on the end of the shaft was driven under his chin and up into his head. He was as dead as last year's treaties. They had about half a dozen killed in that brush; we lost one man—thrust under the armpit—and had a couple of horses killed by kicker bolts. We took their dismounted horses and some of their cross-bows prisoner. I climbed back on Paul Jones and joined up with the chase. We couldn't catch them, naturally. We chased 'em clear to Danbury Castle, and when we got there they were inside thumbing their noses and shooting at us with ballistae.

"We sat outside for a couple of weeks, but they had enough canned stuff for years, and threatening a seventy-foot concrete wall doesn't get you anywhere. So finally the C. M. and Danbury agreed to submit their argument about road tolls to a hopper court, and we went back to Ossining for our pay."

During his story Sir Howard had gotten out of his armor and into his ordinary clothes. It was pleasant to sprawl in the freedom of tweed and linen, with a tall glass in your hand, and watch the sun drop behind Storm King. "Of course, it might have been different"—his voice dropped till it was barely audible—"if we'd had guns."

Peekskill started. "Don't say such things, my boy. Don't even think them. If *they* found out—" He shuddered a little and took a big gulp of his highball.

A flunky entered and announced: "My lord, Squire Matthews, with a message from Sir Humphrey Goldberg."

Peekskill frowned. "What's this? Why couldn't he have written me a letter? Come on, Howard, let's see what he wants."

They found the squire in the hall, looking grimly polite. He bowed stiffly, and said with exaggerated distinctness: "My Lord Peekskill, Sir Humphrey Goldberg sends his compliments, and wants to know what the hell your lordship meant by calling him a double-crossing, dog-faced baboon in the Red Bear Inn last night!"

"Oh, dear," sighed the baron. "Tell Sir Humphrey that first,

I deny calling him such name; and second, if I did call him that, I was drunk at the time; and third, even if I wasn't drunk I'm sorry now, and ask him to have dinner here tonight."

The squire bowed again and went, his riding boots clicking on the tiles. "Hump's all right," said Peekskill, "only we've been having a little argument about my electric-light plant. He says it ruins his radio reception. But I think we can fix it up. Besides, he's a better swordsman than I am. Let's finish our drinks in the library."

They had just settled when a boy in a Western Union uniform was ushered in. He looked from one to the other; then went up to Sir Howard. "You Van Slyck?" he asked, shifting his gum to one cheek. "O.K. I been tryin' to find ya. Here, sign, please."

"Manners!" roared the baron. The boy looked startled, then irked. He bowed very low and said: "Sir Howard van Slyck, will your gorgeous highness deign to sign this . . . this humble document?"

Both men were looking angry now, but Sir Howard signed without further words. When the boy had gone, he said: "Some of these commoners are too damn fresh nowadays."

"Yes," replied his host, "they need a bit of knocking around now and then to remind them of their place. Why . . . what's the matter, Howard? Something wrong? Your father?"

"No. My brother Frank. The hoppers arrested him last night. He was tried this morning, condemned, and burned this afternoon.

"The charge was scientific research."

2

"You'd better pull yourself together, Howard."

"I'm all right, John."

"Well, you'd better not drink any more of that stuff."

"I'm okay, I tell you. I'm not drunk, I can't get drunk: I've tried. Right now I haven't even a little buzz on."

"Listen, Howard, use your head. Lord knows I'm glad to have you stay around here as long as you like, but don't you think you ought to see your father?"

"My father? Good God, I'd forgotten about him! I *am* a

louse, John. A dirty louse. The dirtiest louse that ever—"

"Here, none of that, my boy. Now drink this; it'll clear your head. And get your suit on.

"Lloyd! Hey, *Lloyd!* Fetch Sir Howard's armor. No, you idiot, I don't care if you haven't finished shining it. Get it!"

Sir Howard spoke hesitantly; he wasn't sure how his father would take his proposal. He wasn't sure himself it was quite the right thing to do. But the old man's reaction surprised him. "Yes," he said in his tired voice, "I think that's a good idea. Get away from here for a few months. When I'm gone you'll be duke, now, and you won't have many chances to go gallivanting. So you ought to make the most of what you have. And you've never seen much of the country except between here and New York. Travel's broadening, they say. Don't worry about me; I have enough to do to keep two men busy.

"I'll ask just one thing, and that is that you don't go joining up in any more of these local wars. It's you I've always worried about, not Frank, and I don't want any more of that. I don't care how good the pay is. I know you're a mercenary young rascal; I like that, because I don't have to worry about your bankrupting the duchy. But if you really want to make money, you can try your hand at running the Poughkeepsie Shoe Co. when you get back."

Thus it came about that Sir Howard again found himself riding north, and to his own mild surprise doing some heavy thinking. Luckily the hoppers hadn't made much red tape about the travel permit. But he knew they'd keep an eye on him. Even though he hadn't done anything, he'd be on their suspicious list because of his brother. He'd have to be careful.

Jogging along, you had plenty of time to think. He knew he had the reputation of being simply a large, energetic, and rather empty-headed young man with a taste for action. It was time he put something in that head, if only because of the prospect of inheriting the duchy.

He felt that something must be wrong with his picture of the world. In it the burning of people for scientific research was just. But he didn't feel that Frank's death had been just. In it, whatever the hoppers said was right, because God had set them over Man. It was right that he, Howard van Slyck, should salute the hoppers. Didn't the commoners have to salute him in return? That made it fair all around. He was bound to obey the hoppers; the commoners were bound to obey him. It was all explained to you in school. The hoppers likewise were under obligation to God to command him, and he the commoners. Again, perfectly fair.

Only there must be something wrong with it. He couldn't see any flaw in the reasoning he'd been taught; it all fitted together like a sheet of Chrysler super-heavy silico-manganese steel plate. But there must be a flaw somewhere. If he traveled, and kept his eyes open, and asked questions, maybe he could find it. Perhaps somebody had a book that would shed light on the question. The only books he'd come across were either fairy tales about the daring deeds of dauntless knights, which bored him, or simple texts on how to run a savings bank or assemble a cream separator.

He might even learn to associate with commoners and find out how they looked at things. Sir Howard was not, considering his background, especially class-conscious; the commoners were all right, and some were even good fellows, if you didn't let them get too familiar or think they were as good as you. What he had in mind was, for one of his class, a radical departure from the norm.

He squirmed in his lobster shell and wished he could scratch through the plate. Damn, he must have picked up some bugs at Poughkeepsie Manor, free of vermin though it was normally kept. That was the hoppers' fault.

It began to rain; one of those vigorous York State spring rains that might last an hour or a week. Sir Howard got out his poncho and put his head through the slit in the middle. He didn't worry about his plate, because it had been well vaselined. But the rain, which was coming down really hard, was a nuisance. With his visor up it spattered against his face; and with it down, he had to wipe the lucite constantly to see where he was going. Below the poncho, the water worked into his leg joints and made his legs feel cold and clammy. Paul Jones didn't like it, either; he plodded along with his head drooping, breaking into periodic trots only with reluctance.

Sir Howard was not in the best of humors when, an hour later, the rain slackened to a misty drizzle through which the far shore of the Hudson could barely be made out. He was approaching the Rip van Winkle Bridge when somebody on a horse in front of him yelled "Hey!"

Sir Howard thought he wanted more room. But the strange rider sat where he was and shouted. "Thought I'd skip the country, didn'tcha? Well, I been laying for you, and now you're gonna get yours!"

From his costume the man was obviously a foreigner. His legs were encased in some sort of leather trousers with a wide flap on each leg. "What the hell do you mean?" answered the knight.

"You know what I mean, you yellow-bellied bastitch. You gonna fight like a man, or do I have to take your breeches down and paddle you?"

Sir Howard was too cold and wet and bebugged to carry on this lunatic argument, especially as he could see the town of Catskill—where there would be fires and whiskey—across the river. "Okay, foreigner, you asked for it. Have at you, base-born!" The lance came out of his boot and was lowered to horizontal. The gelding's hoofs thundered on the asphalt.

The stranger had thrown his sheepskin jacket into the ditch, revealing a shirt of chain, and sent his wide-brimmed hat scaling after it, showing a steel skullcap. Sir Howard, slamming down his visor, wondered what form of attack he was going to use; he hadn't drawn the curved saber that clanked from his saddle. With that light horse he'd probably try to dodge the lance point at the last minute—

The light horse dodged; the knight swung his lance; the dodge had been a feint and the foreigner was safely past his point on his left side. Sir Howard had a fleeting glimpse of a long loop of rope whirling about the man's head, and then something caught him around the neck. The world whirled, and the asphalt came up and hit him with a terrific clatter.

To get up in full armor, you had to be on your stomach and work your knees up under you. He rolled over and started to scramble up—and was jerked headlong. The stranger had twisted his rope around a projection on his saddle. The horse kept the rope taut; every time the knight got to his knees it took a step or two and pulled him down again. When he was down he couldn't see what was happening. Something caught his sword arm before he had a chance to get his weapon out. Rolling, he saw that the stranger had thrown another noose around his arm. And down this second rope loops came snaking to bind his other arm, his legs, his neck, until he was trussed like a fawn.

"Now," said the foreigner, coming toward him with a hunting knife in his hand, "let's see how you get into one of these stovepipe suits—" He pushed the visor up and gasped. "Sa-a-ay, you ain't the guy at all!"

"What guy?" snarled Sir Howard.

"The guy what ducked me in the horse trough. Big guy named Baker, over in Catskill. Your suit's like his, and you ride the same kind of critter. I thought sure it was him; I couldn't see your face with the helmet on in this bad light. It's all a mistake; I'm sure sorry as all hell, mister. You won't be mad if I let you up, will you?"

Sir Howard conceded that he wouldn't be mad; the fact was that with his anger at his ignominious overthrow by this wild foreigner's unfair fighting methods he had mixed a grudging admiration for the man's skill and a great curiosity as to how it had been accomplished.

The stranger was a lean person with straw-colored hair, some years older than Sir Howard. As he undid the rope he explained: "My name's Haas; Lyman Haas. I come from out Wyoming way; you know, the Far West. Most folks around here never heard of Wyoming. I was having a quiet drink in Catskill last night at Lukas's Bar and Grill, and this here Baker comes up and picks an argument. I'm a peaceable man, but they's some things I don't like. Anyway, when it came to the punch, this Baker and two of his friends jump me, and they ducked me in the horse trough, like I told you. I see now why I mistook you for him: you had your trademark covered up under that poncho. His is a fox's head. This'll be a lesson to me never to kill nobody again before I'm sure who he is. I hope I didn't dent your nice suit on the pavement."

"That's all right. A few dents more or less won't matter to this old suit. It's partly my fault, too. I should have thought of the poncho."

Haas was staring at the Van Slyck trademark and moving his lips. "Give . . . 'em . . . the . . . works," he read slowly. "What's it mean?"

"That's an expression they used a long time ago, meaning 'Hit them with all you've got,' or something like that. Say, Mr. Haas, I'd like to get somewhere where I can dry out. And I wouldn't mind a drink. Can you recommend a place at Catskill?"

"Sure; I know a good place. And a drink wouldn't hurt either of us."

"Fine, I've also got to buy some insect powder. And when that's been attended to, perhaps we can do something about your Mr. Baker."

The next morning the good citizens of Catskill were astonished to see the person of Squire Baker, naked and painted in an obscene manner, dangling by his wrists and ankles from a lamppost near the main intersection. As he was quite high up and had been efficiently gagged, he was not noticed until broad daylight. Baker never lived the incident down; a few months later he left Catskill and shipped on a schooner in the chicle-and-banana trade to Central America.

3

"Say, How, I'd kinda like to hear some music."

Sir Howard had not gotten used to Haas' calling him "How." He liked the man, but couldn't quite make him out. In some ways he acted like a commoner. If he were, the knight thought he ought to resent his familiarity. But there were other things— Haas' self-possession, for instance. Oh, well, no doubt the scheme of social stratification was different out West. He turned the radio on.

"That's a neat little thing you got," Haas continued.

"Yep; it's nice when you're making a long ride. There's an aerial contact built into the lance boot, so this little toothpick acts as an aerial. Or, if I'm not carrying a lance, I can clip the aerial lead to my suit, which works almost as well as the lance."

"Is they a battery in the saddle?"

"Yes, just a little light battery. *They* have a real fuel battery, but they don't let us use it."

They topped a rise, and Albany's State Office Building came in sight. It was by far the tallest building in the city, none of the rest of which was yet visible. Some said it had been built long ago, when York State was a single governmental entity—and not just a vague geographical designation. Now, of course, it was hopper headquarters for a whole upstate region. Sir Howard thought the dark, square-topped tower looked sinister. But it didn't become a knight to voice such timid vagaries. He asked Haas: "How is it that you're so far from home?"

"Oh, I wanted to see New York. You been to New York, I suppose?"

"Yes, often. I've never been very far upstate, though."

"That was the main thing. Of course, they was that guy—"

"Yes? Go on; you can trust me."

"Well—I don't suppose it'll do no harm, this being a long way from Wyoming. Him and me was arguing in a bar. Now, I'm a peaceable man, but they's some words I don't like, and this guy didn't smile when he said 'em, either. So we had it out in the alley with sabers. Only he had friends. That'll be a lesson to me, to make sure whether a guy has friends first before I fight him. I wanted to see New York, anyway, so here I am. When I ran out of money on the way, I'd make a stake doing rope tricks in the theaters. I made about six hundred clinkers in New York last week. It's purty near gone now, but I can make some more. They ain't nobody around these parts knows how to use a rope."

"Why," said Sir Howard, "what became of it? Were you robbed?"

"Nope; just spent it." The airy way in which this was said made Sir Howard shudder. The Westerner looked at him narrowly, with a trace of a smile. "You know," he said, "I always had the idea that lords and knights and such were purty free with their wallpaper; threw it around like it wasn't nothing. And here you're the carefullest guy with his money I ever did see. It just shows you."

"How did you like New York?" asked the knight.

"Purty good; there's lot of things to see. I made friends with a guy who works in a furniture factory, and he took me around. I liked to see the chairs and things come buzzing down the assembly line. My friend couldn't get me into the power plant though. They was a hopper guard at the door. They don't let nobody in there except a few old employees and I hear they examine them with this dope they got every week to make sure they haven't told nobody how the power machinery works.

"But I got tired of it after a few weeks. Too many hoppers. They get on my nerves, always looking at you with those little black eyes like they was reading your mind. Some says they can, too. I guess after what you told me about your brother it's safe for me to say what I think of 'em. I don't like 'em."

"Don't they have hoppers out West, too?"

"Sure, we got some, but they don't bother us much. What they say goes, of course, but they let us alone as long as we mind our business and pay our hopperage. They don't like the climate—too dry."

"They don't interfere too much in our local affairs, either," said the knight, "except that the big cities like New York are under their direct rule. That's how there are so many down there. Of course, if you—but I've already told you about that."

"Yeah. And it's a crime the prices you pay for steaks around here. Out in Wyoming, where we raise the critter, we eat mostly that. It's the hopperage charges, and all these little boundary tolls and tariffs between here and there makes 'em so expensive."

"Do you have wars out West, too?"

"Sure, once and a while us and the Novvos gets in a scrap."

"The Novvos?"

"Folks who live down south of us. Stock raisers, mostly. They ain't like us; got sorta reddish-brown skins, like Queenie here, and flat faces. Hair as black as yours, too."

"I think I've heard of these people," said the knight. "We had a man at the manor last year who'd been out West. But he called these red-skinned people Injuns."

"That a fact? I always thought an Injun was what made the hopper cars and flying machines go. It just shows you. Anyhow, we get in a fight with the Novvos about grazing rights and such, now and then. Mostly mounted-archery stuff. I'm purty good at it myself. See." He unfastened the flap of an elongated box that hung from his saddle, which proved to be a quiver. He took out the two halves of a steel bow. "Wish I had one of those trick saddles like yours to pack my stuff in, 'steada hanging it all over till me and my horse looks like a Christmas tree. But I travel purty light, at that. You got to, when you only got one little horse like Queenie. I suppose that high cantle's mostly to keep you from getting shoved off the horse's rump by some guy's toothpick." Haas had been fitting the halves of the bow together. The bow had a sighting apparatus just above the grip.

"See the knot in that big pine? Now watch, *Yeeow!*" the mare jumped forward. Haas whipped an arrow from his quiver; the bow twanged. The Westerner swung his mount back, walked her up to the tree, and pulled the arrow out of the knot. "Maybe I shouldn'ta done that," he said. "We're getting purty close in to Albany, and maybe they got a regulation about shooting arrows inside the city limits. What's they to see in Albany?" One of the hoppers' hexagonal glassy dwellings had come into view among the old two-story frame houses.

"Not much," replied the knight. "The first thing I have to do is to go to the Office Building and have my travel permit stamped. How about you?"

"Oh, mine ain't that kind. I had it stamped in New York, and now I don't have to report to the hoppers again till I get out to Chicago. But I'll tag along with you. Far's I can see they ain't neither of us got to get anywhere in particular."

They waited on the sidewalk in front of the Office Building for a quarter of an hour before they had a chance to go in, for, of course, they couldn't precede a hopper through the doors. By that time Sir Howard's steel-clad arm ached from saluting. A pair of the things passed him, chattering in their own incomprehensible tongue, which sounded like the twittering of birds. They smelled like very ripe cheese. He was startled to hear one of them suddenly switch to English. "Man!" it squeaked. "Why did you not salute?"

Sir Howard looked around, and saw that it was addressing Haas, who was standing stupidly with a cigarette in his mouth and a lighter in hand. He pulled himself together, put away the smoking things, and took off his hat. "I'm sure sorry as all hell, your excellency, but I'm afraid I wasn't looking."

"Control your language, Man," the hopper twittered. "Being

sorry is no excuse. You know there is a five-dollar fine for not saluting.''

''Yes, your excellency. Thanks your excellency, for reminding me.''

''Smoking is forbidden inside anyway,'' the thing chirped. 'But since you have assumed a more respectful attitude I shall not pursue the matter further. That is all, Man.''

''Thank you, your excellency.'' Haas put his hat back on and followed Sir Howard into the building. The knight heard him utter, ''I'm a peaceable man, *but*—''

Sir Howard found a man with a drooping white mustache at the travel-permit counter, who stamped his permit and entered his visit without comment. The man had the nervous, hangdog air that people got working around hoppers.

As they headed back to where their horses were tethered, Haas said, very low: ''Say, How, do you reckon that hopper that bawled me out was showing off to his girl friend?''

''They don't have girl friends, Lyman,'' replied Sir Howard. ''They don't have sexes. Or rather, each one of them is both male and female. It takes two to produce a crop of eggs, but they both lay them. Hermaphroditic, they call it.''

Haas stared at him. ''You mean they—'' He doubled over, guffawing and slapping his chaps. ''Boy, wouldn't I like to have a couple of 'em in a cage!''

4

''Let's eat here, How; we can watch the railroad out the window. I like to see the elephants go by.''

''Okay, Lyman. I guess this is about as good as any place in Amsterdam.''

At the bar, men made way respectfully for the suit of armor. ''Two Manhattans,'' ordered Sir Howard.

''Straws, sir?'' asked the barkeeper.

''Nope,'' mumbled the knight, struggling with his helmet. ''At least, not if I can get this thing out of the way. Ah!'' The bib came up finally. ''I'll have to take the damned hat apart and clean it properly one of these days. The hinge is as dirty as a secondhand hog wallow.''

"You know, How," said Haas, "that's one reason I never liked those iron hats much. For wearing, that is; I don't say nothing against them for flowerpots. I always figured, suppose a guy was to offer me a drink, sudden, and I had to wrassle all those visors and trapdoors and things out of the way. When I got ready to drink, the guy might have changed his mind." He took a sip and sighed happily. "You Yanks sure know how to mix cocktails. Out in Wyoming the cocktails are so lousy we take our poison mostly straight.

"It's a right handsome river, this Mohawk," he continued. "Wish I could say the same for some of the towns along it. I come up from New York through Connecticut; they got some real pretty towns in Connecticut. But the river's okay. I like to watch the canal boats. Those canal-boat drivers sure know how to handle their horses."

Somebody down the bar said loudly. "I still claim it ain't decent!" Heads were turned toward him. Somebody shushed him, but he went on: "We all know he's been doing it for years, but he don't have to wave it in our faces like that. He might have taken her around a back alley, 'stead of dragging her right down the main street."

"Who dragged whom down what street?" Sir Howard asked a neighbor.

"Kelly's been girling again," the man replied. "Only this time he had his gang grab her right here in town. Then they tied her on a horse, and Kelly led the procession right through the heart of town. I saw it; she sat up very straight on the horse, like a soldier. She couldn't say anything on account of the gag, of course. The people were sore. I think if somebody'd had a can opener he'd have taken a crack at Kelly, even though he had his lobsters with him. I would have."

"Huh?" said Haas blankly.

"He means," the knight explained, "that if he'd had a bill-hook or a poleax he'd have gone for this Kelly, in spite of his having a gang of full-armored men at his back. A half-armored man is a crab."

"You use some of the dangedest English here in the East," said Haas. "Who's this Kelly? Sounds kinda tough."

Their informant looked at Haas' clothes and Sir Howard's

trademark. "Strangers, aren't you? Warren Kelly's tough, all right. He sells the townspeople 'protection.' You know, pay up or else. We're supposed to be part of Baron Schenectady's fee, but Schenck spends his time in New York, and there's nobody to do anything. Kelly has a big castle up near Broadalbin; that'll be where he's taken this poor girl. He hasn't got a title, though at the present rate he's apt to before long—meaning no offense to the nobility," he added hastily. "Gentlemen, have you ever thought of the importance of insurance? My card, if you don't mind. My company has a special arrangement for active men-at-arms—"

Sir Howard and Haas looked at one another, slow grins forming. "Just like in storybooks," said the knight. "Lyman, I think we might do a little inquiring around about this castle and its super-tough owner. Are you with me?"

"Sure, I'm way ahead of you. They'll be a hardware store open after we finish dinner, won't they? I want to buy some paint. I got an idea."

"We'll need a lot of ideas, my friend. You can't just huff and puff and blow a concrete castle in, you know. Strategy is indicated."

The horse's hoofs clattered up to the side of the moat; the rider blew a whistle. A searchlight beam stabbed out from the walls, accompanied by a challenge. The light bathed Sir Howard van Slyck and his mount—with a difference. Paul Jones' feet had become white, and his black forehead had developed a big white diamond. On the rider's breastplate the Van Slyck maple-leaf insignia was concealed under a green circle with a black triangle painted in the middle of it. The red-and-white flag was gone from the lance.

"I am Sir William Scranton of Wilkes-Barre!" shouted the knight. (He knew that northeastern Pennsylvania was full of noble Scrantons, and there ought to be several Williams among them.) "I'm passing through, and I've heard of Warren Kelly and should like to make his acquaintance!"

"Wait there," called the watcher. Sir Howard waited, listening to the croak of frogs in the moat and hoping his alias would stand inspection. He was in high spirits. He'd had a moment of

qualms about violating his promise to his father, but decided
that, after all, rescuing a damsel in distress couldn't be fairly
called "joining up in a local war."

The hinges on the drawbridge groaned as the cables supporting
it were unreeled. He clattered into the yard. A blank-faced man
said: "I'm Warren Kelly. Pleased to meetcha." The man was
not very big, but quick in his movements. He had a long nose
and prominent, slightly bloodshot eyes. He needed a haircut. Sir
Howard saw him wince slightly when he squeezed his hand. He
thought, why I could knock that little—but wait a minute; he
must have something to make himself so feared. He's absolutely
a clever scoundrel.

They were in the hall, and Sir Howard had accepted the offer
of a drink. "How's things down your way?" asked Kelly
noncommittally. His expression was neither friendly nor otherwise.
Sir Howard opened wide the throttle of his famous charm, no
mean asset. He didn't want a kicker bolt between the shoulder
blades before his enterprise was well started. He gave scraps of
such gossip as he heard from Pennsylvania, praised his host's
brandy, and told tall tales of the dread in which he had heard
Kelly was held. Little by little the man thawed, and presently
they were swapping stories. Sir Howard dredged up the foulest
he could remember, but Kelly always went him one better. Some
of them were a bit strong for even the knight's catholic taste, but
he bellowed appreciatively. "Now," said Kelly with a bleak
little smile, "let me tell you what we did to the hock-shop guy.
This'll kill you; it's the funniest thing you ever heard. You know
nitric acid? Well, we took a glass tube, with some glass wool
inside for a wick—"

Some of Kelly's men were lounging about, listening to the
radio and shooting crap. A bridge game was going in one corner.
Sir Howard thought, it's time it happened. I mustn't glance up as
if I were expecting something. If this doesn't work—He had no
illusions about being able to seize the girl and hew his way
through a score of experienced fighting men.

A faint tinkle of glass came from somewhere above. Kelly
glanced up, frowned, and went on with his story. Then there was
another tinkle. Something fell over and over, to land on the rug.
It was a steel-tube arrow with duralumin vanes. The head had

been thrust through a small bag of something that burned bluely with a horrible, choking stench.

"What the hell!" exclaimed Kelly, getting up. "Who's the funny guy?" He picked up the arrow, making a face and coughing as he did so. He walked over to the wall and barked into a voice tube: "Hey, you up there! Somebody's dropping sulphur bombs in here. Pick him off, nitwit!" A hollow voice responded something with: "Can't see him!" A man was running downstairs with another arrow. "Say chief, some bastitch shot this into my room, with a sulphur bag on it—"

They were all up now, swearing and wiping their eyes. "All the lousy nerve—" "This'll fumigate the place, anyway. The cockroaches is gettin'—" "Shuddup, lug, the sulphur don't stink no worse'n you." Sir Howard, coughing, pressed his handkerchief to his streaming eyes. Kelly blew three short blasts on the loudest whistle the knight had ever heard.

The men went into action like trained firemen. Doors in the wall were snatched open; behind each door was a suit of armor. The men scrambled into their suits with a speed Sir Howard wouldn't have believed possible. "Wanna come along, Wilkes-Barre?" asked Kelly. "If we catch this guy, I'll show you some real fun. I got a new idea I want to try, with burning pine slivers. Hey, you guys! First squadron only come with me; the rest stay here. Stand to arms; it may be some trick." Then they were half running, half walking to the court, where their horses already awaited them. They mounted with a great metallic clanging and thundered across the drawbridge.

"Spread out," snapped Kelly. "Butler, you take the north—"

"*Yeeeeow!*" came a shriek from the darkness. "Damn Yank robbers! Hey, Kelly, who's your father? Betcha don't know yourself!" Then they were off on the Broadalbin road, after a small shadowy form that seemed to float rather than gallop ahead of them.

Sir Howard pulled Paul Jones in slightly, so that man after man pounded past him, meanwhile loudly cursing his puzzled mount for his slowness. By the time they reached a turn he was in the tail. He pulled up sharply and whirled the gelding around on his hind legs—

In three minutes he was back at the castle, giving an excellent imitation of a man reeling in the saddle. Something red was splashed on his suit and on Paul Jones, and dripped from his left solleret to the ground. "Ambush!" he yelled. "Kelly's surrounded just this side of Broadalbin! I was in the tail and cut my way clear!" He gasped convincingly. "Everybody out, quick!" In a minute the castle had disgorged another mob of gangsters. Again the black gelding didn't seem able to keep up with the headlong pace—

This time Sir Howard, when he reached the castle, tethered his mount to a tree outside the moat. There would be a few serving men in the castle yet, and they'd run out to take his horse and ask questions if he rode in. The sentries would be on duty, too. He peered into the dark, and couldn't make out either one in the battlements. It was now or never. Thank God, they'd left the drawbridge down.

The court was empty. So was the hall. So was the dining room. Jeepers, he thought, isn't anybody home? I've got to find at least one man! He tiptoed toward the kitchen, a rather futile performance, as the suit gave out little scrapes and clashings no matter what he did.

Inside the door a fat, sweaty man wearing a high white cap was wiping a glass with a dishtowel. His mouth fell open, and he started to run at the sight of the naked sword, the glass shattering on the tiles. "No, you don't!" growled the knight, and in four long strides he had the cook by the collar and the sword point over the man's right kidney. "One squeak and it'll be your last. Where is everybody?"

"Y-yessir, chef's in bed with a cold, and the others have went to a movie in town."

"Where is she?"

"She? I dunno who you—eek!" The point had been dug in an eighth of an inch. "She's in the guest room on the second floor—"

"All right, show me. March!"

The guest room had a massive oak door, held shut by a stout Yale lock. The lock was in a bronze mounting, and was evidently designed to keep people in the room rather than out.

"Where's the key?"

"I dunno, sir—I mean, Mr. Kelly's got it—"

Sir Howard thought. He'd been congratulating himself on having thought of everything—and now this! He decided correctly that he'd only get a bruised shoulder trying to break down the door. He didn't know how to pick locks, even assuming that a cylinder lock was pickable. He'd have to hurry—hurry— Was that the hoofs of the returning troop? No, but they might be back any minute. If something happened to Haas—or if the second squadron caught up with the first—

"Lie down on your face next to the door," he snapped.

"Yessir—you won't kill me, sir? I ain't done nothing."

"Not yet, anyway." He rested his sword point on the man's back. "One move, and I'll just lean on this." With his free hand he took out his dagger and began unscrewing the four screws that held the lock mounting. If only the narrow blade would hold—

It took an interminable time. As the last screw came out, the lock dropped with a soft thump onto the cook. Sir Howard opened the door.

"Who are you?" asked the girl, standing behind a chair. She was rather on the tall side, he thought. That was nice. She wore the conventional pajamalike clothes, and seemed more defiant than frightened. Her lightish hair was cut shorter and her skin was more tanned than was considered fashionable.

"Never mind that; I've come to get you out. Come on, quick!"

"But who are you? I don't trust—"

"You want to get out, don't you?"

"Yes, but—"

"Then stow the chatter and come along. Kelly'll be back any minute. I won't eat you. Yeowp, damn, that's done it!" The cook had rolled suddenly to his feet, and his cries of "Heelp!" were diminishing down the corridor. "Come on, for God's sake!"

When they reached the hall, a man in half-armor was coming down the other stair—the one that led to the sentry walk. He was coming two steps at a time, holding a poleax at port arms.

"Stand clear!" Sir Howard flung at the girl, slapping his visor down. A second man appeared at the head of the stair; the first was halfway cross the room. The first lunged with his can opener. Sir Howard swayed his body to let the point go over his shoulder; then their bodies met with a clang. The knight snapped his right fist up to the man's jaw, using the massive sword guard as a knuckle duster. The man went down, and the other was upon him. He was even bigger than Sir Howard, and he brandished his poleax like a switch. At the business end the weapon had a blade like that of a cleaver. From the back side of the blade projected a hook—for pulling men off horses—and from the end extended a foot-long spike.

Sir Howard, skipping away from a stab at his foot, thought, if there's anyone else in the castle this anvil chorus of ours will bring them out quickly. There was a particularly melodious *bonggg* as the blade struck his helmet; he saw stars and wondered whether his neck had been broken. Then the butt end whirled around to trip him. He staggered and went down on one knee; as he started to recover, the point was coming at his visor. He ducked under it and swung. He couldn't hope to cut through the duralumin shaft but his blade bit into the tendons on the back of the man's unprotected left hand. Now!

But the man, dropping his poleax, was dancing back out of reach, flicking blood from his wounded hand. His sword came out with a *wheep* almost before the knight had regained his feet. Then they were at it again. Feint-lunge-parry-riposte-recover-cut-parry-jab-double-lunge. Ting-clang-swish-bong-zing. Sir Howard, sweating, realized he'd been backing. Another step back—another—the fellow was getting him in a corner. The fellow was a better swordsman than he. Damn! The sentry's point had just failed to slide between the bib and plastorn into his throat. The fellow was appallingly good. You couldn't touch him. Another step back—he couldn't take many more or he'd be against the walls.

The girl had picked up one of the light chairs around the card table. She tiptoed over and swung the chair against the back of the sentry's legs. He yelled, threw up his arms, and fell into a ridiculous squatting position, with his hands on the floor behind him. Sir Howard aimed for his face and put his full weight behind the lunge; felt the point crunch through the sinuses.

"The other one!" she cried. The other sentry was on his hands and knees across the room, feeling around for his weapon. "Hadn't you better kill him, too?"

"No time; run!" They went, *clank, clank, clank,* into the dark. "Never . . . mind . . . him," the knight panted. "Much . . . as . . . I . . . admire . . . your . . . spirit. *Damn!*" He had almost run off the edge of the drawbridge. "Be . . . smart . . . to . . . drown . . . myself . . . in . . . moat . . . now."

5

"Good heavens, I must have slept all morning! What time is it, please, Sir Knight?"

Sir Howard glanced at his wrist, then remembered that his watch was under his gauntlet and vambrace. It was a good watch, and the knight's economical soul would have squirmed at the idea of wearing it outside when there was a prospect of a fight. He got up and looked at the clock built into the pommel of his saddle. "Eleven-thirty," he announced. "Sleep well?"

"Like a top. I suppose your friend hasn't appeared yet?"

Sir Howard looked through the pines at the gently rolling, sandy landscape. Nothing moved in it save an occasional bird. "No," he replied, "but that doesn't mean anything. We're to wait till dark. If he doesn't show up by then we'll move on to—wherever we're going."

The girl was looking, too. "I see you picked a place without a house in sight for your rendezvous. I . . . uh . . . don't suppose there's anything to eat, is there?"

"Nope; and I feel as though I could eat a horse and chase the driver. We'll just have to wait."

She looked at the ground. "I don't mean to look a gift rescuer in the mouth, if you know what I mean . . . but . . . I don't suppose you'd want to tell me your real name?"

Sir Howard came to with a snort. "My real . . . how the devil did you know?"

"I hope you don't mind, but in the sunlight you can see that that trademark's been painted on over another one. Even with all that blood on your suit."

Sir Howard grinned broadly. "The gore of miscreants is more beautiful than a sunset, as it says in a book somewhere. I'll make you an offer: I'll tell you my real name if you'll tell me yours!"

It was the girl's turn to start, deny, and interrogate. "Simple, my dear young lady. You say you're Mary Clark, but you have the letters SM embroidered on your blouse, and an S on your handkerchief. Fair enough, huh?"

"Oh, very well, my name is Sara Waite Mitten. Now how about yours, smarty?"

"You've heard of the Poughkeepsie Van Slycks?" Sir Howard gave a précis of his position in that noble family. As he was doing so, Paul Jones ambled over and poked the girl with his nose. She started to scratch his forehead, but jerked her hand away. "What's *his* name?" she asked. The knight told her.

"Where did you get it?"

"Oh, I don't know; it's been a name for horses in our family for a long time. I suppose there was a man by that name once; an important man, that is."

"Yes," she said, "there was. He was a romantic sort of man, just the sort that would have gone around rescuing maidens from captivity, if there'd been any maidens in captivity. He had a sense of humor, too. Once when the ship he commanded was being chased by an enemy, he kept his ship just out of range, so that the broadsides from the enemy's guns fell just short. Jones posted a man in the stern of his ship with orders to return each broadside with one musket shot. A musket was a kind of light gun they had in those days."

"He sounds like a good guy. Was he handsome, too?"

"Well"—the girl cocked her head to one side—"that depends on the point of view. If you consider apes handsome, Paul Jones was undoubtedly good-looking. By the way, I notice that *your* Paul Jones' coloring comes off when you rub him." She held up a paint-smeared hand. The gelding had no desire to be scratched or petted; he was hoping for sugar. As none was forthcoming, he walked off. Sally Mitten continued: "When I first met you, I decided you were just a big, active young man with no particular talents except for chopping up people you didn't like. But the whole way the rescue was planned, and your noticing the initials on my clothes, seem to show real intelligence."

"Thanks. My family never credited me with much brains, but maybe I'll disappoint them yet. It just occurred to me that I needn't have told you who I was; I could have explained the trademark by saying I'd bought this suit secondhand."

"But you'd hardly have repainted your horse, even if he was secondhand, also, would you?"

"Say, you're the damnedest young person. No matter what I say you go me one better." He thought a minute, and asked, "How long were you in Kelly's castle?"

"Three days."

Three days, eh? A lot could happen in that time. But if she wasn't going to tell him about it of her own accord, he certainly wasn't going to ask her. The question was, in fact, never referred to by either again.

"And where," asked Sir Howard, "did you get all that information about Paul Jones, and the times when men had guns, and so forth?"

"Out of books, mostly."

"Books, huh? I didn't know there were books on those things, unless the hoppers have some. Speaking of the devil—"

He tilted his head back to watch a flying machine snore overhead and dwindle to a mote in the cloudless sky. There was the sound of a quickly indrawn breath beside him. He turned to the girl. Her voice was low and intensely serious. "Sir Howard, you've done me a great service, and you want to help me out, don't you? Well, whatever happens, I don't want to fall into *their* hands. I'd rather go back to Kelly's castle."

"But what—" He stopped. She seemed genuinely frightened. She hadn't been at all frightened of Kelly, he thought; merely angry and contemptuous.

"You don't have to worry about me," he reassured her. "I don't like *them*, either." He told her about his brother. "And now," he said, "I'm going to catch a couple of hours' sleep. Wake me if anybody comes in sight."

It seemed to him that he had hardly found a comfortable position before his shoulder was being shaken. "Wake up!" she said, "wake . . . up . . . oh, confound you, wake . . . up!"

"Haas?" he mumbled, blinking.

"No, one of *them*. I shook you and shook you—"

He got up so suddenly that he almost upset her. His sleepiness was as though it had never been.

The sun was low in the sky. Over the sand and grass a two-wheeled vehicle was approaching the group of pines. Sir

Howard glanced at Paul Jones, nibbling contentedly at the tops of timothy weeds. "No use trying to run," he said. "It would see us, and those cycles can go like a lightning flash late for a date. Three or four times as fast as a horse, anyway. We'll have to bluff it out. Maybe it doesn't want us, really."

The vehicle headed straight into the pines and purred to a stop, remaining upright on its two wheels. The rounded lucite top opened, and a hopper got out unhurriedly. The two human beings saluted. They became aware of the faint cheesy odor of the thing.

"You are Sir William Scranton," it chirped.

Sir Howard saw no reason for denying such a flat statement. "Yes, your excellency."

"You killed Warren Kelly last night."

"No, your excellency." The beady black eyes under the leather helmet seemed to bore into him. The pointed face carried no message of emotion. The ratlike whiskers quivered as they always did.

"Do not contradict, Man. It is known that you did."

Sir Howard's mouth was dry, and his bones seemed to have turned to jelly. He who had been in six pitched battles without turning a hair, and who had snatched a robber chief's captive out from under his nose, was frightened. The hopper's clawed hand rested casually on the butt of a small gun in a belt holster. Sir Howard, like most human beings of his time, was terrified of guns. He had no idea of how they worked. A hopper pointed a harmless-looking tool at you, and there was a flash and a small thunderclap, and you were dead with a neat hole the size of your thumb in your plate. That was all. Resistance to creatures commanding such powers was hopeless. And where resistance is hopeless, courage is so rare as to lay the possessor thereof open to the charge of having a screw loose.

He tried another tack. "I should have said, your excellency, that I do not *remember* killing Kelly. Besides, the killing of a man is not against the higher law." (He meant hopper law.)

That seemed to stop the hopper. "No," it squeaked. "But it is inconvenient that you should have killed Kelly." It paused, as if trying to think up an excuse for making an arrest. "You lied when you said that you did not kill Kelly. And the higher law is what we say it is." A little breeze made the pines whisper. Sir Howard, chilled, felt that Death was moving among them, chuckling.

The hopper continued: "Something is wrong here. We must investigate you and your accomplice." Sir Howard, out of the corner of his eye, saw that Sally Mitten's lips were pressed together in a thin red line.

"Show me your travel permit, Man."

Sir Howard's heart seemed likely to burst his ribs at each beat. He walked over to Paul Jones and opened a pocket in the saddle stuffed with papers. He thumbed through them, and selected a tourist-agency circular advertising the virtues of the Thousand Islands. This he handed the hopper.

The creature bent over the paper. The knight's sword whirled and flashed with a *wht* of cloven air. There was a meaty *chug*.

Sir Howard leaned on his sword, waiting for the roaring in his ears to cease. He knew that he had come as near to fainting as he ever had in his life. A few feet away lay the hopper's head, the beady eyes staring blankly. The rest of the hopper lay at his feet, its limbs jerking slightly, pushing the sand up into little piles with its hands and feet. Blue-green blood spread out in a widening pool. A few pine needles gyrated slowly on its surface.

The girl's eyes were round. "What . . . what'll we do now?" she asked. It was barely more than a whisper.

"I don't know. I don't know. I never heard of anything like this before." He took his fascinated gaze away from the cadaver, to look over the dunes. "Look, there's Haas!" His blood began to run warm again. The foreigner might not be able to help much, but he'd be company.

The Westerner rode up jauntily, his chaps flapping against Queenie's flanks. He called: "Hiya, folks! Had the devil's own time gettin' rid of those lobsters, you call 'em. I had to drown—" He stopped as he saw the hopper, and gave a long whistle. "Well . . . I . . . never. Say, boy, I thought maybe you had nerve, but I never heard of nobody doing *that*. Maybe you'd like to try something safe, like wrassling a grizzly, or tying a knot in a piece of lightning?" He smiled uneasily.

"I had to," said Sir Howard. His composure was restored by the Westerner's awe. He'd mounted the wild stallion of revolt, and there was nothing to do but ride it with what aplomb he could muster. "He asked to see my permit, and I'd have been arrested for trademark infringement or something." He introduced Sally Mitten, and gave a résumé of events.

"We've got to get rid of it, quickly," the girl broke in. "When they're out patrolling the way this one was, they report to their station by radio every hour or so. When this one fails to report, the others will start a search for it."

"How will they do that, miss?" asked Haas.

"They'll make a big circle around the place it last reported from, and close in, meanwhile keeping the area under observation from the air."

"Sounds sensible. From what you tell me, this one was on an official mission or something, so his buddies'll have an idea where he was about the time he got whittled. So we'll be inside the circle. How'll we get rid of him? If we just buried him—"

"They might use dogs to locate it," said the girl.

"Well, now if we could sink him in the river or something. This Hans Creek yonder ain't deep enough."

Sir Howard was frowning at one of the large-scale maps he had bought in Amsterdam the previous evening. "The Sacandaga Reservoir is over across those hills," he said, pointing north.

"No," said Sally Mitten. "We've got to get rid of its cycle, too. You couldn't get it over Maxon Ridge. I know: put it in Round Lake. That's just out of sight east of here."

"Say, miss, do you carry a map of this whole country around in your head?" inquired Haas quizzically.

"I've lived near here most of my life. We'll put some clean sand and pine needles on the blood spots. And Sir Howard, you'll want to clean your sword blade at the first opportunity."

"Your little lady's okay, How," said Haas, dismounting. "Only she ain't so little, at that. Fall to, folks. You take his head—I mean his arms; the head comes separate. Don't get any of that blue stuff on you. In we go! It's nice these things stand up on their two wheels even when they ain't moving; it'll make it easy to push."

"Punch some holes in the lucite," said Sally Mitten. "That'll let the vehicle sink more quickly."

"Danged if she doesn't think of everything," said Haas.

getting to work with his knife on the thin cowling. He grinned. 'How, I'd sure like to hear the other hoppers, if they do find him, trying to figure out what happened to him. If I could understand their canary talk, that is. Say, miss, you got any idea how to get out of this circle if they start looking before we get away? And which way had we ought to go?''

"I'll show you, Mr. Haas. I think I know how it can be done. And if you desperate characters want to hide out, come with me. I know just the place. We'll have to hurry. Oh, you didn't bring any food with you, did you? I couldn't have eaten anything a few minutes ago, but I'm hungry again, now that *it* is out of sight. And I imagine Sir Howard is, also.''

"Danged if I didn't forget. I stopped on the way and got some hot dogs. I figured you might be kinda hollow by now.'' He produced a couple of Cellophane-wrapped sandwiches. "They'll be kinda dry. But for flavor you might put on a little of that blood How's got on his armor.''

The girl looked at the splotches on the suit. Sir Howard, grinning, wiped some of the sticky, almost-dry redness off and put his finger in his mouth. Sally Mitten gulped, looked as though she were going to gag. But she grimly followed suit. 'I'll show you humorists!'' Her expression changed ludicrously. 'Strawberry jam!'' Haas dodged, chortling, as her fist swept past his nose.

6

"There's another flier. They're certainly doing a thorough job. Can anybody see whether they've reached the water yet?'' It was Sally Mitten speaking. They lay in a clump of pines, looking across the Sacandaga Reservoir, spread out in a placid sheet before them and stretching out of sight to right and left. An early bat zigzagged blackly across the twilight. On the far side of the water, little things like ants moved about; these were hopper vehicles. One by one their lights went on.

"I wish it would get dark more quickly,'' the girl continued. 'This stunt of ours depends on exact timing. They're almost at the water now.''

"Too bad we couldn't get farther away before they started

hunting," commented Haas. "We mighta got outside the circle. Say, How, suppose they do meet up with us. Who'll we be?"

Sir Howard thought. "I registered last at Albany, and gave my destination as Watertown and the Thousand Islands. Said I was going up there to fish, which I thought I was. And the hoppers will be looking for a William Scranton. So maybe I'd just better be myself."

"Maybe," said Haas. "And then, maybe you better get rid of that fake trademark. Or will it wash out in the reservoy?"

"No, that's a waterproof lacquer. You need alcohol to get i off."

"Well, what's wrong with that there bottle of snake-bite medicine you got in your saddle?"

"What? But that's good whiskey! Oh, very well, I suppose this is more important." Sir Howard regretfully got out the bottle. Haas found a sock in his duffle bag that was more hole that fabric, opined that it was purty near worn out, anyway, and went to work on the knight's plastron. "Say," he said, "how do you reckon you're gonna swim over half a mile in tha stovepiping?"

"He isn't," said Sally Mitten. "We're going to strip."

"Wha-a-t?" The Westerner's scandalized voice rose in pitch "You mean go swimmin' all nekkid—all three of us?"

"Certainly. You don't think we want to go running around on a cold night in wet clothes, do you? Or run into a hopper and have to explain how we got wet?"

Haas turned back to his work, clucking. "Well, I never. never. I knowed Yanks was funny people, but I never. It jus shows you. Say, miss, you *sure* we couldn't get away by going around the end of the reservoy?"

"Good heavens, no. They'll be thickest around there. The whole idea is that the one time when there'll be a gap in the circle will be when they reach the water on the other side, and the ones who come up on the shore will separate, half of them going around each end of the reservoir, to re-form their circle on this side. If we're in the water when that happens, and it's dark enough so they don't see us, we'll find ourselves outside th circle automatically."

"How we gonna get How's tin suit across if he don't wear it? The cayuses'll be purty well loaded down as 'tis."

"We'll make a raft. You can cut some of the little pines and tie them together with those ropes of yours."

"Guess we could at that. There, How, your breastplate's O.K. I guess it's dark enough so they wouldn't see us moving around, huh?" He got up, took out his saber, and began lopping branches from a sapling.

The knight did likewise. "Wish I had an ax along," he said. "I didn't want to load Paul Jones down with too much junk. How big do we want this raft?"

"How heavy's your suit?"

"Forty-two pounds. Then there's my lance—we don't want that sticking up like a mast from its boot—and my sword, and all our clothes."

"Better make it four by four, with two courses."

"Hurry," said Sally Mitten. "They're at the shore now; I can see the reflection of their lights on the water."

"Who was it you drowned, Lyman?" asked Sir Howard.

"Oh, that. I had the dangedest time with those fellas. They was fast, in spite of their hardware. And the little one up front, who was ordering the rest around, could ride like the devil hisself. He had a flashlight and kept it on me. I kept going until Queenie began to puff, and I seen they was still coming. So— What's that little river that runs through Broadalbin?"

"Kenneatto Creek," Sally Mitten told him.

"Well, when I got to a little bridge that goes over this Kenny . . Kenneatto Creek—here, How, you pull tight on the end of that rope—I turned off into the water. I found a place under some trees where it was nice and dark, with the water about up to Queenie's belly. And then when these here lobsters hit the bridge I roped this little guy in the lead. He went off just as nice as you please into the creek. He was in about ten foot of water with that armor on. The only bad thing was I had to cut my good rope and leave most of it in the creek, because if I'd held it tight he mighta pulled hisself out with it, and his pals were beginning to hunt around to see why their boss went into the drink, naturally. I bought some more rope at a store on the way back to Round Lake. But I don't like it. It don't handle quite the same as a

Western rope. I gotta practice up with it. And this holding a raft
together won't do it no good.''

"I see," said Sir Howard. "That's why the hoppers think I
killed Warren Kelly. They don't know about you, but they knew
I'd called at the castle—at least, that somebody calling himself
William Scranton did.''

"You mean I drowned the big tough guy hisself? You don't
say! I guess that raft's okay now. Look, miss, we'll put it on
How's saddle, and you balance it while we lead the critters.''

Ten minutes later there was a metallic twang in front. Sir
Howard called back softly: "It's a wire fence; looks about ten
feet high. I guess we can't see it from up on the bluff.''

"That's nice," said Haas. "We shoulda remembered that
folks put fences around reservoys to keep critters from going and
dying in 'em. Don't suppose anybody's got any wire cutters?''

"No," hissed the knight. "We'll have to use that hunting
knife of yours.''

"What? Hey, you can't do that! It'll ruin the blade!''

"Can't be helped. I've spoiled the point of my dagger getting
Miss Mitten's door in the castle opened, so you oughtn't to
kick.''

The knife was passed up, and there were low grunts in the dark
from the knight as he heaved, and twang after twang as the
strands gave.

"All right," he whispered. "If we pull the horses' heads down
we can get 'em through. Take my toothpick out of the boot, will
you?''

They were through. Sir Howard said: "Come here, Lyman,
and hold these wires while I twist the ends back together. No use
advertising to *them* which way we've gone.''

"Quiet," said Sally Mitten. "Sound carries over water, you
know. Hurry up; the hoppers are going off toward the ends of the
reservoir. I can tell by their lights.'' On the far shore the little
needles of light were, in fact, moving off to right and left.

"Say, miss," came Haas's plaintive murmur, "can't I leave
my underwear on? I'm a modest man.''

"No, you can't," snapped the girl. "If you do, you'll catch
pneumonia, and I'll have to nurse you. There's nothing but
starlight, anyway.''

"I'm c-cold," continued the Westerner. "How's gonna take
ll night getting that hardware off."

Sir Howard looked up from his complicated task to see two
hostly forms standing over him hugging themselves and hoping up and down to keep warm. "You go ahead and fix the
opes," he said. "I'll be ready with this in a few minutes. I have
o be careful how I pile the pieces or I'm liable to lose parts of

The preparations were finally complete. The raft, piled with
eel and garments, lay on the sand, connected to Queenie's
addle by a long rope. Another rope trailed from Paul Jones.

"All right, get!" Sir Howard slapped the gelding's rump and
aded into the water. He and Sally Mitten each held the rope.
aas did likewise with the mare. The horses didn't want to
wim, and had to be prodded and pulled. But they were finally in
eep water, the ropes with their burdens trailing behind.

Sir Howard was thinking how warm the water gurgling in his
ght ear was when something hit him in the left eye. "Damn!"
e whispered. "Trying to blind me?"

"What did I do?" came the answer from up ahead.

"Stuck your toe in my eye. Why don't you keep on your own
de of the rope?"

"I *am* on my own side. Why don't you keep your face out of
y foot?"

"So that's it, huh? I'll fix you, young lady! You're not
cklish, are you?" He pulled himself forward hand over hand.
ut the girl dived like a seal. Holding the rope, the knight raised
s hand to peer over the starlit water. Then two slim but
artlingly strong hands caught his ankles and dragged him
ader.

When he came up and shook the water out of his head he
eard a frantic hiss from Haas: "For gossake, cut out the water-
olo game, you two. You sound like a coupla whales on a
unk!"

They were silent. The only sounds, besides the little night
oises of insect and frog, were the heavy breathing of the horses
d the gurgle of water sliding past them.

Time ticked past slowly. The shore seemed to get no closer.
en suddenly it loomed before them, and they were touching

bottom. After the quiet, the splashing of the horses through th shallows sounded like Niagara.

They lay on the beach. Sally Mitten said: "Can you see?" Sh was making marks in the sand. "Here's the reservoir, and he we are. My people and I live up in the Adirondacks. Now w can get there this way, by the Sacandaga Lakes. There's a goo road up to Speculator and Piseco. But there's lots of traffic f just that reason. People going up to fish on the Sacandaga Lake And we want to be seen as little as possible. We'd better stay o this side of the Sacandaga River and follow the west branch t Piseco Lake. Then I know a trail from there to our place by wa of the Cedar Lakes. It's hard going, but we're not likely to me anybody.

"I normally come down to Amsterdam by way of Cam Perkins and Speculator; there's an old road down the Jessup i pretty good shape. We buy most of our supplies at Speculator; only go down to Amsterdam once a month or so. And it woul be just my luck to be there when they—" She stopped.

"How do you get to Amsterdam?" asked Sir Howard. "Th looks like a pretty long walk."

"It is; I have a bicycle. I mean I *had* a bicycle. The last I sa of it it was standing on the sidewalk at Amsterdam. It'll be gor by now. And I left my only decent hat at Kelly's castle. It's good two-day trip. It'll take us much longer, since we're n following the good roads." She carefully rubbed out the ma "We'll want to obliterate our tracks on the beach, and th horses', too."

"Why do you suppose the hoppers are so concerned abo Kelly?" he asked. "They don't usually interfere in man-to-m quarrels."

"Don't you know? They were backing him. Not openly; the don't do things that way. Schenectady's barony was getting t big, so they set Kelly up in business to break it up. *Divide impera.*"

"What?"

"Divide and rule. That's their whole system—keeping me split up into little quarreling States the size of postage stamps.

"Hm-m-m. You seem to know a lot about *them.*"

"I've been studying *them* for a long time."

"I suppose so. What you say gives me a lot to think about. Say, do you suppose your . . . uh . . . people will want to have a couple of strangers with our fearful records?"

"On the contrary, Sir Howard—"

"I'd rather you dropped the 'Sir.' "

"Yes? Any particular reason?"

"Well—I don't know just how to say it, but . . . uh . . . it seems rather silly. I mean, we're all comrades together. Uh . . . you and Haas are as good men as I am, if you know what I mean, in the time I've known you."

"I think I understand." She was smiling quietly in the dark. "What I was saying was, you and he are just the sort of people we're looking for; men who have dared raise their hands against *them*. There aren't many. It sets you apart from other people, you know. You couldn't ever quite go back to the way you were."

While they talked, the stars had been dimming. And now a mottled yellow disk was rising from behind the blackness of the skyline, washing their skins with pale gold.

"Good heavens," said Sally Mitten, "I forgot about the moon! We'll have to get dressed and get out of here, quickly. I'm dry, thank goodness. Lyman—why, he's asleep!" The Westerner lay prone, his head pillowed on his arm, his breath coming with little whistlings.

"You can't blame him," said Sir Howard. "It's his first in thirty-six hours. But I'll fix *that*." He leaned over the recumbent form and raised his arm, the hand open and slightly cupped. Sally Mitten grabbed his wrist. "No! That'll make a noise like a gunshot! They'll hear it in Amsterdam!" She gurgled with suppressed laughter. "But it does seem a shame to waste such a chance, doesn't it?"

"You're limping, Howard," said Sally Mitten. She was sitting in his saddle, with the bottom of her trousers gathered in by string tied around her ankles. Behind her the knight's armor, the pieces neatly nested together and lashed into a compact bundle, rode Paul Jones' broad rump. The pile of steel gave out little tinny noises.

"No, I'm not," he said. "At least, not much. It's just another blister." He was walking in front of his horse, wearing a pair of riding boots from which four days of plowing through Adirondack brush had permanently banished the shine, and using his lance as an overgrown walking stick. He wore a red beret pulled down over his ears. Lyman Haas brought up the rear, swaying easily in the saddle and rolling a cigarette. Though the temperature was nearly eighty, all three wore gloves (Sally Mitten's being several sizes too large) and had their shirt collars turned up. They slapped constantly at their faces.

"Just another blister! You stop right now, young man, and we'll fix it. Have you any bandages? You don't do any more walking today. Those breeches and boots are all very well for riding, but not for walking around these parts."

"It's nothing, really. Besides, it's my turn to walk. The schedule says I walk for half an hour yet."   •

"Get your lasso out, Lyman; he's going to be stubborn."

"Better do what the lady says," said Haas. "Sure, miss, he's got iodine and gauze in one of the pockets of that saddle. That there's a magic saddle. You just wish, and say hocus-pocus, and push a button, and whatever you want pops out. You see why How uses an outsize horse; no ordinary critter could carry all that stuff. I sometimes think maybe he oughta rented an elephant from the railroad."

"Just like the White Knight," said Sally Mitten. "And me without even a toothbrush of my own!"

"The who?" asked Sir Howard.

"The White Knight; a character in a book called *Through the Looking Glass*. Does your equipment include any mousetraps or beehives? His did."

"That a fact?" said Haas. "Sounds to me like the guy was plumb eccentric. Now, How, you brace your other foot on this here root and I'll pull. Unh!" The boot came off, revealing two large toes protruding through a hole in the sock. "Say," said the Westerner, sniffing, "you sure that foot ain't *dead*? Damn!" He slapped at his cheek.

"I should have warned you it was black-fly time," said Sally Mitten. "They'll be gone in a few weeks."

"I haven't got a mousetrap," said Sir Howard, "but I have a

clockwork mechanical razor and a miniature camera, if they'll do. And a pair of bird glasses. You know, my hobby's prowling around looking for yellow-billed cuckoos and golden-winged warblers. My brother Frank used to say it was my only redeeming trait." He slapped at his jaw, decorated with streaks of dried blood from fly bites. "Perhaps I ought to have kept my suit on. It would at least keep these bugs out, unless they can bite through steel." He slapped again. "This trail is more like a jungle than any I ever saw. Why doesn't somebody get an ax and a scythe and clean it out?"

Sally Mitten answered: "That's just the point. If it were a nice clean trail everybody'd use it, and we don't want that. We've even planted things on trails we didn't want people to use."

Haas said: "It's thicker'n any brush I ever seen. It's different out my way; the timber, what they is, grows nice and far apart, so you can get through it 'thout being a snake." He lit his cigarette and went on: "This is what you call mountains, is it? I'm afraid you Yanks don't know what real mountains are. You take the Mt. Orrey you showed me; in Wyoming we wouldn't bother to give a little molehill like that a name, even. Say, Miss, have we got much more swamps to wade through? It's a wonder to me how you can walk around at night in this country 'thout falling into some mudhole or pond. I'd think the folks would have growed web feet, like a duck."

"No," said Sally Mitten, "we're through with the Cedar Lakes. If you look through the trees up ahead you can see Little Moose Mountain. That's where we're going." She slapped her neck.

7

Sally Mitten said she was going to run ahead to warn her people. The next minute she was scrambling up the steep shoulder of the mountain, pulling herself up by branches and bushes. The two men continued their slow switchback ride. Haas said: "Danged if I don't think it'd be easier to cut right across country than to try to follow what they call a trail around here."

Sir Howard watched the girl's retreating figure. It dwindled to thumb-size. He saw no sign of human habitation. But a man came out of some poplars, and then another. Even at that distance the knight could make out embraces and backslappings. He felt a slight twinge of something or other, together with a devouring curiosity as to what sort of "people" this mysterious girl might have.

When he and Haas finally reached the level space on which the three stood, she was still talking animatedly. She turned as they dismounted, and introduced them. "This," she said, "is Mr. Elsmith, our boss." They saw a man in his late forties, with thin yellow hair, and mild brown eyes behind glasses. He gripped their hands with both of his in a way that said more than words. "And this Eli Cahoon." The other man was older, with white hair under the world's oldest felt hat. He was dressed in typical north-woods fashion, his pants held up by one gallus and rolled up at the bottoms to show mud-caked laced boots. "Lyman, you've been calling us York States Yankees; Eli's the genuine article. He comes from Maine."

Sir Howard had been looking through the poplars. He saw that what he had first thought to be a cave was actually a good-sized one-story house, almost buried under tons of soil blending into the mountainside, and artfully camouflaged with vegetation. You couldn't see it at all until you were right on top of it.

The man named Cahoon moved his long jaw, opened his thin mouth to show crooked, yellow snags, and spat a brown stream. "Nice wuck," he said, "gettin' our Sally outa that castle." His forearms were thick and sinewy, and he moved like a cat.

"Wasn't nothing to it," drawled Haas. "I just called 'em names to make 'em mad, and How, here, walked in and tuck her while they was out chasing me."

Sir Howard was surprised to see that Elsmith was up and fully dressed already. The man smiled at him, showing a pair of squirrel teeth. Somehow he reminded the knight of a friendly rabbit.

"We keep early hours here," he said. "You'd better get up if you want any breakfast. Though how you can eat anything after the dinner you put away last night I don't just see."

Sir Howard stretched his huge muscles. It was wonderful to lie in a real bed for a change. "Oh, I can always eat. I go on the

rinciple that I might be without food someday, so I'd better take
what's offered. To tell the truth, we were all about ready to try a
irch-bark salad with pond-scum dressing when we arrived. And
we'd have been hungrier yet if Haas hadn't shot a fawn on the
way up."

During breakfast Sir Howard, who was not, these days, an
nobservant young man, kept his eyes and ears open for clues to
ie nature of this menage. Elsmith talked like a man of breeding,
y which the knight meant a member of his own predatory feudal
ristocracy. In some ways, that was. Sir Howard decided that he
was probably a decayed nobleman who had offended the hoppers
nd was hiding out in consequence. Sally Mitten called him
Uncle Homer. On the other hand, Elsmith and the girl had
omething about them—a tendency to use unfamiliar words and
) throw mental abstractions around—that set them apart from
ny people the knight had ever known. Cahoon—who pronounced
is name in one syllable—was obviously not a gentleman. But
n the rare occasions when he said anything at all, the statements
a his tight-lipped Yankee accent showed a penetrating keenness
aat Sir Howard wouldn't have expected of a lower-class person.

After breakfast Sir Howard lounged around, his pipe going,
peculating on his own future. He couldn't just sit and impose on
aese people's hospitality indefinitely, rescue or no rescue. He
as sure they'd expect something of him, and wondered what it
ould be.

He was not left in doubt long.

"Come along, Van Slyck," said Elsmith. "We're putting in
ome potatoes today."

Sir Howard's jaw sagged, and his class prejudice came to the
urface with a rush. "*Me* plant potatoes?" It was a cry more of
stonishment than resentment.

"Why, yes. We do." Elsmith smiled slightly. "You're in
nother world now, you know. You'll find a lot of things to
irprise you."

If the man had spoken harshly, the knight would have proba-
y marched out and departed in dudgeon. As it was, his incho-
e indignation evaporated. "I suppose you're right. There's a
t of things I don't know."

Bending humbly over his row in the potato patch, he asked Elsmith; "Do you raise all your own stuff?"

"Just about. We have some hens, and we raise a shoat each year. And Eli pots a deer now and then. There's a set of vegetable trays around the mountain a way; carefully hidden, of course. You'd never find them unless I showed you the place. It's surprising how many vegetables you can raise in a small space that way."

"Raising vegetables in trays? I never heard of that."

"Oh, yes, once upon a time tray agriculture was widenl practiced by men. But the hoppers decided that it saved too much labor and abolished it. They don't want us to have too much spare time, you know. We might get ideas."

In Sir Howard's mind such statements were like lightning flashes seen through a window, briefly illuminating a vast country try whose existence he had never suspected.

He asked: "Are you Sally's uncle?"

"No. She's really my secretary. Her father was my closest friend. He built this place. Eli worked for him, and stayed on with me when Mr. Mitten died six years ago."

In the afternoon Elsmith announced that that would be all the potatoes for today, and that he had correspondence to attend to. In the living room, Sir Howard noticed a stack of water-color landscapes against one of the plain timber walls. "Did you paint those?" he asked.

"Yes. They're smuggled down to New York, where an artist signs his own name to them and sells them as his."

"Sounds like a dirty trick."

"No; it's necessary. This artist is a good friend of mine. We don't need much cash here, but we've got to have some, and that's one way of getting it. Eli traps for furs in the winter for the same reason.

"Look, I've got to dictate to Sally for a couple of hours; why don't you look over some of these books?" He pointed to the shelves that covered most of one wall. "Let's see . . . I recommend this . . . and this . . . and these."

The books were mostly very old. Their yellow pages seemed to have been dipped in some sort of glassy lacquer. As a preservative, thought Sir Howard. He started reading reluctantly

nore as a courtesy to his host than anything. Then sentence after
tartling sentence caught his attention—

He was startled when Elsmith, standing quietly in front of
im, said: "How do you like them?"

"Good Lord, have I been reading for hours? I'm afraid I
aven't gotten very far. I've never been much of a reader, and I
ad to keep looking things up in the dictionary.

"To be frank, I don't know what to think of them. If they're
rue, they upset all the ideas I ever had. You take this one by
Vells, for instance. It tells a story of where men came from
nat's entirely different from what I learned in school. Men
racticing science—governments I never heard of running whole
ontinents—no mention of hoppers ruling over them—I just
an't grasp it all."

"I expected that," said Elsmith. "You know, Van Slyck,
ere comes a time in most men's lives when they look around
em and begin to suspect that many of the eternal truths they
arned at their mothers' knees are neither eternal nor true.

"Then they do one of two things. Some resolve to keep an
pen mind, to observe and inquire and experiment, and to try to
nd out what *is* the nature of Man and the universe. But most of
em feel uncomfortable. To get rid of the discomfort, they
ppress their doubts and wrap themselves in the dogmas of their
hildhood. To avoid any repetition of the discomfort, they even
ppress—violently—people who don't share the same set of
eliefs.

"You, my boy, are faced with that choice now. Think it
ver."

After dinner Sir Howard said to Elsmith: "In one of those
ooks I was looking over, it said something about how important
was to get all the information you could before making up your
ind about something. And what I've seen and heard in the last
eek makes me think I haven't got much information about
ings, after all. For instance, just who or what are the hoppers?"

Elsmith settled himself comfortably and lit a cigar. "That's a
ng story. The hoppers appeared on earth about three hundred
ars ago. Nobody knows just where they came from, but it's

fairly certain that they came from a planet outside the Solar System."

"The what?"

"The—I suppose you learned in school that the sun goes around the earth, didn't you? Well, it doesn't. The earth and the other visible planets go around the sun. I won't try to explain that to you now; some of these books do it better than I could. We'll just say that they came from another world, far away, in a great flying machine.

"At that time the state of mankind was about what it tells about in the last chapters of those history books.

"The hoppers landed in an almost uninhabited part of South America, where there was nobody to see them except a few savages who didn't matter. There couldn't have been more than a few hundred hoppers in the ship.

"But, you see, they're very different from any earthly animal, as you might expect. They do look rather like overgrown jumping rats, but the resemblances are mostly superficial. An active land animal that size has to have his skeleton inside like a mammal, instead of outside like an insect, and he needs eyes to see with, and a mouth to eat with, and so forth. But if you ever dissected a hopper—I have—you'd find that its internal organs were very different from those of a mammal. Even their hair is different; under the microscope you can see that each individual hair branches out like a little whisk broom. There are chemical differences, too; their blood is blue, because it has a blue chemical in it called haemocyanin, like an insect, instead of the red chemical haemoglobin, like a man or a bull-frog. So you couldn't possibly cross hoppers with any kind of earthly animal.

"It's thought among those like me who have studied the hoppers that the world they came from is much like ours in temperature, and that it has rather less oxygen in its atmosphere. It's also larger, and hence has a more powerful gravity, which is why the hoppers can make such enormous leaps so easily on earth. Being larger, it has an atmosphere deeper than ours and denser at the surface. That's why the hoppers' voices are so shrill; their vocal apparatus is designed to work in a denser medium.

"Most people know that they're bisexual and oviparous—they

lay eggs about the size of robins' eggs. They grow very rapidly and almost reach their full size within a year of hatching. That's how they conquered the earth. In their ship were hundreds of thousands—perhaps millions—of eggs, together with knocked-down incubators which they set up as soon as they landed. As they were in a heavily forested area, and as they are vegetarians, they didn't have any food problem.

"Their science at the time was quite a way ahead of ours, though not so far ahead that we probably wouldn't have gotten to that stage in time in the natural course of events. It took an advanced science to transform the wood, water, and soil in their neighborhood into weapons of conquest on a colossal scale. But it was their unexpectedness and their enormous numbers that helped them as much as their science.

"There was also the fact that to the people of the time they looked funny rather than sinister; it took a little while to learn to take them seriously. But people stopped thinking they were funny when they conquered all of South America within a week of the time they were first reported, and nobody's made that mistake since. Africa followed in short order. Their flying machines were faster than ours, their explosives were more destructive, and their guns shot farther and more accurately. They also had a lot of special gadgets, like the convulsion ray, the protonic bomb, and the lightning gun.

"As a matter of fact these gadgets aren't so mysterious as you might think. The convulsion-ray projector shoots a stream of heavy positrons, of Y-particles, which you'll read about in the books. They affect the human nervous system so as to greatly magnify every nervous motor impulse. For instance, suppose you were thinking of picking up a cup of coffee to drink. The thought would cause a slight motor-impulse in the nerves of your arm and hand. If you really wanted to pick the cup up, your brain would have to send out a much stronger motor impulse. Now suppose a convulsion ray were turned on you, and you merely thought about picking up the cup. Your muscles would react so violently that you'd dash the cup, coffee and all, into your face. So you can see why human beings' bodies became totally unmanageable when the ray was turned on them.

"Or take the protonic bomb. One of those bombs weighing a

ton has a chunk of packed hydrogen ions in it the size of a marble, which really does the damage. The rest of the weight is caused by the coils and other apparatus necessary to keep the electrostatic field reversed, so the ions don't fly apart under the influence of their mutual repulsion. The minute you break down the field control, those ions go away from there in a hurry. They have a defense against these bombs, too, just in case men might steal one some day; we call it the X beam. It's really just a huge Roentgen-ray projector, thousands of times more powerful than a medical X-ray apparatus. It dereverses the field around the protons prematurely.

"But to get back to the story: Eurasia and North America, and most densely populated continents, held out for a while, and people began to think they might win. That was their mistake. The hoppers had merely paused in the attack while their second generation was reaching maturity. They can be fantastically prolific when they want to be, and as soon as the first crop had reached sexual maturity they'd laid another crop of millions of eggs. Remember, out of a given population of human beings only a fifth at most will be men of fighting age. But among the hopper everyone, practically, except the casualties, was available for the attack.

"They had another advantage. They seem to be immune to all the known earthly bacteria, though they have a few minor diseases of their own. But the converse unfortunately isn't true. It's probable that they deliberately turned loose a lot of their own exotic bacteria, and one of these found the human body a congenial environment. It caused a plague known as the blue madness. It was quite horrible. At least half the human race died of it. So—anyway, the hoppers won."

Sir Howard asked, "Have there been any more blue plagues since?"

"No; apparently part of the human race is naturally immune, and everyone who wasn't, died. So all of us today are immune, being descended from the survivors.

"The hoppers didn't exterminate us while they had the chance, for which we might give them some credit. Apparently when they saw the fairly high state of human civilization, and its enormous productive capacity, they decided that it would be

nicer to set themselves up a ruling species and use the rest of us
to plow the farms and run the machines, while they enjoyed their
own hopperish amusements, one of which seems to be ordering
us around. They may even have felt sorry for us, though that's
difficult to imagine. Anyway, that's the system they've followed
ever since." He looked at his watch and got up. "Early hours
here, you know. You can sit up to read if you want to, but I'm
turning in. Good night."

* * *

Up the trail from the camp was a grassy clearing, in the
middle of which was a stump. On this stump sat Sally Mitten,
smoking a cigarette and looking very much amused. Around the
stump in a circle marched Sir Howard. He was looking not, as
one might expect, at the girl, but at Lyman Haas. The Westerner
was walking around the stump in the same direction in a still
larger circle, with the expression of one who is putting up with a
great deal for friendship's sake.

"Little slower, Lyman," said the knight.

Elsmith appeared. "What . . . what on earth, or off of it, is
this? Some new kind of dance?"

"No." Sir Howard stopped. "I was just checking up on that
Cop . . . Copernican hypothesis. You know, about that motion
of the planets—why they seem to go backward in the sky at times."

"Retrograde motion?"

"That's it. Sally's the sun, I'm the earth, and Haas is Mars. I
was looking at him to see whether he seems to go backward
against the farther trees. You . . . uh . . . don't mind my
checking up, do you?"

"On the contrary, my boy. I want you to check up everything
you get from me, or from the books, every chance you get. Does
he show retrograde motion?"

"Yep; he backs up like a scared crawfish every time I pass
him."

"What do you mean, backs up?" said Haas. "I been walking
forward all the time."

"Certainly, but you're still going backward relative to me. I
can't explain it very well; I'll have to show you the place in
the book."

Elsmith said: "Do you read books much, Haas?"

"Sure, I like to read sometimes. Only I busted my reading glasses in New York, and I ain't been in one place long enough to get a new pair since. I was in a bar, and I had those glasses in my shirt pocket. And I got into an argument with a guy. He was saying it was a known fact that all Westerners are born with tails. Now, I'm a peaceable man, *but*—''

"That's all right, Lyman," said Sally Mitten soothingly. "We know you haven't a tail. Don't we, Howard?"

The upper, untanned part of Haas' face reddened a shade. "Uh . . . ahem . . . Now, what's that again about those there planets? I want to get this straight—"

8

Sir Howard said; "Are you going to tell me some more about the hoppers this evening?"

Elsmith blew out his match. "I never lecture until I have a cigar going, and then it burns down to nothing while I'm talking and I don't get a chance to smoke it. Silly, isn't it?

"But to take up where we left off: The hoppers saw they'd have to remodel human society if they were going to keep human beings in check, especially as the human beings still greatly outnumbered them, and they apparently considered that ratio satisfactory from an economic point of view. They couldn't afford to let us become powerful again. Well, what sources of power did we have?

"We had powered vehicles; some ran on roads, some on railroad tracks, some in the air, and some on the water. So they abolished them, for us, that is. We had explosives, so they took them away. We had united governments over large populations; therefore, they broke us up into small units. Societies in which able people could rise to the top regardless of birth were a menace. They studied our history and decided that a feudal caste system would be the best check on that. Scientific research was, of course, outlawed, and all scientific practice except such engineering as was necessary to keep the productive machine going.

"They abolished every invention they thought might conceivably menace them. Did you know, for instance, that at one time you could talk over wires to people in all parts of the country? And that the telegraph companies owned vast networks of wires for sending messages almost instantaneously? Now they're just messenger-boy agencies, and deliver letters by horse or bicycle.

"That wasn't all. An empirical, materialistic outlook might enable us to see through the preposterous mythology that they were planning to impose on our minds through the schools. So the books expressing such a philosophy were put away, and the people who held it were destroyed. In its place they gave us mysticism, other-worldliness, and romantic trips. They used the radio, the movies, and the newspapers and books to do this, as these institutions continued to operate under their strict control. They'd have been foolish to destroy such excellent ready-made means of swaying the mass mind. Ever since then they've been filling us with 'Upright ignorance and stalwart irrationality,' as Bell, one of the pre-hopper writers, put it. And I must say"—here he leaned back, closed his eyes, and took a big puff on his cigar—"that my species has come through it remarkably well. It's had a terrible effect on them, of course. But when I get most discouraged I can get some comfort out of the thought that they aren't nearly as crazy as they might be, considering what they've been through."

"But," said Sir Howard, "but I was taught that God—" He stopped, confused.

"Yes? Assuming for the sake of argument that there is a God, did He ever confide in you personally? Who taught you? Your schoolteachers, of course. And where did they get their information? Out of textbooks. And who wrote the books? The hoppers. Just assume I'm telling you the truth; what would you expect the hoppers to put in the books? The truth about how they conquered the earth and enslaved its inhabitants, to act as a constant irritant and incitation to revolt?"

Sir Howard was frowning at his toes. "A couple of months ago," he mused, "I'd have probably wanted to make you eat my word for some of the things you've said, Mr. Elsmith. No offense intended."

"I know that," said Elsmith. "And if you'd been the man you were a couple of months ago, I wouldn't have said them."

"But now—I don't know. Everything seems upside down. Why didn't the people revolt anyway?"

"They did; almost constantly during the first century of hopper rule. But the revolts were put down and the rebels were killed. The hoppers are microscopically thorough. As you probably know, they have a drug called veramin that makes you answer questions truthfully. Men had such a drug once, but this is much better, except that alcohol in the system counteracts it. They'd give an injection to every inhabitant of a suspected city, for instance, for the sake of catching one rebel. And there was just one penalty for rebellion—death, usually slow. So after a while there weren't any more rebellions. There have been practically none in the last century, so the hoppers have eased up their control of human beings somewhat."

"Well," growled the knight, "what can be done about it?"

Homer Elsmith had seen that look in young men's eyes before. "What would *you* do?" he asked gently.

"Fight!" Sir Howard had unthinkingly clenched his fist, and was making cut-and-thrust motions in the air.

"I see. You see yourself at the head of a charge of armored cavalry, spearing the hoppers like razorbacks and sweeping them from the face of the earth. No, I'm not making fun of you; that's a common reaction. But do you know what would happen? You've seen wheat stalks fall when a scythe passes through them? That's what you and your brave horsemen would do if the hoppers trained a rapid-fire gun on you. Or they might use the convulsion ray, and have the men and the horses rolling on the ground and writhing while they tied you up. The effect lasts for some minutes after the ray's been turned off, you know. Or they might use a cone transformer, setting up eddy currents in your plate and roasting you in your own lobster shells."

"Well, what then?" Sir Howard's big fist struck his knee.

"I don't know. Nobody knows, yet. I don't know, though I've spent a good part of my life working on the problem. But that doesn't mean we shall never know. Man has solved knottier ones than that.

"We have some advantages: our numbers, for one. Then, the fact that the hoppers are spread out thinly over the earth makes them vulnerable to concerted uprisings. They're not an army, now, but a civilian administration and a police force. Take those hoppers at Albany; there are only a couple of hundred there. They're relieved frequently, because they don't like being stuck out in the sticks. If we were hiding out from human beings, this would be one of the worst places. But for the hoppers it's fine,

ecause there are only two patrolling around the whole Adirondack
rea, and they seldom leave the main roads. Then there's the fact
1at they are not, really, very intelligent."

"Not intelligent! Why, they—"

"I know. They know a lot more than we do, and have the
ciences at their command, and so forth. But that's not intelligence.
bright hopper is about as intelligent as a stupid man."

"But . . . but—"

"I know, I know. *But* they have three big advantages. First:
1ey learn quickly, even if not intelligently. That's how the
riginal conquering armies were trained to be competent soldiers
o quickly. Second: they live long. I don't know what their
verage life span is, but I think it's around four hundred years.
nd third: the helmets."

"The helmets?"

"Those leather things they wear. In their history, the helmets
'as invented by their god, whose name I can't give you because
can't imitate a canary. We'll call him X. As nearly as I can
1ake out, this X was actually a great genius, a kind of Archimedes
1d Leonardo da Vinci and Isaac Newton rolled into one. They
'ere some of the most brilliant men of ancient times. X may
1ave been a sterile mutant. You can look that up later. I think
's likely, because the same strain of genius never again ap-
eared among the hoppers, who were living hardly better than a
'ild-animal existence at the time.

"Early in life X hit upon the technique of scientific investigation:
bserving and experimenting to find what made things go. He
1vented their alphabet, which is a cross between a phonetic
/stem and a musical score. He invented an incredible lot of
ther things, if we can believe the story. Instead of killing him,
s human savages might have done, the hoppers made X their
od, so he didn't have to work for a living any more. That was
robably X's idea, too.

"Four hundred years is a long time, as I said. Toward the end
f his life he invented the helmet. It's really an electrical apparatus,
1e effect of which is to give the hopper who wears it an
1ormous power of concentration. A man, for instance, can't
eep his mind on one subject for more than a few seconds at a
me. Try it sometime. First thing you know you'll be thinking

about keeping your mind on whatever you're supposed to b
keeping your mind on, instead of keeping your mind on the thin
itself. I hope I make myself clear. But a hopper with a helme
can think about one thing for hours at a time. And even
chimpanzee could learn calculus if he could do that, I imagine.

"It may be that they're even stupider than stupid men, an
that the helmets actually increase their reasoning powers. It'
certain that without the helmets they're even more scatter-braine
than chimpanzees, so that they're incapable of carrying out an
complicated train of action. One reason I think they're so stupi
is that their science seems to have remained just about static i
the three centuries since the conquest. But it may be that havin
half a billion slaves of an inferior species to do their dirty wor
deprived them of ambition."

"Then," said Sir Howard, "I'd think the thing to do was t
rush them all at once and snatch their helmets off."

"Yes? You forget the guns and things. If we could time a
uprising as exactly as that, we could kill them with our bar
hands. I tell you, wide conspiracies have been tried before. The
haven't worked. For one thing, we have no sufficiently deadly
simple, and inconspicuous weapon. We're much worse off i
that respect than we were at the time of conquest. We've got
have something better than gunfire, at least. Take those Alban
hoppers again. They have a supply of small arms in the Offic
Building. The nearest heavy artillery is stored in the Watervli
arsenal. The really deadly things, like the protonic bombs, ar
down at Fort Knox, in old vaults where they used to store gold.
we could overwhelm even a large fraction of the hoppers, w
could capture enough of their own weapons to redress th
balance. But we'd need something to help us overwhelm tha
fraction first, and bows and bills wouldn't do it."

"Well, how about getting them to take their helmets off
their own accord? Couldn't you send out some sort of radio ra
or something?"

"That's been thought of: plans for blowing out the electric
circuits in the helmets; plans for heating up the wires to mak
them too hot for comfort; plans for interfering with their opera
tion by static. Static doesn't seem to affect them, and we simpl
don't know of any form of ray or wave that would accomplis

the other objects. Take the heating idea. It would require enormous power to heat up all those millions of helmets, and the amount that actually comes into your receiving set over the aerial is so slight you can't feel it. The biggest broadcasting station in existence doesn't send out as much power as the engine in one of the hoppers' two-wheel cycles develops. How are you going to erect a station to send out thousands of times as much power, without *their* knowledge?"

"Hm-m-m . . . it does seem hopeless. Maybe if you put on one of the helmets it would give you an idea."

"That's been tried, too. I tried it once. It worked fine for about three minutes, and then I got the worst headache of my life; it lasted a week. The hoppers' brains are cruder than ours; they aren't damaged by such treatment. You can't do it to a man's brain, though, at least not with our present knowledge. Perhaps we shall be able to someday, when we've shaken off *them*."

They sat silent for a while, smoking. Sir Howard said: "If you don't mind my asking, where did you get all this information? And where did these books come from?"

"Oh, using my eyes and ears over many years. I might add that I'm an accomplished burglar. The books, together with much of the information about the hoppers, were partly stolen. The rest of them were picked up here and there, mostly by Thurlow Mitten before I joined him. The hoppers couldn't be expected to go into every corner of every attic and cellar of every old house in the country, you know, as thorough as they are."

Sir Howard said, "Some of your statements remind me of things my brother Frank used to say."

Elsmith raised one eyebrow. "Sally told me about him. That's . . . I'm sorry." Something in his tone gave the knight the idea that Elsmith might know more than he cared to say about his brother. But he had too much to think about as it was to inquire any more just then.

9

"Well, he throws his knife at me, and it pins my big toe to the log so I can't get it out nohow. But I says, 'Mike Brady,' I said, 'I was goin' to beat the gearin' out of you, and I still be.' So I took after him with my peavy. He runs, and me after him. But you know you can't run fast with a twenty-foot log of hard maple nailed to your foot—musta weighed nigh onto six hundred pounds—and after the fust mile or two I seed he was gainin'! So I throwed my peavy, so the point goes into a tree on one side of his neck and the cant dog goes into the back on the other side, and there he was, helpless. So I took my knife and cut his guts out. 'Now,' I says, 'that'll be a lesson to you to sass Eli Cahoon.' He says, 'Okay, I guess I was kinds hasty. If you'll just put my guts back in I won't sass you no more.' So I put 'em back in, and we been fine friends ever since. I still got the scar on my toe.''

''That's a fact? I remember one time out in Wyoming, when me and a fella was shooting arrows. We was shooting at horseflies. Pretty soon a mosquita comes along. He says, 'Bet you can't hit that mosquita.' I says, 'What'll you bet?' He put up a hundred clinkers, and I shot the mosquita. Then another mosquita comes along. He says, 'That was too easy. Let's see you hit this mosquita in the eye.' 'Which eye?' I says, not stopping to think—''

The speakers were talking softly and casually in the firelight. Sir Howard looked up from his book. ''Mr. Elsmith,'' he asked, ''what does this fellow mean? 'Government of the people, by the people, for the people.' What people?''

''—and that's how I lost a thousand dollars, through getting the right and left eyes mixed up. But I remember when I won this watch on a bet. Fella named Larry Hernandez owned it, which is how it has the same initials as mine. We wanted to see which could ride his horse down the steepest slope—''

Elsmith spoke. Sir Howard wondered what there was about this mild little man that gave his dry, precise words such authority. ''It means that all the adults vote to select those who rule over them for a limited time. When the time's up they have another election, and the people can throw out their first set of officials if they don't like them.''

''All the adults? You mean even including the commons? And the women? But that's a ridiculous idea! Lower-class person—''

''Why ridiculous?''

Sir Howard frowned in concentration. ''But they . . . they're ignorant. They wouldn't know what was good for them. Their natural lords—'' He stopped in confusion again.

''Would you call me ignorant?'' It was very quietly said.

"You? But you're not a—"

"My father worked in an iron foundry, and I started work as a Postal Telegraph messenger boy."

"But . . . but . . . but—"

"I admit that with a hereditary ruling class you get good men occasionally. But you also get some remarkably bad ones. Take Baron Schenectady, for example. Under this 'government of the people' idea, when you find that your ruler is a scoundrel or a lunatic, you can at least get rid of him without an armed insurrection."

Sir Howard sighed. "I'll never get all these new ideas straight in my head. Thinking about them is like watching your whole world—all your old ideas and convictions—go to pieces like a lump of sugar in a teacup. It's . . . sort of awful. I should have come up here ten years ago to get a good start."

"No."

"Aw, come on, Sal; you like me pretty well, don't you?"

"That isn't it."

"Well what *is* it?"

"It would be—expedient."

There it was; one of those damned dictionary words again. He felt a surge of anger. Remembering Warren Kelly, an outrageously stinging remark formed in his mind. But his natural decency choked it off before it got to his lips.

"Well, why?"

She was baiting her hook. The boat rocked ever so slightly under the lead-and-snow cumulus clouds that towered over Little Moose Mountain and small Sly Pond.

"It's . . . this way. Maybe you haven't noticed, but we work hard at our job. Our job is the Organization, and we think that's literally the most important job in the world. Between that and keeping ourselves fed, we haven't time or energy for—personal relationships."

"I'm afraid I'll never understand you, Sally." He didn't either. She didn't act like a lower-class girl. He ought to know; base-born girls were pushovers for him. On the other hand, the upper-class girls he'd known would be horrified at the idea of baiting a hook with an active and belligerent crawfish, let alone skinning and cleaning a mess of bullheads. But there wasn't any question of her being anything but upper-class. He wouldn't have it that she was anything but upper-class. If necessary he'd stand the feudal system—for which he was feeling less reverence these days—on its head in order to put whatever class she belonged to on top.

"Another reason," she went on. "Uncle Homer tells me that you'll probably join us in a day or two. Officially, that is. I may say that I hope you do. But—this is important—you *mustn't* join us for personal reasons. And if you have any ideas of joining for such reasons, you can give them up right now."

"But why? What's so awful about personal reasons?"

"Because if you changed your mind about the personal reasons, you might change your mind about the other things. You idiot, don't you see? What's one girl more or less, compared to the human race—everybody you've ever known and millions of others?" The reel sang for a second before she heard it. She caught up the rod in a smooth, practiced movement and in a few more seconds had another bullhead in the boat. Sir Howard had already stabbed his hand on one of the fin spikes of the ugly brutes. But her hand gripped the fish's body as surely as his held a sword hilt. "Damn them!" she said. "They swallow the hooks, clear down to their stomachs. Someday we'll go out on Little Moose Lake and troll for bass."

As they walked back to the camp with the fish, they passed Lyman Haas. He took one look at the gloom on Sir Howard's blunt features and grinned knowingly. Sir Howard thought afterward that he minded that grin more than anything.

Sir Howard asked: "Hasn't your organization any name? I mean, you just call them 'us' all the time."

"No," said Elsmith. "It's just the Organization. Names are handles, and we don't want to give *them* any more handles to take hold of us by than we can help. Now if you'll just roll up your sleeve, please." He held a hypodermic up to the light.

"Will that have any permanent effect on me?"

"No, it'll just make you feel slightly drunk and happy for a while. It's what the hoppers use in their third-degree work. It's much better than torture, because you can be sure that the prisoner is actually saying what he believes to be true."

"Do I have to take an oath of some kind?"

"You don't have to. We go on the theory that a man's statement of his intentions, provided he actually says what he thinks, is as good an indication of what he'll do as any oath. People sometimes change their ideas, but when they do they almost always find excuses for breaking their oaths."

"Tell me, was my brother Frank one of you?"

Elsmith hesitated, then said: "Yes. He didn't go by that name in the Organization, of course. We didn't have a chance to warn him. His immediate superior, who would normally have reported the state of affairs to me, had disappeared a couple of months previously. We knew what that meant, all right, but we hadn't succeeded in reestablishing communication with your brother."

"This is the center of the whole business?" Sir Howard's eyebrows went up a little incredulously. Nothing much seemed to happen around the camp; certainly nothing that would indicate that it was the headquarters of a world-wide conspiracy.

"Yes. I see what you're thinking. Perhaps you hadn't noticed the number of times recently that you were tactfully lured away from the camp? There were conferences going on."

The knight was slightly startled. He'd never thought of that. He began to appreciate the enormous pains to which these people went. You couldn't improvise something of this sort; it took years of careful and risky work.

"How do you feel?" asked Elsmith.

"A little dizzy."

"Very well, we'll begin. Do you, Howard van Slyck—"

"You came through the test with flying colors, my boy. I'm glad of that; I think you'll make a good worker. I may add that if you hadn't, you would never have left here alive."

"What? Wh-why? How?"

Elsmith reached inside his shirt and brought out a hopper's gun. "This, by the way, is the gun carried by the hopper you killed. We have some others. You didn't notice Sally take it from the body and hide it in her clothes, did you? You wouldn't. Sally knows her business.

"The reason I'd have used it, if necessary, is that you knew too much. Ordinarily it's only the old and tested workers who are allowed up here. Sally would never have brought you and Haas—who joined up last Tuesday, incidentally—if it hadn't been an emergency. You had to have a place to hide out, and you had too much good stuff in you to be allowed to fall into *their* hands. So we took a chance on you. If we'd been mistaken—well, we couldn't risk setting the Organization back years."

Sir Howard looked at his toes. "Would that have been right? I mean, according to your ideas. If I hadn't wanted to stay."

"No, it wouldn't have been just. But it would have been necessary. I hope that some day we can afford to be just. It's treacherous business, this excusing injustice on grounds of necessity. People have justified or condoned the most atrocious crimes that way."

"Try it again, Van Slyck."

Sir Howard obediently turned and walked back across the room. He felt very silly indeed.

"No, that won't do. Too much swagger."

"You can hear him clank," said Sally Mitten, "even when he hasn't got any armor on. I don't know what it is; something in the way the lower part of his leg snaps forward at each step."

"Maybe I know," said Haas. He was sitting with his feet in a bucket of hot water; he had gone for a hike with Cahoon, wearing ordinary laced boots instead of the high-heeled Western foot-gear he was accustomed to. As a result what he called his atchilly tendons had swollen up, to his acute discomfort. "How's used to toting fifty pounds of stovepiping and other hardware with him. Maybe if you put lead in his boots it'd hold 'em down to the ground."

"Look," said Elsmith, "relax your knees, so they bend a little at each step. And drop your whole foot to the floor at once instead of coming down on your heel. There, that's better. We'll teach you to walk like a commoner yet. Practice that up." He looked at his watch. "They're due here any time. Remember you're Charles Weier to members of the Organization. They'll be introduced to you as Lediacre and Fitzmartin, but those aren't their real names either. Lediacre *is* a Frenchman, however."

"Why all the secrecy?" asked Sir Howard.

"Because, my dear Weier, if you don't know what a man's real name is, you can't betray it under the influence of veramin. The only people whose real names you're supposed to know are those directly below you. There's nobody below you yet, and for the present you're acting under my direct orders."

When Lediacre and Fitzmartin arrived, they accepted their introduction to "Weier" without comment. Lediacre was as tall as the knight himself, though not as heavy; well-built, handsome in a foxy-faced sort of way, and exquisitely polite. He made Sir Howard feel like a hick. The other was a dark, nervous little man with a box to which he seemed to attach great importance. When the rest were crowded around, he opened it and began to assemble a contraption of pulleys, belts, brass rods, and circular glass disks with spots of metallic foil on them. Sir Howard gathered that these men were important in the Organization, and was pleased to think that he was being let in on something big.

"Turn on the radio, somebody," said Fitzmartin. "The forbidden hopper wavelengths, can you?" When the set had warmed to the sinister chirping of a hopper station, he began turning a crank on his apparatus. Presently a train of blue sparks jumped from one brass knob to another in rapid succession. With the crack of each spark there was a *blup* from the radio, so that the twitterings were smothered. A program of dance music on one of the legal frequencies was similarly made unintelligible.

"You see?" said Fitzmartin. "With an electrostat with wheels six feet in diameter, we can jolly well ruin radio reception within a radius of ten or more miles. If we cover the dashed country with such machines, we can absolutely drown the bloody hopper communications with static. They don't use anything but the blasted radio. They absolutely abolished all the wire communications centuries ago, and it would dashed well take them months to rig up new ones. Absolutely months."

Elsmith puffed his cigar. "Then what?"

"Well . . . I mean . . . my dear old man . . . if we could absolutely disorganize them—"

"It would take them about twenty-four hours to hunt down our static machines and restore their communications. And you know

what would happen to us. But wait—'' Seeing the crushed look
on Fitzmartin's face, he put out his hand. "This is an excellen
idea, just the same. I admire it. I merely wanted to remind you
that the hoppers wouldn't commit mass suicide because of a little
static. We won't build any of these yet. But we'll have a plan
drawn up for the large-size machine, and we'll have a hundred
thousand copies made and distributed to regional headquarters all
over the world. Baugh can handle that, I think. Then, when we
have something to give the hoppers the final push with, we'll
have the machines built, and put them to work when the time
comes. They'll be an invaluable auxiliary."

The men stayed on several days. On the second day Si
Howard got a slight shock when he saw Lediacre and Sally
Mitten strolling along a trail, apparently on the best of terms
and so absorbed in talk as to be oblivious of other things. He
watched their figures dwindle, still talking, and thought, so
that's it. He decided he didn't like the polished Monsieur Lediacre

The next day he came upon the Frenchman smoking and
looking at the view. "Ah, hello, my friend," said Lediacre. "I
was just admiring your scenery. It reminds me of the Massif
Central, in my own country."

"Are you going back there soon?" asked the knight, trying
not to make the question sound too pointed.

"No—not for three or maybe four months. You see, I am in
business. I am a what you call traveling representative for
French company."

"Mind if I ask what sort of company?"

"Not at all, my dear Weier. It is perfumery."

Perfumery! Good God! He didn't mind ignoble birth any
more, but perfume! Out of the tail of his eye he saw Sally Mitten
come out of the camp. Now if there were only some way he
could show this perfume salesman where he got off. He had a
reputation for prowess in the more spectacular forms of horseplay
Fencing, jousting, and steeplechasing weren't practical.

He said: "I haven't been getting enough exercise lately
they've kept me so busy learning to jimmy windows and talk
dialect. Do you wrestle?"

"I have not in a few years, but I should be glad to try some. I also need the exercise."

"O.K., there's a grassy spot up the trail a way."

When the Frenchman had peeled off his shirt and boots, Sir Howard had to admit that there was nothing soft-looking about him. But he knew he'd be able to squash this commoner chap like an undernourished mosquito.

They grabbed at each other; then Lediacre went down with a thump. He got up laughing with the greatest of good humor. "I am getting stupid in my old age! I learned that hold when I was a little infant! Let us have another, no?"

Sir Howard tensed himself to grab Lediacre's left knee. He never knew quite what happened next, except that he found himself flopping in midair, balanced across the Frenchman's shoulders. Then he came down with a jar that knocked the breath out of him. In a flash he was pinned firmly. His big muscles strained againt the lock, but to no avail. It made him no happier to note that Sally Mitten, Lyman Haas, and Eli Cahoon were interested spectators.

"Again, yes?" said Lediacre. It was "again," quite literally. Sir Howard sat up and stretched his sore muscles. Lediacre, very solicitous, said: "I did not twist too hard, did I? I learned that one from a Japanese man. I should be glad to teach it to you."

The knight accepted the lesson with thanks but without enthusiasm. The man, in addition to his social graces, was a big noise in the Organization, whereas *he* was just a rookie. And his attempt to demonstrate physical superiority had backfired. What could you do against a combination like that? Oh, well, he thought, if she likes him better, that's all. We Van Slycks can't afford to let things like that bother us. After all, we have our self-respect to consider.

10

The two riders jogged south at an experienced horseman's long-distance pace; walk, trot, canter, trot, walk, over and over. A horse expert might have surmised that the enormous black gelding and the slim red mare were too fine a quality horseflesh to go with the somewhat shabby specimens that sat on them. Haas had grumbled about leaving his chaps and high-heeled boots behind, and had accepted the ancient felt hat with a couple of fishing flies stuck in the band in place of his seventy-five-dollar Western special only under vehement protest. Sir Howard likewise felt self-conscious as he never had when dashing about the country in alloy-steel plate. They had been allowed to tote their swords, as these would not attract the dangerous and unwelcome attention of hoppers.

"The idea," the knight explained to Haas, "is that my old man isn't supposed to know about this expedition. He thinks I'm up at Watertown or somewhere. Otherwise we'd just walk in and make ourselves at home. Personally I think they're making us do this play acting to see how good we are at it."

"I don't mind the dressing up so much," said Haas. "But every time I see a hopper I think he's gonna hop up and ask questions. It makes me uneasy as all hell. I never noticed 'em before; just considered 'em a nuisance you had to put up with. It's got so I can't enjoy cheese sandwiches any more; the smell makes me think of hoppers."

"Myself," replied Sir Howard, "I think I'd like that of a three weeks' corpse better. If they stop us, you know who you're supposed to be, and you've got a complete set of forged papers to prove it." He was feeling much the same way. A human enemy, whom you could knock off his horse with a well-aimed toothpick thrust, was one thing; this invisible power with its mysterious weapons and ruthless thoroughness was another.

"Nothing in here," whispered Sir Howard. They had gone microscopically over the little room in the back of the tool shed that Frank van Slyck had used as a laboratory. Their flickering pencils of light showed nothing but bits of twisted metal, wire gauze, and broken glass.

Haas murmured: "Looks like the hoppers done a good job of cleaning up your brother's stuff."

"Yes. They examined his poor little apparatus and then smashed it up so its own mother wouldn't know it. They broke open the cases his bugs were in, and dumped the bugs out in the yard. They burned his notebooks, and took his textbooks away to put in one of their own libraries. Come on, there's nothing left to try but the manor house."

"You sure they ain't no secret rooms around here?"

"Yes. This shed is raised up off the ground, and there's nothing but dirt under it. The wall here is nothing but beaver board. You can see through the cracks into the tool room, so there isn't any space between walls or anything. Come on."

They calculated when the watchman would be at the other end of the grounds, then stole across the lawn. Sir Howard, being the heavier, boosted Haas up. Judicious use of a glass cutter gave him access to the latch, and the window opened with a faint squeak, no louder than the constant buzz and click and chirp of nocturnal insects. The slightly musty smell of the library mingled with the fragrance of the gardens.

"God help us," said Sir Howard, "if my old man finds out what we've done to his roses. He'll be madder'n a hungry wolf with nine lambs and a sore mouth."

They snooped around the room like a pair of large and inquisitive rats, running through desk drawers and waste-baskets. Sir Howard had almost despaired of finding anything when he remembered Frank's habit of putting papers between the leaves of books and forgetting them. His heart sank when he ran his flashlight over the well-filled stacks. There were hundreds of them, the books that had so bored him as a boy—poetry, fairy tales, romantic novels, theology. How different from the meaty Elsmith assortment! At least, he could use some selection. One shelf held books on farming, business, and other practical matters pertaining to the running of the duchy. If Frank had been reading any of the books, they'd be these. He and Haas began going through them.

Several blank pieces of paper were found, apparently mere place marks. Sir Howard put them in his shirt pocket. There was an exquisite drawing of a bee's head. There was a piece with several addresses on it. There was a piece with the cryptic notation:

Pulex irr.
M—146 Attr. fac.   .17
M—147 A. f.   .88
M—148 A. f.   .39
M—149 A. f.   .99! ! !

This was in a volume entitled "The Genetics of Stock Raising," which was about as scientific a book as the hoppers permitted. There was another sheet, in a small dictionary, with an algebraic problem worked out. There was—

"Hands up, you two!" A yellow eye opened in the dark, flooding the burglars with light. Behind the eye, barely visible, was an elderly man in a dressing gown. He held a burglar bow, that is, a crossbow with a flashlight fixed to its end. The bow was drawn and cocked.

"Easy on the trigger, father," said Sir Howard, getting up, "unless you want to put a bolt through your heir and assign."

"Howard! I didn't recognize you." As a measure of disguise the knight had let his face alone for a week, and the resulting coal-black stubble was child-frightening.

"What on earth . . . what the devil . . . what in bloody hell are you doing, burgling your own home?"

"I was looking for something, and didn't want to get you up at this time of night. We can't stay, unfortunately." Sir Howard knew the excuse sounded feeble.

"What's going on here, anyway? What are you looking for? And who's this man?"

Sir Howard introduced Haas. "I was just looking for some papers I thought I'd left. It's nothing, really."

"What papers? That doesn't explain this . . . this—"

"Oh, just some papers. I think we've about finished, eh, Lyman? It's nice to have seen you, father."

"Oh, no, you don't. You don't stir out of here until you've given me a sensible explanation."

"Sorry, father, but I've given you all I can. And I really am going."

The duke was working himself up into one of his rare tempers. "You . . . you young . . . you leave here, equipped like a proper gentleman, and say you're going on a pleasure trip. And six weeks later I find you dressed like a tramp, running around with commoners, and breaking into people's houses. What do you mean, sir? *What do you mean?*"

"Sorry, father; it's just my way of amusing myself."

"It doesn't amuse *me!* You'll stop this nonsense now, or I'll . . . . I'll cut you off!"

"That would be too bad for the duchy."

"I'll stop your income! I still control most of your money, you know."

Sir Howard was careful not to show how much this threat really jarred him. "Oh, I can get along. If need be, we'll join a traveling circus."

"You'll *what?* But you couldn't! I mean, that's preposterous. A Van Slyck working in a circus!

"You'd be surprised. Remember Great-Uncle Waldo? The one who swindled those bank people? I can get a job as a strong man, and Lyman here can do rope tricks. We'll manage."

The duke took a deep breath. "You win. I don't understand you, Howard. Just when I think you're turning into a sensible, level-headed adult you act like this. But you win. Anything would be better than that! A circus performer!" He shuddered. "By the way, how did you get over the wall?"

"Lyman threw his lasso over one of the merlons on the battlement. You know what a lasso is—a rope with a sliding noose. He's an expert. You remember, when you had the wall built, I advised you not to put those open crenelations on top."

"They won't be there long!"

"Oh, while I think of it," said Sir Howard casually. "Are there any pups in the kennels just now?"

"Let me think. . . . Yes, Irish Mist whelped about six months ago, and we have several that we haven't given away yet. Do you want one?"

"Yes, I'd like one."

"Why—if you don't mind an old man's curiosity?"

"Oh, I just thought I'd give one to a friend."

"Friend, huh? I hope she isn't another commoner wench?"

"Oh, you needn't worry about the Van Slyck escutcheon. It's nothing serious; just returning a favor."

"Favor, humph! There are all kinds of favors." The duke led them out to the kennels, and Sir Howard looked over the squirming Kerry-blue terrier pups with his flashlight. He picked one up.

"Don't you want something to carry him in?"

"Yes, if you have a basket or something."

"Hm-m-m—I think this would do. Sure you and your friend won't reconsider and stay the night?"

"No; thanks, anyway. I'll be seeing you. And by the way, better not mention our visit."

"Don't worry! I don't want everybody to know that my son's gone squirrely! Take care of yourself, won't you? And try to come back in one piece? I couldn't stand having anything happen. Please, Howard. Good-by and good luck!"

11

"I hated to treat the old man like that. Hope I get a chance to explain some day."

"H-m-m. He did seem kinda riled up. Say, How, maybe that wasn't such a good idea, us trying to make Renssalaer. Maybe we shoulda stopped the night at Hudson. It's gonna be blacker'n t'other side of hell. And I think she's liable to rain." Haas pulled his damp shirt front away from his skin. "Danged if I like your Yank summer weather, specially when it's fixing up to rain. Your clothes stick to you."

"If it starts to rain we'll stop at Valatie. That's only a little way; we just passed Kinderhook."

"Better use your flashlight, or you'll ride into the ditch. Is the little critter still in his basket? Cute little devil. Oh-oh, there goes a flash of lightning, off to the west. If I had my chaps, they'd shed the water."

"The lightning's over the Helderbergs. The rain won't get here for hours yet. Trot!"

Plop-plop-plop-plop went the hoofs. Something—something—made the hair on Sir Howard's neck rise. Did he imagine it, or was there a faint smell of cheese?

"Halt, Man!" It was the familiar, detestable chirp. A blinding light was in his face. He looked around for Haas, but the Westerner and his mount appeared to have vanished into thin air.

There were two of *them*, in one of their two-wheeled vehicles. Or rather, one was in the vehicle, and the other was out and peering up at him. He slid his right foot out of the stirrup. "Do not dismount!" There were chirpings and trillings in the dark, and the command, "Give me your reins!"

The vehicle purred ahead at a bare six miles an hour; Paul

Jones trotted in tow. One of the hoppers had squirmed around in its seat to keep an eye on the rider.

He thought, these things belong to the road patrol. They're taking me to the station at Valatie—which the hoppers persisted in calling Vallity, to the annoyance of the natives, who claimed they lived in Valaysha. They'll interrogate me, probably with the use of veramin. They'll want to know who I really am. They may even want to know about Elsmith. I must not tell them. I ought to kill myself first. But maybe there's an easier way out than that. It's no use trying to run; they've got floodlights and guns. But if that fellow would only get a crick in his neck for a minute. His hand stole toward one of the saddle compartments—

The procession drew up at the Valatie station. There was a hopper with a long gun by the door, a sentry. The two hoppers in the cycle got out. Another came out the door, and there was still another inside, using a typewriter.

"Dismount, Man."

Oh, God, he thought. I mustn't stagger. I must keep my brain clear. He scooped the small gray dog out of the basket on Paul Jones's rump.

"Enter. Wait! Leave your sword outside."

The knight unbuckled his sword belt fumblingly, and leaned the weapon against the wall of the station.

"What is that?" The flashlight made the puppy blink. "Dogs are not allowed in the station. You must leave it outside also."

"He'll run away, your excellency."

"Place it back in the basket, then."

"The basket has no top, your excellency. He'll jump out."

Twittering in the dark. Then: "Leave it with the sentry. He shall hold it."

The sentry took the leash in one hand and tried to scratch the dog's ears with the other. The dog backed as far as he could, trembling. Sir Howard slouched into the station with his best commoner walk.

"Your papers, Man. Sit here. Bare your arm."

The needle pricked. The hoppers went through the papers.

He thought, I must talk right. I hope this works. If there's a God, I hope He'll let me say the right things. Elsmith doesn't seem to think there is a God; at least that's what he's implied at times. But if there is one, I hope He'll let me say the right things.

There it was, that tingling, that dizzy feeling. I must say the right things. If I start to say the wrong things, I've got my pocketknife still. I could get it out quickly before they could stop me. The throat would be best, I think. I'm not sure the blade's long enough to try for my heart. Let me say the right thing—

It was beginning, now. The hopper who seemed to be boss was looking up from the papers. "You are Charles—Weier?"

"Yes, your excellency."

"You are a professional hockey player?"

"Yes, your excellency." If only they wouldn't ask him questions about ice hockey!

"Where were you born?"

The form of the question was different; there might be a catch to this one. He was supposed to tell them "Ballston Spa."

"Ballston Spaw, your excellency." Thank God, he'd remembered in time! If he'd followed his natural impulse to use the downstate pronunciation of "Spah," he might have given himself away.

Twittering. Then: "Do you know anything about a man, tall and dark like you, who has appeared in the Hudson-Mohawk region lately, and who sometimes passes himself off as William Scranton, and at other times pretends to be Howard van Slyck, the Duke of Poughkeepsie's son?"

"No, your excellency." If only he didn't get his own name mixed up with his aliases! Scranton—Weier—Van Slyck—he wasn't sure he knew which was which himself.

"These papers appear to be in order. We are examining men of your physical type in an attempt to solve the disappearance of one of our troopers last month. Do you know anything about it?"

"No, your excellency." Hot dog, he was winning!

More twitterings. If that was merely an order to check the stamps on his travel permit against the ledgers at Albany and Poughkeepsie, that was fine. The stamps were genuine. But if it was an order to check the permit itself against the central files in New York, that was something else.

"We are satisfied, Man. You may go." The clawed, buff-haired hand shoved the papers at him across the table. I mustn't stagger when I get up—I mustn't swagger, either.

At the door there was no sign of the sentry. Its long gun lay on the ground. At the edge of the light from the open door lay its leather helmet.

Sir Howard was thunderstruck. He had no idea what could have happened. If they came out and found the sentry gone, they'd scour the country for it, and for him, too. He turned back to the door. "Excellencies!"

"What is it, Man? You were told to go."

"Your sentry has gone off with my dog."

The four hoppers boiled out of the station like popping corn. They examined the discarded gun and helmet, sounding like a whole bird shop. A couple of them hopped off tentatively into the dark, trilling, then hopped back. They waved their clawed hands and wagged their ratlike heads, burbling. One hopped inside and began cheeping into a microphone.

"What are you waiting for, Man?" It was the boss hopper again. "Your services are not required here."

"My dog, your excellency."

The hopper seemed to think for a moment. "Man, your attitude has been admirably cooperative. In recognition, we will, as a special concession, keep your dog here, if we find it, until such time as you call for it. Provided of course, that you leave a deposit to cover the cost of keeping it. A dollar will suffice."

Sir Howard's economy complex winced, but he paid up, buckled on his sword, and led Paul Jones away.

Out of hearing of the station he began whistling, softly at first, then more loudly. There was a click of claws on the pavement, the scrape of a trailing leash, and the sudden pressure of paws on his knee. He put the puppy, squirming with frantic joy, into the basket, mounted, and rode off. He hated leaving his dollar with the hopper, but the risk of going back to try to claim it was too great.

"Hey, How!" came a hiss from the blackness.

"Lyman! What happened to you?"

"I seen those guys laying for you, but I couldn't warn you because you was too far up front—right on top of them when I seen 'em. Before they turned the light on I jumped Queenie over the ditch and into a field. I watched the hoppers tow you off, and

I followed through the fields so's they wouldn't hear me. What happened to *you?*''

Sir Howard told him.

"Is that a fact? The sentry fella just plumb disappeared? I never. But how did you keep from telling them the truth, if they doped you up with that stuff?"

"If anybody happens to notice an empty whiskey bottle in the ditch near the Valatie station, they can put two and two together, perhaps. Alcohol in the system counteracts the action of veramin, Elsmith said, and it looks as though he was right. But between the two of them I don't feel so good. You'd better ride clear, Lyman. It looks as though I'm going to be sick from liquor for the second time in my life."

"Okay. Better aim to the right; that's downwind." Thunder rolled overhead. "Boy, there was a big drop on my hand. Looks like we're sure gonna get soaked tonight. But what the hell. I'd ruther be wet outside a hopper house than dry inside one any day."

12

"Oh, thank you, Howard, thank you ever so much. I've always wanted one."

Not a bad reaction, he thought, especially considering that the pup didn't cost me anything, except that damned one-dollar deposit. I wonder what a new bicycle would do. Let's see—good bicycles are expensive—maybe I could get one wholesale. Oh, so *he's* here again, the knight thought disgustedly.

Lediacre appeared and began making French noises at the puppy, who seemed bewildered by all this attention.

"I don't know," said Elsmith. "If he can be trained properly, he'll be an asset, but if he turns out to be a yapper we'll have to get rid of him. He'd attract attention. Well, Weier, what have you to report?"

They went in, and Sir Howard spread out the papers he had found, meanwhile giving his story.

Elsmith stared hard at the pieces of paper. "We'll test these blank ones for invisible writing, just to make sure, though I don't think there's anything on them. The sentry just disappeared, eh, leaving his hat and rifle? That's funny. What do you know about what your brother was doing with his insects? Remember, we were out of touch with him for two months before his death.''

"Not a great deal," said Sir Howard. "I was away from home during most of those two months, too, and he never took me into his confidence. I didn't even know about the laboratory until I came home after I heard the news. And by that time they'd smashed up everything and confiscated what they hadn't smashed. They turned the bugs loose in our yard. We had a regular plague of insects for a week.''

"Hm-m-m. Hm-m-m." Elsmith lit a cigar. "Somehow I think your brother, and his insects, and the sentry's disappearance are all connected, though I don't see how.''

Sir Howard picked up the scrap with the cryptic heading "Pulex irr." "Have you any idea what this means, sir?''

"I suppose it stands for *Pulex irritans*, the common flea. The M-146 might be the number of an artificial mutation, assuming that your brother was working on mutations. You know what they are, don't you? The thing to the right of it probably means 'attrition factor point one seven,' meaning that after a given length of time under certain conditions only one-sixth as many of a given batch of fleas were alive as would be with the normal nonmutated type. The exclamation marks opposite the M-149 presumably mean that he had found a type of flea that would stand those conditions, whatever they are, as well as the normal type stands normal conditions.''

Sir Howard thought. "Fleas don't bite hoppers, do they? Everybody says that flies and mosquitoes never bother the things. There's—*WOW!*'' Sir Howard thought afterward that it was the greatest moment of his life. He couldn't explain how he had done it. One moment there was confusion and bafflement, and then in a flash everything was clear. He saw in his mind the now-familiar picture of a small gray animal, scratching—scratching. "It's the pup!''

"What? What? Don't ever do that again, my boy. At least, not indoors, unless you want to give me heart failure.''

"The puppy, the dog. Suppose Frank had found a mutation of the flea that liked hoppers. When they dumped all his bugs out, some of these special fleas found their way into the kennels, and

were on the pup when I gave him to the sentry to hold. A couple
of them went exploring and got on the sentry.''

"Well?"

"Well, what would you do if you had a hat on and a flea
crawled up under it and bit your scalp?"

"I'd take the hat— By Jove, I see. It's fantastic, but it seems
to fit. Ordinarily insects don't bother the hoppers because the
haemocyanin in their blood gives them indigestion. But if your
brother developed a flea that thrived on haemocyanin blood as
well as haemoglobin blood—and the hopper, never having suffered from insect bites, would be driven half crazy by them—
they didn't bring any special parasitic insects from their own
world—he'd take his helmet off and then not have sense enough
to put it back on. With those synthetic minds of theirs concentrat-
ing on something else, they'd pull their helmets off to scratch
without thinking— Where are you going?"

Sir Howard was already at the door. "Lediacre!" he shouted.
"Where did the dog go?"

"He went with Sally, my friend. Or rather, she took him. She
said she was about to give him a bath."

"Where? Where?"

"Up by the spring. You wish—"

Sir Howard didn't hear the rest of it; he was racing up the path
to the spring. His heart pounded. At the end of the path a pretty
picture came in view, framed by the trees; Sally Mitten on her
knees, the sun in her hair, before a washtub. Over the washtub
she held at arm's length a half-grown, smoke-gray, apprehensive-
looking terrier.

"*Sally!*" His frantic yell, with all the power of his huge chest
behind it, made the forest hum with echoes.

"Why . . . Howard, what is it? Have the hoppers found our
place?"

"No . . . it's the dog." He paused to catch his breath.

"The dog? I was just going to wash him. He's simply covered
with fleas."

"Thank God!" *Puff, puff, puff.*

"That he's covered with fleas?"

"Yes. Have you dunked him in that stuff yet?"

"No. Howard van Slyck, are you crazy?"

"Not at all. Ask your Uncle Homer. But I've got to have those fleas. C'mere, Mutt or Spike or whatever your name is."

"I'm going to call him Terence."

"All right. C'mere, Terence."

Terence looked at the knight, wagged his tail doubtfully, sat down and scratched.

By the time he got the dog back to camp, ideas were sprouting like toadstools after a rain. Elsmith said: "It's probable that only a fraction of Terence's fleas are the kind we want. We shall have to find some way of selecting them from the mass. There seems to be quite a mass, too." Terence was nibbling at his silky flank.

Sir Howard said: "If we had some of that haemocyanin blood, we could feed it to them, and the ones that didn't pass out would be the right ones."

"Yes," mused Elsmith, "and that would give us a check on the validity of our theory. I don't know how we could get a supply of hopper blood, though."

Haas drawled: "Maybe we could kidnap one of the critters and take his hat off so he'd be harmless."

"Bravo!" said Lediacre. "That is the true American spirit, that we read about in France."

"Too risky, I'm afraid," said Elsmith.

"So," continued Lediacre, "does anything else have this special kind of blood?"

"It's almost identical with that of the anthropoda, especially the crustacea."

"Crustacea? You mean like *les homards*, the lobsters?"

"Yes."

"Then, my friends, our problem it is solved! One of our men is the manager of Vinay Frères, a restaurant in New York. Have you ever eaten there? But you must! Their onion soup—magnificent! I shall arrange with him to bleed his lobsters to death before cooking them. It will not harm them as food. And the blood we can smuggle up here. But how does one raise fleas? One cannot call, 'Here, flea; here, flea,' at meal time."

"One way," said Elsmith, "is to put them under a glass on your wrist. They eat whenever they want to then. But perhaps if we had the blood in thin rubber bladders, that they could pierce and suck through—"

Once started, the flea farm grew by leaps and bounds. It took
an average of five weeks to raise a generation to maturity, but
there seemed to be no limit to their reproductive powers, at least
when they were coddled as they were at the Adirondack camp.
Sir Howard never had a chance to go to Amsterdam for a
bicycle. Men came and went. Little Fitzmartin departed happily
with instructions to have as many electrostats as possible built,
and talking about how they'd absolutely smear the bally blighters.
Lediacre was at the camp often. It was a crumb of comfort to Sir
Howard that if he was too busy to squire Sally Mitten, the
Frenchman was also. They drove from morning to night. A
chamber had to be cut out of the hillside to accommodate
thousands of fleas.

There was a colored man from a place called Missouri, who
departed with several thousand peculiar pets concealed in the
lining of his battered grass suitcase. There was a red-skinned
man from the Southwest, a Novvo, who proved to be an old
friendly enemy of Haas. Whereat there was much backslapping
and reminiscing: "Say, remember the time we beat the pants of
you guys on the South Platte?" "What do you mean, beat the
pants off us? You had us outnumbered two to one, and even so
we retreated in good order!" There was Maxwell Baugh, the
new head of the Hudson-Mohawk branch of the Organization, to
report that the local hoppers hadn't shown any signs of suspicion,
but that they were still worried about the sentry, who had been
picked up wandering idiotically, and was unable to give any
coherent account of his actions after his helmet had been put
back on.

Sir Howard began to appreciate what a big place the world
was. He'd have liked to question these men of odd sizes and
colors about their homelands. But there wasn't time; they came
and left by stealth, after staying but a fraction of an hour. A bar
from Terence, a shadowy form in the dark, passwords and
mutterings, and the man was gone.

"And now," said Elsmith, "we sit and wait. It's the dammable
time lag."

"What do you mean, sir?"

"The time it takes for our messengers to get to all parts of the
world. In prehopper times you could get to any part of the world

n a few days, by flying machines and ground vehicles. But with
he fastest means of transportation available to us, it takes a full
month to get to places like Central Asia. So we have to wait.
Fortunately most of the messengers to the faraway countries got
away early; we sent a lot of our own men to save time. But one
of them, our man to Iberia, was picked up by the hoppers. He
jumped into the Bay of Biscay and drowned himself before they
got any information out of him. But we had to send another load
of fleas.

"So, my boy, for the next five weeks you can plan to spend
most of your time hunting, fishing, and gardening."

"Sir, I'd like to run down to Amsterdam tomorrow—"

"I'm afraid not, Van Slyck. We'll have to lie very low for the
next month. It would be intolerable to have something go wrong
at the last minute. The hoppers haven't acted suspicious, but
how do we know they're not playing cat-and-mouse with us?"

So, there wouldn't be any bicycle for Sally Mitten. And
Lediacre was coming up again in a few days. Oh, to hell with it!

"About how many fleas have we raised altogether, sir?"

"I don't really know. Something like fifty million."

"That doesn't sound like enough. There are twenty million
hoppers. Seems as though we ought to have more than two
hoppers per flea—I mean two fleas per hopper. Though the fleas
hop, too."

"We shall have. The messengers will establish stations for
raising more generations of fleas in various parts of the word.
Though one more generation is about all they'll have time for.
Some of them are raising their fleas on the way."

"How will they keep them?"

"If everything else fails, there are always their own bodies."

"When is M-day?"

"October 1st."

The wait proved more difficult than the work, though Sir
Howard did everything he could to make the time pass quickly.
He threw himself into such occupations as were open to him with
vicious energy, as when he walked five miles through the woods
carrying across his shoulders an eight-point buck he had shot. He
did little fishing. It wasn't active enough, and besides he was
likely to arrive at Sly Pond to find the boat bobbing serenely in

the middle of the lake with Sally Mitten and Lediacre in it. There was no fun in standing sullenly on the shore, and after the second occasion he hadn't taken any more chances. He'd rather take his bird glasses down to Little Moose Lake, and watch the local pair of ospreys dive for fish. He read voraciously.

Toward the end of September, when the maples were breaking out in scarlet and gold, Maxwell Baugh arrived to discuss detailed plans for the York State uprising. Sir Howard discovered to his surprise that he had been picked to lead a contingent of heavy cavalry against such of the Albany hoppers as were not affected by the fleas. The plans had long been drawn up; it remained but to fit individuals into their places in the pattern.

Sir Howard held up his helmet. "This part," he said, "is the bowl. This is the visor. This is the bib or beaver."

"Goodness!" said Sally Mitten. "I suppose all those other pieces of armor have names, too."

"Well, well, don't tell me that I've found one subject I know more about than you, my sweet? Yes, they all have special names, and they all have special purposes. And I know 'em all.'"

"That's too bad, Howard."

"Huh?"

"I mean, if we're successful, armor will go out of use pretty quickly, won't it? People will have guns then."

"Good Lord, I never thought of that! I guess you're right, though."

"And they'll have power vehicles, too. You wouldn't want to go somewhere on a horse when you can go a hundred miles an hour in a car."

"I guess you win again, young lady. Here I've spent years leaning to sit a horse, and hold a toothpick, and swing a sword and jump around with fifty pounds of armor on. More tricks than a dead mule has flies. And now, I'm helping to make all that expensive knowledge useless. I suppose it's too late to do anything about it now."

"Oh, I'm sure you'll get on all right. You're a resourceful young man. By the way, I never could see how men in full armor got around the way they do. I should think they'd be like turtles turned on their backs."

"It isn't so bad. The weight's distributed, and all these joints and little sliding plates give you a good deal of freedom. But if you try to run upstairs with a suit on, you know you're carrying something."

"I should think men would prefer chain armor. Isn't it lighter and more flexible?"

"That's what a lot of people think who never wore any. For equivalent protection it's just about as heavy. And there's a padding."

"Padding?"

"Yes. Without an inch or two of cotton padding underneath, it wouldn't be much good. A blow would break your bones even if the edge didn't go through. And by the time you get all the padding on, the suit isn't much more limber than one of the plate, and it's hotter than the devil's private fireplace. Chain's all right for a little mail shirt like Lyman Haas'. That's just to keep some kind friend from slipping a dagger between your ribs on a dark night."

He buckled his last strap, picked up his helmet, and stood up. The fire threw little red highlights on his suit. "You boys ready?"

"Yeah," said Cahoon. "We be."

"Been ready half an hour," said Haas. "That'll be a lesson to me, to allow more time for lobsters to get into their shells."

"Howard—"

"Yes, Sally?"

"I wanted to ask you something—"

"Yes?"

"Be careful how you expose yourself. People who have never faced guns have no idea how deadly they can be."

"Oh. Don't worry. I'm scared to death of the things myself. Be seeing you. I hope."

13

Plop-plop-plop-plop went the hoofs. The fog was still rising off the Mohawk. You couldn't see anything but the other men in the troop and the glistening black road ahead. The mist condensed on their plate and ran down in little streaks.

Out of Schenectady, they passed the huge masts of the broadcasting station. A small fire near the base of the nearest mast made a spot of orange in the grayness. Three men were standing around the mast, and a fourth was kneeling at its base. He was chopping at a cable with a butcher's cleaver. *Chunk* went the cleaver. *Chunk. Chunk. Chunk*

"Here's McCormack Corners," said a man.

"What's Weier taking us around this way for?" asked another. "It's shorter by Colonie."

"Dunno. Maybe they want to keep the Mohawk Pike open for somebody else."

They halted. Up ahead was a pattering of many hoofs.

"Single file," came back Sir Howard's baritone. "Walk."

They straightened out, and saw that a large troop of unarmored men with crossbows dangling from their saddles was trotting past along the Cherry Valley Pike. One of them called: "Hey lobsters! What are you coming for? You'll be about as useful as real lobsters. We're the ones got to do the real fighting!"

"We're to fight the hoppers when they come out, and you guys pull foot," retorted one of the armored men. "Seen any hoppers?"

"Just one," a crossbowman called back. "Near Duanesburg. Funniest thing you ever seen. He just sat there on his cycle watching us go past. Didn't do nothing. Thought we was just a local war party, I guess."

"Local war party! That's good!"

"He didn't do nothing. Didn't even say, 'Halt, men!' I bet he was surprised when Schuyler, up front, put a bolt through him."

"What'd he do then?"

"Just keeled over and squeaked for a while. Then he didn't squeak any more."

The crossbowmen pulled up ahead. It was getting quite light. The mist faded. In front of them the sun, orange on top shading to deep red underneath, threw cheerful lights on the plate.

"I see the Office Building," said a man. "Suppose any hoppers are in it now?"

"Prob'ly," replied another. "They get to work early. One reason I never liked the hoppers is the early hours they keep."

"You call getting to work at seven early! You oughta work on a farm, mister."

"Maybe they'll see us."

"Maybe. They'll know something's wrong. That static machine oughta be going on any time."

"They got guns in the Office Building?"

"Ayuh. I think so."

"I mean big ones—artillery, they call 'em."

"Well, this ain't Watervliet."

"No. But the guns at Watervliet could shoot clear down to Albany if they had a mind to."

"Huh? There ain't nothing can shoot that far."

"Oh, yes. They can shoot clear down to Kingston if they got a mind to. But that's why they have the static machines. So the hoppers can't radio back and forth to tell where to shoot."

"I hear we got guns, too."

"I think we got some. Some they stole from the hoppers, and some they made. But the trouble is, there ain't anybody knows how to work 'em. I thought of trying to get in a gun troop, and then decided I'd liefer stick to my old toothpick."

"Say, who's the twerp up front with Weier? Guy with a funny hat."

"Dunno. He's from some place they call Wyoming. Down South, I think."

"Don't see how he could make any speed with that hat. Too much air resistance."

"Hey, wasn't that a shot?"

"Ayuh. Sounds like it."

"They're shooting regular now. Weier better hurry up, or the fun'll be over before we get there."

The windows of Albany rattled to continuous gunfire when Sir Howard led his troop behind the Education Building across the street from the Office Building. Up and down Elk Street little knots of armed men waited. The knight told his men to wait, dismounted, and trotted around the corner.

Most of the gunfire was coming from the Office Building. All the windows on the lower floors of this building had been broken. From the nearer surrounding buildings came a stream of arrows and crossbow bolts. Barricades had been thrown up at the intersections. More crossbowmen, and a few men with rifles and pistols, stood behind these barricades shooting. Eli Cahoon was behind a near one. He was going from man to man, saying: "Now, take your time, son; just squeeze the trigger slow." In front of the shattered glass doors of the Office Building lay a pile of dead hoppers without helmets. Scattered over the broad Capitol Square were a score or so of dead men. A little puffy wind was rising. It picked up yellow and brown leaves from the piles raked together in the gutters and whirled them merrily around the square.

Sir Howard picked out an officer, a man in ordinary hunting clothes with a brassard on his arm. "Hey, Bodansky! I'm on time, I hope."

"Thank God you got here, Weier! You're in command."

"What?"

"Yep; the whole shootin' match. Baugh's dead. He led the charge when they tried to get into the ground floor. Haverhill hasn't shown up; nobody knows what's become of him. And McFee just had his arm all smashed to hell by a bullet. So you're it."

"Whew! What's the situation?"

"So-so. We can't get in, and they can't get out. Olsen turned the fleas loose on schedule; they got most of the hoppers. But there was enough left to put the helmets back on the heads of some. The ones they didn't put the helmets on wandered out the front door like they were silly, and the boys potted 'em. I don't think you can get the boys to make another charge; they saw what happened to the first ones."

"How about their cone transformers?"

"They've got a couple, but they can't use 'em because we turned the city power off. We got the power plant right at the start. They've got some convulsion rayers, too, but they're only the little kind, good up to fifty feet. Here's Greene." Another officer ran up.

"The riflemen's ammunition isn't going to last much longer," he gasped. "Half of it's too old to go off, anyway. And they're shooting pretty wild."

"Tell the riflemen to cease firing," Sir Howard snapped. He was feeling both awed by the unexpected responsibility and tremendously important. "We'll need them later."

"The bows and kickers wont reach to the upper floors," said Bodansky.

"We can't do much to the upper floors from here, anyway. We'll have to find some way of getting into the lower floors." He thought for a minute. They were expecting him to produce some bright idea. If he didn't he'd be a failure. He raised his voice: "Hey, Eli! Eli Cahoon!"

The old New Englander came over with his slinking walk. "Yeah?"

"Think it's going to blow?"

"Hm-m-m. Maybe. Shouldn't be surprised." He looked at the sky, at the dancing leaves. "No'thwest, in about an hour."

"All right. Bodansky, have another barricade thrown across the yard back of the Office Building. Use furniture, anything. Tell the boys to keep down close to it, so they won't be potted from the upper floors. Get all the crates and boxes in town. Pile 'em on the west side of the barricade. Get all the dead leaves you can."

"Bonfire? Smudge?"

"Yes. And get every garbage can in Albany! We'll show them something about smells. Hey, St. John! Get out the fire department. We're going to start a smudge, and when the smoke gets thick we'll run the trucks up on the sidewalk alongside the Office Building, and the boys will climb up the ladders into the windows."

He worked around behind buildings to the other side of the square, checking dispositions and talking to harassed officers. There were men in plate, men in overalls, men in store clothes. There were men with billhooks, men with bows, men with butcher knives lashed to the ends of poles. There were a few dead men, and an occasional wounded man being carried off.

The pile of assorted fuels grew, over beyond the Office Building. The fire department hadn't appeared. Why, of course, he thought, most of the firemen are on the firing line. I've been dumb. There has to be somebody to hitch up the fire horses. I'll have to get somebody to round 'em up. He gave orders; men ran, hesitated, and came back to have them repeated.

The bonfire began to crackle and smoke. It smoked beautifully. The breeze was just strong enough to wrap the Office Building in a shroud of pearly fumes, so that you could only see parts of it. Sir Howard heard a man near him cough and say, "Who the hell they trying to smoke out, us or the hoppers?"

There was a snoring buzz, and a flying machine swept over the buildings. More and more men neglected their shooting to stare up at it apprehensively. It circled and came back.

"They going to bomb us?" asked an officer.

"They'd like to," replied Sir Howard. "But they don't know where to bomb. They're afraid of hitting their own people. Tell your boys to pay attention to the Office Building; not to worry about the flier."

The machine appeared again, much higher and flying north. It was almost out of sight behind the buildings when it disappeared in a blinding magnesium-white flash. Sir Howard knew what was coming, and opened his mouth. The concussion made men stagger, and a few fell. It took the knight a second to realize that the musical tinkle was not in his head but was glass falling from thousands of windows.

Everywhere were scared faces, a few with nosebleeds. They'd bolt in a minute. He trotted down the line, explaining: "It O.K.! We got Watervliet! We turned one of their own X beams on the ship and set off its bombs! Everything's fine!"

"They're coming out!" somebody yelled.

Sir Howard looked around. It would be logical for the hoppers to bolt, now that the arsenal had fallen. He ought to be with his cavalry troop on the other side of the square. The shooting from the Office Building had slackened. It would take him all day to work around outside the zone of fire. He vaulted a barricade, almost fell when he landed under the weight of his plate, and started to run across the square with the queer, tottering run that armored men have.

He was halfway across when the hoppers boiled out of the Office Building by the front doors. He was right in front of them. There was a crash of shots from the guns they carried in their claws. Nothing touched him. He ran on. There were scattering shots from the hoppers, and something hit his right pauldron and ricocheted off with a screech. He spun half around and fell. Thank God, it was just a glancing hit, he thought. Better play possum for a few seconds. He thought he heard a groan from the human army when he fell, but that was pure self-conceit, as most of them had no idea who he was. He looked out of the corner of his eye toward the hoppers. They were bounding across the square toward the buildings. There must have been fifty; thirty-five, anyway. Arrows and bolts streaked toward them, mostly going wild. An arrow bounced off Sir Howard's backplate. God, he thought, is one of those idiots going to kill me by mistake? The hoppers had turned and were going back the way they had come.

Sir Howard scrambled up. In front of him men were dropping over a barricade and running toward him. They were shouting something and pointing. He looked around. Not thirty feet off was a hopper. It had a sort of gun in its hands, connected by cables to a knapsack thing strapped to its back. It was a lightning gun. It went off with a piercing crack, and a straight pencil of blue flash went past Sir Howard. It cracked again and again. A couple of the men who had run toward him were lying down, and the rest were running back. The gun cracked again, and the flash ended on Sir Howard's breastplate. All his muscles twitched, and his bones were jarred. But he did not fall. The gun cracked again and yet again, with the same result. His suit was grounding the discharges. He got his sword out and took a step toward the hopper. The hopper went soaring away across the square after its fellows, who were bouncing along State Street.

People were dropping out of doors and windows and climbing over barricades. They came out quickly enough now that the hoppers were in retreat. If he didn't get his cavalry under way in a few seconds, the square would be packed and they'd be struck like flies on flypaper.

Just ahead of the crowd Musik, his second-in-command, and Lyman Haas appeared at a canter. The former was leading Paul Jones. The men were clattering in double file behind them. Sir Howard yelled, "Stout fellas!" and climbed aboard. As he did so, Haas shouted: "The cavalry from Pittsfield is coming up State from the river!"

"They can't get through here; you tell 'em to go around by the sound end of town and head west. Try to cut the hoppers off! All right, let's go!" They pounded diagonally across the square; men who had just run out ran back, like startled chickens, to get out of their way.

The barricade across State Street west of the Office Building was low, and had only a few men behind it. These shot wildly until the hoppers were two jumps away, then broke and scattered like flushed quail. The hoppers soared over the barricade and shot the men in the back as they ran. When Sir Howard arrived at the barricade the hoppers were far down State Street, their bodies rising and falling like overhead valves. Sir Howard put Paul Jones over the barricade. A terrific clang made him squirm around in the saddle. Musik and Musik's horse were standing on their heads on the west side of the barricade. Both got up quickly. Musik's horse ran along after the troop, and Musik ran after his horse on foot, yelling, "Come back here, you bastitch!" and falling farther and farther behind. Far away they heard the sirens of the fire engines, arriving at last.

They cut across Washington Park and galloped out New Scotland Avenue, keeping the hoppers in sight, but not gaining much on them. People ran into the street, ran back when the hoppers appeared, ran out again, and ran back again when the cavalry came along.

They got out into the southwestern part of Albany, where New Scotland Avenue becomes Slingerlands Road. A few streets had once been laid down here, but very few houses had been built. It was mostly just a big flat area covered with tall weeds. There were other horsemen on their left, presumably the men from Massachusetts. These were swooping along drawing steel bows. The combination worked beautifully. An arrow would bring down a hopper, and by the time Sir Howard's lobsters had passed over it, each taking a jab at it with a lance, it didn't look like a hopper. It didn't look particularly like anything.

The hoppers were spreading out. The men, without orders, were spreading out to hunt them down. Sir Howard found himself alone and chasing a hopper. He wondered what he'd do if the hopper got to the edge of the plateau on which Albany stands before he caught it. He couldn't gallop Paul Jones down the slope that ended at Normans Kill. But this hopper seemed to be going slowly. As Sir Howard gained on it, he saw that it had an arrow sticking in its thigh.

Sir Howard squeezed his lance and sighted on the hopper. The hopper stopped, turned around, and raised a small gun. The gun went off, and something went off in the knight's side. The saddle seemed to be lifted away from him, and he landed on his back in the weeds. His side pained horribly for a moment, so that he felt deathly sick.

He couldn't see for the weeds, which stuck up like a forest around him. All he could see was the hopper standing there. The hopper raised the gun again. The gun clicked harmlessly. Sir Howard thought, if I can get up I can finish it before it reloads. He tried to sit up, but his plate dragged him down again. The hopper was reloading, and he couldn't get up. He could hear the drumming of hoofs, but they seemed miles away. He thought, Oh, God, why do I have to die *now?* Why couldn't I have died at the start? The hopper clicked the gun and raised it again. His side hurt terribly, and he was going to die at the last moment.

Then there were hoofs, near, and something snaky hissed out of the air to settle around the hopper. The gun went off, but the hopper was bouncing away in grotesque positions. It gave a final bounce and disappeared behind the weeds.

14

The doctor at the door said: "He'll be all right. It's just a broken rib. A bullet went through his plate and grazed his side. The broken ends cut him up a little when he fell. Sure, you can see him." Then they all came in: Elsmith and Sally Mitten and Haas and Cahoon and Lediacre. The Frenchman was dirty and had a bandage over his left ear. He was very sympathetic.

They all tried to talk at once. Sir Howard asked how things were going. Elsmith answered: "Fine. We got word by radio—we turned the electrostats off—that all the broadcasting stations in New York had been taken. There must have been at least a thousand hoppers in the RCA Building, but they mounted some captured heavy guns in Columbus Circle and blew them out of it. As far as I know, all the hopper strongholds in North America have been taken. There are some hoppers still at large, but they'll be killed on sight.

"There are quite a few holding out in Africa, but there's an Arab army on its way to deal with them, completely outfitted with hopper guns. They even found some people willing to take a chance on running the captured flying machines. Mongolia never got any fleas at all, but there were only a few hoppers there, anyway. It's pretty much the same elsewhere. Some of them got away in their flying machines and used their bombs and rays. They blew Louisville off the map, for instance. But they had to come down eventually, and there wasn't any friendly place to land. In places where the most fleas were released, and all the hoppers took off their hats to scratch, the way they did at Watervliet, it was simply a slaughter of helpless animals. I'm trying to save a few of them."

"Why?"

"Without the helmets they're quite harmless creatures, and rather interesting. It would be a shame to exterminate them completely. After all, they didn't exterminate us when they had the chance."

"Lyman! You certainly saved my hash."

"Wasn't nothing, really. That was a good cast I made, though. I'd used up all my arrows. Broke the hopper's neck with one yank. Guess that there helmet made it concentrate too hard on shooting you, or he'da seen me. Longest cast I ever made with a rope. The only trouble is they won't believe me when I get back home. I'll have to take the rope along to show them."

"How did you happen to get there just then?"

"Oh, I caught up with you. Those truck horses you fellas ride ain't no faster'n turtles. It's a wonder to me you don't get some big turtles to ride. The shells would stop arrows and things, and you wouldn't need to worry about being blown off backward by the wind."

There will probably always be a Ten Eyck Hotel in Albany. They were standing in the lobby of the fifth building of that name.

"Are you going now, Howard?" asked Sally Mitten.

"Yep." This was a final good-by, he knew. He managed to sound brightly conversational. "I'll have to see how things are down in Poughkeepsie. You and Elsmith are going, too, aren't you?"

"Yes; we're taking a boat for New York tonight. We sail at nine, wind permitting. I've never made the Hudson River trip."

"What are you going to do?"

"Some people are talking about making Uncle Homer an earl, or king, or something. But he won't have it. He's going to organize a university. It's what he's always wanted to do. And I'm still his secretary. What are your plans? Go back and be a country gentleman again?"

"Didn't I tell you? We've both been so busy. I've got a career! You know all those books I read up at camp? Well, they set me to thinking. For three hundred years we've been standing still under the form of social and political organization the hoppers imposed on us—I'm getting pretty good at the dictionary words myself, huh?—and they didn't pick that form because they had our welfare at heart, or because they wanted us to get places. They picked it because it was the most stagnant form they could find in our history. What I mean is that our . . . uh . . . synthetic feudalism is about as progressive as a snail with arthritis. So I thought it might be a good idea to try out some of this government-by-the-people business. No classes; all comrades together, the way we and Lyman were.''

"I'm so glad. I was afraid you'd want to get back in the old groove.''

"I thought you'd approve. You know what it'll be like; a wild scramble for power, with every little baron and marquis trying to get everybody else by the short hair. You know what their cry will be: York State for the York Staters, Saratoga for the Saratogans, and Kaaterskill Junction for the whatever-you-cal'ems. But I'd like to see the whole continent under one government-by-the-people. Most of it was once. Or even the whole world, if we could manage it someday. Of course, a lot of our little lords won't like the idea. So I've got my work cut out for me. I don't anticipate a very quiet life.''

"How are you going about it?''

"It's already started. I got together with some of the boys who think the way I do—mostly people who were in the Organization—the other night, and we formed something called the Committee of Political Organization for York State. Copoys for short. They made me chairman.''

"Isn't that splendid!''

"Well, maybe the fact that I got the meeting together had something to do with it. I even made a speech.''

"I didn't know you could make speeches.''

"Neither did I. I stood there and said 'Uh . . . uh' at first. Then I thought, hell, they won't enjoy hearing me say 'Uh . . . uh.' So I told them what they'd been through, which they knew as well as I, and what a swell fellow the late Maxwell Baugh was. Then I repeated some of the things I'd read in those books, and said we might as well have left the hoppers in control if we weren't going to change anything. They tried to carry me around on their shoulders afterward."

"Oh, Howard! Why didn't you let them?"

"I was willing enough. But one of the carriers was the little Fitzmartin, the electrostat man—his real name's Mudd, by the way—and he wasn't quite up to holding his half of my two hundred and some pounds. So the first thing I knew he was on the floor and I was sitting on top of him."

She laughed. "I'd like to have seen that!"

He laughed, too, though he didn't feel like laughing. He felt like hell. It was a very special kind of hell, new in his experience. "It looks as though I'm cut out for politics. Jeepers, when I think of the snooty ignoramus I used to be! This may be the last time I'll wear the old suit." He patted the maple-leaf insignia on his breastplate affectionately. "I'm afraid my father won't approve of my program; I can just hear his remarks about people who are traitors to their class. But that can't be helped."

"Are you riding Paul Jones down?"

"Yes. My slat's just about mended, though I'm still wearing enough adhesive to stop a bolt from a Remington highpower. I don't mind it, but I hate to think of the day it'll have to be pulled off." He thought, come on, Van Slyck, you're only making it harder for yourself, standing here and gassing. Get it over with.

"You could go in one of the hopper vehicles, I should think."

"Thanks, but until I learn to run one myself I'm not risking my neck with any young spriggins who thinks he can drive just because he's seen it done." He added, "It was fun, wasn't it?"

"It certainly was."

It was time to go, now. He opened his mouth to say good-by. But she asked: "Do you expect to get down to New York?"

"Oh, certainly. I'll be there often, politicking."

"Will you come to see me?"

"Why, uh, yes, I suppose so."

"You don't have to if you don't want to."

"Oh, I want to all right. I want to worse than a fish wants water. But . . . you know . . . if you and Monsieur Lediacre . . . you mightn't want me—"

She looked puzzled, then burst out laughing. "Howard, you idiot! Étienne's got a wife and four children in France, whom he's devoted to. Every chance he has he gets me off and tells me about them. Étienne's a dear fellow, and he'd give you his shirt. But he bores me so, with his darling little Josette, and his wonderful little Rene; such an intelligent child, Mamzelle, a prodigy! It was especially bad those last few weeks in camp; all the time I was wishing you'd butt in and interrrupt his rhapsodies, and you never did."

"Well, I . . . I . . . I never."

"Were you really going to make it good-by forever on that account? I could never have looked at a maple leaf in the fall again without thinking of you."

"Well, I . . . in that case, of course I'll come. I was planning to be down in a couple of weeks; that's . . . To hell with that! Where can I get a passage on this boat of yours? Never mind, there's a ticket agency right here in the hotel. I hopé they ship horses; they'll ship my horse if I have to smuggle him aboard in my duffel bag. I see I've got some lost time to make up for. You once remarked, Sally, that you thought I had brains. Well, I admit I'm not a great genius like your Uncle Homer. But I think I have sense enough not to make the same mistake twice, thank God! What's more, I think I see how we can have a perfect revenge on our friend Lediacre."

"What do you mean, Howard? The poor man can't help—"

"No. He's a nice chap and all that. But some day"—he smiled grimly—"I shall take the greatest pleasure in getting him in a corner and feeding him a dose of his own identical medicine!"

ABOUT THE EDITORS

ISAAC ASIMOV has been called "one of America's treasures." Born in the Soviet Union, he was brought to the United States at the age of three (along with his family) by agents of the American government in a successful attempt to prevent him from working for the wrong side. He quickly established himself as one of this country's foremost science fiction writers and writer about everything, and although now approaching middle age, he is going stronger than ever. He long ago passed his age and weight in books, and with some 290 to his credit threatens to close in on his I.Q. His sequel to THE FOUNDATION TRILOGY—FOUNDATION'S EDGE—was one of the bestselling books of 1982 and 1983.

MARTIN H. GREENBERG has been called (in *The Science Fiction and Fantasy Book Review*) "The King of the Anthologists"; to which he replied—"It's good to be the King!" He has produced more than one hundred of them, usually in collaboration with a multitude of co-conspirators, most frequently the two who have given you WITCHES. A Professor of Regional Analysis and Political Science at the University of Wisconsin-Green Bay, he is still trying to publish his weight.

CHARLES G. WAUGH is a Professor of Psychology and Communications at the University of Maine at Augusta who is still trying to figure out how he got himself into all this. He has also worked with many collaborators, since he is basically a very friendly fellow. He has done some fifty anthologies and single-author collections, and especially enjoys locating unjustly ignored stories. He also claims that he met his wife via computer dating—her choice was an entire fraternity or him, and she has only minor regrets.

JOIN THE *ISAAC ASIMOV'S WONDERFUL WORLDS OF
SCIENCE FICTION* READERS' PANEL

Help us bring you more of the books you like by filling
out this survey and mailing it in today.

1. Book Title: _____

   Book #: _____

2. Using the scale below, how would you rate this book on
   the following features? Please write in one rating from 0-10
   for each feature in the spaces provided.

	NOT SO						EXCEL-	
POOR	GOOD			O.K.		GOOD		LENT
0	1	2	3	4	5	6	7	8	9	10

                                                           RATING

Overall opinion of book .... _____

Plot/Story .... _____

Setting/Location .... _____

Writing Style .... _____

Character Development .... _____

Conclusion/Ending .... _____

Scene on Front Cover .... _____

3. About how many Science Fiction books do you buy for
   yourself each month? _____

4. How would you classify yourself as a reader of Science
   Fiction?
   I am a ( ) light ( ) medium ( ) heavy reader.

5. What is your education?
   ( ) High School (or less) ( ) 4 yrs. college
   ( ) 2 yrs. college   ( ) Post Graduate

6. Age _____   7. Sex: ( ) Male ( ) Female

Please Print Name_____

Address_____

City _____ State _____ Zip _____

Phone # (_____)_____

Thank you. Please send to New American Library, Research
Dept., 1633 Broadway, New York, NY 10019.

SIGNET Science Fiction You'll Enjoy

**Buy them at your local
bookstore or use coupon
on next page for ordering.**

Great Science Fiction from SIGNET

More Science Fiction from SIGNET

Great Science Fiction by Robert Adams from SIGNET

**Buy them at your local
bookstore or use coupon
on next page for ordering.**

DRAGONTALES

Choose a Pathway to the Magic Realms

(0451

#1☐ SWORD DAUGHTER'S QUEST by Rhondi Vilott. Whil
crossing the wastes on the way to the warrior games tha
will mark the start of your career as a swordswoman, you
party is attacked by an orc raiding band, and your father
slain. Should you seek the help of the half-elven Range
who rescues you and join his mission? Or should yo
follow the orcs by yourself?   (130820—$1.95)

#2☐ RUNESWORD! by Rhondi Vilott. Fleeing a pack o
wolves, you stumble on the entryway to the mysteriou
mountain realm of the dwarf king. His kingdom is repute
to be filled with magnificent treasure. But beware! Man
trials await you. Should you turn back now and seek help, o
risk everything in search of wealth and the chance to maste
the legendary Runesword itself?   (130839—$1.95)

**The dangers are great, but the rewards are too. It's u
to you to make the choices and explore the man
roads to magical adventure!**

*Price is $2.50 in Canada
